the

great

indoors

the great indoors

SABINE DURRANT

Riverhead Books

a member of Penguin Group (USA) Inc.

New York 2005

RIVERHEAD BOOKS

Published by the Penguin Group

Penguin Group (USA) Inc., 375 Hudson Street, New York, New York 10014, USA •
Penguin Group (Canada), 10 Alcorn Avenue, Toronto, Ontario M4V 3B2, Canada
(a division of Pearson Penguin Canada Inc.) • Penguin Books Ltd, 80 Strand, London
WC2R 0RL, England • Penguin Ireland, 25 St Stephen's Green, Dublin 2, Ireland
(a division of Penguin Books Ltd) • Penguin Group (Australia), 250 Camberwell
Road, Camberwell, Victoria 3124, Australia (a division of Pearson Australia Group
Pty Ltd) • Penguin Books India Pvt Ltd, 11 Community Centre, Panchsheel Park,
New Delhi–110 017, India • Penguin Group (NZ), Cnr Airborne and Rosedale
Roads, Albany, Auckland 1310, New Zealand (a division of Pearson New Zealand
Ltd) • Penguin Books (South Africa) (Pty) Ltd, 24 Sturdee Avenue, Rosebank,
Johannesburg 2196, South Africa • Penguin Books Ltd, Registered Offices:
80 Strand, London WCR 0RL, England

Library of Congress Cataloging-in-Publication Data

Durrant, Sabine.
The great indoors / Sabine Durrant.
p.   cm.
ISBN 1-57322-295-X
1. London (England)—Fiction.   2. Antique dealers—Fiction.
3. Single women—Fiction.
4. Loneliness—Fiction.   5. Cats—Fiction.   I. Title.
PR6014.U77G74   2005   2004050781
813'.6—dc22

Printed in the United States of America
1   3   5   7   9   10   8   6   4   2

This book is printed on acid-free paper. ∞

Book design by Chris Welch

"You want to have some fun?
Walk into an antique shop
and say, 'What's new?'"

—*Henry Goodman*

the

great

indoors

the drawing room

"Remember that in a social situation a sofa
never pulls its full weight."

THE ESSENTIAL HOUSE BOOK, *by Terence Conran*

MARTHA'S SISTERS sometimes say that her furniture is
her real family. They also say she doesn't like children. Martha
gets annoyed by this. "I have nothing against children," she
says, though secretly it is the glibness of the phrase that disturbs her, as if one could feel about children as one does about
raw fish or Russian films. Because the truth is she does quite
like her nephews and her niece, and even the occasional off-
spring of one or two of her friends. It is more that children
don't fit into her world: the small rented flat she has come to
call home, "her space," with its few carefully chosen objects, its
soft creamy sofa, its ash-blond seagrass, its aura of oatmeal and
sand. And children have no place at all in her shop.

Martha Bone Antiques is, for the most part, like the grave: a fine and private place. During the week Martha can renovate and distress in peace, visited mainly by dealers who can be relied upon to be aloof. But the shop is also next door to a cafe, and on weekends it's subject to a certain amount of overspill. Martha is not averse to these Pokers and Browsers—who fall in love with things and shell out so easily for them—or even their husbands, awkward and too big for themselves, like teenage boys visiting relatives at Christmas. But children are a different matter. Martha would prefer to sit quietly over her accounts on a Saturday, but she has learned that a sharp intake of breath from the corner isn't enough. Instead, at the first sight of a grumpy chocolate-rimmed face or a small pair of muddy boots, she jumps up, shuts off her vintage radio, and discreetly (or so she likes to think) *hovers* until the small people (what a phrase that is, she thinks) make faces and leave smears on her eighteenth-century gilt mirrors (French), or jump on the Victorian armchairs (tastefully reupholstered in gingham or plaid), or climb up the nineteenth-century rocking horse (still in its original paintwork, as its label is delighted to announce).

"Sorry," she says then. Her tone is light, but her grip on their clambering ankles like steel. "Bit fragile," she adds. She ruffles their hair and steers them to the door and outside, where their scooters and bikes lie flat and abandoned across the pavement like dead horses on a battlefield.

On this particular Saturday, though, the shop is childless and shut. There is a sign on the door that says, "Closed due to unexpected family circumstances." It is a very small sign, and the woman who is peering through the window, eyes squinting in irritation as she tries to make out the exact proportions of a cherrywood cupboard, can be forgiven for missing it. It is a tag, really, a brown tag, the same brown tag that Martha uses to price her distressed or renovated items. In her neat flowing scroll, she draws a customer's attention to an artifact's attractions while drawing it away from the price. If the woman could only read it from the step: "An unusual and delightful 19th-century French cherrywood armoirette, £1,200."

Martha's labels are threaded with a piece of green and brown tartan ribbon, which she then attaches to a piece of furniture. Without thinking, befuddled by anxiety, at three o'clock in the morning, she has slipped a piece of this ribbon through this label, too. But there was nowhere on the door to tie it, so she stuck it to the glass with a piece of tape. It is a charming ribbon, but it looks forlorn and useless here. "Pretty and unusual 19th-century family circumstances: English."

◆

MARTHA AND HER STEPBROTHER, Ian, are standing in the sitting room of their parents' house. Ian is wearing a suit, but he has taken off his shoes and is curling and uncurling his maroon nyloned toes against the shag of a Persian rug. The lower rims of his eyes are pinker than they should be, and there are traces of dried spittle along the middle of his lower lip, a ragged line of dashes; otherwise there is little to tell that he has been up all night. But he has one of those faces that always looks as if it has been up all night: the skin along the neck translucent and papery, an extra couple of creases under the eyes. Martha itches to get out some sandpaper when she looks at him, to rub him down with beeswax. He hasn't had bad eczema for years, but he's chafing his hands up and down against the rough edge of his jacket pocket.

It is ten o'clock in the morning, seven hours since Ian rang Martha to tell her of his father's death, and they have gone beyond the immediacy of the situation. Martha wonders if they actually ever inhabited it. When she got his phone call, she was flooded not only with shock, but with a kind of panic that, since he had called *her*, something special was expected of her, that there was something in the situation only she could respond to. She got to the hospital within twenty minutes of his call and saw, through the revolving doors, Ian sitting in his suit in a plastic chair. His pale, gingery head was bowed and moving in a rhythmic way. She thought he was saying something, or sobbing maybe, but when she had passed through the doors, she realized he was rolling his lower lip between his thumb and finger back and forth, as if he was . . . *humming*.

"Ian," she said, putting her arms out. She expected a moment then when she would sit down next to him. But he jumped up, greeted her as if she were a colleague convening at a sales conference. "Excellent," he said. He looked at his watch. "You've made very good time."

"I'm so sorry, Ian." She put her hand on his shoulder.

He tapped it rather patronizingly. "Well. Yes. Anyway. Shall we?"

In Martha's Volvo Estate, he sat with his knees to his chin. She had moved the seat forward the day before to make room for a Welsh dresser. She kept saying, "Ian, you can move the seat back. There's a thing under the seat you pull." But he said, "No. No. I'm perfectly happy here, thank you."

He had been in a restaurant in Croydon with some clients when his cell phone rang. After his father's first heart attack, they'd thought . . . but anyway. Ian had left the car at the office and had a drink or two. "Not more than that. Only two. But you can't be too careful. You can't risk it, can you? The restaurant called me a mini-cab. Left! Left!"

"What?"

"Go left here! You don't want to go down Garratt Lane. The congestion where it meets the Wandsworth One Way System is . . . murder."

"Ian," Martha said gently. "It's four o'clock in the morning."

"West Hill's just as bad. It kills me why they don't add an extra lane."

"Ian," she said again.

She drove to his father's house in Wimbledon, the house Graham had lived in with her mother before she died—the house that Martha herself had lived in as a child. "Ah, the family home," Ian said as she pulled up outside 10 Chestnut Drive (though, in fact, he had never lived there at all). The house was looking unloved. The Virginia creeper, which her mother would prune hard twice a year, was sagging and bearded after three years of neglect, hanging off under its own weight in patches. The paintwork on the windows was peeling and the curtains in the bay window, pulled closed, were sagging in the middle.

In the hallway, Ian and Martha stood for a moment. She smelled cat's piss and old dust and unaired clothes. Ian took off his shoes. Martha was reminded of Ian's wife, who put plastic coverings over the furniture when she vacuumed, who sang, "Shoes!" when anyone came to the door. She said, "Is Julia . . . ?" Ian, still bending, said, "She's going to wait until the twins are up. It seemed unnecessary to, you know, disrupt their routine."

Over the banister, Graham's coat was hanging, discarded and empty. When Ian was lining up his shoes under the radiator,

Martha picked it up and quickly hung it on a peg. The pockets felt heavy with change. Ian turned around. "Right," he said. There was scurf in his pale eyebrows. His lips were drained of color. For a moment, he froze, as if lost. Martha felt a surge of compassion. Now is when I should take control, she thought. But, in that moment, she froze, too. Why had they come? To check that the house, abandoned so fast, was okay? To thank the neighbors for their quick action? To feed the cat? Or was it something more elemental? Maybe Ian needed to see the house's emptiness for himself. Maybe only then would his father's death sink in.

She said, "Would you like a shower?" with an idea in her head of a stripping down, an immersion, some kind of rebirth.

Ian looked at her, and then stared, as if he'd noticed her for the first time. He said, "Are you in your pajamas?"

Martha looked down. A band of pale skin flashed between pink fabric and her sneakers. A thread of ribbon trailed out of the V of an old sweater. She crossed her arms, suddenly self-conscious. "I was in a hurry," she said.

"Oh. Well, would *you* like a shower? I could check if the water's on. You look a little . . ."

"No. No. I'm fine."

"Okay then. Well, I suppose I'd better get organized."

He started down the stairs to the basement kitchen, muttering about "arrangements." Martha followed. Catching sight of herself in the fish-eye mirror on the way down, she was the one who looked grief-stricken, her face hollowed out, her features sharp, shadows looming under her eyes, her short brown hair sticking out at the back.

In the kitchen, the scene of so many family meals in Martha's past, Ian made lists. Martha put the kettle on. Ian said, "We'll need to get moving with The House." She said, "Tea. Strong tea with sugar." He said, "Coffee if there is any. With milk."

She opened the fridge, but there wasn't any milk. Just three open jars of Coffee-mate. The sugar bowl was empty but a pile of sugar packets sat in a saucer by the sink. The cupboard above gaped open to reveal several tins of cat food (cod and salmon flavor) and twelve tins of baked beans (some containing frankfurters). Her stepfather appeared to have become increasingly eccentric in his kitchen organization. Anything used regularly—mugs, plates, pans, utensils—had come out of the shelving and onto the Formica top so the room looked like something that had been turned inside out: the galley of a ship after a storm. It struck Martha that it's only when people retire, and have the time for it, that they become most hung up on convenience and obsessed with time-saving devices. Maybe you start thinking that if you eke time out, don't fritter it away on tasks like cooking, or spreading hard butter, then somehow it will last longer.

Ian took a couple of sips of his sweet Coffee-mated drink, put the mug back down on the table, and said, "Right. Let's get moving." Then he sat on the stairs outside the kitchen, in the gloom, winding the spiral wire of the old-fashioned phone around his fingers, to call relatives, his sister in Vancouver, an uncle and, at eight A.M., when it was "decent," Martha's own two sisters. Stepsiblings of the bereaved. Stepdaughters of the deceased. Involved and yet not involved, like Martha herself, family by virtue of accident and death and divorce.

Martha said she could call them. But Ian replied that he wanted to do it. "It is, after all, my . . ."

"Father who has died," Martha finished for him.

He gave her an odd look.

"Place," he said.

◆

BUT THAT WAS ages ago. And here they are, still waiting.

"That's the problem with Stanstead. You really want Gatwick. A"—Ian is standing, legs apart—"you can check in at Victoria Station if you want, and get the train. Luggage and everything. B: There's long-term parking. You get straight on the bus and into the terminal. It's very fast, very efficient."

Martha says, "So, that's good."

"Although, even with business, there's no way to avoid air traffic control."

"No, of course not."

"Or weather."

"No!"

"You can leave home in the morning and there's clear skies all over Gatwick, but what you can't see is that ridge of low pressure over Alicante. Fog. Electrical storms."

"No, that's true."

"I mean, take this summer . . ."

Martha feels a wave of exhaustion for the first time this morning. She feels sorry for Ian, for losing his father. But also, for being so *awful*. It strikes her how unfortunate it is that the aspect of his personality that's so alienating—forced pomposity, labored smugness—is really, in fact, just insecurity. She thinks back to the day her mother died. He doesn't know what he's doing, she thinks.

God, she wishes his wife would get here. Or even her sisters.

Because they will be so much better at comforting than she is. Geraldine, the maternal one, will clutch Ian to her bosom; she will assume a certain type of grief from him and, not noticing behavior to the contrary, will receive it. Her younger sister, Eliza, the businesswoman, will simply match him with her efficiency. But Martha herself is no good at relationships. Sometimes, unexpectedly left alone in a room with a good friend, she finds herself at a loss for words. So how on earth is she supposed to cope here? His hands are going chaff-chaff against his pockets. But he's telling her about the holiday he "and the family" have just had in Florida in a tone that would be condescending if the subject matter wasn't so bland. He's saying, "Look, it was expensive but you can't put a price on memories you make for the children, can you?"

One thing Martha does have against children is the sentimentality they can bring out in their parents. She says sharply, "Do ten-month-olds have memories?"

Ian says, "Absolutely. Of course they do. And you've got to fill them with golden moments. In my opinion, holidays are the single most important thing. Holidays full of golden moments. After all, when I look back, when *one* looks back, what does one remember about one's childhood?"

"Divorce?"

"Holidays. That's what one remembers. Cornwall, before my mother died. Susie and me, Father and Mother. Dad would take us fishing and we'd muck around in rock pools and, um . . . you know, where's that picture? The day we went fishing for mackerel? It's here . . . isn't it . . . ? Or has it been moved?"

He has started fiddling with the photographs on the mantelpiece, but they are mainly of grandchildren now, or of Graham and her mother, holding hands in front of a pretty view, on one of the many jaunts they took after Graham retired from his job "in concrete." Happiness second time around for them both. Ian stops looking. His hands hang down. There is no sign of Graham's first family here. Ian says, "Perhaps it's upstairs."

Martha says, "I'll go and look." She feels a strong need to leave the room, to splash water on her face, maybe even to scream silently at her own reflection. But Ian says, "No. No. I'll go."

"It might be in the . . . in the desk in the bedroom? I know Mum used to keep a load of photos in there. Ones she wanted to reframe and . . ."

"Ok-ay," Ian says. "To the Master Bedroom."

She looks around the room. She has drawn back the drapes, but it is still dreary. Graham's easy chair is matted with cat hair. This house has been lived in by people who grew up in the war, who made the most of what was already there. Martha's generation strips out the old floorboards and replaces them with new, refits perfectly decent bathrooms, redecorates, replaces. Before Martha, on the mantelpiece, is a small chipped statue of the Virgin Mary. Martha studies this with an antique dealer's critical eye. An interesting piece of kitsch, or too damaged to be worth attention? Martha's mother lived by her religion and so does Martha, only her god is a household god, the god of small, desirable things.

She sighs. This isn't her mother's home anymore. It is a collection of rooms, of stuff, letters and albums and paintings and books and furniture, stuff to be sorted, stuff to be chucked, stuff to be allocated, divided up, chosen, rejected, selected. It was bad enough sorting out the jewelry, what will it be like with a whole house? Geraldine, she knows, has always had her eye on the chesterfield. Eliza will want *The Boy*, a late-nineteenth-century portrait that hangs above the fireplace, left to their mother by an aunt. It is, Martha estimates, worth several thousand, though of course it is the sentimental value that Eliza will talk about. There is a Penwork tea caddy with brass lion feet, which is even more valuable, but she suspects her sisters don't know this and will find the tug on their heartstrings subsequently diminished.

When Ian first left the room, Martha heard a clattering and a creaking of boards overhead, but it's quiet now. After a few minutes, she calls up, "Ian? You okay?" Still silence, but she waits a little while longer before going upstairs to look for him. And then, turning the corner, through the doorway of the bedroom she sees him sitting on the big cast-iron bed with something in his lap, and she asks, "Did you find it?" He raises his head then and she sees that the object he's holding isn't a picture at all but a sweater, a tatty green lambswool V-neck, the one Graham used to wear for gardening. And then she sees his face. It's knotted up and twisted. "Oh no," she says, and she goes to him, and finally holds his heaving shoulders while he weeps.

◆

"I AM NOT taking the cat."

"Matty. Be reasonable." Eliza rubs her chin with the heel of her hand. "It's the least you can do. Ger, Matty is now saying she won't take the cat."

Martha is kneeling on the floor by the fridge, with rubber gloves on, her face glowing white in the artificial light, handing items of food up to Eliza. Eliza is sitting on a stool, dressed in her usual black, her long, slim legs crossed at a jaunty angle so that she looks like an office worker waiting at the bar for an early evening drink, rather than someone involved in clearing out a kitchen.

Geraldine has come in with her arms full of sheets—a jumble of horrible brown and navy polyester. She is on her way to the washing machine. She pauses, her tilted bulk swaying, and says, "Oh, Matt."

Martha's thighs are aching, the knees of her cotton pajama bottoms gray with dirt. Reaching into the back of the fridge, she says, "I'm not 'now saying' I won't take the cat. At no point did I say I *would* take the cat."

"Matt-ski." Eliza's tone is wheedling, coaxing. Her mouth is pouted, one of the exaggerated facial expressions she uses to hide her detachment. She's accustomed to getting her own way, but in this case she doesn't really care. She sees Martha looking at her and straightens her mouth. In an ordinary voice, says, "Come on. Someone's got to." She pauses over a jar of tartar sauce. Her polished nails scratch at the label. "October 'eighty-seven. Shit. No wonder he was under the weather."

"Eliza!" Geraldine has started stuffing the washing into the machine. When she bends you can see the white elastic stitching in the fabric of her blue leggings; the seams stretching. Straightening up, she releases an "ouf" of breath—not an indication of real pain or discomfort, but an imitation groan like the one their mother used to give, a sign that Geraldine feels put-upon. She is large and soft, slack-muscled, round-shouldered. If Martha's sisters were lamps, Eliza would be an Anglepoise, elegant and angular, Geraldine one of those made from Chinese ginger jars, with a circular base and a top-heavy shade. She has the same curly hair as Eliza, but hers is flyaway across the crown. Today, with the low sun in the window behind, she looks as if she's wearing a halo.

Martha says, "Can't we give it to the neighbor?" Eliza grimaces at the jar of tartar sauce. "The *cat*," Martha adds.

Geraldine is setting the machine's controls. "No, we can't. They're away a lot." She clamps her hands to her waist. "Look, *I'd* take him if it wasn't for the dogs."

Eliza says, "And you know *I* can't because of Gabriel's asthma."

The washing machine has started its preliminary gurgling, and Geraldine is on the way to the door again. "And Ian can't because Julia couldn't have hairs in the house, it would give her a nervous breakdown. Not to mention Ian and his eczema." There is some sudden shouting upstairs, a high-pitched scream, and a man's voice yelling, "STOP FIGHTING, YOU TWO." She says, "Look, fine, whatever. We'll have him put down."

Martha knows this is her cue. But she doesn't say anything. Geraldine hovers for a moment, fiddling with the crucifix around her neck. Then she raises her chin (they all have "the Bone chin," but Geraldine more than the others) and barrels up the stairs toward the noise. Yawning, Eliza says, "Oh fuck it, let's chuck the whole lot."

Martha sits back on her haunches. There's a hole in one of the rubber gloves and the fingers on that hand are clammy. "That's probably best in the long run."

It is the middle of the afternoon now and her sisters have picked up the house and shaken it. Geraldine arrived first with her husband and three kids. "Has it come as a terrible, terrible shock?" she said, kneeling at Ian's feet. (Geraldine's questions often include the answers: a way of ensuring that the world comes out as she expects.) Her husband, Greg, a bulky man whose jowls move as he walks, had followed her in, steering Ivor, their middle one, by the back of the head. The others had already run off. "Sorry about the invasion," he said, pumping Ian's hand up and down. When he planted a kiss on her cheek, Martha smelled a faint, not unattractive smell of sweat.

Eliza arrived shortly afterward. Geraldine greeted her at the door. Greg and the children were in the garden so Martha and Ian were left alone for a minute. They sat in silence listening to Geraldine and Eliza in the hallway, talking as if nothing had happened. Geraldine said something about liking Eliza's trousers, but was leather really practical with a small child? Eliza said, "You just sponge them down. Honestly, they're to die for." Martha and Ian looked at each other and smiled. It was the first time, she realized, she had broken rank.

Now Eliza has finished tying up the garbage bags and is standing on a chair beginning an assault on the top cupboards. She says, "I suppose Ian called you because you were closest to the hospital." She has a tower of baked bean cans under her chin. She adds with her lower jaw at a funny angle, "Ugh. Imagine living off these!"

Martha is emptying her bucket into the sink. She glances up. She hadn't thought of that, which is probably why Eliza, who likes to make a virtue of her "openness," has reminded her. But of course Eliza is right. It was convenience that led Ian to ring her first, nothing else. She feels foolish and grubby and tired. Her eyes are at midriff level. Eliza's stomach, between her black leather trousers and black T-shirt, wrinkled up as she stretches, is flat and brown.

"You're very slim again, Eliza," she says. "How do you do it?"

"You know me, living on my nerves. Oh, and running after an eighteen-month-old!"

"Of course." Martha puts the bucket in the cupboard under the sink.

Eliza's gotten down from the chair and has chucked the cans on the counter. "Oh fuck it," she says, looking at the chaos. "I suppose we are being useful?"

Martha snaps off the gloves and sits down on a chair. "You've got to do something," she says.

Eliza sits down, too. "God," she says.

There is a pause. The house has been full of noises—shouts and the clattering of feet on stairs—but is quiet for a moment. Eliza spins the thick silver rings on the middle finger of her right hand a few times, then says, "I rang Daddy before I came. He was very sorry to hear."

"How is he?" Martha hasn't called her father "Daddy" since he left their mother. Old enough to have been aware of the tensions he created and the misery he left behind, she is imbued with too strong a sense of him as a husband, and an ex. The divorce seemed to have passed her younger sister by and she is always caught out by Eliza's lack of self-consciousness about him.

"Fine." Eliza's tone is light. She slips her silver ring onto a different finger.

There is a silence, which Martha breaks. "How's work?" Eliza is in financial PR, which always sounds to Martha like a contradiction in terms.

"Oh, you know. The usual. Long hours . . ."

"Thank God for Denis. Voltaire?"

Eliza rolls her eyes.

"Ah." Martha smiles. She takes this to mean Denis's Ph.D. is still not going well, but, the only member of her family who didn't go to university, she doesn't feel in a position to comment further. "Jolly good."

Eliza says, "Everything all right on your end? The shop still a hive of activity?"

"Yep." Martha runs her finger along a knot in the table. "Look, it's because of *that* I can't take the cat. You know that, don't you? It'll scratch the furniture, leave hairs . . . You know, this is my living we're talking about."

Eliza dabs at a spot of rust on her shirt, licking her finger and rubbing. She doesn't look at Martha. "But it's only for a night or two. You can keep him upstairs."

"I don't want it upstairs." Martha remembers the hair-strewn easy chair and shudders. "There's merchandise up there, too."

"You could sell him, make a feature of him. A delightful old cat: genuine fleas."

Martha doesn't answer.

"Well, whatever." Eliza gets up and looks out the window. Martha stays at the table for a bit in case she comes back. Eliza has started whistling in a bored way. Martha feels her own face fix. Geraldine's oversensitivity may sometimes be hard to take, but Eliza's refusal to bend to the feelings of others is equally infuriating. The newness of Eliza, the sharpness of her; the little sister they all tugged around and spoiled, who has now put her family behind her, the successful professional woman with no time to waste. Even her house, a modern palace of sharp corners and bright halogen lights, is architect-designed. Martha says, "Anyway," and leaves the room.

Halfway up the stairs, she meets Julia, Ian's wife, coming down with a wastepaper basket in each hand. Julia is wearing camel trousers and a white shirt. She has straight blond bangs that form a line across her forehead. Everything about her is smooth and shiny and brittle, like a Dresden shepherdess. "Goodness, gracious, the stuff everywhere." She wrinkles her nose. "How can people live like this?" Julia has a thing about dust mites.

Martha says "Ssssh," though she doesn't know where Ian is. He could be anywhere. They are all over the place, the lot of them, children and dogs and bereaved relatives, in and out of rooms, somehow licensed now to take the house over as never before. Not even at Christmas. She can hear Geraldine shout to Greg in the garden from a top window. Patrick and Ivor, two dark heads, two enormous pairs of sneakers, are sprawled on the rug in the sitting room, fiddling with their Game Boys. Anna, the youngest, is playing with a doll on the stairs, reprimanding it for something. She looks up when she sees Martha. She still has the round, flushed cheeks of a baby, her mouth always part open, her hair silky fine. She cocks her head and says, "Auntie Matt?"

"Yes?" Martha sits on the bottom step. She likes to think she talks to children as equals. (Geraldine, she's noticed, says "Ye-es?" to her children, giving the word two syllables as if to demonstrate patience, or, if distracted, "What?" to demonstrate the opposite.)

"How bad is shark repellent bat spray?"

"Umm."

Patrick, eight, yells, "I've told you. Bad enough to kill you."

Julia comes back up the stairs then with a black garbage bag in her arms. "Martha. All this in here: it was at the back of the ironing cupboard. It seems to be yours. Just letters and old . . . things." She is shaking her head; her bangs sway. "Shall I just chuck it?"

Martha hesitates. Her bag of mementos. She had forgotten all about it. Letters, papers, rubbish, really.

Anna says, "Kill you like you're really dead?"

"It's just clutter," says Julia. "Clutter is the enemy of a clear mind. There was an article in *Good Housekeeping* the other day, the three rules of a well-organized life: chuck, chuck, chuck."

"Kill you like Graham is dead?"

"Actually, I . . ."

Geraldine is coming down with more sheets. She gives Martha a pointed look over the linen.

"I'll keep it," Martha says, then adds, "The letters, not the cat."

❖

NO ONE FANCIES COFFEE-MATE, so the tea is black. No teapot, either, or cups, just mugs. Julia has gone to collect the twins from her mother's so Geraldine is sitting next to Ian, the chief mourner, on the chesterfield. She is holding his hand and talking again about "the end." She shakes her head and says she thought Graham was so much better and Ian, who is in his shirtsleeves, with the tears coming easily now, says how busy he's been at work and how last weekend he hadn't been able to make it to Dad's, and that if the Quinces next door hadn't had his cell phone number from the last time, then . . . Geraldine squeezes his hand, puts her other hand on top, and says, "You were there. That's what counts."

Eliza has decided against the cat-haired easy chair, and is sitting in a hard frame chair with a tapestry seat. The cat, who turned up a few hours ago, has also decided against the easy chair and is on Eliza's knee. She is stroking it, with firm rhythmic strokes from the top of its head to the base of its tail. It is purring, arching its body into her hand so that its back goes up like a wave. It is also drooling onto her leather-clad leg, which she doesn't seem to have noticed. She says, after a while, "I suppose we'd better start sorting through some of the things." Her eyes flit to *The Boy* above the fireplace. "Working out who's getting what. Furniture . . . things like that."

Geraldine's spare hand grips the corner of the chesterfield. "Eliza!"

"And then there's the crematorium. Shall I call them? Ian, would you like me to do that?"

Martha, from her cross-legged position on the floor, sees what's coming. "Eliza, um . . . Ian—"

Ian interrupts. "I think my father would have preferred a burial. I've already discussed it with my sister. There is, as you know, the double plot in Putney Vale cemetery where my mother's buried."

The cat leaps off Eliza's lap. Geraldine, who is still clasping Ian's hand, looks away, out the window, her lower lip twisted. She is wearing a white T-shirt and you can see the indentations of her bra across her back. Martha feels a tug of tenderness toward her. Their mother's ashes were scattered, at her request, at a local scenic spot: Pen Ponds in Richmond Park. She and Graham met there. It was their place. Perhaps she imagined the same for Graham. But such were the messy unforetold complications of the second marriage. Naturally, Ian would choose to lay his father with his mother; the bones of his mother, Martha found herself thinking, not the mother of the Bones.

Geraldine recovers. "The most important thing, Ian, is that he knew you were happy. That was what mattered to him; he knew that you and your sister were both settled. You must hold on to that. I remember talking to Mummy when she was very ill and she said, you know, 'Thank God you're all happy and in stable relationships; you've got Greg and Eliza's got Denis and Martha's got David . . ." She stops. There is a moment of silence in which Martha thinks she can hear the atoms clashing in her ears. Geraldine adds quickly, "And of course the antique shop."

Ian is unaware of what has just been said. He looks up. "Yes, I know. And he was a terrific father. I respected him. Loved and respected him. You can't ask for more than that."

Martha doesn't look up to see if her sisters are exchanging glances. She hopes they aren't, but knows that they are.

❖

IT IS PAST EIGHT P.M. when Martha finally makes it back to the shop. She parks the Volvo outside, in a loading bay, unlocks the front door, and then gets her bag of mementos from the trunk. The door has swung closed when she gets back so she has to push it with her foot, as a result of which the label on the door announcing the unexpected circumstances twirls to the floor like a helicopter seed coming down from a sycamore tree.

She left a lamp on in the back of the shop, on a table in the section that is mocked up to look like a child's bedroom. There is a sleigh bed, and a painted cupboard with gingham panels in the doors, and a little chest of drawers, and the rocking horse in its original paintwork. The Victorian sprig quilt on the bed looks so soft and inviting, the scene so peaceful in the low glow of the small light, she sits for a moment on the bed and rubs her eyes. After a few minutes she gets up, unlocks another door in the side wall, and heaves the garbage bag up the flight of stairs behind it and into her flat. Almost to her surprise, it is just as she left it. Her space, her haven: still and serene and ordered. Everything as it should be, everything as it was. She plumps up the new linen cushion on her Howard sofa, straightens the kilim, and stuffs the bag of letters out of sight under the kitchen table. And then she goes back down the stairs and back to the car to get the cat.

CHAPTER TWO

the bedroom

"When buying a double mattress, two people
should lie on it side by side to see how
firmly it will support two bodies."

BEDROOMS AND BATHROOMS, *by Nonie Niesewand*

FOR THE SECOND DAY in a row, Martha is awoken by the
phone ringing.

"Oh good, you're up," Geraldine says.

Martha reaches out to nudge the alarm clock into view. It
says 9:35 A.M. "Um," she says.

"What, don't tell me you're still in bed? It's almost ten,
Matty. I've already been to Mass. Sorry, but lucky for some."

Martha doesn't say anything. She can hear Geraldine's house
in her ear, the hollering of small children and the racket of dogs
and the zap and crackle of the television. She imagines Geraldine standing by the sink piled with dishes, the table still scattered with wet Krispies and spilled milk from breakfast.

Geraldine says, affronted, "Do you want to call me back?"

Martha yawns, putting the receiver against her chin to muffle the sound. "Can I just wake up a bit?"

"Okay," says Geraldine stiffly, hanging up.

Martha lays her head back into the pillow. The room seems unnaturally dark and quiet. She can see the shape of her chest of drawers, but none of the objects on it. She likes to tidy them in her mind—moving the lamp a couple of inches to the left, regrouping the pot that holds her earrings, and the jug, and the little pile of antiquarian books, positioning them just right. Things in groups of three are always best. But this morning it is too dim to make out the decorative touches so she gets up to pull the curtains apart and sees that there is a blanket of fog outside. Next door's garden is white and ghostly, swathed as if in smoke. Even from here she can smell the sharp tang of it. She pulls up the sash and breathes in the air, which is damp and heavy like churned-up earth. But as she does, there's a flurry of fabric next to her and a brush of warmth against her hand and she has to slam the window shut before the cat jumps out.

"Oh fuck," Martha says. "I'd forgotten about you."

The cat stares at her and then, losing its balance, leaps off the sill and stalks off as if it was going to do that all along. The night before, it padded around her flat, its arthritic body slunk low to the floor, nostrils quivering, investigating every corner for rats or demons. In the end, Martha shut it in the kitchen, with some food, and an attractive dusky pink and sage plaid Welsh blanket that once adorned the end of her bed but that she has since put aside to sell. The cat dabbed at it, as if trying to get glue off its pad, and then, when a claw entangled in a thread (and broke it, damn it), shot back as if electrocuted.

It is tabby and white, this cat, with balding patches between its ears, and a saggy underbelly. It is large, overweight probably, but its bones are knobbly, its fur thin. There are cats that Martha knows she could warm to. A black cat with pea-green eyes could be an asset, curled in a ball on the end of the mushroom-colored sofa, with a red collar to match the threads in the curtains. But this old thing brings nothing to the party. It will molt, scratch at the furniture. She'll take it to Battersea Dog's Home as soon as she is dressed. "You're the boss," she says to herself as she steps into the shower. She closes her eyes and puts her head back, feeling the water needle her face, stream through her hair. "I'm the boss," she says loudly to nobody in particular. Or maybe to the cat. Or maybe, across London, to her sisters.

Because, what is this but just another example of them trying to assign a role to her? This time the role of the lonely old cat woman. Thirty-eight, single, and childless: she should have something to love. Well, I'm fine as I am, she thinks. I've got plenty to be lavishing my love on as it is. An image of the beautiful buffet deux corps she is in the process of restoring comes unprompted into her head.

Martha finishes her shower, dresses quickly, and slowly makes her bed, smoothing the seagull-white Durham quilt under the top pillows, laying the dove-gray pashmina throw at the perfect angle across it. She casts her eye over the sitting room. It looks cozy and serene this morning, with the gloom outside, the curtains pulled, and side lights on, a cream cube against the hoary September day. She plumps up the linen cushions on the sofa. They don't need it—they haven't been sat on since she plumped them up last night—but the act of doing it satisfies her; it makes her feel as if the day is going to be fine. She considers them, running her hands over the slubbed texture—how delicate their scalloped edges; how perfect the whole ensemble—and goes into the kitchen. She doesn't like to inspect the makeshift litter tray behind the door, but she left some cat food in a Spode saucer and all that is left of it now is a rim of brown dried-on smears. She holds the saucer at arm's length and runs it under the tap, her nose wrinkled.

After this, she needs a cup of coffee, but when she sniffs the carton, the milk has that artichoke smell of milk on the turn. Recently, since the introduction of late-night shopping, she has developed a routine whereby she shops on Saturday nights. She has the supermarket all to herself then. But last night she was too tired. So she grabs her purse, goes down the stairs and into the street.

Right outside the shop is the cafe, which is just opening, and beyond that, Sustainable Forests, the secondhand bookshop, which is closed on Sundays. But Martha turns left to where on weekdays a halfhearted market straggles—a couple of vegetable stalls, a man selling knock-off CDs, a barrow of ready-mixed flowers. She passes the tatty estate agent, the chemist, and the gift shop, and reaches the end of the street, then turns right again into Balham High Road. The supermarkets aren't yet open, so she crosses over by McDonald's and turns down a smaller road to the corner shop. Here she buys some milk, a paper, a sliced brown loaf, and a carton of orange juice with the label "no pulp." The woman who takes her money smiles at her and then Martha thinks, See, here I am, a single woman in control of her life, buying Sunday breakfast, with the paper—and time to read it—in a place that knows me.

The fog is lifting a little now. The air feels warmer, and

there's a patch of blue above Martha's head, the clouds around the edges like smoke. It's not yet autumn after all, but one of those interim days with warmth still in the air. Back on Balham High Road, a family is trying to cross the street. One of the children is in a stroller and the other is being made to hold on to the father's hand, but he's pulling on it, his legs scraping across the ground, wailing. For a stomach-clenching moment, Martha thinks the man is David. There's something about the size of him, the set of his shoulders, the hair. But of course she knows it can't be and when she passes, weaving in front of them between cars, she sees that this man is much younger. And David couldn't have done all this so quickly. Not children with someone else. Not so soon. Then she walks, more quickly, toward the flat.

She can hear the phone ringing as she climbs the stairs. But it isn't Geraldine. It's Ian.

"Hel-lo," he says, in a dull singsong.

Martha puts the plastic bag on the table and sits down. "How are you, Ian? I was going to call. Are you all right?"

"Under the circumstances. Quite beneficial that it's Sunday. I don't think I'd be much of an asset at the office today."

"No, of course not. I mean, it's only twenty-four hours. You must be just . . ."

"Right. Yes. Well, I was just calling to thank you. It was kind of you yesterday, to pick me up from the hospital. Much appreciated. And for everyone's help during the day. Obviously, what with one thing and another, there's rather a lot to do, arrangements to make, etcetera."

"Honestly. It was nothing. I, we, were glad to. We've got to sort the house out. In fact, I'll come round later this week."

"But also taking Kitten. I really appreciate it. I know once Hilly died, you know, my father"—there's a pause, after which Ian's voice sounds less pompous—"really loved that cat."

Martha scours the kitchen with her eyes. The cat isn't there. She moves, with the phone under her chin, to the sitting room and it isn't there, either. Or in the bedroom. She says, "Well . . ."

"He's all I've got left of him."

Martha is looking under the sofa. And behind the curtains. "You don't think you and Julia . . ."

"Not with the eczema."

"No, of course not."

She is looking in the bathroom now, behind the shower curtain. In the space under the bath. Ian is saying, "So I've been to the hospital, sorted things out there. And I've found a funeral home in Merton that's quite reasonable. Copewell and Paine, they're called."

Martha straightens up and bangs her head. "Really?" she says. "Are they really called Copewell and Paine?"

There's a pause and then Ian shouts a laugh. "Do you think they're having me on? Actually, I called a few. To get quotes." He laughs, more hysterically. "There I was talking about types of wood and linings—would I like red crushed velvet? I don't know—and my father's just there in the hospital."

"Oh God," Martha says. "Not crushed velvet."

"Anyway, the church has an opening on Friday." He hoots again. "Huh! An opening! Can you believe it? I don't know. And I wondered . . . Well, I know what good taste you've got. Julia is always saying you have impeccable taste. 'Martha and her good eye,' she says. 'Martha and her perfect little flat.' Could you be in charge of the flowers? I wouldn't know where to start. Something simple, obviously. What do you think? Just one big garland saying 'Dad,' or 'Grandad,' or would 'Father' be more dignified?"

"Or just a wreath?" Martha says, back in the kitchen now. "Of course." Maybe the cat has gone downstairs. Maybe it even got out when she went to the shop, to tear into the road, to be run over: all that's left of Ian's father squashed in the gutter. She says, "Ian, I better go. Can I call you later?"

The cat (Kitten—*that's* what it's called) has gotten into the shop, but no farther. It is curled up on the sleigh bed, like a hedgehog. Martha feels a thud of relief when she sees him snailed there. He looks almost attractive: an antique cat on an antique cot. But as she gets closer she notices the ugly nest of hairs his coat has rubbed onto the Victorian sprig eiderdown, and recovers herself. "Hey," she says, giving him a poke. He untucks his head and looks at her, but there is a moment before he realizes that she's serious. He stares at her accusingly before unfurling and flopping onto the floor. "Go on," she says, nudging him with her leg. He skittles to the door. But once beyond it, he lollops ahead of her slowly and regularly, pausing on each wooden step as if the stairs have already become routine. So casual is he, you might even think this old cat feels just as at home here as she does.

◆

ACROSS SOUTH LONDON, Geraldine is sitting on the stairs of her large Victorian house in Kingston with her coat on. The front door is wide open and Gregory is scrunching in and out to the car. He has collected the dogs and tied the bikes to the roof and he is rounding up the children now, switching off the video, confiscating Game Boys, chucking cushions in a hap-hazard manner back onto sofas, and Legos into boxes. He shouts, "This. House. Is. A. Wreck," but it's like a celebration when he says it.

He passes her again. Despite his size, he is all energy. He spends his week at a desk job at a newspaper, moving articles about war in foreign places around a page, and on weekends it's as if he wants to see some action of his own. "Come on, Ger," he says. "Old girl." This designation used to be a joke but it's part of the language between them now. In turn, sometimes Geraldine calls Gregory "Dad," and she's noticed that he dwindles a little bit each time she does, so that even though she's being ironic the irony eats away at her sense of him as anything else. A husband or a news editor or, God forbid, after all this time, a lover.

She says, "All right, I'm coming. I just want to give her an-other minute or two."

Gregory chucks the car keys into the air and catches them. He says, "Why don't you call *her*?"

But Geraldine resents Martha for the number of times she rings her. The whole point is that Geraldine is supposed to be the protective one, not the needy one. Eliza's out of her reach. You get her when she wants you to. Ms. Self-sufficiency, she is; she neither demands nor gives. But Martha has this vulnerabil-ity she herself doesn't even seem to notice. If only *Martha* would call *her*. She says, "It's just she said she'd ring back. It's been over an hour now."

Gregory throws his keys into the air again, but this time, just before he catches them, he mimes lobbing them with an invis-ible tennis racket onto the driveway. "More than," he says.

"More than an hour, not over an hour." He has an unfussy attitude toward his family—mother gaga in a nursing home, brother overseas, Christmas, birthdays, duty visits, duty calls—but firm ideas about language. It exasperates him how Geraldine messes around with it. Never hungry or tired, she is "starving wharving" or "knacker-acker-ooed." "Fancy a coff?" she'll ask him, shortening or lengthening perfectly decent words. Sisters, language, children: she never leaves anything alone. He puts the keys back into his pocket. "Maybe she's forgotten."

Which is, of course, what Geraldine worries about. Martha forgetting. Martha forgetting to do this, or that. Martha forgetting to look after the cat. Martha, all on her own in that grotty neighborhood, ironing her antique linen bedsheets into crisp white envelopes, forgetting to look after herself.

She says, "I'll ring Eliza. Is that all right? Have I got time to quickly ring Eliza?"

Gregory says, "Quickly to ring." He goes back into the playroom, where she hears him shout, "Telly *off*." There are noises of horseplay with Patrick, squeals from Anna, but Ivor sidles out into the hall, one hand rubbing his neck from behind, a recent nervous habit. The skin beneath his lower lip is reddened and raw. Geraldine has started dialing, but she puts her spare arm around her middle son. In many ways he reminds her of Martha, a middle child, too: always disgruntled, always observing. She kisses his head. She is not going to ask what's wrong now. Sometimes having children is like having your nerve ends exposed. She holds him tight while she talks on the phone to Eliza.

"Listen," she says. "That thing I said. Was it awful? Did you see Matt's face? About David and her being settled? God, I'm stupid."

Eliza says, "Oooh. There we go. Higher? Higher? Oooooh."

Eliza must be in the garden, which has so much tasteful wooden equipment Geraldine calls it The Princess Diana playground (her way of telling Eliza she thinks Gabriel is spoiled).

"Well," Eliza says, her voice closer to the receiver. "Fuck it, Ger. She jilted him. Wedding date set. Apartment waiting for her in Geneva. I said it then and I'll say it now: she's her own worst enemy. Anyway, it's two years already. We can't be treading on eggshells forever."

"I just wish she'd meet someone else. But all she does is stay in that dark old shop all day."

"I know. She's mad."

Geraldine continues: "What else does she *want*? David was nice, reliable, good-looking, interesting job. All those great holidays they went on. Those charming parents down in Sussex. Do you remember that time he got us all Center Court tickets at Wimbledon and bought that cooler of strawberries and champagne? How many men think of doing things like that? Greg wouldn't, that's for sure."

Eliza laughs. "I don't think she even appreciated it at the time."

"Anyway, according to Greg, who played squash with him last week, he's seeing someone else now. Called Maddy. She works at the auction house, too. In Oriental Miniatures. Legs up to her armpits."

Geraldine's throat feels tight. She is awash suddenly and hugs Ivor a little closer. Ivor pulls away and says, "I want to watch telly."

Eliza sounds unmoved. "Have you spoken to Ian?"

Geraldine blows her nose. "No, but I must. Are we just going to let Ian take charge of it all, just because he's a man?"

"He is in the business, I suppose."

"Quantity surveying?"

"Etcetera. Etcetera." Eliza imitates Ian via Yul Brynner in *The King and I.* Geraldine laughs more than the impression deserves to keep Eliza's attention. She can tell she's only got half of it.

Eliza says, "There are one or two things . . . not that I mind what I get, but some odds and ends do have, well, sentimental value."

An image of *The Boy* comes into Geraldine's mind. She knows Eliza wants it and has always wanted it and that somehow always wanting is her claim to getting it, but she feels a twist of resentment. She thinks about the chesterfield and Mummy's little lacquered desk and the mahogany three-legged table.

Eliza says, "Can't imagine Ian or Susie caring much about the art, do you? They can share the easy chair."

Geraldine laughs. Ivor is sitting on the step between her legs now, his head at eye level, and she has started combing through his hair with her spare hand, checking for lice while she's got him. "Yes," she says. "I know. Goodness, I must call Dad. He'd want to know. Not that it affects him, but . . ."

"It's all right, I've called him already."

"Oh really?" Geraldine likes to believe it's her role to think of things like that.

"Briefly. Yesterday. Didn't I tell you? He was looking after the girls so he had his hands full. Eloise had a meeting in Marseilles."

"How was he?"

"Fine. He said he's coming over soon to get something for the boat."

"Oh." Geraldine rests her chin on Ivor's head. "Right." She

wonders who he will stay with. Last time he stayed with Eliza ("closer to town," he said, but he's always had an easier relationship with his youngest). She says, "He probably should stay with me this time because of the baby."

There is the sound of wailing on the other end. Eliza says, "We'll figure it out. I don't know. I'd better go. Cheer up, Ger. And don't worry about Martha. She can look after herself."

Geraldine wonders, *Can she?*

Greg comes back into the hall, raising his eyebrows. Geraldine dials before he can say anything. Patrick and Anna hurtle past him as he stands there, looking at her, rubbing the bit of his head where the hair is thinning. She's so soft on everyone, and anxious. The women at work, with their bobbed hair and boots, like Eliza, have such *edges*. Geraldine next to them seems frayed and fuzzy. When she was working, when she had the orchestra and her cello to think about, she was more self-possessed, more purposeful. She should spend more time on herself. She'll be too warm in that old coat now that the sun's broken through. And he wishes she wouldn't let Ivor drip over her so much. It's not surprising he's so clingy. "Come on, chap," he says in a hearty whisper, jabbing playfully at Ivor with an outstretched finger. "Let's wait for Mum in the car, eh?"

Geraldine watches them go, Ivor's face sheepish, half-pleased. There is a triangle of shirt hanging out of the back of his trousers. She resists pulling him back to tuck it in, to wrap him in her arms again.

Martha answers on the second ring. "I was just about to phone you." She sounds irritated.

Geraldine says, "So you're up now, are you?" She means it as a joke, but it doesn't come out that way.

"I'm up. I had to get breakfast and then Ian rang."

"Ian rang?"

"Yes. He wanted to ask me about flowers."

"Did he mention anything else?"

"Like what?"

Geraldine can see Greg gesticulating at her from the car. He is pretending to pull out his hair—what's left of it. "Like furniture," she says. "Odds and ends. Pictures. That sort of thing."

"So you've spoken to Eliza."

"Just briefly."

Martha says, "Isn't it a bit soon? Shouldn't one at least wait until he's buried?"

"It's just that if we're going to be fair about all this . . ." Geraldine trails off.

Martha says, "Oh right."

The conversation is not going the way Geraldine intended. Martha can be so prickly. And not just about David, either. When their mother died, Geraldine knows her own grief seemed excessive to some people, Greg for one, but she finds tears come easily and that the depletion she feels afterward calms her. Anger was Eliza's form of release. But Martha was so closed: *impenetrable.* There was one occasion when Geraldine caught her crying. It was several months after their mother had died, and they were shopping together, chatting about normal things, and an assistant squirted them, as they passed, with perfume, and after a while Geraldine noticed Martha had gone quiet and become very interested in a rack of hosiery. When she turned, her face was pale and Geraldine was sure she had been crying, but Martha rubbed her cheeks roughly and said she was fine. In the car home, she just said, "Mum's perfume. O de Lancome." Geraldine tried to hug her when they parted later, but Martha just mumbled something about how she'd got it all wrong. Geraldine, who hadn't liked to say anything but had thought it was Tresor, said, "No, they probably don't bother spraying you with old ones."

Now she says, "Matt, I wasn't ringing about that. I was ringing to see if you were okay, and that Kitten's settling in."

"Kitten is fine."

"Don't forget, you mustn't let him out. Not until he feels at home."

"Geraldine. I am not keeping the cat. I'm going to go down to Battersea Dog's Home this afternoon. They take cats and I'm sure they'll find it a good home."

Geraldine feels a smart of panic. "You can't do that."

"It's better than having him put down, which is what you were suggesting yesterday."

"I wasn't serious, and anyway, no it's not. They'll put him down there anyway. He'll just have a miserable life in a cage for a few weeks before they do that. Staring out behind a glass wall at the people trooping past. I mean, who's going to choose him when there are kittens and—"

"Attractive cats."

Geraldine laughs despite herself. "Martha," she says pleadingly.

"Or dogs, for that matter. I've never really got that. Do you think people go all the way to Battersea Dog's Home planning on a Doberman or a red setter and then when they get there, they think, 'Oh actually, that ginger tom's rather sweet. Maybe we need a cat instead.'"

This time Geraldine just says, "Martha?"

"Oh God."

Geraldine knows Martha has given in by the tone of her voice.

"All right. Okay. God, I'm so bullied. I won't take it to Battersea Dog's Home, but I'm not keeping it. I'm not going to be a mad single woman with a cat. I'll put a note up in the shop window. Okay? Will that do? I'll find a nice home that way. It'll take longer, but I'll keep it until then."

Geraldine can see Greg getting out of the car, striding up to the front door to get her. "Yes, yes, I'm coming, I'm coming," she says. "Thank you, Matty." By now Greg is standing in front of her and she can see his shoulders rising and falling. His breathing is ragged and there is a rash of sweat on his brow. He really should get his cholesterol checked. Sometimes, she thinks there are so many people to worry about, she's going to cave in completely.

◆

KEITH AND KAREN have a small baby that they carry, discreetly, in a papoose. It is navy blue with a tartan lining, this papoose—or "sling," Karen calls it—and the baby is so tiny it looks like another fold in the fabric, only its wine-colored face visible, scrunched against Keith's T-shirt, hair so dark and primeval it still looks wet from the birth canal.

"How old is she now?" asks Martha, peering, as she puts an espresso for her and two decaf lattes for them down on the cafe table. "How many weeks?"

Keith says, "Two" at the same time Karen says, "Three," and they laugh. Keith and Karen are Martha's kind of parents.

Martha sits down between them. "And are its eyes open yet?" It's her favorite newborn baby joke. Keith bends his head. He has had his hair cut scalp-short, to camouflage his balding crown, and he looks younger. He says, "Oh yes. Won't be long before she's out in the world on her own. It's just a matter of weaning her and getting enough strength into those legs. As soon as she can manage the catflap, she'll be out of here. Did you know, by the way, that mother cats eat their kittens' excrement?"

"No!" says Martha. She laughs. Keith is a biology teacher and his dropping of arcane pieces of knowledge into the conversation is one of the things she loves most about him. She raises her eyebrows at Karen, who smiles back. It is the first time she has met them out of their house since their baby was born. It's a relief to find things between them unchanged. Other people she knows—not Eliza, who approached pregnancy and childbirth like a design issue, but Geraldine certainly—went in butterflies and came out caterpillars. Geraldine started carrying this big fabric bag with pictures of nursery animals on it. But here are Karen and Keith, with just this papoose and a small black backpack between them, seeming to indicate that all that fuss is just a matter of choice, not circumstance. The baby seems to have fitted in as neatly as the legs on a dovetailed table.

Karen has her elbow on the table and she's leaning her cheek on her hand. Her freckly face is pale; there are shadows under her orange-flecked eyes and her hair, which when it catches the light is the color of toffee, is looking faded, as if the redness has been spun out of it. But she has lipstick on, which turns her mouth the same hue as her freckles. She says, "Is your cat past the child-rearing stage?"

"It's not 'mine.'" Martha shields her eyes with her hand and makes her voice sound anguished. "And it's male, anyway." She takes her hand down. "You don't think a little furry friend for the baby? A kitten for Kit?"

This time when Keith and Karen speak at the same time, they say the same thing. "No."

Martha sighs. "Thought not. Oh well, I've put a note up now and hopefully pet lovers will be flocking to my door."

Keith says, "Must be odd, a stepfather dying. I mean, how do you feel? Grief-stricken? You weren't that close to him. Relieved? You don't have to worry about him. Guilty?"

Martha doesn't answer. She looks at Keith closely. He nods. "Yeah. I can see it's tricky."

Karen, who has detached the baby from Keith's chest, is breastfeeding, her little finger coaxing the baby's mouth onto her nipple. She says, "He loved your mum, though. That's important, isn't it?"

Keith, watching Karen, says more to her than to Martha, "Of course he did. Yes."

Martha, feeling left out, says, "Hm."

Karen is her real friend. She has known her since school. But Martha also feels a sense of ownership toward Keith. They met on a train when she was traveling in India. When she got back she introduced him to Karen, and a few months later they started going out. They have opinions about her life and her family; they talk around her and about her. They joke about her sisters: "How's Ms. Control?" they ask about Eliza. "Geraldine been on the phone in tears lately?" When she was going out with David, and was setting up her shop, she saw less of them. There was so little time what with all the dinner parties and the concert recitals and the trips abroad. "Your handsome jeweler," they called him, or "Mr. Right," though she was never sure they meant it. Once, the four of them went away for a country weekend. On the Sunday, David wanted to try out an expensive restaurant in the local village. Karen and Keith slipped off for a picnic. David thought they were nice "but a bit odd." Karen and Keith never referred to the weekend again.

Only occasionally does Martha worry that, behind the jokes and the banter, they notice how little she opens up herself.

Keith is looking at Karen. He reaches out his arm and very gently sweeps a strand of hair away from her eyes. Martha clears her throat and looks at the floor. In India, Martha and Keith held hands on a boat in Cochin. There was a kiss. He was a mess then, all over the place, hadn't known what he wanted from life. He asked her too many questions, looked into her eyes as if he wanted to know her. And that absurd batik hat he wore—like a teapot lid! Looking at him now, she feels a twinge. That kiss is never mentioned, and she rarely remembers it. Now, with a sudden unexpected pang, she wonders what it would have been like if she'd let it go further . . .

She sighs. No, how much safer it is like this, with herself between them, the cataloger—*the curator*—of their perfect relationship. They are a threesome. Things in groups of threes are always best. She leans forward as Karen passes the sated baby back to her father. "And where would you be without me?" she says to this tiny scrunch of life. "Nowhere, that's where."

By the time they finish their coffee the baby has started stirring, and Keith, after trying to bounce it up and down a bit, suggests they go for a walk across the common. It's quite warm when they come out of the cafe, and there are lots of families with children and buggies and bikes striding around in a haphazard Sunday manner. It is one of those autumn days that could be mistaken for spring. The mist has lifted, but it's still smoky at the top of the trees. The leaves haven't yet turned, but the trees don't look quite right—a little too green.

Keith, Martha, and Karen strike off diagonally across the grass toward the pond, not very fast because Karen is walking in a slow, lopsided way. Martha slips her arm into hers to hurry her along and says, "We should go out soon, shouldn't we, you and me? Leave Keith at home with the baby. Or how about a shopping trip?" Karen gives a wan smile. Martha realizes they've talked about nothing but herself all day. She racks her brain for the right sort of question. After a few paces, she says, "So, are you getting any sleep? Is she sleeping through the night yet?" Keith makes a spluttering noise, even though he's a bit ahead, and Karen says shortly, "No."

"Oh God. Are you exhausted?"

"Not yet. Not really. I'm sure I will be, but it's still weird and . . . it is quite nice at night. Quiet, everyone else asleep, just me and the baby."

"And Keith."

"Well, no, actually. He's sleeping on the sofa."

"Too right I am," says Keith from up ahead.

Martha looks at Karen to see if she's serious. She looks from one to the other, from Karen wobbling along next to her, to Keith, also walking with unnaturally small steps, his dark shaved head bent forward, in front. She's sure this can't be right, that parents shouldn't sleep apart. Something must have gone wrong between them. They fall into step with Keith, who has stopped to rearrange the straps, and Martha puts her arm through his, too, and the three of them are linked together, with Martha in the middle, but she has this odd feeling that something is awry.

After that things don't go quite as they should. The three of them would usually go to the movies in the early evenings on Sundays. Today, Karen is insistent that the baby shouldn't change anything. Kit will just sleep, she says. "It'll be dark and babies don't mind loud noises. They're used to the womb.

Think of the digestive system—do you think even Jean-Claude van Damme can throw up anything noisier than that?" But when they get there, they find babies do change things after all. Their choice, a new British thriller "exploring the interplay between sex and drugs in a Glasgow tenement," is adult rated. "We can't let children into that," says the boot-faced woman at the desk. "She's three weeks old," says Keith. "Exactly," says the woman, turning to the next customer.

Martha is about to suggest a meal, when she notices again how out of focus Karen's movements seem, and says, trying out the idea, that perhaps they should call it a night. Karen and Keith both look grateful. They kiss her and she watches the two of them amble arm in arm down the street toward the Tube. They stop, and Karen bends over Keith, fiddling again with the blasted sling thing. Martha corrects herself: it's no longer two of them. There are *three* of them now.

❖

SHE GETS HOME earlier than she was expecting, in that dusty trough of mid-evening. The light isn't blinking on the answering machine—her sisters have clearly given up on her—and the cat is uncomfortably asleep under the kitchen table. It is half on the black garbage bag and appears to have attempted to get to its contents; there are papers, scruffed, scratched, over the floor. Martha bends to pick them up: a couple of yellowing party invitations, a bus ticket, a ski pass, the invitation to Geraldine's wedding, a box of matches with a phone number scrawled across the lid. She gathers them up and puts them back in the bag.

She sees David's writing on an envelope and her stomach

lurches. Under it is a Valentine's card: a black-and-white post-card of a couple kissing. David was always big on the romantic gesture. Why has she kept all this stuff? Leaving David was Martha's Big Mistake: two years on she knows that now. She doesn't need reminding. She stuffs the debris in but as she does so, she sees something else—an old red and white plastic bag from the Notting Hill Record and Tape Exchange, letters from an earlier life. She burrows her hand into this and pulls out a piece of lined paper. Blue school ink. Doodles. "Don't walk away in silence" scrawled across the top of the page, like an epi-graph. She laughs out loud. It is a long time since she has thought about this. Her first love. Her big boyfriend before David: Nick Martin. Another nice man. Another nice man she left. Where does that leave her?

She goes to the sitting room where the table lamps are still on from the morning and now bounce light against the dark windows. She puts on a CD and pulls the curtains closed. Then she stands in the doorway in her perfect home. Maybe the linen cushions on the sofa are too bland, or perhaps the dove-gray throw isn't as attractive as she thought against the pure white Durham, but there seems to be something unfinished about the place tonight, something not quite right.

It must be the cat.

◆

IN THE MORNING she hangs a sign in her shopwindow:

KITTEN

Attractive and unusual tabby seeking
new home on death of owner.
Inquire within.

CHAPTER THREE

the work space

"Anyone who works at home without the luxury of a
dedicated workroom or office knows how difficult it
can be to combine working and living space."

GOOD HOUSEKEEPING: COMPLETE HOME BOOK,
by Linda Gray

SOMEBODY IS a little in love with Martha. His name is Jason
and he is an expert in furniture restoration. It is Monday, his
day for checking in.

"Helllooooo," he calls through the letterbox. "Wakey, wakey,
rise and shine."

He rings the bell. After a minute or two, he sees the flat door
open and Martha comes through to the front of the shop. It's
not that she's beautiful, because she isn't. Her hair is not *full* like
the girls down at the golf club. It's flat and brown, a cap of hair
like on a Russian doll, only her features aren't rounded but
sharp. She's in jeans as usual, and her feet are bare. They are
knobbly feet. No nail polish. She gets to the shop door and
reaches up to unbolt the top lock. Her eyes are puffy and she

looks anxious. She often does. Maybe that's what draws him to her. She is wearing a blue man's shirt, but there is a button missing halfway down and, as she stretches, he has to will his eyes away from the slight gape in the material. She smiles at him through the glass, and then he remembers that of course it isn't the anxiousness that draws him to her at all but this. The mouth, pulled in at the corners, even as she widens it, as if she's self-conscious of the slightly crooked teeth behind.

She opens the door. "Hello. You're early."

"Am I? Sorry. Is it . . . ?"

"No, it's fine." She looks irritated at the apology. He turns away. The market stalls are setting up. He sees his own breath warming the air. He adjusts the belt on his jeans. "Early bird, me."

She steps out. "Nice day. I hadn't realized."

"Is it?" Jason looks up at the sky, which is a dark blue. But it's the kind of dark blue that can merge subtly into dark gray clouds, and there are some of them collecting at the end of the road. "Maybe for September," he adds.

"Are you in the loading bay? Have you got the buffet deux corps?"

"What?"

"The buffet deux corps."

"The . . . oh yeah, 'course. When have I ever let you down?"

"Good," says Martha. "Shall we . . . ?" She gestures to his van.

He doesn't move. "You all right?" he says. "Keeping well?"

"I'm fine," she snaps. Then adds, as if as an afterthought, "You?"

"Fantastic."

"And when we've got that in, do you have time to look at a little three-legged fruitwood table?"

"*Naturellement,* I've always got time for you," he says. He mimes the theatrical doffing of a feather hat. Finally, he forces himself to turn away. Opening the back of his van, he says "wanker" to himself under his breath. He can never talk, or react, normally when he's with her. "Fuck," he adds, catching his fingers in the door. "Fuck, fuck, and fuck."

Martha comes out after him and helps him carry the buffet. At one point, Jason walking backward into the curb, they almost drop it. They get into a bit of a muddle fitting it through the doorway. Finally it's in and Martha inspects the new door catch and the new back legs. After a bit she says, "Great."

He's not sure if she means it. "Really? Is it okay?"

"Yup."

"And you think the stain here isn't too obvious?"

"Beautiful, Jason. Very good job." At last.

He clears his throat. "Right. Where do you want me?" Somebody else might use that as an opportunity to make a rude joke, but she doesn't. And they go down to the basement, where he drops down onto his haunches and studies the fruitwood table. He wonders if she even knows he exists. She's saying something, but it's only about the table. "Is it even worth it?" he thinks, and then realizes by the sudden silence that he has said that aloud.

"Don't you think so?" she says. "I thought it just needed a new joint and some TLC."

"Yeah. No. You're right. I can fix it."

The two of them haul it up the stairs, wrap it in the big gray horsehair blankets Jason carries around with him, and lift it gently into the van. Martha wipes her hands on her jeans. "Right."

Jason says, "Better go. Things to do, people to see."

Martha leans forward and he flinches, but she's only flicking some of the dust from the basement stairs off the shoulder of his T-shirt. "Sorry," she says, jerking back. Sometimes he thinks she knows how he feels and is teasing him. "Bit of dirt," she says. "Filthy down there."

"Yup. Better get on."

She puts her hands in her pockets. "Well, see you."

"Okeydokey, chokey lokey," he says, backing away and getting into the van. "Catch ya later."

"Bye." She waves him off. He glances back in his mirror just before he pulls out into the main road, and she's still standing there, with the early sun on her face and that tower of mottled dark lilac clouds she hasn't yet noticed behind.

Martha is only watching to check that the van doesn't go too fast over the bump at the end of the street and damage the fruitwood table. She thinks of Jason as an extension of her shop, as a tool, no different really from her sanding machine, but today when she saw the grubby cobwebs on his T-shirt she remembered David. He hated getting his hands dirty or ruining his clothes. He used to dust himself down with the brush he kept on his hall table; quick, efficient strokes, like the dabs of a feline tongue.

She turns and goes back into the shop. Bugger, she thinks, I never asked Jason if he wanted a cat.

◆

APRIL ARRIVES AT ELEVEN A.M. in a flurry of apologies. "Sorryimlate, sorryimlate, sorryimlate, Tube," she says, flinging some item of clothing with a fluffy edging over the back of the rocking horse. "Overslept. Alarm clock, blah blah. Tube, blah blah. You know. Nightmare." April is taking a year off from a school in Manchester where she is getting a degree in furniture and product design—failed coursework, serious overdraft—and is helping Martha while she figures out what to do next.

Martha says sardonically, "Ah, the cavalry."

April was one of only two applicants who answered an ad Martha placed in the window earlier in the summer. The other was a sensible middle-aged woman in search of an "outside interest" with which to fill the hours when her children were at school. She would have been fine, diligent, a sensible choice who, on quiet days, would have studied up on *Miller's Antique Guide*. April was none of those things, and didn't. When she first came in, she told Martha that she wanted to transform the way people look at their homes, not simply as somewhere to sleep and eat, but as a temple to their inner selves. Martha asked her where she lived and she said, "a squat in Collier's Wood," and then the two of them laughed for a good full minute. So Martha employed her, giving her too-short and too-tight T-shirt and the hooded sweatshirt the benefit of the doubt. It hasn't taken her long to realize that April isn't a great deal of help, but nonetheless, Martha enjoys her company. On one level, she reminds her of herself at twenty: sloping around, hopeless, pursuing a vague interest in antiques. But on another, she's more like the person Martha wishes she *had* been. On the plump side, doughy even, her face still freckled with adolescent acne, April dresses and flashes herself about with the careless confidence of youth.

Now she's clapping the tips of her fingers together, looking around the shop like a new arrival checking out a party. She is wearing very low-slung, very flared trousers made out of what looks like tent material, which don't exactly draw attention away from the roll or two across her stomach and which, more to the point, will trip her on the basement stairs. Her eyebrows are plucked into a thin, high arch. "So. What's happening?" she says, pulling her pale curtain of hair back and tucking it into the neck of her top. "It's Monday. Why're we open?"

Martha tells her about Graham's death and having to close the shop on Saturday. April's face twists in sympathy. "Ohhh-noo. Ohhh. Poor you. OOoh."

Martha says, "Well, not really. Poor other people. Poor Ian, his son."

April says, "Oh-aw. Bless."

"So anyway," continues Martha. "I thought we might as well open today. Could you get to work on that pine corner cupboard downstairs? The off-white eggshell? The glaze and the paintbrushes are in the storeroom."

"Cool."

"Good."

"Jason been?"

"Yup. Been. Gone."

"Moonsick?"

"Don't be ridiculous." April has this thing about Jason fancying Martha. "He's a . . . he's a . . ."

"He's a what?"

"A *furniture restorer,* for God's sake."

Martha gets up, flicks April's fluffy thing over her arm, and hangs it on a hook on the door. She finds April a marvel, the way she dresses, the way she talks about sex. Even at twenty, Martha was nothing like that. She was with her teenage sweetheart Nick Martin then. He was off at college but he'd come down on weekends to visit her. You'd hear that Ducati he had vrooming down the main road toward her turning, hours before he actually got there. Did she greet him with April's abandon? She didn't, did she? If April's sexuality is like a Louis XIV four-poster—ornate, flamboyant, upfront—hers has always been a Swedish cabinet, pure white, enclosed.

She says, sitting back down, "Anyway, I'm off radar. Late thirties and moonsick do not go together."

"Oh," says April. "Don't be dippy."

"I mean it." Martha suspects April is just teasing her anyway. A woman of thirty-eight must look over the hill to her. A spinster of the parish. "There's more to my life than men. Now get on."

April still stands in the middle of the shop, unconcerned. She says, "I went to see that new thriller set in the Glasgow ganglands last night. Have you seen it?"

"Funnily enough, no."

"It's brilliant. You've got to."

"Yes. So I've heard. Adult rated. Cupboard?" Martha quite enjoys the person she becomes in April's haphazard company: organized for once, efficient. In their odd way, she feels they connect, that she has a better relationship with her than with most of the people in her life.

"Oh. How about coffee? What would you say to a cup of coffee?"

In her head, Martha says, "Hello, cup of coffee," but it isn't her voice, it's Nick Martin's voice. She says, "Oh, okay."

April goes next door to the cafe and Martha stays sitting where she is. Now that she's seen Nick's letter, he keeps coming into her head. For a moment he's fleshed out, at seventeen, in the shop in front of her, the cocky young boy in the jeans and leather jacket, a packet of cigarettes in his top pocket. Rothman's. Roth

Man, he used to call himself. She tries to adjust her image of him, to add on twenty years, but she can't do it. Nick Martin. God. They used to lie on the floor, eating toast, listening to songs about anarchy. He was full of moods and anger (his dad had just left, too), but when he sang along, he'd punch the air with his arm and then let it fall across her shoulders, turn it into a caress. "You make me feel safe," he said once. She shakes her head, straightens her back, swivels her legs around until they're under her desk. "Right," she says.

First she rings Darling Buds in Tooting and orders a large wreath of plain white lilies for Graham's coffin. Then she phones Ian, who is at home, to tell him she's done so and to discuss the Arrangements further—service at the church, 12 P.M.; internment at the cemetery, 1 P.M.; drinks and snacks at "the family house," 1:30 P.M. And then she leaves a message on Geraldine's answering machine, passing those details on.

Also at Ian's request, she rings Eliza at work. Eliza says, "Oh Lord. Friday."

"Is that a problem?"

"Um. I was hoping for Saturday."

"Well . . ."

"No, no, I know. It was only that there's a meeting. But forget it. Friday's fine. I'll be there. I'll probably bring Gabriel, if that's all right with everyone."

Martha says, "Whatever." She smiles at April, who is dancing back into the shop with the cappuccinos. She rounds her eyes as she takes one from her and mouths, "Thanks."

Eliza is saying something about Geraldine. Martha, who is peeling off her foamy lid, says, "Sorry, missed that. What did you say?" Eliza tells her about a series of phone conversations she has had with their oldest sister, culminating in one earlier today in which Geraldine broke down in tears. Traditionally, when one of the sisters is cross with another, she rings the third to tell her—a kind of sibling bagatelle.

"Typical, isn't it?" Eliza says. "Everything comes down to her. My stepfather, my tragedy." Martha realizes that this is her cue to begin a lengthy and unsparing examination of Geraldine's character, but a woman in high-heeled boots has come into the shop with a pert expression on her face. April is leaning against the door to the cellar taking noisy sips from her coffee. You can tell from the woman's stance that this irritates her, that she was expecting more formal attention. She looks like the kind of woman who wants the latest old thing—whatever her friends, or magazines, have been talking about. So Martha says, "Oh, poor old Geraldine. She does get upset by things," which stems Eliza's flow and makes her say, with slightly disappointed sympathy, "Yeah, I know." The woman has gone straight to the armoirette and has called April over with some searching questions. "Is it French? Has it been stripped? What are these darker marks? What exactly is an 'armoirette'?" April is answering with a defensive certainty that would not inspire Martha with confidence: "Absolutely. Definitely not. They are the marks of extreme age. This is a very interesting piece, smaller than your average armoire."

"Martha?"

"Sorry, Eliza. I'd better go."

She puts the phone down and is about to go to April's aid when it rings. She vacillates for a second, thinks it might be Ian, and picks up. It's Geraldine. Geraldine says, "I've had a very upsetting conversation with Eliza. I mean, why is she always so—"

Martha cuts her off, too. "I'm a bit busy here, Ger. Can I ring you back?"

"Oh. All right. But, listen: has anyone rung Philip, Mum's godfather? I know he'll be so upset not to be invited. And what about their bridge friends? The Howards?"

Martha says, "That's a good idea, Ger. Why don't you ring them?"

"Yes, okay."

"Anything else?"

"I can't believe we're having the party at the house. It's practically falling down. And we have to start clearing it, sorting who has what. . . . I'd be perfectly happy to have it at mine."

"I think Ian would like it to be at the house."

Geraldine sighs. Her tone goes flat. "I just am beginning to feel . . . what would Mummy want?"

Martha says gently, "Mum's not here, Ger. Really, it's only what Ian wants that matters. And his sister, of course."

"Is Susie coming?"

"God, I'm not sure. I expect so. Though Vancouver is a long way. I don't know. I forgot to ask. Cheer up, Ger. Look, I'd better . . ."

The woman in boots opens the door to the armoire, closes it, and opens it again, testing the lock. Then she starts poking around inside, feeling the weight of the shelves. April has put her hand in her pocket and is standing by a little too proprietorially. She is holding her coffee cup at an angle and it might be about to spill. Martha says, "I've really got to go now, Ger."

Geraldine says, "Okay. See you on Friday. Speak to you before then. Oh and . . ." She speeds up and this last bit comes out in a rush. "Greg had a drink with David and told him Graham died and David wants to come to the funeral."

"*How* much?" the woman in heeled boots is saying.

"I thought I better mention it to you first." Geraldine laughs nervously. "So it doesn't come as too much of a shock. Martha? Are you still there?"

"I've got to go."

April is holding on to the price label by the ribbon, for security, for protection, and is smiling tightly. "*How* much?" the woman repeats. Martha feels an urge to grab the label, tear it up, and stamp on it. She doesn't want to think about David. But she says, "Can I help you?"

"I was just telling your assistant. I tried to come on Saturday, but you were closed."

"Yes. I'm sorry. My—" Martha doesn't mean to say what she says next. She means to say "stepfather." But she is feeling so tense, suddenly so defensive, she says, "My father died on Saturday." April turns her head a few degrees like a startled bird. Martha has put her hand over her own mouth as if to stop herself from saying anything more. April says, "But . . ." and then Martha, coming to her senses, says, "Sorry. That came out wrong," and she is about to backtrack, but the woman in boots has put her hand on her arm and is saying, "No, no, don't apologize. Please. God. Awful. I'm so sorry." She has stepped away from the armoire. There is nothing imperious about her now at all. She just looks kind. "God, and here I am barging in and demanding service, and trying to haggle."

Martha says, "No, no, actually . . ." But April interrupts, "He had been ill off and on," she says, her eyes on Martha's. "But no matter how prepared one is, it still comes as a terrible shock." She puts her arm around Martha's shoulders and holds her against her bare midriff protectively—or warningly.

"How awful. I'm sorry. The death of a parent . . ." Then she opens her bag and gets out her checkbook. "Look, I love this cupboard. It's just what I've been looking for. I'm often passing and what with parking . . . I don't often . . . but from now on I'm going to tell all my friends about you. . . . Here." She holds out the check, but before Martha can do anything about it, or say anything more, there is a clang and the door opens again.

All three of them turn to see a tall, thin man with straggly brown hair and a lopsided face that seems to be all bones. He is stooping to get in through the doorway. He is probably in his thirties, but to April's mind he looks much older. Martha notices his eyes—one is green and the other is different, bluer. The woman in boots notices his clothes. Nothing matches: he is wearing a thin paisley shirt with orange swirls on it, a tan corduroy jacket with too-short sleeves, and blue trousers that may, because of the fabric, have once belonged in a suit. And the kind of shoes her godchildren wear—like tennis shoes only they come up over the ankles. They have stars on the side, which would be no good for tennis. And these ones are red. He is carrying a small brown leather suitcase, which he puts down on the floor. He says shyly, in a voice that is deep and serious, slightly faltering, "Sorry. Am I . . . am I interrupting?"

There is a pause. He is not what any of them would expect to see in Martha's shop. He is too nervous to be a dealer, too . . . too untidy to be a customer. Martha braces herself for a sales pitch—vaccuum cleaners, maybe? So, there is a moment when the three women struggle to register him. And in that moment, the woman in boots takes control. "No, not at all. I'm going." Turning back to Martha, she says, "I'll send my builder with his van." She presses the check into Martha's hand and then cups it with her own. "Take care," she says. On the way out the door, she says quietly to the newcomer, "Poor girl. Her father died on Saturday." The tall man says, "Oh," and rests his eyes on Martha again. The shop door clangs as the woman leaves. Martha stands there with the check balled in her palm.

April, breathing out, says, "Sorry. Can I be of any assistance?"

The man is stooping slightly. He looks panicked, sways his head to one side to avoid a wrought-iron chandelier, ducking lower than he needs to as if to avoid being attacked by low-flying objects.

"Are you looking for anything in particular?" April adds.

The man moves to the left and straightens. His Adam's apple protrudes when he talks. He says doubtfully, "A kitten?"

April looks at Martha and then back to the man and says, "A what?"

"A kitten. Have I come to the . . . er . . . ?"

Martha clamps her hands together. "Kitten, of course," she says.

April looks at her, nonplussed. The man jerks his head back fractionally. Martha, pulling herself together, realizes two things: firstly that April doesn't know about the cat; secondly that, in the light of her father's supposed death, the man might expect her to sound more subdued. With effortful diffidence, she adds, "Kitten, yes. Gosh, you're quick. I've only just put the note up."

The man has made a couple of tentative steps into the shop. "I was passing and . . . um . . . Was it your father's, then?" He's moving his weight from foot to foot. He's put his fists deep into his jacket pockets. "The note said death of owner . . . um . . ."

Martha closes the cupboard and locks it. She darts April a look. "That's right."

"So . . . it must have been . . . was it very sudden?"

Martha looks down at her shoes. She semi-winces, gritting her teeth and half-closing one eye. "He had been ill off and on . . ." she begins.

The man says, "He couldn't have been expecting it, then. If he'd just taken on a cat, I mean."

Martha draws a pattern on the floor with her toe. She says slowly, "Ah. He hadn't exactly just taken it on. The cat's quite . . ."

"Oh?"

"No. Kitten has been around awhile. You see, he's been called Kitten ever since he was a kitten." Martha turns and widens her eyes at April, who shrugs and, heading for the cellar steps, says brightly, "Cool. Well, I'd better get on with that cupboard."

Martha turns back to the man. "So it's definitely a kitten you're looking for?"

The man has taken something out of his pocket, something round and soft, a ball, a squishy ball, which he's rolling around in one hand. He says, "I've . . . er . . . promised my daughter a thing, er, kitten. It's her, um, thing, birthday. Problem is, the pet shop says, not really the right time of thing. And we don't want a pedigree or anything. Just a stray. Is it . . . is it still available?" He smiles for the first time and it's a nice gentle smile, though his teeth are stained.

"Yes. It's definitely still available. But it's . . ."

The man is looking at her hopefully.

"It's tabby."

He puts his head on one side as if considering it. "Tabby. Now you've thrown me." She thinks she has put him off but then she realizes he's joking, which is surprising because, along with the nerviness there is something unusually formal about him. She can imagine him wanting a 1970s-style reclining chair on a metal frame that someone might have told him would be "good for his back." Or perhaps a weathered-wood reading lamp with a directional hinge. Or a wicker lobster pot, like the one he had as a child, to keep his keys in . . . "Tabby's probably fine," he says.

"But it is a slightly older kitten? Not in the first flush of . . . kittenhood. Though there are lots of advantages to that. Very nice nature. Spayed. Inoculated. Save on bills?"

He smiles again, but more absentmindedly, then looks at his watch. It is a Casio digital watch with a scratched face. The thin black strap makes his wrist look delicate. There are dark hairs on the bones. "Well, it's, er, can my daughter see it? Could I bring her back after school? She's at Kelmscott, just around the corner."

"We're open till five."

The man bends to pick up his suitcase. The leather bows out at the sides as if it is very full. There is a corner of purple fabric sticking out of one edge. He says, "Five would be okay. Can we come then? We have a thing to do first. Um. That would be very kind." He turns. "It's here somewhere, is it? Hiding?"

Martha laughs. "It's upstairs."

He smiles again. "I see. Well, see you later. Five-ish? And, um . . . ." He moves as if to make a step closer to her but then falters. "Sorry about your father."

"Thank you," she says.

After he's gone, she screams with exaggerated embarrassment down to the basement, "Aaaargh." April comes to the foot of the stairs. "*So* sorry about your dad," she says solemnly and then snorts with laughter. "Sold to the woman in the boots," she whinnies. Martha remembers the money then and guiltily unfolds the check in her hand.

CHAPTER FOUR

the stairwell

"There is nothing like the sound of several small
children thundering up and down an old, bare,
wooden staircase to give you a sudden
renewed taste for fitted carpets."

THE COUNTRY HOME, *by Judy Spours*

AT LUNCHTIME, Martha sets off in her Volvo for the auction viewings in Chelsea. But she doesn't find anything worth bidding on. She is later than usual and she doesn't even meet anyone she knows. Usually, there's some fellow misfit: Melissa, a shop owner from Notting Hill, and her yapping dog; or Bill and Steve, two dealers from Brighton. But today, there are only unknown faces, and even though she's tempted by a one-armed nineteenth-century marble angel, it is hugely overpriced and nothing else grabs her. At any rate, not with her mother's house swirling around in her mind—all those bits and pieces that no one will want but will assume can be left for her to take care of.

It's quiet in the shop in the afternoon. There are a couple more coffee runs, interspersed with a bored at-loose-ends visit from Nell, the woman who runs Sustainable Forests, the secondhand bookshop. She throws herself on a daybed. "God, business is slow," she moans, fiddling idly with the edging on an antique cushion. "Not here!" sings April. "But you have to know your sales technique." Martha shoots her an admonitory look. Nell says, "Rent's going up. Have you heard?" Martha says she hasn't. Nell says, "Well, be warned. That's all."

At four, Martha sends April home. At five she opens the door, looks up the street a few times, and then turns the OPEN sign to CLOSED. She is still pottering about in the shop ten minutes later, straightening the patchwork cushions on the two-seater, watering the miniature terra-cotta pots of ivy that decorate the wine table, testing out some of her new stock of "Room Colognes" ("Lavender in the Wind," particularly aromatic), thinking to herself how happy she can be alone in her shop, with her beautiful things, when the letterbox clatters, and turning, she sees two noses pressed low against the door, with a darker shape behind them. Ah, the odd man, she thinks, and his daughter. No, not daughter clearly—his *children*.

She goes to let them in and indeed there he is again, still with his little suitcase, his hair lankier than before, his corduroy jacket buttoned up wrong, and next to him, *below* him, two small children: a boy and a girl.

"Hello," she says.

The two children stare at her. The girl is older than the boy. She's got very straight hair with severe short bangs, and big dark brown eyes that gaze at Martha suspiciously. She's wearing a duffle coat and tights with multicolored stripes, but a thin summer dress. It's as if all her seasons are muddled. The boy is wearing tracksuit bottoms and a jacket with a teddy bear on the pocket. Both of them are carrying tiny plastic bags the size of paperback books, which appear to be decorated with pirates.

The man says, "Say hello." There is something odd about his complexion.

"Hello," the girl says dully. The boy still stares.

He hadn't said two children. He'd said one. Well, just as long as they didn't touch anything. "Come in. Come in." The three of them troop up the steps into the shop, but stop just inside. Martha bends down and, smiling, says, "And what's your name?"

"Hazel."

"And yours?" Her voice is going up at the ends in what she hopes is a jolly manner.

The boy still doesn't answer, but the girl says, "He's called Stanley, but we call him Stan. Except for my Gran, who says his name makes her toes crawl. She calls him Michael, which is his middle name. My middle name is Twig."

The man, the girl's father, says, "No it's not."

"Yes it is. Hazel Twig."

"It's Elizabeth. Your middle name is Elizabeth."

"But you call me Hazel Twig."

"Yes, but that's my name for you. Your real name is Elizabeth. And flesh crawl. Not toes crawl. Your grandmother says Stanley makes her *flesh* crawl."

The girl closes her eyes. "Okay. Flesh crawl."

Martha gives a nervous laugh. They are talking to each other as if she is not here. She says, "Right. Okay. Let's go up, shall we?"

She turns and is about to open the door to the flat when she hears the girl say "Yes, please," and she realizes that she has come up quickly behind her and has slipped her spare hand into hers. It feels warm and sticky. She looks down at it. The nails are bitten and there are traces of pink nail varnish across the middle of them. She says, "So how old are you, Hazel Twig?" and Hazel says, "I'm six and three-quarters and Stan's four. Gran says that's a difficult age, but Dad says he should try being forty."

Martha looks over the child's head to catch the man's eye, but he's not directly behind them like she thought he was. He's farther back in the shop, about to lift the little boy onto the rocking horse. Her grip on the doorknob tightens. Before she can stop herself, she says shrilly, "Ooh, careful. Fragile!"

The boy looks up at her, as does the man. The boy's mouth turns just a fraction at the corner. His eyes are big and brown like his sister's. Their mother must have brown eyes. The man says, "Sorry," and begins to put him down on the floor. Martha releases the doorknob. She says quickly, "It's okay. Just be, er . . . be gentle."

She can hear the horse's hiccuping rock, each creak agonizing to her nerves, as she and Hazel carry on up the stairs. But then Hazel stops.

"Why don't you have carpet?"

"Because I like wood."

"They're a bit hard and scratchy. You might get splinters."

"That's how I like them."

"Why doesn't the light have a shade on it? Why's it just a bulb?" And Martha begins to explain about not being able to find one that's quite right, that overhead light shades are a very tricky area, that she never buys anything unless it's perfect and the perfect overhead light shade has so far evaded her, and then she says, "Look, about this cat, Hazel. He's a really, really lovely cat. But he's not a kitten. I mean, he's kittenlike, he's just not a tiny kitten like on boxes of chocolates, you know?"

Hazel says, "Oh."

"And if it's a kitten that you want, then perhaps we should go downstairs and tell Daddy now that he's not quite what you're looking for—not your favorite kind of cat. In fact, I should have told Daddy this earlier, but there was a bit of a misunderstanding."

"What's a 'misunderstanding'?"

"It's either a lie or a mistake, depending on your viewpoint."

"Oh." Hazel sits down on the wooden stair. "How inconvenient," she says.

Martha laughs. She leans against the wall. "What does 'inconvenient' mean?" she says.

Hazel opens the plastic bag in her hand and brings out a packet of sweets, a tube of pastel-colored sweets in a twist of cellophane. "I don't really know," she says. "Gran says it about Saturdays. The purple ones are my favorite. What are yours?"

Martha sits down next to her and studies them carefully. "Er . . . white," she says. "The white ones are good."

"And the orange ones."

"Yes, I like the orange ones, too. Maybe not as much as the white ones, but they're still nice. You sure you can . . . oh, thanks. You've got a lot of sweets in there, Hazel."

Hazel sighs. "Yeah."

She puts her hand into the plastic bag again and brings out a blue and white packet, and a yellow tube Martha recognizes from her own childhood. "Sherbet Fountain, Milky Way Stars," Hazel recites. She wrinkles her nose. "Milky Way Stars are always a bit stale."

"Maybe you should choose something different next time, then?"

"I didn't choose them." She shakes her head, putting out both her hands, palms up, as if explaining something to an idiot. "It's a party bag."

"What's a party bag?"

"From a party."

Martha says, "Oh. I see. Like a going-home present. Was it fun?"

The girl sighs again. "Not really. The usual."

There's a pause. The girl looks very serious. They can hear muffled giggles from downstairs. Martha thinks, What kind of a child is this, so blasé, and says, "Listen, shall we go and look at the cat? Or would you rather not bother?"

The girl gets up off the bare stair. She says in a singsong voice, "No, let's go."

So they do. They carry on up the stairs and into Martha's flat and together they look in the kitchen ("Not there," sings Hazel), and the sitting room ("Not there"), and finally the bedroom, where on the end of the duvet, on top of Martha's beautiful, delicate, dove-gray pashmina, they find Kitten.

When he opens one eye and sees them, Kitten behaves like a cat that has gotten used to its habitat. He stretches out, his mottled stomach rippling, the tips of his paws and his claws reaching out away from them as he stretches, lengthening his body into a crescent. He tucks his head upside down, revealing his throat to them. Then he twirls over onto the other side, as if he is no longer interested. The girl says, "Oh," and goes up to him cautiously. "He-llo," she says. "Hell-o." She strokes the top of his head with straightened fingers.

Martha resists the temptation to shoo the cat off the shawl. Instead, she says quietly, "He won't bite."

The girl turns, looking irritated. "I know. I'm just letting him get used to me."

Martha says, "Oh, right." And she stands and watches as this girl, this Hazel Twig, massages the cat under his chin and rubs her hand against his back. "Do you know?" the girl says after a bit, "His feet smell just like feet. Like our feet—they have that sort of feety smell."

Martha laughs. "You'd think they'd smell of fur."

"Yeah." The girl bends to sniff some more. "But they don't. They smell of feet." She burrows her face into his outstretched stomach. She stays there a bit, making a cooing, chortling sound, and then she stands up and says, shrugging, "I did sort of want a kitten."

Martha feels a wave of unhappiness come over her. This cat and this little mite, whose mother doesn't dress her properly. She says, "I know. I know. It's just the cat is called Kitten. I think that's where we went wrong. . . ."

"Daddy said it was going to be a kitten."

"I know. It was a misunderstanding."

"A mistake?"

Martha nods her head and then shakes it. "More of a lie."

The girl thinks for a bit and then says, "Why are there price labels on everything?"

"Sorry?"

"All your stuff. It's got tags on it."

"Well, it's a shop."

"Up here, I mean. Why has all your furniture, like your blanket, got prices on it?"

"Well, some of it's from the shop and some of it's going to go back to the shop."

"Why?"

"Because that's my job. I keep things. I sell things. I . . ."

Hazel says, "I wouldn't sell my things. Like my Barbie duvet cover. It's mine. I wouldn't want to sell it."

"Yes. Well, you don't have a shop."

Frown. "Oh. I think I'll go and find my daddy now."

They meet the man and the boy coming up. The boy is grinning, though he stops when he sees Martha, and the same wary look comes over his face. The man says to the girl, "Find the kitten?"

Martha can feel Hazel looking at her. And then Hazel says, "It's a cat. He's nice. His tummy is soft. He gave me a kiss on the nose. And his feet smell like feet."

"He needs a good home."

The man still doesn't look at her. He says to the girl, "Do you want to go back now and think about it? We can call the lady later."

Hazel doesn't say anything. She is still holding her bag of sweets. The boy starts swinging on the banister. He's leaving marks with his sneakers on the wall. He jumps up and down on the wooden stairs and the sound reverberates. The naked bulb hanging from the ceiling sways. Martha thinks the girl wants a kitten: she should have a kitten. She's about to say this, when Hazel says it for her. "No."

Martha says swiftly, "No, I didn't think so." They should all leave her now and she won't have to think about them anymore, or worry why their clothes don't match. She gives a quick smile at the father. His hair is long in some places and short in others. There are smile lines at the sides of his eyes, a neat fan, but also deep grooves between his eyebrows hacked at random. And those odd eyes. Martha makes a small movement with her hands that is meant to urge them down the stairs and out of her shop and off to wherever it is they belong. It's too crowded all of a sudden. It's only a small stairwell, after all. The man nods awkwardly. He makes an abrupt exhalation sound, like a train coming to a halt, and turns as if to go. But the girl hasn't moved. She says, with more panic now, "No." The man, who is holding the boy's hand, turns his head up to her. "No," she says again. She has sat down on the stairs with her little plastic bag of sweets on her lap. "I know I said I wanted a kitten," she says. "But, Dad, would it be all right if I had this cat instead?"

The man is looking up at his daughter. He widens his eyes, which causes the grooves between them to disappear, and he opens up his arms theatrically. His wedding ring spangles in the air. The little boy starts laughing, and the girl has jumped up and is laughing, too. Martha feels something well up inside. It isn't tears, she knows that. It's more like indigestion. Heartburn, maybe. She takes a deep breath. "Well. Whatever," she says.

They don't take the cat that night. There are things to get. Food and a basket ("And toys!" the little girl cries. "Pretend mice, and balls with bells in them."), and both children have school all week so it would be better, their father says, if they waited until the weekend to come and get him. He has come up to inspect the new cat and as he says this, he is rubbing his finger under his tabby chin.

"Kitten," he says, smelling his feet, and the name comes out like an endearment.

Martha says "Fine" to everything. She is feeling sheepish now. The woman who rejected the nice cat. She tells them to come before she opens. On Saturdays, she says, we open at ten A.M. We can get very busy. The woman with a lot of com-mitments. Then she waves them out and watches as they go up the street, the tall awkward man still holding the boy's hand, the girl skipping ahead, a gypsy in her stripey tights and sum-mer frock. But it's not summer. It's autumn. Though it's hard to tell today; bright one minute, stormy the next. And there's something odd about the light. She can't see the sun from here but it must be slanting through a cloud, sneaking low across a garden, because it's hitting the side of the building at the end of the road, striking it orange as the girl and the man and the boy walk past.

◆

MARTHA PLANNED to be in the north of England this week, for the big monthly trade fair that takes place on a for-mer airstrip outside a town called Newark. Usually, she hires a van and buys so much furniture, both from the fair and from local dealers, she has to secure the doors shut with string.

Graham's death means she hasn't gone this month, and the gap in her schedule leaves her this evening with unexpected time on her hands, no string to bind it with. So she goes to bed early, with a cup of coffee and a pad of paper, her head full of lists. There is a lot to work out: the house, all that furniture to be divided up and shifted, with the attendant arguments, no doubt; and the funeral to organize. She could ring Ian and Julia and see if she can help. But as she lies there, a strange lassitude comes over her. She drops the pad and lies back into the pillow (which smells of fresh ironing and violets—Eau de Lit, which she buys in a bottle), flexing her legs into the smooth, cool reaches on the other side of the bed. The movement disturbs

Kitten, who stands up, stretches, and collapses back in a new position against one of her feet. She is about to kick him off when she remembers Hazel smelling his paws. Is she awful to be getting rid of him? Is it so out of the question to think of an old cat living among her old things?

She lets herself dwell on this thought for a moment, and then, her eye catching the nineteenth-century candle sconce on the wall, corrects herself: her *lovely* things.

Under the table in the kitchen still sits the bag of letters, and after a few minutes she gets up and collects it, heaving it up onto the bed. Here is something she can do. She can organize this stuff, sort it into piles, create a catalogue, organize her mind before seeing David on Friday. She starts sifting through it. On the top, there are stiff, white envelopes, with postmarks from Europe (he traveled a lot for the auction house where he worked). Inside are love letters: "My dearest Martha," reads one. "After you left on Tuesday, I took a walk into the old town and found a shop selling embroidered antique fabric. How I wished you'd been with me." His handwriting is impeccable. He always used a fountain pen.

Another reads, "My darling, I think I have found us the perfect apartment. It has floor-to-ceiling windows and a view of the mountains. There is a polished marble counter in the kitchen . . ."

Martha folds the letter and puts it back in the envelope. At the bottom of the bag are other things: bus tickets, concert tickets, postcards, torn-out pages from notebooks, notes passed in class, a great muddle of memorabilia. Some documents have dates, lots don't. There are bits and pieces that mean nothing. She picks out a matchbox with the name of a central London restaurant on it. Why did she keep that? In her other hand is a ticket for an Ian Dury concert . . . oh, that's a different story. That she remembers, not just the music, but the bus ride home, the plush seat rough beneath her knees. She went with Nick and they bought fish and chips and . . .

Because David isn't the only man in her past. For the last two years he has filled up her head, blotting out anything else. The Big Mistake, the Perfect Boyfriend she left on a whim and has spent every other moment since regretting. She has let herself forget Nick. In her head, he has been slotted inside David, like a small Russian doll or marquetry box, inside the next size up, enclosed, superseded. Or maybe he was like a cracked ornament on a shelf, concealed behind the perfect piece, the Ming vase. But now, with an empty evening ahead of her, she separates them, sets them up alongside each other, so that she can assess them clearly.

Nick Martin, the wild kid, the brilliant activist, who didn't even have to try to do well at school. Nick Martin, who listened to music that slightly scared her, who thought he could change the world. He was raggedy and skinny, like Iggy Pop, but when he smiled he looked so innocent and winning you wanted to kiss him. Which she would.

"Auntie" he used to call her. Or sometimes "Mum." "All right, Mum," he'd say when she told him to put on a sweater or take the inhaler he needed for his asthma. They met in a crowd of kids who went to the same school. She didn't understand at the time why he picked her. There were other girls who wore torn fishnet stockings and dyed their hair shocking black. He came up to her in the pub one night and later they found themselves peeling off from the others, and wandering along the

Thames. It was dark, but the water shone orange under the streetlights. "My dad's walked on us," he said. "Left my mum for another woman." Martha knew all about that, by then she felt like an old hand. "You'll feel better," she said. "I'm sure he still loves you. And you'll get more presents at Christmas." He held her hand. "I sound cool," she said, "but it still hurts," and then she told him how bitter she felt because Eliza, her younger sister, had gone to stay with their father in France. She couldn't go because of her bad grades. "I'm crap at everything," she said. When they reached the community center, he kissed her. "You're not crap at this."

He was fumbling. There was a rash of acne at the line of his collar; the soft beginnings of a beard on his face. A few weeks later, she smuggled him into her room. The house was often empty. Her mother had just met Graham, Geraldine was at college, Eliza was on that holiday in France. When they made love, it was the first time for both of them.

They began to see each other every day after school, hang out at each other's house on weekends. There were the gigs—not just Dury but The Undertones, The Buzzcocks, hot, pogoing nights. She often wondered again why he'd chosen her, but she knew now he'd never leave, that she had replaced something in his life.

And then he left for college in another city. He had bought that motorbike by then, the Ducati.

The cat has crept up the bed. He is lying alongside her ribs and purring. A Ducati purr.

The day Nick left she watched it roaring away from her down the street, strained her ears until she couldn't hear it any longer. Of course he came back the very first weekend, and maybe the one after that, but then it became harder. Visits were canceled at the last minute. There were parties, political meetings. When they did meet, he talked about people she didn't know.

She began to feel the disparities in their lives. She was working at a stall in Camden Market, selling Peruvian hats for a friend of a friend. She thought she'd never make anything of herself. He was destined, everyone said, for great things. She began to wonder what they had in common, to remember how much she didn't even like the music they listened to. How she didn't care about "the destruction of the class structure." She felt left out. She identified a fault in her relationship with him, a hairline crack, that would break them apart sooner or later— like in a beautiful Victorian teapot that can never hold water.

The last time they met was "on neutral ground," a cafe in central London. "Do you understand?" she asked. He didn't look up from the table.

"No."

She said, "We've grown apart."

He was fiddling with a box of matches. He said they hadn't, that she wouldn't work at it, that was all, that things weren't always perfect. "It's just like you not to try," he said, with sudden bitterness, tearing the matchbox into shreds. "As soon as things get tough, you give it up. Schoolwork, jobs, it's all the same. Things aren't naturally perfect. You have to try a bit." He was so angry. She used it as an excuse to leave the cafe before she cried, to bolster her determination to finish it. See, he's not even that nice, she thought to herself.

She sighs. She's stroking the cat. If she thought of her relationship with him at all before it was as an object that was damaged, past repair. But, holding it to the light now, she sees potential, new uses it could have been put to. If she stayed with him, worked at it, *used the right glue,* could the relationship have been repaired? Did she leave David for the same reason? Did something go wrong and she just cast the relationship aside? She can't even remember *why* she left David. Decisions, she thinks, are as light as dandelion seeds. Only later do you see how each one, made on a whim, has taken root somewhere.

She is about to close the bag when she realizes she still has the matchbox in her hand. She looks at it. The Cafe Madrid: of course. It arrived in the post a few days after her last meeting with Nick, identical to the one he'd torn up, but complete. She opens the lid. Inside, he's written, "Can we mend it?" She hears her heart in her ears. Is it too late to write back?

A paw stretches out. She looks down at Kitten. What an extraordinary position he is in, hammocked like that in the crook of her arm, like a person in a deck chair. It occurs to her that he isn't so commonplace, that maybe, as cats go, he's quite exceptional.

CHAPTER FIVE

the kitchen

"The great thing about kitchen clutter is that it doesn't
usually hold any emotional attachments."

THE LIFE LAUNDRY: HOW TO DE-JUNK YOUR LIFE,
by Dawna Walter and Mark Franks

KAREN IS breastfeeding when Martha drops in on her the
next morning. She is still in her nightie and sits nursing the
baby in the kitchen armchair, plump and A-line, like an angel
on top of a Christmas tree.

Keith and Karen's house is in a state of flux. There are
swatches of different-colored paint on the walls with pencil
marks underneath saying things like "String" and "Dead
Salmon." The floorboards have been sanded, but the skirting
boards are scuffed. Martha thinks the house has potential.
Keith calls it "a work in progress." Karen, who campaigns for
the homeless, says they are lucky to have a roof over their
heads at all.

In the kitchen, bouquets of flowers are stuffed in inappropriate vases and New Baby cards litter the dresser. A plastic basket is piled high with dry, creased clothes; kitchen towels are soaking in the sink and the dirty dishes are cramped for space on the side. The baby, such a small thing in itself, seems to have created an enormous amount of displacement, the contents of the house splattered like bathwater after a hippopotamus has gotten in. There are clothes everywhere. Keith's computer is on the table; piled up haphazardly are the biology books and dictionaries, all the paraphernalia Keith needs for the textbook he was supposed to have finished this summer. On top of them, precariously, is a camera out of its case.

Martha fusses around, making tea. She feels tender toward her friend, and this tiny baby, so vulnerable somehow in the middle of this chaos. She is chastened, too. She was so self-absorbed on Sunday and yet here is all this upheaval.

She says, "I think I like 'Pickled Herring' best. What about you?"

"What?"

"On the walls."

Karen looks vague. "Oh God, I don't know," she says, and starts telling her about the midwife who's just been to visit and the indignity of having her stitches inspected. "She poked around and then she said thoughtfully, 'Hm, three layers, I see.'"

"Three layers?" says Martha, wincing. "Poor you." She lays Karen's tea down gently at her side and hovers at her shoulder, trying to look more closely at the baby's wrinkled face. "She's very noisy, isn't she? She's really slurping it in. Does it hurt?"

Karen rearranges the baby and with her spare hand carefully moves the mug to the other side of the table out of range of the baby's foot. "Not really. She's got the knack now. Can you pass me that cloth?"

Martha passes it to her and then starts tidying up the books on the table.

"Leave it." Karen gestures to her to sit down. "It doesn't matter." Martha, putting the camera back in its case, takes the chair next to her. She wills her eyes away from the ironing and watches as Karen wraps the cloth around the baby's chest and then maneuvers her into a sort of upright, sagging position. Cupping the baby's tiny boneless chin, she taps her gently on the back as if in congratulation. Karen sees Martha looking and says, "Wind."

Martha says, "I know," though actually it was Karen she was watching. She has never seen her looking so serene or so happy. She says, "Is everything okay between you?" remembering the separate beds, but Karen just smiles and says, "I'm exhausted but it's wonderful," and Martha feels the same pang she felt the other day, the same feeling that Karen and Keith created something without her really noticing.

Families bother Martha. They seem to create so much muddle and complication. Her father's latest children, her little half-sisters, just seemed like gnats to be swatted. You'd be trying to have a conversation with him and they'd be in the way, crying in his arms or wriggling in their strollers. She knew he was proud of them—little Odaline and little Agnes—but even he seemed to prefer them out of the way. "Eloise," he'd call out to the latest Mrs. Bone (an athletic, highly successful French lawyer, a few years younger than Martha). "I think Odaline needs changing," as if it was beyond him.

Geraldine and Eliza both attack family life as a way of

proving something. The other day, Martha saw Geraldine slamming the door of the dishwasher as if she wanted to kill it. But she didn't *say* anything out loud. She seems determined to re-create herself in their mother's image. Her children seem to wear her down, to exhaust her. She often seems exasperated by the dullness of her chosen path. But it's as if she's desperate to make it work, to "make a home" that Gregory—unlike their father—won't want to leave.

All Eliza's energies seem to go into *not* being their mother. *She's* the breadwinner, the one who calls the shots. Denis is the one trailing around the Science Museum on a Saturday morning, when she's away on business. Recently, when she was away at some conference or other, Geraldine said, "I don't know why Eliza *had* a child if she's never going to see him . . ." and much as Martha had wanted to agree, she felt overcome suddenly, like someone adjudicating a tennis match between mortal enemies. Why don't they just enjoy themselves?

"You all right, Martha?"

Karen has wrapped Kit in a small white sheet and put her into the Moses basket.

"I was just thinking about my sisters. They were so on edge with their babies."

"Maybe it was you?"

"What do you mean?"

"I just mean it's hard when someone's watching. It can make you feel self-conscious."

"You think I make them tense?"

"No. But stop tidying."

Martha was fiddling with the books on the table, organizing them into piles without even realizing she was doing it. She looks down into the Moses basket. Kit's fingers are up to her little red, wizened face. For a weird moment, she imagines that Kit belongs to her, that she let that kiss in Cochin develop. She wants to snatch her up. Karen comes up behind her and the feeling goes. She is left with the sense that the world is full of babies that might have belonged to her and don't.

"David's going to be at my stepfather's funeral," she says.

"Oh. Really?" Karen looks concerned.

"And I've found this old bag of letters," she continues. "I've been reading them and I can't stop thinking about the past."

"Oh yes?"

"Somewhere," she says dramatically, "I went wrong."

Karen sits there, still in her nightie, looking worried. "Oh yes?"

"Somewhere along the line"—she's still using the same melodramatic tone—"I may have left the wrong man."

"Which?" Karen is laughing now. "There've been so many. Oh." She stops laughing. "Or do you mean David? Why did you leave him?"

"No. Not David." Martha juggles the marquetry boxes in her head. "Nick Martin."

"Nick Martin?"

"Yeah, but I've lost touch. I had an old number. I tried it this morning, but—" Martha herself laughs now, to pretend she doesn't feel as seriously about this as she does. "But it was out of service."

"Nick Martin. That's going back." Karen thinks for a moment, then says, "Well, if it'll take your mind off seeing David, let's try. Friends Reunited! You know that website where you can track down people at your school? Let's try that."

So they ease past the sleeping baby to the computer and for a good half hour they discover that Penny Hatch is a nurse in Kent, Samantha Toay has four boys, and Helen Cohen imports olives with the husband she met on safari. Their contemporaries at St. Hillier's School for Girls are, it seems, alive and well and thrilled to hear from anyone who knows them! At St. Hillier's School for Boys, there are fewer entries for their year. There is no mention, or sign, of Nick Martin. "Figures," says Karen. "He was never a conformist."

Martha leaves a bulletin by her name saying: "Antique dealer. Keen to track down old friends—particularly anyone in touch with Nick Martin," and adds her phone number. Karen writes by her name: "Charity consultant. Married. New baby. Exhausted." And leaves a photo of Kit.

When they have logged off, mindful of the last part of Karen's bulletin, Martha tells her friend to go up to bed for a bit and says she'll look after the baby. Karen resists, but says finally that maybe she wouldn't mind a quick nap, and to wake her immediately if Kit stirs. "Oh God, she won't stir, will she?" Martha narrows her eyes and pretends to look panicked. "I mean, will she?"

After Karen has gone up, Martha sits and looks at the baby closely for a while. She rocks the Moses basket back and forth gently with the end of her fingers. The wicker feels scratchy, but there is padding inside. The baby makes small, soft snuffling noises—at one point her hands shoot back in the air as if something has startled her. Karen and Keith's baby. She says it in her head, over and over. After a while, she stands up and gets to work on the kitchen. She rearranges the flowers, washes the dishes, and mops the floor. The army of cereal boxes goes into the cupboard. A bottle of olive oil, with a pretty label, and a slim frosted-glass bottle of balsamic vinegar are positioned, decoratively, by the stove. Finally, when all is clean and tidy, she does the ironing. She hums, spreading out the tiny scrunched onesies and folding them, watching the steam rise, hot and white, from the sheets. Before long there are neat, color-coordinated piles across the scrubbed kitchen table. She may know nothing about family life, but just watch her tidy a house.

◆

"OH, MATT. I wasn't expecting you. I was expecting the machine."

"Geraldine."

"Ah. Yes. Um."

"So why ring if you thought I was out?"

"I was just going to leave a message."

"Well, you can leave it with me instead."

"Oh. Yes. Of course. Are you sure you've got a minute? Or am I disturbing you?"

Geraldine is at her most twittery. Martha has just walked into her flat. She is feeling positive, full of action. She has tidied Karen's kitchen. She has *helped out*. The decision to track down Nick Martin has excited her; she is filled with anticipation, with the sense that she might be about to discover something she can mend and beautify (rather as she would have felt if she had gone to the Newark fair after all). She is determined not to be irritated. She says, "No. No. It's fine. I've just popped up to make a cup of tea. April's in the shop. Fire away."

"Ah. Well. I was ringing about Friday. It just struck me that maybe we should all—you, me, and Eliza—visit Pen Ponds on the way to Wimbledon. At eleven-ish? There would be plenty of time. We could have a little ceremony like we had there with Mother's ashes. I realize we won't have Graham's ashes to throw in, but we could take some flowers and scatter the petals.

Or we could take something that belonged to him . . . some personal item. If you think that is a good idea, should we go in one car, us three, or in separate cars? I don't know. What do you think? Also, shall I take the children out of school? I mean, he was their step-grandfather, but it wasn't like they knew him terribly well. Um . . ."

Martha says, "It's a good thing you got me. You'd have filled the answering machine up for the whole day."

"Oh, I'm sorry."

"I'm joking."

"Oh. So what do you think?"

Martha takes in a deep breath but lets it out quietly so it won't sound like a sigh. "Okay. Pen Ponds is a good idea. Item of Graham's? Um. Can't think of anything. Copy of *Concrete News*, shredded? That's a joke. I'll think. Separate cars best. Kids? I don't know. Let them come? It's up to you. Anything else?"

"No. That's it. Are you sure about separate cars? Wouldn't it be nicer if we went together? Us three?"

"No. I think separate cars are a good idea. Because we'll be going straight on to the tea and cakes, won't we, and I don't know how long . . ." Martha breaks off. The dislocation is her way of letting Geraldine know how she feels about David being there. "How long I'm going to stay."

Geraldine says hastily, "No, no, of course. No, I understand. Eliza and I will go together."

Martha is about to put the phone down when she feels Kitten weaving in and out of her legs, hoping for food. "Oh, I almost forgot. Are you still there? One piece of good news. I've found a home for Kitten."

"Really?"

"Yes. A nice man saw my ad, wanted a cat, liked Kitten, there you go. Signed, sealed, and delivered. Actually not delivered, they're coming on Saturday. But the whole thing was much easier than I thought. Isn't that good? Though actually I think I might quite miss him now."

Geraldine says, "Oh, what a relief. Where do they live, nearby?"

Martha has put down some cat biscuits and begun absentmindedly to tidy up the kitchen. But at this she pauses, the carton of milk in her hand, the fridge door open. "That's a good point. I forgot to ask that." She laughs. "Must be quite near because the kid goes to Kelmscott Primary."

Geraldine says, "You don't know where they live?"

"No." Martha replaces the milk and swings the door shut. "I forgot to ask."

"Oh, Martha."

"What do you mean, 'Oh, Martha'?"

"Well, you can't just let Kitten go without checking out where they live. You've got to do a house check."

"Geraldine, I am not doing a house check for a secondhand cat."

There is a long silence. Finally Martha adds, "I mean for a cat. Honestly, Ger."

The phone in her ear fizzes. She can't even hear Geraldine breathe. Martha says, "A cat, Ger. It's not a person. It's not Graham. It's not Mum. It's a cat."

There is a further beat. Then Geraldine says quietly, "Give me their number. I'll do it myself."

Martha sits down at the table. "I don't have their number," she says.

"You don't have their number?"

Martha says, "No."

"You don't have their number. You don't know where they live. They could be anybody. For all you know they don't even have a garden. You're just going to let them waltz off with him. If they do, that is. They might not even come back."

Martha has an image of the little girl with her face in Kitten's fur. And then another of her dancing down the street. "They'll waltz," she says.

Geraldine's voice sounds a long way away. "Well, people don't always do what they say they're going to do."

Martha smooths the tablecloth with her hands. It's linen. The pattern is called Gypsy Print—roses, sprigged together but loosely, as if someone picked them but then dropped them, still bunched, to the floor. "Look, Ger, don't get upset. I'm sorry. They were nice. They seemed to like the cat. But you're right. I'll see what I can do. Maybe I should have asked a few more questions. Found out about a garden. Met the wife. I'll look into it, okay?"

Geraldine says, "You haven't met the wife?"

"No. I haven't. I'm sorry. I've been hopeless."

"It's just . . ."

The cat is on the counter, staring out the window. There is the staccato squeak of blue tits on the tree outside. The cat is making odd chirrupy noises deep in its throat. The roses on the tablecloth look as if they've been scattered, abandoned. They wouldn't last a minute out of water. "I know. I know. It's not just a secondhand cat."

◆

AFTER SHE PUTS the phone down, Geraldine leans at the kitchen sink looking out at the last roses in her garden. She pruned the Gloire de Dijon hard this year and there are six or seven creamy pink blooms on the wall just by the window. But the leaves of the sycamore have begun falling onto the lawn, which is damp even though it's past lunchtime, and the mint has gone to seed. She should get out there; she should be getting on top of things now that Anna is at nursery school. She puts her forehead against the glass. Once she traveled the world with a national orchestra, and now she can't even keep a house together. For a moment, she imagines herself lying on the sofa in Martha's quiet, peaceful flat, no children to bother her, no shoes to tidy, no lunches to pack . . . Sometimes, she thinks, Martha doesn't know how lucky she is.

She turns to the back door and reaches to unlock it while shoving her feet into a pair of suede loafers she keeps by the mat. The dogs hear her coming and start barking up at her, rubbing their wet noses in smears against the glass. It's a jolly good thing Martha hasn't found herself with a dog to look after. How would she cope with that? She opens the door and bends down to wrestle affectionately with them. Montgomery licks her face and she rubs his silk-purse ears. "There you go," she says. Dogs are so uncomplicated, there are no edges with them, no treading around their feelings all the time.

Living on her own has made Martha selfish, that's what it is. And fancy deciding to go to Pen Ponds separately in her car. Now Geraldine will have to go alone with Eliza and . . .

She breathes in sharply. The thought of being alone with Eliza is not a welcome one. Earlier today she found herself doing something she knows she shouldn't have. She doesn't know what came over her, really. She was at the house, putting stickers on the bits and pieces she might take, when her eyes fell on

The Boy. At first it didn't even cross her mind that she herself had any right to the picture. Eliza was the one who always wanted it and what Eliza wanted, Eliza usually got. For years, they'd all colluded in that. Eliza used to say everything was "unfair." Why didn't *she* get the new dress, the new bicycle? Why was everything *she* got a hand-me-down? Geraldine can't remember when the scales tipped, but somehow, to make up for all the unfairness, Eliza began to reap rewards. Neither of the other sisters got a car, but Eliza got the Mini. Eliza got the deposit for her first flat. . . . Standing in the house, staring at *The Boy*, Geraldine felt a flush of irritation. Why couldn't *she* have first dibs for once? And before she knew it, she had taken the picture off its hooks and loaded it into the car.

It's in the corner of the kitchen now, face to the wall. She has suppressed any guilt. Isn't it about time other people—Martha, Eliza—considered *her* feelings? "I'm not a complete doormat, you know," she says.

It's a phrase her mother used to say. This happens more and more these days. Last week, when she was telling Patrick and Ivor she couldn't understand why they didn't put away their toys, she added, as she was walking out, "I. Just. Don't." And the side of her that was only putting on a display of being cross thought, That's our mother talking. And sometimes in the mirror, she sees her mother's face looking back at her, too: the furrows between the eyes, as if she's frowning into the sun even when it's cloudy, the lines pressing down from the nose to the mouth, little pockets on either side of her chin. When she coughs, it's the *ceh-ceh-ceh* her mother used to make, and it's the same when she sneezes.

She goes to the sink to wash her hands and turns them over

to look at her nails—thickening and yellowing, splitting at the corners. Her mother's hands.

She wonders if Martha or Eliza feels the same. Do they sneeze their mother's sneezes? Do they wash their mother's hands? Or is it her burden alone?

"I'm getting old," she tells the dogs.

◆

APRIL IS IN a bad mood. She is reading *Hello* magazine, but not idly or conversationally, not reading out the good parts. She's snapping the pages over, one after the other. Snap. Snap. She has pulled the zipper of her top up to her chin. Martha has bought April coffee and a doughnut (April has a new thing about the cafe doughnuts), and she hasn't drawn attention to the still unfinished cupboard in the basement. There are emotional dramas in April's life, a man up in Manchester that Martha doesn't ask about, that she treads around.

At three P.M., after getting back from taking a pair of metal beds to the sandblaster in Mitcham, Martha waits a few minutes and then asks April (who really *could* be getting on with some painting) if she minds her "disappearing" again for a few minutes. April doesn't look up. "Go ahead," she says, still flicking. Martha wonders if it's something she's done. But she doesn't ask. When she gets onto the street, it is chillier than it felt earlier, so she has to go back through the shop to get a sweater. April is on the phone herself then—laughing and giggling— and Martha feels awful for a moment, awkward and resentful, and left out, and she wishes she had said something after all.

It isn't just Geraldine's disappointment in her that is behind this trip—though she has imagined Geraldine's subsequent phone call to Eliza, Eliza-the-organizer's *horror* at Martha's in-efficiency, the phone call Martha is about to receive from *her*. But it's more than that, more than a preemptive strike. Important as it is to set up a house check for Kitten's sake—she realizes that now—she's also curious. She has the same feeling she gets when she has rejected some oddment—some ladder-back chair or three-legged stool—and finds afterward that she can't get it out of her head, that perhaps it begs a second look.

She has reached Kelmscott Road. The street is always heavily parked, but as she walks along it today, she notices the occasional woman in the driver's seat, reading the paper, or just sitting. Some of the cars have babies sleeping in them, too. It is beginning to drizzle and closer to the school gates, there are groups of people in huddles, clutching their jackets around their necks, heads bowed, chatting.

Martha stops on the outer reaches and puts her hands in her pockets. Nobody seems to notice her. She looks at her watch. It's ten past three. More people arrive: a couple of women with strollers, the occasional man. She moves over, so that she's against the wall, slightly apart from the others, her eyes scanning for the children's father, though it has occurred to her belatedly that maybe their mother comes to get them—that woman over there, perhaps, her hennaed hair piled up in a bun secured by big black artistic knitting needles, her eyes heavy with kohl? Or that creature with the short blond spikes and the sheepskin vest?

A door beyond the gate is opening and a wash of small boys and girls pours through. She cranes her neck, looking now for Hazel and her brother. Children are being plucked from the melee, parents and caregivers swooping like seagulls, bearing them off like morsels from the waves. Small children with big bags, tired faces, and waving arms, disappearing into cars and up the street. No sign of Hazel or Stan. No sign of their father. The crowd is thinning when suddenly a car pulls up next to her, double-parking and tooting, and the teacher at the door peers in and waves and calls something behind her into the building. And then out trot Hazel and Stan, with another girl. Hazel is holding her brother's hand, but she's talking to the girl, her head bobbing self-consciously from side to side, her hair poking in tufts from two pigtails. She's wearing her duffle coat, but the buttons are done up out of sync. Today, her tights are purple with stars. The little boy's face looks pinched and tired. He is trailing slightly behind.

The children's father has gotten out of the car and gone around it to meet them. He has bent down on the pavement, his arms wide open, and the little boy runs into them. The two girls follow. Hazel's mouth is at an angle, as if she's stopping herself from grinning. She sidles up, allows herself to be hugged, and then pulls back and says something to her friend, who giggles. But the man is all smiles as he opens the back door, extends an arm in greeting to the teacher, and steers the children into the car. It is lime green, with a scratch along one side. The trunk is full to the roof with boxes. It is one of those tinny Japanese cars that you wouldn't want to trust on a highway. The man is so tall and thin, when he bends he's like a coat hanger being twisted out of shape. He is still smiling, but as he straightens up, Martha sees him glance at his watch and a blast of worry hits his face.

She has held back until they are bundled into the car. But now, as she starts forward, she sees that another car has come up behind it, its engine idling loudly, and she panics. She runs forward and taps on the passenger window. The man, who has hurried into the driver's seat, looks startled, frowning properly now. She says through the window, "Sorry. Um . . ."

He leans across and opens the door. Then he looks over his shoulder at the buildup behind. There are several cars now. "Yes?" he says. "Yes?"

"Sorry," she says again. "It's about the cat. Have you got a sec?"

The man looks over his shoulder again. A car three down has started tooting. "Er . . . not really," he says. He hurls his leather suitcase off the passenger seat and onto the floor. "Um . . . Get in?" It's not a command so much as a question.

So Martha does. She slams the door and, before anyone says anything, he drives off. They are both looking for somewhere for him to pull over again, but the road is lined bumper to bumper. Martha says, "Sorry, sorry" again, but the man says, "Hang on, don't worry. Ummmmm. Hang on. Ummmm." This *ummm* fills the space between them so that Martha doesn't say anything even though she realizes she's the one who needs to explain. She's got her legs squished over to one side in the way of the gear stick because the rest of the space is taken up with dented plastic Coke bottles and newspapers and a bag stuffed with clothes. The ashtray is open and full.

He says again, "Ummm . . ." Hazel in the back says, rather peremptorily, showing off, Martha thinks, "What about the cat? What is it?" And then to her friend, "She's giving us the cat I told you about."

Martha has twisted around to face the children. She says, "Oh no. Kitten's fine. I just want a quick word with your dad."

The man says, "Er. Gosh. Bit crowded down here, isn't it. Hang on. Just turn a sec . . . Okay. Sorry. Yes." He rounds into a road where there is a free strip of single yellow line at the end, and comes to a halt. He turns to face Martha for the first time. "Goodness. Sorry. Didn't mean to, er . . ."

"Kidnap me," Martha finishes for him, and then feels embarrassed. He has turned to look at her. His extraordinary unmatching eyes hold hers. She feels herself flush. "I'm the one who should be apologizing. Leaping out at you like that."

"Not at all," the man says, turning away. He is freshly shaven. His jacket is brushed with wet sparkles from the rain.

Hazel from behind says, "Dad, you're going to be late. Again."

"I'm so sorry," Martha says. "It's just I wanted a very quick chat about . . . I was talking to my sister about finding a home for the cat, a good home," she corrects herself, "and she asked about a garden and I realized I hadn't asked about that and—"

"We've got a garden," Hazel says, boasting now.

The other girl says, "So do we. And a climbing frame and a sandpit."

The man says, "Er, we have got a garden. If that's it. Er. Is that it?"

Martha feels suffocatingly hot suddenly in her extra sweater. She has closed her fingers around the door handle, about to push. "Yes," she says. "So. Good, I'm glad about that. Um. Just one small thing—"

"We've got to hurry," Hazel says again. "It said three-thirty."

"Yes, er, I know," her father says.

Martha speaks very quickly now. "So would it be all right if I just popped in and checked? A house check, I think is what they call it."

The man frowns.

Martha says, "I wouldn't. It's just my sister . . . she's quite . . ."

"A house check?" he says.

"Yes. A house check."

"You want to check the house?" he says. "Yes. Of course." He looks at his watch. "I'm terribly sorry. We're a bit busy now. I've got a thing."

"No. No. I realize. No hurry."

"You want to check the house. Um. When, er?"

"Anytime, really. Um . . ."

The man says, "Ummm."

"Unless I brought the cat to you. Would that be the thing to do?"

His eyes flick into the rearview mirror, and then at her. "But what if we failed the . . . thing, and you had to take the cat away?"

"Oh."

Hazel says, "Dad. We're going to be late."

"Tomorrow?" he says. "Oh, no, damn. Thing. Look, Friday morning, how's that? Ten-ish? Would that be all right?"

Martha, hot and red and awkward, says that would be fine, even though she knows there's Graham's funeral on Friday, and now Geraldine's Pen Ponds ceremony. But she lets him give her their address, and finally she can get out of the car. She bends in to say good-bye. She keeps her eyes down so she doesn't have to look at him.

"Hope you're not late," she adds, "for, um . . . whatever."

"Kids' party," he says.

"Oh," she says. "Another one! Have fun then, kids."

Hazel looks at her. "We won't," she mouths—grumpy little thing—as they drive off.

Martha has to walk past the school on the way home. It's empty now and the gate is closed. All the parents and children have gone. She is troubled by her encounter. The boy still silent, the girl too big for her boots. And the man? You want to close your hand over his shoulder through his jacket to check that the bones are there.

She turns the corner into her road, the end with houses rather than shops, her hands in the pockets of her jeans, her head bowed against the drizzle.

She stops, mortification suddenly catching up with her. What an idiot she must have seemed to the man, jumping out at him like that. What must he have thought? And how is she going to get out of visiting him on Friday? The world is a wet, cold place, fraught with problems. She shivers. And, defenses down, a new panic thuds into her. Friday. On top of everything, she'll see David again.

Normally, she is adept at keeping the memory of David at bay. But now a dark blue cashmere sweater wet with rain like glitter comes into her head, and for a moment she can physically feel it against her cheek. She can cope with the idea of him. If Karen pushed the point earlier, she could have answered easily. She left him because, after her mother died, she felt stifled, because the list of pluses in his favor became overwhelming, because one day she'd been eating fish and chips and he wouldn't kiss her. She left him because, *she made a mistake.* She's used to this now. The perfect man she threw away. The idea of him is fine, but occasionally the loss of his physical presence overwhelms her. Oh God, Friday. She will see David on Friday.

She is standing there, hot behind the eyes, when she realizes she's staring into a room of a house next to her. The paper lantern in the middle of the ceiling is on, throwing a blank white glow over the whole room. It must be rented, because the decor, swirly carpet and flocked wallpaper, is at odds with the details in the room: the batik rug chucked over the arm-chair, the Che Guevara poster, the windfall of CDs scattered across the floor. It should be a sitting room, but there's a microwave and a fridge in the corner so it must be used as a kitchen, too.

And hurled, headphoned, in a haphazard heap on the sofa is a man—no, a boy—in a scruffy T-shirt, his eyes closed. Martha, with David in her head, is in need of saving and she finds it here. The boy isn't Nick Martin, but it's *like* him, and for a moment she forces herself to imagine she's sitting on the floor next to him, in the layered cotton skirt she used to wear, those big dangly silver earrings she'd brought back from India, his spare hand in her hair . . . It was long then, and blond, dabbed with those ridiculous highlights that made her look like Rod Stewart. She puts her hand up and touches it. No highlights now—short and brown and tidy.

She looks again into the room. The boy's eyes are still closed. And she wouldn't have been wearing those Indian ear-rings. She broke up with Nick *before* she went to India. But, as she stands there looking in, the light flickers, as if the wind is playing across the wires, and after that the electric bulb seems to shine brighter for a few moments, as if it's been given a sec-ond chance.

◆

THE BOY on the sofa has looked up. She thinks she hears him saying something. "Martha, when did you become so neat?"

CHAPTER SIX

the hall

"A hall is pivotal, not only because it provides the
first impression of your house, but also because
it sets the tone for what is to come."

NINA CAMPBELL'S DECORATING SECRETS

MARTHA IS IN charge of the lavatories.

It's Thursday afternoon. She has come round to meet Julia
at the family house, and has found her armed with lists.

"Right," Julia said, after kissing her on each cheek. "One,
vacuuming. Two, dusting. Three, toilets, upstairs and down.
Funny smell."

The estate agent was due any minute. He was coming for an
evaluation. Julia, who was dressed in white jeans with gold buttons, felt she would present "a better front" than her step-sister-
in-law. "Appearances do make a difference," she sang.

Martha left her wielding a duster in the living room where
there are already stickers on some of the furniture. There is

also a large yellowing rectangle above the fireplace where *The Boy* hung (Eliza, she assumes, must have already been along to take it). Now she is taking refuge in the upstairs bathroom. She has cleared the tubes and ointments from the cabinet, scoured the toothpaste stains in the sink, and is squirting mucus-green Mr. Muscle into the lavatory bowl when she hears the front doorbell.

Snippets of conversation reach her up the stairs. "Very much an asset," she hears the estate agent say. Then Julia's tinkling laugh: "Oh, absolutely, absolutely." The man's voice is gravelly. It comes and goes as he explores. "The hall. Very important. One could do with some smartening up." Outside the bathroom, it's suddenly loud: "Obviously in a state of some disrepair. But original features. Extensive garden."

"Yes, yes," tinkles Julia. "Bathroom!"

The door opens. "Good day," the estate agent says to Martha. She nods. He must think she's the maid.

After he's gone, Julia shouts up, "Used to be a policeman." Martha laughs. "Hello, hello," she says to the bath plug. "Open up, open up." She wonders whether, if he goes around for a viewing and the owner doesn't open the door quickly enough, he says, "Stand back," and knocks it down.

When she has had enough of scrubbing the rim of the toilet and has begun to feel resentful toward her sisters for not being there to wield the toilet brush, she goes into her mother's room and sits on the bed. Things have changed up here over the years—when her father moved out, her mother prettied up the bed linen; when Graham moved in, space was made for the Corby trouser press, loose coins reappeared on the bedside table. When her mother died all her little things vanished, her "effects" divided between the girls. (Martha retreated from the battle for the jewelry and settled for the art deco dressing table set, turquoise shell, circa 1930.) But the counterpane has never changed. It is gold with squiggly lines running down it in tufted fabric. As a little girl, she used to run her fingers down the grooves imagining they were rivers or the paths in quiz book mazes. She remembers lying on this counterpane in a towel waiting for her mother to finish bathing Eliza. Sometimes all three girls would mess around on the bed and the phone would ring and it would be Neville, their father, and when their mother talked, her voice was scraggy with irritation.

She gets up and goes into Geraldine's and her old bedroom. It is a guest room now, the poster-strewn cupboards painted lemon, the bunks replaced by twin beds with padded floral headboards. Martha used to listen to her parents through the wall. She had a terrible feeling inside her, scared and horrified, and yet hungry for it. When their voices got loud she would feel herself cringe down, but if they quieted, she would strain her ears to hear them. It was an obsession to hear every detail. She would go and sit on the toilet if it helped. Not hearing was worse than hearing.

She used to think, Why does she shout at him all the time? Why isn't she nice?

From the bedroom window, you can see across the street and down the adjoining road. Once, when she was about thirteen, Martha was coming home from tennis practice and saw her father sitting in the car. They were half a block from the house and she started smiling and walking toward him, wondering why he had parked so far away. It was only when she got closer that she saw he had a girl with him. She knew the girl a bit; she was a few years older at school. Not much older. That's the thing about her father: he always liked the young, the new. It wasn't long after that that he left.

For Martha, the world has suddenly filled with ghosts. Since her foray into Friends Reunited, she has had several e-mails from old schoolfriends—including one from an ex she hardly remembers. But the memories brought back by messages from girls or boys she used to know are nothing compared to the memories of herself that have begun attacking her in the world outside. Earlier in the week, she met a fellow dealer for a drink in Kentish Town. The Tube took her through Camden and she saw herself, age twenty, wending down the platform to the escalator—a day selling South American hats ahead of her. The minicab that took her home drove down Lisson Grove and she caught a flash of green skirt disappearing around the turning toward Alfie's Antiques Market (where a year later she opened her own stall). Then to Hyde Park and the Serpentine Gallery, where a woman in a black scarf was waiting for her auctioneer boyfriend, clapping her hands together to keep warm. The ghosts are indiscriminate. These are not important moments she remembers, though they are *specific*: a definite occasion when she was hurrying to open up at Alfie's, for example, not just any old day. But why that one? Are they moments in which she was outside of herself even then, thinking detached thoughts about her life (Here I am, a woman on a mission, opening up my own stall at Alfie's)? Or are they random? Either way, she feels a sense of immediacy, as if she has opened something up and now her life is happening on two planes at once, as if she could drive around London forever, witnessing different occasions in her past.

It happens when she's least expecting it. Earlier today, she had an early morning appointment at a house on a tree-lined avenue in Clapham Old Town. The house is owned by an elderly Polish couple who have painted the woodwork around their windows red. Once a month, the Collofs find something in a box or under the bed, or in the attic, that they think might make their fortune. This time it was spoons. On previous occasions it has been wooden shoehorns and damask antimacassars. April, who was with her the first time, would kill her if she knew how much she bought. None of it is worth selling, so it stays in boxes at the back of Martha's car. It is not pity—the Collofs are too dignified for that, too contemptuous of Martha's checks as it is ("Ach," Mr. Collof always says, jabbing at the phone directory, "the man from the other shop will offer more"). It is something else, something to do with the light rustling of Mr. Collof's large bulbous thumbs as he rubs the dust off an old leather tie box, clumsy and yet reverent, the way Mrs. Collof wipes her hands on her apron before taking it from him, that touches her, that reminds her of the time when she was starting out, when objects inspired her with the same deference.

Inside, there were more unrelated memories. A sniff of air freshener in the downstairs bathroom that reminded her, acutely, of staying at her grandmother's house. The taste of the Collofs' coffee—a caramelly, sweet taste she now knows is chicory—that pulled her back to Nick Martin's mother's kitchen. And when she spins the silver cutlery in her hands, so worn in parts it's purple, for a moment she expects to see the lamp that used to hang above the kitchen table at home—a gas lantern converted to electric—spinning in miniature in the round pockets of the spoons.

Now, she goes downstairs, past "the study," which used to be Eliza's room (she never had to share), through the hall, where exam results were torn open, and down to the kitchen, full of pop music and shouting and slammed doors. Julia is here folding paper napkins into water lilies. It is like seeing a stranger in the house suddenly, a stranger doing origami. The old lantern above the kitchen table has long been replaced by a round, modern paper shade.

Julia sighs when she sees Martha and, folding a final water lily, extends the sigh into a shudder. "I'll be glad when this is all over."

Martha sits down on the edge of a chair. "How many are you expecting?"

"Oh, about fifty. But I don't mean the funeral tea. I mean, the house. The finances. The clearing up. I can't bear it all sitting here. We have to put it behind us and get on with the rest of our lives."

Martha supposes that "it" means her father-in-law's death. "I guess one does," she says.

"I mean, I know one has to grieve, but at some point you have to let go. I don't think Ian has even recovered from the death of his mother. He never got over Graham marrying Hilly so quickly." She looks up from the paper plates she's been counting. "Do you think I'm being hard-hearted?"

"No. I don't know. People are different. Some people take longer to get over things. Other people find it easy to move on, to be more dispassionate."

"You and I are similar in that way—when Hilly . . . you were much more sensible than the others. You seemed to get it out of your system much more efficiently."

"Did I?"

"And it's not really as if Ian and his father were that close."

"No. Poor old Graham."

Julia looks up. "What do you mean?"

Martha feels a pinch of sadness. She says, "Not having been close could make it worse for Ian, not better."

"Well, I for one will be glad when the house is sold. All this old stuff. I've never been one for dark wood. Like you, I much prefer paler wood, painted and varnished. All those wonderful white Scandinavian cupboards that we both love. You and I are the same that way. I like to think we share the same good taste, don't we? I'm thinking of having the house feng shui-ed, by the way. Do you know anyone good?"

"Not really." Martha looks out the window, at the weeds. She wouldn't admit it aloud, but she thinks her taste and Julia's are poles apart. She believes in an objective standard of good taste: that she has it and Julia doesn't. She agrees that Scandinavian cupboards can be wonderful, but *only if they are genuinely old*. She thinks the spanking new ones Julia buys from Ikea are vile.

"And then there's all this other rubbish. Ian came home with a box of his father's school papers. I mean, what is the point, keeping things like that? All yellowy round the edges. The past is the past, why keep hold of it? And there were these horrible little things in some of the workbooks."

"Things?"

"Yes. Like tiny, tiny insects. You might think they were flecks of dirt. But I saw one of them move. Ugh." She pauses. "So they went straight in the garbage."

Martha thinks how nice to be Julia, to live so fair and square in the present. Julia has an amazing ability to banish anything disagreeable from the scented potpourri of her life. For most people, Martha has heard, IVF is a "roller coaster" of emotion—raised and shattered hopes, messy hormones. But Julia's experience has been as easy and clean as her kitchen floor. And it's not just doctors, or death. Julia is the one person who has never mentioned David to Martha in the two years since they split up. It's as if he simply ceased to exist the instant he left her frame of reference. The present, for Julia, is all. But is that how people see Martha? Is that what she has always done? Is she a woman who leaves, and moves on, without looking back?

"Silverfish," Martha says.

"What fish?"

"Those insects. They like damp places. They have tiny jaws on the side of their heads. They eat the starch in old books."

"Disgusting."

"No. Fascinating."

The new lantern above the table is rimmed with dust. It was her father who bought it. That's the problem with new things, Martha thinks; they don't last.

"They're fascinating," she says again to Julia. "Industrious little creatures who live only on the old, who spurn the new."

"Well, I don't know. No accounting for tastes." Julia has returned to her napkin water lilies.

Martha is about to get up and set to work on her next task—vacuuming—when there is a ring at the doorbell. When she opens the door, on the step is Eliza.

"Just passing," she says airily. She is wearing a suit and her briefcase is leaning against her legs.

"But we're in Wimbledon, Eliza. The city is that way." Martha points to the distant horizon. "How can you be just passing?"

But Eliza is already in the house. "I just thought it might be worthwhile popping in to lay claim to a few things that

Mummy always wanted me to have. To avoid any unpleasant-
ness." She has been folding her jacket over the banister; now
she turns and marches into the sitting room.

Martha follows her in. "Haven't you already been?" she says.

Eliza is standing in the middle of the room with her mouth
open. "What . . . I mean . . . who?" She turns to Martha.
"Where's *The Boy*?" she demands.

"I . . . I thought you had it."

"No, I do not have it. Has Jul—"

"No."

"Well then, who has?"

"Well, it's not me. Aren't those your stickers, then?"

"My stickers," says Eliza, "are blue. Those stickers are green."

Martha sits down on the arm of the sofa. Eliza had sent her
some stickers in the post. She thinks they were red, but to be
honest she hasn't even taken them out of the envelope.

"*Geraldine's* are green." Eliza has started pacing the room,
inspecting every green-stickered object. "Right. If she's having
the bookcase, I'm having the bridge table."

Martha watches her. One of the advantages of working with
objects, she realizes, is a certain sentimental detachment. Chests
of drawers come and go. She has seen the faces of customers
collapse on discovering that a particular table is sold, as if that
table is unique, as if there was one kitchen table in the world for
them. They believe in love at first sight, in the ideal match, while
she recognizes there will be another along at Kempton market
in a couple of weeks. Eliza and Geraldine seem to feel they have
a *claim* over certain pieces, as if they have already exchanged
vows, as they have with their husbands, promised fidelity for
life. Whereas she—what is it with Martha? She recognizes the

value of that Penwork tea caddy over there. She sees its beauty—
and its faults. It would *interest* her to restore it. But her emotions
remain somehow cut off. In her mind, this is a good thing. It
means she won't get hurt. Of course, her sister would say she
has a problem with commitment.

"I don't understand." Eliza is still pacing, occasionally tucking her hair in fury behind her ears. "I spoke to her this morning. She didn't say anything about it then." She stops again by
the fireplace, glaring at the empty space above it. "I'm going to
ring her right now."

"Oh, hello, Eliza. You look smart." Julia has come into the
room holding a can of polish and a cloth.

Martha and Eliza both say, "Geraldine's taken *The Boy.*"

Julia sprays the light switch and begins to rub it. The overhead light flickers on and off. "Oh yes. She dropped in yesterday. It's the only thing she took. Don't know why she wanted it:
hideous thing."

"*I* want it." Eliza has given up any attempt to be civilized.
She's the spoiled little five-year-old stamping her foot. "It's
mine. It's not fair. She always comes first in everything." She
stomps out to the hall and wrestles with her bag, finally pro-
ducing her phone.

"Why don't you ring her later when you've calmed down?"

"Calmed down?" Eliza takes a step toward Martha. Her
voice is trembling. Martha puts her hand on her arm and says,
"I know it's hard. I know you love that picture. Perhaps there's
been some mistake? Perhaps she's taken it for you?" As usual
she has ended up comforting Eliza, when really she wants to
kill her.

Eliza looks torn, but she pulls away. "I'm going to ring now,"
she says, in a more businesslike tone of voice. "You have to sort

these things out at the time. It's a waste of energy otherwise. I'm supposed to be at work, for God's sake."

She dials. She taps her foot. The other two look on. "Geraldine? I'm at the house. Yes, Martha is here. . . . Yes, Julia is here. But what do you think isn't here? . . . Yes, you do know. . . . Think . . . By your silence I assume you haven't taken it 'for me'? You do know what I'm talking about. Geraldine! Geraldine." She holds the phone out and stares at it. "She hung up on me! That. Does. It." Her mouth is set in a grim line. Martha knows that look: Eliza means business.

"Look—" she begins.

But Eliza turns on her. "As for you," she says. "How can you possibly think of giving the cat away without doing a house check first?"

◆

THE CAT AND Martha oversleep. For the cat, this is all in a day's work, but Martha wakes at half past nine in a state. The funeral. Richmond Park. The bloody home visit. The moment she left the man's car she knew she would have to get out of it. She has even wondered if she might not keep the cat herself. But it's too late to do either of those things now. And with both her sisters on the rampage and no time left to maneuver, she'll have to fit the visit in.

She dresses quickly in a dark purple shirt she hasn't had time to iron and her smartest pair of black trousers, skips coffee, and thunders down into the shop. Here she is delayed by a flashing light on the answering machine: April (clever tactic not to have rung upstairs where she would actually have to *talk* to her employer) calling to say she's feeling a bit sick and will be in after the doctor's. Martha gives a sigh that turns into a groan when she notices the white envelope on the doormat. It is from the landlord and, tearing it open, she sees Nell from the bookshop was right: he is suggesting a 30 percent increase in the rent "due to the area being on the up." She thrusts the letter onto her desk, where she will worry about it later, and slams out of the shop. She doesn't even leave a note for April.

The cat family lives in a crossword puzzle of identical streets full of identical late Victorian terraced houses known as "the Nightingale Triangle." Martha has been in one or two of these houses before and they vary only in being laid out either to the left or the right of the staircase and in their owners' varying attitudes toward period detail. The house opposite the cat house is nice. It has linen curtains in the window and the original cast-iron railings are painted not black but an authentic blue-gray. (Martha considers the hacking down of London railings for ammunition a particularly dark moment in the history of the Second World War.) Number 35, where she is heading, also has its railings, only they are chipped and gap-toothed. The lid is off the garbage can and the foxes must have been in to investigate because there are chicken bones in the flower bed. But there is a window box in the bay containing a lonely heather, and as she climbs the steps, she notes favorably that the door still has its original decorative glass panels—even if one of them is cracked—and the door itself is painted a decidedly inauthentic shade of mauve.

She rings the bell, which doesn't seem to work, and there isn't a knocker, so she does that rather awkward slapping thing with the letterbox until she senses the light thud of someone approaching and sees the going-on-forever shape of him fractured through the colored panes.

"Hello," he says cautiously when he opens the door. He is in jeans and a loose-necked gray sweater that sits at an angle across his collarbone, drawing attention to the pallor of his skin and the dark hairs on the knuckle in his throat. He is also wearing glasses, with thick, black rectangular rims, that are the ugliest glasses Martha has ever seen. On his feet—sockless—are some sort of Turkish slippers. He hasn't opened the door any farther and is still looking at her inquiringly, his brow furrowed above the black hook of his specs. "Hello," she says. Then, as he still looks at her, "Cat?"

"Indeed." He's holding the door with one hand, but he draws it back now. "The Home Visit," he says, and the way he says it makes her realize that he hadn't forgotten, that it was just awkwardness that held him up, not confusion. "Hello, Martha," he adds.

"I'm sorry. God." Martha speaks quickly, head on one side, to indicate that she is in a hurry. "And I don't know your name."

"Oh. Fred. It's Fred. Fred." He puts out his hand and she shakes it. She has to step in to do so and he backs against a radiator to make room, his head almost disappearing into a bundle of coats that is hanging there. His handshake is firm, the fingers bony. And then she's in—and she almost wishes she wasn't, it is so crammed in here. The walls are crimson from the dado rail up, but purple beneath, which makes Martha feel even more oppressed, and there is junk everywhere. Bikes and scooters and plastic bags and a black box and what looks like a load of fishing rods. On the stairs there is the little leather suitcase and a trail of shoes and clothes. Higher up, on the landing, she can see more fabric devastation. Dirty washing on its way up? Clean washing on its way down?

"Uh," she says, when there's a crack under her feet. She's trodden on something. She picks up the pieces. There are bits of jagged plastic in her hand. "I'm terribly sorry." She holds them out to the man. He says, "Thunderbird Two. Don't worry. It's just the, er . . . thing . . . middle bit." He takes the pieces from her and looks at them in his hand. "I'll . . . er . . . anyway. Sitting room?"

He goes through a door and she follows. All Martha can think when she goes in is that she has never been in such a hideously decorated room. The walls are fleshy pink, and they clash horribly with everything else—with the cheap marine blue sofa and the reproduction winged armchairs (factory "tapestry" style), and the orangey-fake pine coffee table. And it's not just that, it's the stuff everywhere, too: piles of tatty cushions and toys, and, on the shelves and surfaces, not just books but countless bits of *junk*. There are pieces of pottery and cotton reels and ornaments made by children out of toilet paper rolls and objects that may have landed here temporarily but have taken up dusty residence: a doorknob, a pack of playing cards, a box of batteries, a homemade calendar with a cotton ball snowman on it, his head hanging down at an angle, brown with dust. Martha wants to put her arm out and sweep it all into the trash. Instead she makes a noise, meant to express surprise and interest, if not exactly approval. The man has negotiated a path through the furnishings and is carefully laying the remains of Thunderbird Two on the mantelpiece, alongside a pile of foreign money and some dried-up leaves.

The fireplace is the original marble, Martha can tell, because someone has begun stripping the white gloss paint off it, though they obviously gave up after the right-hand leg. Now it looks streaky and bubbly, like the smokestack on a rusty ocean liner. In the grate are the scuzzy remains of a fire, the coal dissolved into pink dust, shards of charred wood and snippets of burned paper. Martha is very particular about her own fireplace. When not in use, she brushes it meticulously and fills it with pinecones. She buys them from the Conran Shop, where they come ready infused with the scent of orange and cloves.

"So this is the, er, sitting room," the man says. "It's a bit . . ." He sweeps something up off one of the sofas—a packet of children's crayons—and some pieces of paper off the floor, placing them haphazardly on top of a horrendous television in the corner. He adjusts the glasses on his nose and, squeezing past the piano, turns to go out the door again. Martha follows, noticing for the first time the picture on the wall behind her—a large oil of purple horses galloping through white spume. The paint, which is thick and spiked, seems to rear out at her as she passes.

"And this is the kitchen," he is saying ahead of her. She follows, feeling like someone from the council come to investigate a bad smell. She should have a clipboard. Or a collecting tin.

The kitchen is not as bad as she expected—"farmhouse" style, an estate agent would call it. There is a big old oak table, which she wouldn't mind having a closer look at, but the chairs are peculiar. They are made of see-through plastic string on an aluminium frame, which would be interestingly modern if the plastic strings weren't thick with gunk. There is a big clock above the door with the numbers playfully (irritatingly) muddled and more books on a shelf by the oven and children's paintings plastered everywhere and photographs stuck all over the fridge, and piles of newspapers on the table, and a jug with dying tulips in it. But the room looks clean. Clean-ish, anyway.

There are brown splatters behind the oven, maroon streaks in the sink where the water has run down from the taps. And the walls are . . .

"Burnt umber," she says.

He looks at her.

"The walls, I mean."

"Oh," he says. "Er . . . orange, I think."

He studies her from behind his glasses. "Um," he says. There's a fraction of a pause and then he continues with, "We did take the liberty of—" He crosses the room and bends down to indicate a catflap in the base panel of the back door. He opens it once or twice to show her that it works. Martha goes over and says with enthusiasm, "Excellent."

"We bought it yesterday and, um, I got a man to put it in this morning, so you'd see it. Hazel was adamant that it should be here when you came. She was worried . . . I'm not very good with that sort of, um, thing, but the man next door . . . he is." He lets the flap flip shut. It clatters once, then silence.

"It seems fine." Martha looks out through the glass at the top of the door. "Very impressive." The garden, small and over-grown with a lawn as threadbare as the rugs in the sitting room, is dominated by a large phallic Leylandii. Martha thinks Leylandii should be universally scythed to the ground.

Remembering Graham, who agreed with her, she looks at her watch. "Well, I think you've passed," she says.

Fred has crossed the room and is at the kitchen door. "But you haven't even seen upstairs yet."

"I'm sure it's fine."

"What about his sleeping quarters?"

"His sleeping quarters?"

"We've bought a, um, basket. Hazel wanted him on her bed

and I wanted him downstairs, so we've, er, compromised. A basket under the radiator in her room."

"I think," Martha says, "that he would like that very much."

"Good," the man, Fred, says. "Er. Very good."

Martha smiles at him across the kitchen. "I was wondering about keeping him."

He doesn't smile back, just stares at her from behind those black glasses. "They were . . . *we were* . . . very excited about having him."

Martha wonders if this corrected "we" means him and the children or him and his wife, or whether he's a widower (all this chaos). She says, "It's okay. He's yours. I think he'll be very happy here."

Fred says, "Oh. But, er, if you don't want to see upstairs, would you, er, would you like a cup of coffee?"

Martha looks at her watch. Twenty past ten. She should get going. The traffic across to the park can be unpredictable. She mustn't be late for Geraldine. She says, "I really ought to get going. I've got this funeral to go to."

He puts his hands to his glasses. "Oh. I am so sorry. Your father. Of course. Today. Goodness."

Martha thinks, Oh God. Then, she says, "Actually—" She is about to explain how she came to be pretending that day in the shop that her father had died, when in fact it was her stepfather. But a mixture of embarrassment and apathy stops her. Instead, she says, "Okay, well, maybe a quick one."

He nods and fiddles around with a coffeepot on the stove. "By the way, I meant to say . . . I'm very sorry about that."

"Thank you." So now it is too late anyway. He has his back to her so she can wince.

He says, "Excuse me." He's trying to get past her to the fridge.

She moves out of the way—there's a sudden stench of garlic and miscellaneous leftovers—and when the door swings she sees the photographs stuck on it with magnets. There are pictures of Hazel and her brother in swimsuits—laughing, tongues sticking out, sand in their hair; and pictures of them with other children, eating lollipops on a bench. There's one photograph of Fred on his own in some sort of fancy-dress costume, and another of him with a woman. She has blond shoulder-length hair and a pretty face. She is wearing a halter-neck top and she's grinning, one of those open, unself-conscious grins in which the gums show. "Is this your wife?" Martha asks.

The man is returning the packet of coffee to the fridge. He says, "Yes."

"She's very pretty."

He pauses, looks at the photograph as if to consult it, and says, "Yes" again. He moves to clear some space at the table. "Do sit down."

Martha sidles gingerly into one of the plastic-spaghetti chairs. The strings bend beneath her bottom. She doesn't like to lean back, not trusting it to support her whole weight, not wanting to get her black trousers sticky. On the table in front of her, next to a packet of cigarettes, are more of those miniature decorated plastic bags. Party bags, she now knows. While Fred pours the coffee, she picks one up; on it is an overly bright illustration of Winnie-the-Pooh. Inside are sweets and a packet of oversized neon-colored jacks. She says, "Do your children spend their entire lives at birthday parties?"

The man puts some tiny pearl-blue cups and a packet of biscuits on the table and sits down opposite her. He says, "Er, ye-es."

"They must have an awful lot of friends."

"No. No. Didn't I . . . ?"

"When I was little"—she has taken a sip of her coffee, dark and syrupy—"I'll never forget the feeling of *not* being invited. The invitations would be on some of the desks in the morning and you'd see this paper trail across the classroom and you'd walk toward your desk and then when there wasn't one . . ." She breaks off and taps her fingers on the table. She glances up and laughs.

He is looking at her with an impenetrable expression on his face. He passes her the packet of biscuits. They are dried ones with almonds. She takes one and dips it in her coffee. It is heavenly, half melting, half rocky, so that her mouth can't quite close. Fred has crossed his legs. In his jeans, they look like the lanky legs of a teenager. "So why weren't you?"

"Why weren't I what?" says Martha, through a mouthful of biscuit.

"To the parties. Why weren't you invited?"

She swallows. "Well. I'm sure I was. Perhaps there was only one time when I wasn't and it's that that sticks in my mind. You know, like when there's a big family outing to the circus, a huge treat—acrobats and clowns, helium balloons, a car ride in the dark—and all you remember afterward is not being allowed cotton candy."

"Memory is a funny thing."

"Yes. I'm going through a nostalgic phase at the moment, keep remembering things like that. Perhaps it's because I'm cleaning out the family home."

Martha is surprised at how much she is talking. There is something about his stillness, about his expression. She looks down at the table, suddenly self-conscious, tracing the grooves in the wood with her finger. She has forgotten about being in a hurry now. Fred cups his hands over the cigarette packet and taps it up and down on the table. He says, "And your father? Were you, er, close to him?"

"Oh." She looks up. "Yes . . . no . . . not really. I adored him when I was little. Don't all little girls? Love their dad, I mean. But he and my mother separated when I was twelve. She had their marriage dissolved, so we all had to pretend it never happened. We stopped calling him Dad, or I did, and he became Neville. He ran off with a friend of mine."

She waits for his sympathy.

But he just says, "A friend of yours?"

"Well, she had been at my school. Several years ahead."

"So . . . not really a friend?"

Martha pauses before answering. She has believed her own elaboration of this story for so long it takes a moment to adjust. "No, not really," she says. "You're right. Anyway, it didn't last. He met someone else, and then someone else. Now he's married to a French woman, a lawyer, Eloise, and they live in France, near Grasse. He has two little girls—a whole new family. He started afresh, you might say. Always in pursuit of 'the new.' My father, he's incredibly charming, talks to everyone as if he's known them all their life. Very endearing—unless of course you *have* known him all your life, in which case it's unnerving not to be treated differently. Everyone's his new best friend."

"I'm sure people felt the same way about him." Fred's voice is low and gentle.

Martha sits tight and waits for the moment to pass. Fred says, "And the shop—it's yours, is it?"

"Yes. It's mine. My baby."

"Isn't it a bit lonely? Or does that other girl work with you?"

"Oh yes. She does. April—and we get on very well. I suppose I'm a sort of mother figure for her, so that's nice."

"Ah. She confides in you . . ."

"Um. Yes. No. Actually, not really." Martha laughs. Fred looks at her. "Why did I say 'mother figure'? Um. Maybe because she doesn't confide in me." She laughs again, nervously.

Fred says, "Is her own mother dead?"

"No. Actually, I don't know."

"Maybe you're more of a sister figure?" Does Martha detect a flash of gallantry here? "Or does she already have sisters?"

"Gosh. Actually, funny thing, I don't know that either." She feels embarrassed as if she's been caught out. "Maybe I should find out."

Fred looks at her.

"Anyway," she says. "Back to the shop. I like mending things, getting the best out of them, and then passing them on to a good home."

"You don't fall in love with things and find them hard to sell?"

"Sometimes." She picks up the party bag again and tosses it from one hand to another. "Rarely. I seem to lack the sentimental gene."

There's a long silence. Finally Fred says, "The reason my children are always at parties is that I'm a magician."

She's not quite sure if she heard right. "Sorry?"

"I'm a magician." He pokes his glasses back up his nose again. He has picked up the Winnie-the-Pooh bag and is dropping it from one hand into the other, as if weighing it. "That's why they go to a lot of parties. They come with me when I work."

"A what?"

"A magician. A children's entertainer."

"What a strange thing to be. Is that . . . ? Are you . . . ?" Martha breaks off. She is about to ask him if that's all he does but realizes just in time that to a serious magician that might sound rude.

"I'm Mr. Magic."

"Mr. Magic!"

"Simple but it does the trick. They know what they're getting."

"God." Martha leans back against the plastic spaghetti supports and studies him.

"I do some corporate things, but mainly it's afternoon parties. Saturdays. Sundays."

"A magician. Have you always?"

"No. Only quite recently." He clears his throat again. "I was an accountant. In the, er, city. But I was laid off two years ago." He looks up at the sparse patch of grass outside the kitchen and shrugs. "I'd always done a bit of magic on the side, since school. Mr. Magic was supposed to be a stopgap but it's become, well, rather more established, and I can fit it around Hazel and Stan. I'm quite good, you know." He was doing his deep-voice mumbling thing, but when he says this, his voice rises and, with a twitch at the corners of his mouth, he looks at her straight on. "Kids like me. The mums like me. I'm really very popular on the four-to-eight party network."

Martha laughs. She looks across to the fridge. "And what about Mrs. Magic. Is she part of the act?"

He looks down again. He says, "No. Actually, no." He breathes in through a grimace and fondles his cigarettes. "Ah. Yuh. No, Mrs. Magic isn't. She's not with us at the moment. She's, um, traveling, finding herself."

There is a flippant note in his voice that makes Martha think she can add, "Oh, done a disappearing act, has she?" but she regrets her words the moment they are out there. "Sorry," she says. "That was a silly thing to say."

He smiles slightly as if it doesn't really matter. He says he loves Lucy, his wife, and that he misses her and the children do, too. But that you can't make people stay with you if they don't want to. Martha is taken aback not by what he says, but by the fact that he says it at all. The words seem to come out so simply.

He says, "I'm lucky. Some people, when their wives leave them, they lose their children, too."

The topsy-turvy clock on the wall behind him says ten to eleven (actually it says half past four) and Martha knows she has to go. She can hear it ticking now that she thinks about it—reminding her with every new second of her lateness. (She mustn't be late for Geraldine. Geraldine thinks Martha is always late and there are few things more irritating than fulfilling one's family's prophecies.) But maybe it is the rhythm of the clock or the comforting honeyed strength of the coffee inside her, or maybe it is simply the fact that she has molded the strings now with the warmth of her back, because the spaghetti chair seems unfathomably comfortable all of a sudden. And when she gets up to go, it is a wrench to leave.

CHAPTER SEVEN

the garden

"Many contemporary gardeners cultivate their
gardens as a reflection of the inner landscape, its
features used as metaphors for the spiritual life."

IN A SPIRITUAL STYLE: THE HOME AS SANCTUARY,
by Laura Cerwinske

WHEN MARTHA turns her Volvo into the parking lot above
Pen Ponds at ten past eleven, Geraldine is standing at the gate,
a bunch of roses held stiffly in one hand, and an object Martha
can't quite make out clenched in the other. The lot is almost
empty this early, but Geraldine still waves wildly, beckoning her
in and pointing to her own car in the far corner, as if ensuring
that Martha doesn't get lost in the crowd.

Eliza is here, too, though she is way over on the other side of
the lot. Her head is down, her hands are plunged deep in the
pockets of her leather coat, and she's scuffing the leaves with
her feet. For a minute, as Martha bumps the car over the
uneven ground toward her, she thinks Eliza is sulking. She

assumes there has been further trouble over *The Boy*. But when she gets closer she sees that Eliza is talking into a cell phone.

Geraldine ambles across the gravelly mud toward her. "At last!" she calls. "I was about to send out a search party."

Eliza has turned, snapping her phone shut. She says, "Oh, don't be ridiculous, Ger. She's only five minutes late."

"Ten, actually."

"Ten, then." Eliza's jaw is set (so there *has* been further trouble about *The Boy*).

"I was just worried she wasn't coming."

Eliza puts the phone back in her briefcase. She says coldly, "I don't know why you thought that."

"Well, you know what she's like. And she didn't seem that keen in the first place."

Martha says benignly, "I'm here," because they seem to have forgotten this. She moves over to Geraldine, who is wearing a long black velvet skirt over Wellies, and gives her a kiss on the cheek. They are not a kissing family, but it seems appropriate today. Geraldine's skin, pale and powdery under what Martha now realizes with surprise is foundation, smells of warm apricots. Geraldine looks pleased. She gives a sort of half nod and is about to say something, but then looks away instead.

Martha says, "I had to do a cat check. Remember? Check the house. And the garden? Well, it's okay. They have one. And then the traffic. Accident, I think." She kisses Eliza, too—she finds herself instinctively moving up a social gear and doing both cheeks for her.

Eliza says, "There's always an accident."

Geraldine says, "Well, I don't know why you had to do the house check today."

"*You* told her to do the house check." Eliza is wearing the charcoal Armani suit she often wears to work; her thick curls are tied back. She looks as sleek and elegant as she always does, but something dangerous is gliding under the surface.

Geraldine glares back, but her lower lip wobbles. "And *you* agreed with me."

"Anyway." Martha moves so that she is standing between the two of them. "Shall we get on?"

They set off down the path toward the ponds. It is a sullen day—the sky is slate and dirty cream in horizontal layers, whipped in places into darker peaks. Some deer graze over on one side, and a seagull flies low across the scrubland, wings flashing oyster-white against the gray. They seem miles from London and yet, in the silence, you can hear it on the wind— the boom of a jet heading for Heathrow; the squeal of a distant police siren. An Alsatian noses past them, followed by a middle- aged man in a mauve anorak. A woman, also in a mauve anorak, tramps up the hill some way behind him. The air smells of curry powder and fennel: bracken, Martha supposes.

She says, "You haven't brought the dogs, then?"

"No." Geraldine looks unfamiliar in her foundation. "Of course not."

"Oh." There is a pause. The three of them are walking alongside one another on the path, only Martha is in the middle, in the dip where rainwater collects, and she keeps having to leap over the puddles. She is lolloping to keep up. Eliza and Geraldine are both walking furiously. Geraldine's boots are thick with mud. Eliza, typically, appears to have found the easi- est, driest path on which to walk. "Of course not," Martha adds. "Stupid of me, sorry."

"I couldn't think what of Graham's to bring," Geraldine says.

"He wasn't the sort of man that one associated with anything in particular. Nothing stood out, do you know what I mean?"

Martha says, "Concrete, of course." Beat. "But that would be hard to disperse."

"I wondered about a book, or, you know, an atlas? Because he liked traveling, and they did a lot of that together. . . . But you can't really scatter a book."

Eliza says, "Don't be ridiculous."

Martha is still a little behind. The leaves on the path are skipping low to the ground like tumbleweed. "You could pull out the pages and hurl them to the wind."

Geraldine says, "Yes, but that would be littering, wouldn't it?"

Eliza has picked up a stick and is thrashing the grass as they pass. "You can't be too careful where sentimental value is concerned. It would be a shame to take an object that somebody else loved. I mean, sometimes you have to take other people's feelings into account. You can't just storm ahead taking what you like in life."

Geraldine says, "No, you can't, can you. Sometimes there has to be a bit of give-and-take. It's the *assumption* some people have that they can take what they like that annoys me."

Martha speeds up to get between them again. She says, "Easy, you two."

They both glare at her. "What?"

She says, "Let's keep ourselves out of this, shall we? Let's try and keep this nice."

"I just think . . ." Geraldine's lower lip is going again.

Martha puts her hand on her arm. "So what did you choose in the end?"

"*Choose?*"

"I mean for Graham," Martha adds warningly.

"Oh. This—" She holds out the small bottle in her hand. "His aftershave. Eau Sauvage. It's easy to pour, it'll disperse easily. I thought it would do, don't you?"

Martha suddenly wants to laugh. She knows she should be feeling calm. She says, "What if it poisons the ducks?"

The woman who was plodding up the hill toward them passes. Her head is down and you can hear the pant of her breathing. There is something resigned in the heavy roundness of her shoulders. Martha turns her head and sees that the woman's companion—husband?—in his matching anorak, has already reached the parking lot. But he's not looking this way. Martha thinks, Why hasn't he waited? Why aren't they walking together? Why would anyone want a relationship when they are always so *hard*?

Geraldine says, "Obviously it's not *actually* Graham's aftershave. I didn't have time when I was in the house to rummage through the bathroom cabinets."

Eliza says, "Oh no? Busy doing other things, were you?"

Geraldine ignores her. "But I know it's the one he used—certainly recently, anyway; we gave him some for Christmas only last year, and Greg happened to have some."

This time Martha does laugh. "Sorry," she says, turning the laugh into a cough.

They reach the ponds. From a distance it looks like one, but up close you see there are two: a pair of murky pools, a breeze ripping over them, edged with reeds with a bank wide enough for a path between. There's a tree here, too, its bark thick and gnarled like a picture of a tree in a fairy tale. A flurry of ducks is paddling in the shallows, and a couple of swans glide toward the shore, hopeful for bread.

It was summer when they came here, five years before, to scatter their mother's ashes. It was a Saturday and sunny, and the place was alive with dogs and children. The swans were bread-sated and superior, away by the other bank. But the ducks were still busy and bobbing and the water glinting, spangled with chips of light. And even though Martha and her sisters were unbearably sad, furious with loss, still in the filthy thick of it, that day they laughed a lot. Geraldine stopped in her tracks, stricken suddenly with what they were doing. "Do you think we need a permit?" she said, and Eliza roared as if that was the funniest thing she had ever heard. And they stood together on the path between the ponds, trying to disperse their mother's ashes, forgetting the other walkers and the wind, which had blown all gusty, scattering pearly dust across their feet, and Greg, Denis, and David waiting solemnly for them up at the parking lot.

But today it is all wrong. And all over that stupid picture, that stupid Boy. Why do they both care so much? She feels a tug of irritation, but then sees that Geraldine's gotten mud on the hem of her best velvet skirt, and she feels sorry for her. "Where do you think, then?" she says cheerfully.

Geraldine says, "Ummm. Well, obviously it'll have to be over there."

She points to the tree in the middle of the path between the ponds, where they stood last time.

Martha says, "Okay," snapping her fingers, and the three of them walk across the sandy earth and hover together under the branches.

Geraldine says, "Shall I . . . or . . . would you . . . ?"

Eliza shrugs. "No, no, you." Martha just nods and puts her hands in her pockets.

Geraldine unscrews the cap of the Eau Sauvage and shakes the bottle over the water. Some of it lands on the bank by her feet and Martha's nostrils flood with the intense perfume-stench of peppery nutmeg. She hasn't thought about Graham properly for ages, not even in this week after his death; in fact she hasn't thought about him at all, but for a moment she has him in her head not as an idea, a concept (The Stepfather, The Man Who Brought Her Mother Happiness, Mr. Corby Trouser Press) but as a person: Graham in his best suit and smart side-burns neatly kissing his bride in front of his children outside the church, two pursed lips meeting like birds pecking on dry earth. Before Sunday lunch, in the garden, poking about with his stick as he talked to whomever he could find to listen about whatever local planning application had most recently excited his indignation. And then, at their mother's funeral, an old man with skin as dry as paper, wet-eyed. He was a funny old chap, but he loved their mother.

She looks at Eliza and then at Geraldine to see if they are still glaring at each other. But for a moment, they aren't. And for a few moments the three of them stand there quietly, looking down, as Eau Sauvage mingles with the tame water at their feet.

◆

AFTER THE Richmond Park ceremony and before the church ceremony, the three sisters join husbands and children in a cafe in Wimbledon village. There are nine of them—five adults, four kids—and, once in, they fill a great slice of the restaurant, scraping two tables together and clattering across more chairs. Martha can see respectable groups of twos and threes looking up from their papers or their conversations in irritation as Eliza trills, "Oh, but make that a skinny one," and Geraldine hisses back, "Aren't you skinny enough already?"

Eliza's husband, Denis, disorganized as ever, shoulders hunched, raises his arm to greet Martha, like a policeman stopping traffic. "All right?" he says, plonking himself down next to her and swinging Gabriel onto his lap. Martha is very fond of Denis. (The fact that he loves Eliza makes her like her sister more.) Today, he is in an Oxfam tweed coat and black trousers with an overwashed shine to the knees. Gabriel is wearing an immaculate blue duffle coat with wooden toggles.

"Yup," she says.

Denis musses the front of his hair. "I hear there's been a bit of trouble over the . . ."

"Best to keep out of it—" she begins to say (both sisters have been trying to get her on her own all morning). But Eliza brings over a high chair then and there is soothing and negotiation to be done as Gabriel goes rigid when they try to put him in it. Martha turns to Ivor on the other side. Geraldine has cut her children's hair for the occasion. Anna across the table on her father's knee looks sweetly tomboyish in her short bob, and Patrick, with his high pink cheeks and mole-dark widow's peak, like a miniature marine. But Ivor's cut has given his six-year-old face, which has begun its lengthening, thinning process, a pinched, raw look. The skin above his ears is white and exposed. He is wearing dark green corduroy trousers that match his brother's, only his are a little too large and are rolled up at the ankles. He is chewing the sleeve of his shirt.

"How's school?" she asks.

He doesn't hear her, or if he does he doesn't look up. The high chair has been abandoned, Gabriel is back on Denis's knee, and everyone is talking loudly. The trip to Richmond Park has become, for Eliza, the subject of anecdote now. The brief armistice between her and Geraldine is over and she is hurling cruel jokes, sheltering behind everyone else's laughter. "And then we couldn't even remember where we'd scattered Mum's ashes!" Geraldine says quietly, "Eliza, how would I have forgotten that?" but her youngest sister is determined to ignore her. While this is going on, Martha watches Greg catch Ivor's eye and frown, making a flipping gesture with his hand. Ivor stops chewing his sleeve and puts his arm down on the table. He keeps his eyes low.

"It's okay," he says.

"Working hard?"

"Yup."

"And then Geraldine got aftershave all over her hands . . ."

Martha bends toward him and whispers, "Good to be skipping school for the day, though, isn't it?"

Ivor looks at her. The skin below his lip is chapped and he keeps running over it with his tongue.

Geraldine arrives at the table with some mugs. "I did not get aftershave on my hands. Hot chocolate. Skinny latte for the stick insect." She puts the mugs down and goes back to the counter.

Eliza says, "And Martha kept going on about how much the dogs would be enjoying it!"

Ivor has said something. She has to ask him to repeat it. "Do you like Harry Potter?" he says.

"I haven't read it yet," Martha answers. "Have you?"

"Everyone at school has."

"That doesn't mean you have to."

"No, but they say you're a Slytherin if you don't."

"Oh dear."

"Patrick's a Gryffindor."

"Is he?" She doesn't have to say any more because Geraldine, who has just conducted a hissed conversation with Greg involving several frowns and darting looks in Martha's direction, is at her shoulder. "Just to warn you," she hisses, "Greg told David to meet us here. Sorry. Tactless idiot. I wish he'd told me he was going to do that. He doesn't seem to get it. Ivor! Stop licking your mouth."

Ivor stops but rubs it with his hand instead. Martha says quietly, "Oh, Geraldine."

"I know. I know. He is the limit." Geraldine says this with some bitterness. "Would it be awful? Is it too much for you to bear?"

"Here?"

"Apparently."

They are talking under their breath, but Eliza has noticed that something is up and is looking at them from across the table. She probably thinks Geraldine is getting Martha on her side about *The Boy*. But it's not *The Boy* but The Man. Martha takes a gulp of her tea. It's still so hot she can feel it scalding her on the way down. She gets up and pushes her chair back. "I'll meet you at the church. I need to check on the flowers anyway."

"Oh, please don't."

But it's too late. Martha is easing out past Denis. "I'm just going to go and check on the flowers." Everyone stares at her. Greg is looking uncomfortable, Geraldine anguished. Ivor is still staring at the table, and without thinking, she hears herself say, "Do you want to come?" To her surprise, he wrinkles off his chair and scrambles over to her. "Okay," he says. She is aware of the whole cafe watching as they leave. Once outside, suddenly, she wants to run—to scream, to hide—but here's Ivor at her side, hovering, plodding. She wonders why on earth she asked him to come. He is not what she needs right now. She says, "Actually, why don't you go back inside?" But he says he doesn't want to, so she sets off at a pace that she knows is a little too fast, in the hope that he will change his mind. He half-runs to keep up. Clumsy, awkward, charmless little thing. She quickens. He starts to run properly and trips. He doesn't actually fall over, it is really more of a stumble, but he gasps and any color there is drains from his face. Martha stops. She takes his hand. "Sorry," she says.

They walk slowly together down the main street, and just before they turn off, they pass a shop selling gifts and toys—one of those places designed for the panicked purchasing of last-minute thought-free presents. In the window, next to a pile of slogan-embroidered cushions ("Home Sweet Home"; "I'd Rather Be Fishing") there's a collection of Harry Potter merchandise. Martha, on impulse, pulls Ivor through the door and to the counter, where she asks the assistant to point out "the most sought-after Harry Potter thing." The assistant ums and ahs and finally says, "The Harry Potter wand is very popular."

"I'll have one of those, then, please," Martha says, thinking what a day it's been for magic wands. To Ivor, she says, "I met a magician today."

Ivor says, "Uh?"

"Mr. Magic. Ever heard of him?"

Again Ivor just says, "Uh?" which she takes to mean no.

"Maybe his fame hasn't yet reached Kingston."

While the assistant wraps the wand, Ivor continues to stand

by her, still unresponsive. But when Martha hands over the money, the assistant says to him, "What a kind mummy, eh?"and he looks at her.

Martha laughs. "Actually," she begins. But the assistant interrupts. "Doesn't he look like you?" she says. And it stops Martha short. Busy contemplating the idea, she lets the mistake lie.

Outside the shop, Martha puts the parcel in his hand. Ivor looks blank again. Martha says, "I just don't think a Slytherin would have one of these. Do you?" and at last he grins and says that maybe a Slytherin wouldn't.

Then he adds, "You didn't buy batteries. It's no good without them."

◆

THE CHURCH IS farther out of Wimbledon village than Martha remembers, and when they get there she finds that they are not in time to check the flowers after all. The rough patch of grass that is used as a parking lot is three-quarters full and the short private lane is crammed with vehicles on both sides. In the small churchyard, where squirrels dart up yew trees and down ancient mossy tombs, you can just pick up the groaning yawn of the organ. A brace of elderly women in feathered hats has just gone in and a couple of young undertakers in suits are having a cigarette, leaning against the far side of a black sedan. She hasn't been to many funerals, but it always surprises her that it's all in a day's work for them. She wonders whether they go out and get drunk every night to drown other people's sorrows.

She smiles as she passes and one of the young men nods before chucking his cigarette on the ground and twisting it out with his foot. She and Ivor go through the big open oak door into the church. It smells of polish and sap, like the inside of a wooden box. For a moment she wavers, wondering which side to sit on before remembering that it's weddings that like a nice divide, your side versus mine; funerals are egalitarian, democratic, pacifist. She slips her hand through Ivor's arm and guides him up the aisle to a pew on the right. Julia is in the front with the twins. Next to her is a thin, tanned woman with long blond hair and spikey bangs who Martha realizes (though she is much changed) is Susie, Graham's daughter, who now lives in Vancouver. Across the aisle there are other people with faces formed from the same mold as Ian and Susie's—the sloping chin, the hawk nose: relatives of Graham's first wife. They are all perched on the other side. So there are divisions in funerals, after all, Martha thinks. At least when a second marriage is involved.

She and Ivor are sitting under stained glass windows of Saint George and Saint Francis. The vicar is fiddling about at the altar, and there is a general creaking of pew, but otherwise it's subdued. The couple who moved in next door to Graham, the ones who travel a lot, sidle in next to her. The pew gate rattles shut. The music seems to get louder, more formed, and through it she hears murmuring and the clopping of heels, and there is her family at the door of the vestry, Gabriel on his mother's hip, Patrick and Anna pressed against their mother's legs, Geraldine crossing herself, and behind them all, the unmistakable figure of David.

Quickly she turns her head to face the pulpit, lowers her face to study the service sheet. He is wearing a dark coat over a dark suit and a white shirt, and glasses—little round glasses. Ivor is tugging at her sleeve. "They're here," he says loudly. She lowers her head. She hasn't seen those glasses before. "I know," she says.

The first time she saw him was in this church for Geraldine's wedding. June. She and Eliza were wearing oyster taffeta, which had clumped over Martha's thighs like fabric cellulite, and they were clutching posies. They were waiting for Geraldine on the porch, and Eliza, peering, told Martha that the best man—Greg's oldest friend from school—had made it after all. "So much for being stuck in Geneva," she said.

Martha wasn't interested. She said, "Sssh."

"Sssh," someone says now. The congregation comes to its feet and turns to the back of the church as the pallbearers—Ian at the front, in blue, with the undertakers alongside him—walk the lily-laden coffin to the front. Ian looks like a celebrity with his bodyguards. They reach the front, the coffin is laid down, and Ian turns, with a poignant crooked smile, to join his wife in the front row. He shakes out his shoulder before he sits down.

They stand to sing "Jerusalem," and Martha tries to concentrate, to renew the intensity of her emotions in the park. She fails.

It was later, after the wedding ceremony, when she met David properly. She was standing at the opening to the tent that took up most of their mother's garden when he came up behind her and said, "Ah, the naughty little sister, I presume," and she said no, that people always think that because she is shorter than the other two, but actually, she is "the naughty middle sister."

He put out his hand. "David Ford."

She put her hand out, too, suddenly conscious of the bunching drag of taffeta across her thighs, "Martha Bone."

They talked a little about his job at the auction house. He told her he was in jewelry, which made her laugh. She imagined him running his hands around a beautiful woman's neck, clicking the diamond earrings off her ears and slipping them into his pocket. He said there was a lot of that, that he was nifty at fingering sapphire-encrusted cuff links, too, but that his main interest was Elizabethan. 1559–1603. "Personally, I don't go for flashy and shiny," he said. "I go for ornate and rare."

He asked her about her stall at Alfie's, and after a while, when she was tired of the formality of their conversation, she teased him about the to-ing and fro-ing that had gone on before the wedding, the would-he-make-it-or-wouldn't-he? She said, "So is it really possible to 'get stuck' in Geneva?" and he laughed, with his eye on her, as if he wasn't used to having his movements questioned, and later, when she went off to dance with Denis, she felt his gaze following her as if she'd caught his interest.

◆

BRING ME MY BOW OF BURNING BLERGHGH. The woman from next door has stopped singing and is blowing her nose. She rolls her eyes at Martha. It's true, Martha thinks, that funerals conform to a strange pattern: the closely bereaved so stiff-backed and stoic and the people on the outskirts dissolving or, like her, not even able to engage, their minds elsewhere. Loss itself doesn't happen here. None of them, not even Geraldine, cried during their mother's cremation. And yet there was some third cousin twice removed gulping uncontrollably five rows from the back. Loss catches up with you at unexpected moments, in a supermarket, walking through the perfume section of a department store.

They sit again. Susie goes up to the lectern to read a poem

that she wrote when she was a little girl about her father. "Oh Dad/When I am sad/You're there/On the stair/Mother, father, both," and the trite sentimentality and for a moment the image of Graham as a young widowed dad make her own throat catch. She knows this feeling, high and acute, is imagined emotion, romanticized, no better than detachment. It is the thought of other people's grief that has gotten to her, not grief itself. And she is doubly contemptuous of herself, because all the time she is also aware of thinking something mundane and trivial and frivolous and nothing to do with Graham's death at all. She's wondering where exactly David is sitting and whether he can see her.

Martha is first out of the church, first to the burial ground. She prepared her tactics during Communion. No hanging around, no chance to be collared.

❖

PUTNEY VALE CEMETERY is large and impressive. It stretches up a hill and is edged on two sides by the brambled wilderness of Wimbledon common. But a third side is banked by the rush and scream of the highway, and the high formal gates, which once led into it from the highway, have been closed off. Now you have to enter via a road behind the supermarket, which feels oddly undignified, like meeting death through the back door.

Martha parks before the entrance, outside a newsstand, and enters the cemetery on foot. Farther in, it is wild and Victorian. You can get lost among the broken angels. But down this end, in the modern part, where the rows are ruler-straight, the highway roars in your ear and you imagine that, if you strain, you can pick up the beep of the supermarket checkout through the fence. A couple of cars roll past her on the cemetery road and she steps off onto the grass. The ground is sodden and clay sticks to her shoes. She passes the row of most recent graves— no headstones and the earth still heaped high and round, like duvets over sleeping forms. She plods on toward the older rows. There are headstones in white and black and pink, heart-shaped, book-shaped, plank-shaped. She stops to read a dedication, self-conscious with cars purring past behind her. There are tidy miniature Leylandiis and fabric violets in pots. She is aware of herself as a woman in mourning looking at a dedication. Most of the deceased are memorialized as Beloved Fathers and Mothers, Much Missed Sons and Precious Daughters. She feels a stab of self-pity. What would she be? Martha Bone: Quite Good Antique Dealer. Sister, at a push.

A hundred yards ahead, one of the graves in an established row has been opened, and standing there already is the priest from the church and Graham's globe-trotting neighbors. The black funeral car arrives and more cars pull up as she tramps across, rather ungainly as the ground is even more boggy here. And then coming up behind her and pulling in just ahead she sees Eliza and Denis's car and behind them Geraldine and Greg's. They're parking and they're all clambering out and she sees the children and her sisters and then, coming out behind them, David.

There is no getting away from it now. She walks toward them. (A woman in mourning who has been looking at dedications heading toward her ex.) But then a hand grabs at her shoulder. It belongs to an old man, with bags under his eyes like reflections, thick dark eyebrows, and spindly hair: Walter, Graham's brother from Borehamwood. He leans on her as if his balance is a little dodgy, and says, "Are you the second wife?" His voice creaks. Martha smiles. Geraldine and David have joined the graveside now. "No. She's dead. I'm her daughter."

Walter looks up at the sky. "Both dead," he says with some surprise. "The other one, years ago, wasn't it? Poor bugger. Never thought I'd outlive him. I'm not what you might call sparking on all eight cylinders."

"You look all right to me," Martha says.

"I'm in between and out," he says, patting his pockets. "Up and down like a fi-fo-fum. Now where the bloody hell did I put my tobacco?"

Martha takes his arm—his jacket smells of damp and smoke—and together they hobble to the graveside. "Bloody things, funerals," says Walter. They stand behind Ian and Julia. She organizes it so that other heads hide her from David. Walter whistles when he breathes. He has shaved, but has missed a whole swath of whiskers below one side of his nose. He leans with both hands on his stick.

The priest begins. His words almost get lost, with the traffic in the distance. Ian is standing with his arms behind his back. She watches his fingers scratching inside his cupped palms.

And now the priest is shuffling back and Ian has thrown—ungainly, thudding—the lilies into the grave, and people have started turning away, doubtful as to what to do next, and Ian is crying and has stepped back in the direction of Martha, so she is, once again, the first thing he turns to—only literally not metaphorically this time—and she puts her arms around him and hugs him, and then Julia and then Susie, too. She looks up to check on Walter, who's still standing beside her, but when she raises her head she realizes that Walter has wandered off toward his car and that the person next to her is David.

Susie has released herself and is being hugged by Julia. Martha scans for somebody else to embrace, but there isn't anyone close enough. She has nowhere to go.

David says, "Hello."

He looks trim in his narrow black coat, both terribly familiar and strange. His hair is much shorter, more fashionable than it was two years ago, and Martha finds herself feeling strangely betrayed by this. His face is close-shaven, but she can still make out the line where the stubble grows. His Sunday beard. The creases in his cheeks when he moves his face, as if the skin only just fits. The slightly crooked front tooth. The way his eyebrows fan out at the far corners. She knows if she breathes in she'll smell limes.

The highway roars in the air between them. "Hello," she says back. There's a lull and then the screech of a motorbike, and for the few moments after that she feels she can pick out the sound of each vehicle that passes, as if all of her nerve endings have been sensitized.

◆

GERALDINE, who is putting two of her children into the car with her back to all this, is not having a good funeral. The effort to maintain a brave front while inwardly *in pieces*—a swirling mess of guilt, fury, resentment—is almost more than she can manage. She might have known that Eliza would react the way she did about Geraldine taking *The Boy*. But she expected more support from Martha. In the car earlier, Greg said he thought perhaps Martha's refusal to take sides could be construed as neutrality, but Geraldine told him that in families there is no such thing as neutrality. "Martha," she said through gritted teeth, "is cold."

"Grrr," she says now to nobody in particular. She gets into the front seat and—typical—sees she has gotten mud all over her best skirt. "Is it too much to ask for you to behave yourselves for two hours?" she snaps.

She buckles her seat belt. "We'll have something to eat in a minute," she says over her shoulder. She says it like a reprimand because they've done nothing but fight since they got there. That piece of Harry Potter plastic rubbish is the main problem. She pokes the wand away in the glove compartment. You'd think Martha would know: buy one for all three or none at all. Hopeless: you can tell she has nothing to do with kids.

"Nwwwwwwww," says Patrick. "But I'm starving."

"Won't be long," she says. "You can wait a few more minutes. We'll get going as soon as your father . . ."

She can see him through the window. He is standing in the middle of the road chatting away with a woman she doesn't recognize. She has blond hair and is wearing a slim houndstooth coat. He has Anna by the hand, except that she's bored—and overtired—and she has put both her hands in his and is swinging, like a one-sided attempt at that game Geraldine and Martha used to play when they were little, crossing arms and spinning around against each other's gravity until you were so dizzy you fell over. But Anna isn't gaining any speed. She looks more like a pendulum, and as Geraldine watches she sags down, her dress riding up, until she's almost on the ground. Greg doesn't seem to notice. He carries on chatting, regardless of his bungee-jumping arm.

They are lucky that he is here at all. Last night from the bath he asked her, cajoling, if there was a "three-line whip." It's one of the military expressions he grew up with and never grew out of, along with OC, as in, "Okay, old girl, you're OC picnic; I'm OC bikes."

The first time he used this, she thought he was saying "eau si." And, as when he'd actually said, "You're OC contraception," she imagined he was referring to some new sophisticated French barrier method. Later when she learned he meant Officer in Charge, she wondered if she would have slept with him at all if she'd known. Military jargon in relation to lovemaking seemed rather dubious to her; not quite—to use another of his catchphrases—"the thing."

Anyway, last night she told him it *was* a three-line whip. She had been sifting through the bathroom cabinet looking for Christian Dior at the time, or she would have asked him how he thought he could possibly *not* turn up—a family occasion, after all. But Greg's head was buried under the water anyway, floating, disembodied, in a mesh of soapy bubbles. And then he rose, shaking a spaniel head, squeezing his nose with his thumb and forefinger, and said, "Okay. But I'll have to go in this weekend to make up."

Geraldine sighed and said fine, but because she hadn't articulated the feelings this aroused in her—a faint perplexity at the idea of herself and her relatives as something separate from Greg—she felt disgruntled. It wasn't as if he was doing her a favor. It hadn't exactly been a treat for her, either, for God's sake, having to sit stiff-backed in the church while their mother was edited out of Graham's life, with Eliza spitting at her at every available opportunity.

"Get off," Ivor says in the back.

"Get off," Patrick says, imitating him, twisting his voice into a taunt.

"Just stop it. Both of you." Geraldine turns and removes Patrick's ankles from Ivor's knees. "Stop irritating Ivor," she says. "Leave him alone, will you? Just for one minute."

Ivor looks at her. He should be grateful, but his face has that sheeted look. She says, "And you—Stop. Sucking. Your. Sleeve."

She turns back and leans her head against the window. It feels cold against her cheek like a turned pillow. She finds she is biting back tears. A car has come up behind Greg and the woman on the graveyard road and they jump apart. Greg waves good-bye and then strides toward the car. He thrusts Anna, giggling now, into the back and gets into the driver's seat. Before he opened the door, the car had felt warm and still, like in an airplane. But he brings new stirred air with him and outside noises.

"Let's go. God, terribly nice woman, that neighbor of Graham's. Camilla Quince. You remember her?"

Geraldine quietly says, "Yes. Away a lot."

"That's the one."

He is making a three-point turn, with lots of jerky, urgent yankings of the wheel, as if thinking he is Starsky. He says, "Three children, fund manager, wonderful woman." He has his eye in the rearview mirror and has started driving off when he adds, "Looks after herself, too, by the looks of it." And then, his voice stretching out with mock intrigue, "A-hoh. Nothing to worry about there, then."

Geraldine scrabbles to see behind her. People are drifting toward cars; many have already left. She sees the woman in the houndstooth—what does he mean, look after herself?—sidle into a Spider sports car with a man in a trendy asymmetrical jacket. "What do you mean?"

"Very cozy," he says, in the same voice. "I don't think you needed to get in such a flap about the cafe after all."

And it is only then that Geraldine tears her eyes away from the houndstooth—this infuriatingly perfect Camilla Quince—and sees Martha and David walking alongside each other toward Martha's car. They are walking a little bit apart—you could fit a third person between them, a small one, a child maybe, if you tried—and they're both looking at the ground.

"Oh God. Oh . . . I . . . We . . ."

"I think he's all right for a lift if that's what you're worried about."

"Oh, but . . ."Geraldine has pulled down her window and is straining to look behind. "Do you? You don't think we ought to check?"

Greg is turning out of the graveyard now, swooping behind Wellmart. "No," he says. "I don't."

"Oh." Geraldine turns again but they have gone from view. "Oh, but stop, can't you? Go back." She meant to orchestrate the meeting, to chaperone Martha and then subtly drift away. She hadn't meant it to be like this. She is annoyed with Martha, but she hadn't meant to *betray* her.

"Too late."

Geraldine slumps forward.

"What?"

"Well, do you think they are all right?"

"Of course they are all right."

She groans. Greg says, "They'll be fine."

"I know, but."

"What?"

"Is he still with Maddy Long Legs?"

But Greg has turned his attention to his wing mirror now. He waves at the Spider as it overtakes them in the outside lane. He says, "We don't have to stay long, do we? I might be able to make my afternoon meeting, if I try."

They drive the rest of the way in silence and when they get to the house, there are cars everywhere so they have to park quite a long way down the road. The front door is ajar and there are people in the hall. Geraldine keeps a bright smile on her face as she hangs up their things on the hall pegs (other coats are being taken upstairs, but she doesn't care). My house, she is chanting in her head, full of strangers. She looks out the front door again to see if Martha is coming. The kids, who seem to have left their hunger in the car, tear into the garden. Greg strides ahead of her into the sitting room and is accosted by a former colleague of Graham's who reads Greg's newspaper and has a few points of issue to raise about the front-page articles relating to Northern Ireland. Greg looks uncomfortable and his eyes flail frantically in Geraldine's direction, but she hasn't forgiven him for the car yet and anyway, he is within the danger zone, a few feet from Eliza. Instead she crosses to where Julia is standing, an infant car seat hooked over her arm like a supermarket basket. Ian is serving drinks, another car seat at his feet, and Julia is greeting guests like a hostess at a cocktail party.

Geraldine hadn't expected so many people, so many faces she doesn't know, or to feel so sidelined. The table by the back door is laden with shop-bought sandwiches (shrimp salad; turkey and cranberry sauce) dolled up on doilies. If only somebody had asked her, she could have made their mother's Coronation Chicken—at a fraction of the cost. Ridiculously overelaborate napkins, too. Julia notices her, and Geraldine says, "Magnificent spread!"

Julia whispers, "Marks and Spencer."

Geraldine says, "I'd never have guessed."

"Ah! So *you* must be the second wife." At the top of the steps down to the garden stands Graham's brother, Walter, who is wiping his mouth with a large red handkerchief. His knuckles are round and purple; his hand movements as he puts a whole sandwich triangle in his mouth exaggerated, as if he's not convinced he won't miss.

"Sorry?" she says, going over to him. It is one of those oddly warm, cloudy autumn days; the air is still beneath the low sky. Quite a few of the guests have wandered down the steps and are standing in clumps on the grass. Occasionally, at the other end, a small child involved in Denis's game of cricket hurtles sideways to the ground.

"Second wife, are you? First one died, know that. Tragic." Walter shakes his head. There are beads of froth at the corners of his mouth, which he wipes again.

She says, "His second wife died, too, didn't you know that?"

He looks at her. "It seems I did," he says. His eyes look faded and milky. He says, "Losing your memory is said to be one of the hardships of old age. Sometimes I find it makes life easier. Wh-oops—"

He has lost his balance, an arm flailing toward her, and Geraldine grabs him. She helps him down to the garden bench at the bottom of the steps, where two elderly women in hats are sitting with their bags on their knees. They make room for him and he settles in comfortably. Geraldine leaves him outlining his own funeral plans with them.

She hovers by the bay tree. It's warm here, but nicer than in the house. She wonders about hauling the kids in and getting them to eat something, but they're playing cricket on the grass. She sees Greg over by the hydrangeas, talking to that ghastly Mrs. Quince again. He is sweeping the dried-up flowers backward with one hand in a display of some imaginary sporting prowess or other, and doesn't catch her eye. Nobody needs her. Inside the house there is chatter and laughter. She cricks her head so she can see through the cloakroom window, past the open door, into the hall. Where are Martha and David? People are coming out with plates of food (hungry work, grieving). Plates with special clips at the side for fixing your drink. None of them is Martha and David. Where are they? What are they up to?

And then, just as she feels she can bear the suspense no longer, she sees Martha coming through the door into the sitting room and she is about to charge back in and find out everything, when someone blocks her way.

It is Susie, Ian's sister, and she's saying, "So, Geraldine. A lot of water under the bridge since we last saw each other."

Geraldine, craning, says, "Yes. Absolutely."

"Must be ten years. So—" Susie, who has hair down to her bottom and earrings in the tops of her ears, is giving the sandwiches on her plate close attention. "Life treating you well?" She lifts a piece of bread and removes the slice of ham from inside. As Susie straightens, Geraldine spots Martha's head in the distance. But she can't see David. Is he with her? Has he come in behind? "Life's okay," she says.

Susie is not moving away. She has folded her piece of ham

into neat quarters, and is eating it with little bites. "So—three kids, is it?"

"Yes. Three. You haven't . . . ?"

"No. Not yet. We're waiting, my boyfriend and I. We want to get as much out of life as we can first, you know? Really enjoy each other." Martha has come to peer out into the garden. She is pink in the cheeks. Her eyes look bright. Geraldine tries to catch her attention but fails. Susie is saying, "I mean, kids are one thing, but a good relationship is something else, do you know what I mean?"

Geraldine is about to say something sharp like, "Well, don't leave it too long," or, "Eggs don't last forever," when she pulls herself together. She says, "Of course," and she means it sympathetically—Susie, the orphan now. But, as she looks at her kindly, *charitably,* she feels an unexpected pang of envy. Susie, only a few years younger than she is, was the one they all laughed at, gawky and gray and suburban. She wore hair clips and brown cords and ill-fitting turtlenecks. And now look at her! It is not just the tan, or the hair, or the clear complexion (not smothered like Geraldine's in Almost Nude, which is making her skin sweaty and the back of her neck feel dirty), but something more than that, something *free.* Geraldine used to imagine herself so radiantly fortunate: a golden person, with her looks, her music scholarship, her marriage, shimmering with good luck. Like that Mrs. Quince over there. And now? Well, now she is blustered about, blistered with worry—her children, Ivor's problems at school, her husband, her sisters, Eliza and her bloody picture, *Martha and David.*

She has been moving gradually up the steps, with Susie following her, and now she's reached the door at the top. There are peals of laughter from deep in the sitting room; the funeral is becoming raucous as if the pressure of keeping somber has become too much, as if life has started bouncing back before the earth has even settled. "Yes," she says. "Good idea. You wait for as long as you can," and maybe she said it with just a little too much conviction because, before she knows it, Susie has launched into an account of this fantastic exercise regime that Geraldine must try, and how much more energy Susie herself has felt since she stopped "combining," and how the one thing she has learned since she moved to Vancouver is the importance of quality of life. And then she says something Geraldine doesn't quite catch. "Sorry," she asks, leaning toward her. "I need *what*?"

But when Susie repeats it, one of those strange lulls falls upon the gathering, so that her voice is louder than necessary. "More time for yourself!" she says. And there is a short while before the noise level rises around them again as if the whole room needed a minute to get used to the suggestion.

CHAPTER EIGHT

the basement

"Some people have an irrational nervousness
of cellars, thinking of them as Hades-dark
caves dripping with water."

NATURAL HOUSEKEEPING, *by Beverly Pagram*

THE DAY after the funeral is a Saturday when, as Martha has already told Fred and his family, Martha Bone Antiques gets very busy.

So it is early, before opening, that she draws up outside 35 Nightingale Road and disembarks with a large cardboard box in her arms.

She stopped en route at the pet shop, which apparently opens even earlier than she does, and bought a blue plastic ball with a bell inside it. Because of the cat box and her car keys and the need to rattle on the letterbox, she is holding the paper bag containing the belled ball between her teeth when Fred comes to the door. It's not strictly necessary—she could have laid the bag *on* the box, or even fitted it in her pocket—but today, for various reasons she hasn't yet admitted to herself, she is light-hearted.

"Ah," he says.

"Egh." She makes a gesture with her head in greeting and then throws the bag, with a thrust of her chin, in the direction of his hands. "A present."

"A present?" he says, just catching it.

Martha moves past him into the house. "You'd better close the door," she says, putting the box down on the floor.

He has taken the ball out of the bag. "Just what I've, er, always wanted," he is saying when Hazel hurtles down the stairs, followed by her brother. "Is it the cat? Is it the cat?" she yells.

"Special delivery," says Martha.

They open the box in the kitchen, but Kitten doesn't get out immediately. He blinks up while Hazel pokes him and Stanley waves the ball in his face. When he finally gets out, he does so in a rush and scurries over to the corner between the oven and the sink.

"Oh dear, I hope he's not too traumatized," says Fred. "Do you think he misses your dad?"

"My *dad*?" says Martha, before remembering just in time. "Oh no. He was hardly ever in."

"And also of course he was in France."

"Yes. That's right. So in fact, he hadn't seen him for a while. I've been looking after him until he came back. . . . Anyway."

Luckily, no one seems to be listening. Fred is spooning some vile-looking cat food into a child's plastic bowl and trying to coax the cat out of its corner. Martha, who learned a few things during her pet shop stop, tells him about this dried food you can buy that's much better for their teeth and doesn't smell. "All in all it's much more tasteful. And they graze at it rather than gobbling it up all at once. It means you can put a great mound of food down and go away and leave him."

Fred looks up. "We don't intend to go away and leave him," he says.

"Ah. Yes." Callous Martha laughs.

The cat, tempted by the revolting smell, creeps out from its hiding place and buries its face in the child's bowl. They watch him eat. Then Fred says, "Ah, coffee"—not so much a question as a statement—and starts fiddling at the stove. He says, with his back to her, "Found out any more about your employee?"

"Who?"

"April, is she called?"

"What do you mean?" Martha is frowning at the back of his legs.

He turns around; his eyes look embarrassed. "I only mean, you know, on the confiding front."

"Oh, I see. No. No, I haven't."

He turns back. "That's a shame."

Martha wants to say, "What business is it of yours?" (what business of his to even *remember* April's name?), and anyway *I've been at my father's funeral,* but her good mood takes over and she throws the ball for Kitten instead. He looks after it with disdain as it rolls, tinkling, under the table.

"I want to take a picture!" Hazel has jumped up and is opening cupboards. Fred hands Martha her coffee. "Er, in here, I think," he says, opening the drawer in the table. A whole lot of stuff tumbles out, loose string, old bills, leaking sunscreen, and scrunched-up tea towels. No camera. "Oh," he says sheepishly.

He leaves the mess and starts opening the drawers under the counter.

"You need a clutter consultant."

"A clutter consultant?" He has found the camera on top of the books and is holding it out.

"I read about them in an interiors magazine. If you don't mind me saying," she adds, feeling unusually open suddenly, "your house seems to be full of waste."

Fred laughs. He says, "Waste not, want not."

She leans back in her chair. "I'm serious. It's got potential. There's style here somewhere. It's just buried beneath a lot of junk."

Fred smiles. "And what junk might that be?"

"Er. Well, this—" She fingers some crumpled children's drawings that came out of the drawer and are now on the table. "And—um—some of the ornaments in the other room. Every surface seems to be covered. And, um, speaking personally, I might, um"—she decides to take the plunge—"think of finding another home for the picture."

"What picture?"

"The one in the sitting room? You know, of the horses?"

"You don't like it?"

"Do you want me to be honest?"

"Of course."

"I hate it."

Fred says, "Oh. How sad."

Martha puzzled over this comment later that day and still couldn't decide whether he meant his own taste or her response to it.

Kitten is struggling, on his back, in Hazel's arms, so a

photograph needs to be taken quickly. Fred obliges. Kitten scurries off. But after that, Hazel wants to take a picture of Martha. "Oh no, I'm terrible in pictures," Martha says. But she can't get out of it without being rude, what with Hazel jumping up and down in front of her, making her sit in a chair, all eager and excited.

"Dad, Dad," she says. "Stand next to her."

Fred sits down in the chair beside Martha. He leans in toward her. She can smell the cigarette smoke on his clothes. There is a pulse in his neck. She forces a smile.

"And Stan! Go on. Get in the photo, too." Stanley has clambered onto Martha's lap. He tucks his legs up and leans his head back against her arm, and she feels the looseness in it, the weight of him, against her. "There! That's lovely!" Hazel has taken the picture and turned back to the cat. Fred hasn't moved, is still sitting close to her. Martha thinks if she turns her head she'll see him looking at her. Stan is warm, surprisingly solid, against her chest. She slips him off her knee and gets up. "Right," she says. "Well, I'll leave you all to it."

But Stanley is still standing next to her, tugging at her jeans. He tries to whisper in her ear. "What?" She can't hear so he moves across to Fred, still sitting, and whispers to him instead. Fred, standing up, says, frowning, "He wants to show you something. I don't know what. He says it's a surprise. It's in the playroom. But, Stan, Martha has a shop to open up, remember. She's a very busy woman."

Martha says, "It's okay. I can spare a few secs."

Stan pulls her into the hall to a door that if she had noticed at all she presumed led down to a cupboard or a cellar. Stan opens it and there are some steps. She and Hazel follow Stan down and she finds herself in a sort of converted basement.

The walls are slightly peeling but painted yellow; there are squares of carpet on the floor and a small curtainless window providing natural light. An old sofa takes up most of the room, but there are also shelves piled up with grubby toys, and a jumble of boxes, clearly containing junk. It smells dank. Martha doesn't imagine anyone spends much time down here.

"This is from my mum," says Stan, going over to a desk in the corner.

"The computer?" says Martha, following him.

"No." It's Fred, who has come down behind them. "He means the e-mail."

Martha looks at Fred and her heart gives a small lunge. He rolls his eyes and makes a grimace. Stan is sitting on the stool next to her, staring at the screen. She sees a line or two, some exclamation marks, a row of kisses, and looks away. Hazel begins reading it out. Something about a boat trip.

Martha moves away, past the boxes of junk, through all the muddle, to the door, and starts climbing the stairs. She doesn't want to listen. It feels like trespassing. She doesn't want to know. She saw Stan's expression and she wants to forget it. Kitten is at the top of the steps, sniffing at the door. "Bye, cat," she says.

At the door, she is about to shout a cheery good-bye to everyone else, but Fred has followed her up. "Sorry," he says. "I didn't realize."

"It's not your fault. I just . . . well, I've got to get on."

He says, "We've got photographs to scan in and send to her now: that will keep us busy."

"Bye," she says.

"Well, I'll think about your suggestion."

"My suggestion?"

"About the clutter."

"Oh, good." She turns away again. "You can start with the basement. I bet there's stuff you don't even know you have down there. Bye."

"And . . . um."

She's at the gate. She's got a shop to open, beautiful objects to think about. "What?"

"Thanks for Kitten. Come and visit him anytime."

"Okay." But as she gets back into her car, she is already putting Fred and his disorganized, broken-down family out of her mind. The whole time she was in the house she had forgotten, but now she thinks ahead to the main business of the day, something shiny and attractive and not in need of attention: David.

◆

"HELLO," he said at Graham's graveside. "You don't have any tissues in your car, do you? I seem to have rather plastered my shoes in mud."

"Oh, your poor brogues." Martha was glad for an excuse to look down at the ground. David's stiff black leather brogues were caked with clay. "I might have some in the glove compartment."

They walked back together to her car and he sat next to her on the passenger seat, scraping the dirt off, knocking the soles against the door until little circles of soil fell out of the decorative puncture holes. They talked first about important things—his job, Graham's death, the durability of leather stitching. Martha kept looking surreptitiously at his face: the slanting eyes, the long lashes, the loose mouth. She watched his Adam's apple move up and down as he talked. David's social manner is polished, his conversation the verbal equivalent of a French courtier doffing his hat (which was the bit of him her mother liked). But Martha has always seen the muscle twitching in his cheek, and known, through the layers of further education and auction house training, how important it has always been for him to be liked. When she thinks back to their time together, it is moments of embarrassment that tug at her the strongest: the aitches he dropped in conversation with taxi drivers; the over-enthusiastic laughter at other people's anecdotes; the way he would, if feeling awkward, hold his hands flat between his knees and twitch his legs.

She knows, too, that with his clothes off he talks differently. He cries out high at orgasm.

"How's your new girlfriend?" she asked boldly. "Maddy, is it? Very long legs, I've heard."

Head bowed, concentration on a coin-sized area of leather. "Hm. Fine." Pause. (A pause Martha is later to interpret as "telling.") "I think."

A little while later, as she jabbered on about this or that friend of his ("So Quentin? Is he still in Old Masters?"), he turned and gave her the kind of look that is working hard to draw attention to itself as a look. "What?" she asked.

"Nothing." He smiled, flicking his thumbnail against his teeth. He narrowed his eyes. "It's just good to see you, that's all."

The story is that Martha left David but you could argue it didn't happen that way. He was the one who wanted her to get married, have his children, follow him to Geneva, to give up the shop, to change. He was the one who moved away.

"You back, then?" she said, thinking all this. "For good, I mean."

He put his shoes back on, pulling the laces so tight the leather creaked. "For now," he said.

She took him to the station. He had paid his respects and had a departmental strategy meeting to get back for.

"Diamonds and pearls?" she said.

"Important clocks."

"Time waits for no man," she said.

Getting out, he asked if they could meet and she nodded without giving herself permission first. When he kissed her good-bye, his face smelled not of limes, but strangely new, of nutmeg.

◆

SHE HAS ARRANGED to see David at a bar by the river at Wandsworth Bridge. Their rendezvous is not until the evening, but she spends the day getting ready. For some people this might mean manicures, the trying on of clothes, elaborate hair preparations. Martha gets to work on a nineteenth-century Virginia table, waxing every inch of its mahogany surface until its complexion gleams.

The shop is quite busy but in a quiet moment she calls Karen.

"Guess who I'm seeing tonight," she says.

"I don't know . . . Nick!"

"No. Not Nick. David."

"David! Oh God, of course, did you see him at the funeral?"

"I did."

"And?"

"Oh. I don't know. It was weird." Martha fills Karen in on the events of the day before.

"And what about Nick? Is he no longer the ex-boyfriend you want to track down, the love of your life who escaped?"

Martha, holding the phone under her chin, is polishing some reproduction eighteenth-century wine goblets. "Maybe David's a diversion from that. Or maybe it's closure. One of those, anyway." She places the sparkling goblets on the mahogany table, so shiny she can see their reflection. "Have I told you about this odd man I've met?"

"No."

"He's a magician. He's adopted the cat."

Karen makes a noise, a sort of up-and-down sexual-intrigue sort of noise, at the back of her nose.

"Absolutely not," says Martha. "He's got two children, and a wife somewhere, and I'm not interested in him at all. Not in that way. But I like him. . . ."

"Oh." Karen sounds disappointed and starts telling her about the e-mails she has received since they placed their bulletins on Friends Reunited. She hasn't been contacted by any pushy ex-boyfriends, but she has heard from the same girls as Martha, equally keen to meet up with *her.* "There is talk," she tells Martha, "of a reunion."

Martha shudders. "Can't do reunions," she says. "Not with my life in the mess it is. They'll all be married with hundreds of children or great jobs."

"You've got a great job."

"Not great in the right way. Not 'Oh, how impressive, you must get to see the world,' dollar-signs-in-the-eyes kind of great. More sort of 'Oh, how . . . quaint.' No, I can't do reunions."

"What about me? I'm in the voluntary sector; that's not exactly high stakes, either."

"Yes, but you get to tell them about Kit and it doesn't matter what your job is. You're a rounded human being. You've created a life; anything else is extra."

Karen laughs as if Martha is joking. "If you still want to track down Nick," she says, "a reunion might be the only way."

A customer has come in who needs policing. Her shoulder bag is hanging at a dangerous, glass-flicking level. "I'll think about it," says Martha.

An hour later, she is ironing some monogrammed linen sheets (beautiful, but limited to customers with the initials EJS), and not thinking about it, when Eliza drops in.

"Afternoon," she says casually, standing in the doorway with Gabriel on her hip. He's already reaching for the antique decoy ducks gracing the side table.

Martha puts down the iron and comes over to kiss her. "Hello. This is a nice surprise." It's a surprise, anyway: her sister doesn't usually venture this far into the suburbs. She ruffles Gabriel's hair and tucks his reaching arm away from the ducks. "Just passing?"

"Yes. Just thought I'd . . . yes."

"Good. How nice. Would you like some tea?"

"That would be nice. Where's your girl?"

"April? She doesn't work every Saturday. She has a life!" Martha puts the kettle on. April talks about movies and bars, but Martha can't visualize her at them. She has an image in her head of a Victorian clockwork toy, slowly winding down and lying down in its box. When she turns around she sees that Eliza has put Gabriel on the ground and given him a decoy duck to chew on. Eliza is looking around at the furniture appraisingly. "I wouldn't mind a table a bit like that," she says, gesturing to the Virginian mahogany. She looks at the price tag and raises her eyebrows. "Presumably, you'd give it to me at cost."

"I thought you preferred things new," says Martha. "Modern and hard-edged."

"Maybe." Eliza has flicked the price tag to one side and already looks bored at the idea. "Anyway, listen. Have you spoken to Geraldine?"

"About what?"

"About *The Boy*? Have you told her?"

"Have I told her what?"

"That it's mine."

"No." Martha takes the duck from Gabriel, wipes the spittle off it, rubs at the bite marks, and puts it back on the table. "No, I haven't. If you want it so badly, you have to deal with it yourself. I'm not going to be drawn into the middle."

"I just think she's being very childish."

Martha doesn't answer. She is trying unsuccessfully to steer Gabriel away from the rocking horse.

"Don't *you*?" says Eliza.

"I think you should sort it out for yourselves. Sorry, this rocking horse isn't really for children."

Eliza tuts and grabs Gabriel. "Well, it just seems very insensitive to me. You both knew that Mummy always wanted me to have *The Boy*. It's the sentimental value that counts. Anyway, I'm above it all now. One of us can be mature. If she fucking wants it, she can have it. But perhaps you could ring her to tell her I've arranged a van to pick up the chesterfield this afternoon."

"But Geraldine wants the chesterfield . . ."

Eliza smiles sweetly, and kisses the head of her son. "I know."

◆

DAVID IS WAITING for her in the pub when she gets there. It's a wet, drizzly evening, so there is no chance of sitting outside. You can't even see the river from his table; just the rain streaking down the window. Martha has run from the car. It doesn't matter about her hair—it'll dry—but her sneakers are wet and she worries they might begin to smell. That's one thing you could never forget about David: his very sensitive nose.

"Martha." He stands up and smiles as she walks toward him. He's wearing chinos. His dark hair is wet and slicked back. They kiss politely, on each cheek. He goes to the bar to get her a drink—"white wine?" he volunteers before she can ask. Oddly, she hasn't drunk much wine since they split up; more beer or the occasional cocktail. But wine was what, as a couple, they drank. She nods. "Lovely," she answers. He is sniffing it as he brings it back to the table. "Very nice head," he says.

They never really sat in pubs when they were an item. Maybe to begin with, but after those initial skittish dates, it was all restaurants and dinner parties, little weekends away. When he picked her up, the first thing he'd utter was a checklist— "passport, toothbrush, lipstick?"—as if she couldn't be relied upon to keep it together. He would read the guidebook to her on the plane, or, if they were just going to dinner with people he knew, deliver a symposium on their life and work in the car. "She's an Oxford double first," he'd say. "He was at Linklater's; now he's a top VC." Martha was too flattered at his assumption that she knew what any of it meant to ask.

Over the years since then, she has discovered that a double first doesn't really exist, not in any technical sense, that Linklater's is a firm of lawyers, and that a VC is only a Venture Capitalist. When they first began to date, she saw herself in his eyes as this fresh, quirky, interesting woman. She can't remember when that changed. Take that country weekend with Karen and Keith. Martha wanted to go on the picnic, too, and should have joked him out of the posh restaurant. But she didn't. They picnicked; she dined à deux with him. It was as if by surrendering her own opinions and tastes to his, she kept herself separate. Being the person he wanted her to be protected the person she really was. It was wrong, wasn't it? She can be different now. She's older and wiser, after all.

"So," she says sparkily (like the girl he first met). "Tell me everything about Maddy Long Legs."

"Ah." He grins. "I suppose Greg told Geraldine, who—"

"Told me. Yes. Is it going well?"

He casts her a look from under his eyelashes. "Let's just say, the jury's out on that one."

"Oh? Trouble in paradise?"

He curls his lips. "I think that's enough about my personal life. I haven't seen you for two years."

Martha looks at the floor.

"Martha?" There's a serious note in his voice she's not sure she's ready for.

"Hm."

"It's two years. I thought you might have made contact."

"I know. I'm sorry."

"You just sort of dropped me. One minute, we were practically engaged. The next—nothing. . . . It wasn't easy, you know. Everyone wanted to know where you were. . . ."

"I'm sorry."

"I think I deserved an explanation."

"You did." Martha looks up.

He takes a sip of his wine. "I mean, it's water under the bridge now."

"Yes, of course."

"But . . ."

"David, all I can say is that I think I just panicked. We seemed so complete, so finished, like one of the perfect but terribly valuable necklaces you handle all the time but which I would never dare wear. It seemed easier to put it away in a drawer and forget it. And then the shop—"

"I was the one who encouraged you to set it up."

"I know. You were brilliant." She has spilled some of her wine and she traces a twirl across it with her finger on the table. He came early to pick her up from the antique market one day with a business proposal in his briefcase. They sat in a coffee shop and planned. He looked at properties with her. He kept his enthusiasm when she panicked. She puts her finger in her mouth. "But you wanted me to sell it."

"To come to Geneva with me."

"I know."

He clears his throat. "Well, as I say, it's all done and dusted now. And I'm just delighted to see you looking so well. And to have this chance to chat, to catch up."

"Absolutely," Martha agrees.

He is looking so nice. His hair is clean, his shirt beautifully ironed. There is a tiny spot of blood just under his jaw to show he's just shaved. She feels a flood of well-being flow through her. "Anyway," she says. "You're not in Geneva anymore."

"No. It was great. I met some very interesting clients. But there was this opening in the main office here. . . . You know what I'm like."

"Yes."

"And you? How's the shop?"

Martha tells him about the Pokers and Browsers, the increasing preponderance of middle-class mothers, their passion for pine. She tells him she's taken on some help. He says April sounds a bit too "kooky" for his liking. "She's a bit like how I was," Martha says, "only more liberated." David asks, mock-salaciously, if April has a boyfriend and Martha says she doesn't know. "Good family?" Martha doesn't know that either.

"Bit worrying. She could be anyone." Martha ponders this. Fred asked her about April, too. But how different their approaches: Fred interested on April's behalf; David protective on hers. To change the subject, she tells him everything about the Battle of *The Boy*. She's been worrying about it off and on all day, but now she camps it up for his entertainment. She has her sisters tearing at each other's throats. She has Geraldine sobbing, locking the picture in the car while Eliza tries to break in. He laughs. "Eliza hasn't changed, then," he says.

They don't talk so much about David. It's like the early days of their relationship, when Martha had so much to say, when he'd smile at her oddities without trying to change them. It's a shock when he says he has to leave. He looks at his watch and fidgets. It's not yet nine P.M. Martha thought they'd have all evening. She says, "Oh, have you got to go?" and he says yes, that really he does. His mouth makes the shape of regret. The confidence she'd felt earlier—the bandying of Maddy—drains. "Life goes on," she says.

When he kisses her good-bye, in the rain, by her car, she senses the warmth of his skin. She feels a pang of nostalgia, for the inside of his car, for her youth, for the girl she was when they first met. He says, "What's that smell?"

"My feet," she says.

At home, she gazes at the garbage bag of letters, a bundle of her past. She wonders if there are any answers in there. Maybe, if she went through it, reading every word of every letter from David, she would find the objective truth; she would see why she left him and whether she'd been right—or wrong. But the first thing she sees is from Nick—it's a piece of lined paper torn out of a notebook, with some lyrics from a song on it, and she starts wondering about him instead. It seems easier, more rich with potential. There might not be a Maddy Long Legs in his life. She looks him up in the phone book. There are eight N. Martins. She rings three of them. One Nicola, one Norman, one disconnected.

When she goes to bed, the flat feels empty. She misses the cat.

◆

"MARTHA! MARTHA, I KNOW you're there! Wake up. Wake up!"

Martha fumbles for the phone. "Ur?" she manages.

"She has gone and taken the chesterfield."

"Oh." Martha pulls herself into a sitting position. "Yes. Geraldine."

"You *knew* about this?"

"She was here yesterday. Sorry"—yawn—"bit early. She mentioned it."

"She was there yesterday? With you? It sounds like you've been ganging up against me." Geraldine gives a brittle laugh.

"No. Not at all. I told her I thought you wanted the chester-field. Listen, it's a bit early for this. I'm still asleep."

"It's half past nine, Martha. Some of us, it may surprise you to learn, have been up and about with our children since six o'clock."

"I'm sorry. I just don't think a picture and a couch can be that important. I think you should try and sort it out."

"It's the principle. I just wanted both of you to think about me for once."

"Sweetie, I think about you all the time."

Geraldine doesn't say anything for a minute. When she does, her voice sounds tearful. "I want her to apologize, that's all."

Martha fluffs the pillow behind her head. "But what for? You took *The Boy*. I hate to admit it, but you did start it."

"I want her to apologize for . . . for . . ."

"For being her? She is what she is. That's the thing about Eliza, she's not going to change, she's always been like this. Remember that brand-new bicycle she got? Remember the car? This is what she's like."

Geraldine laughs, too. "Yes. I suppose it is. Still, I'm not giving it back. And that's final."

"Okay. Point taken."

She's about to hang up. But Geraldine says, "Martha?"

"Yes?"

"Friday?"

"What about Friday?"

"David. What happened?"

Martha breathes in deeply. "We talked. It was nice. End of story."

"Really?" Geraldine's voice is dull with disappointment.

"Really."

Martha doesn't feel a twinge for lying. She wants to keep her excitement close to her chest. She finishes the conversation by telling Geraldine she won't ring Eliza on her behalf, that if Geraldine wants the chesterfield she'll have to go round, with

The Boy in tow, and get it. And after she's hung up she has the un-usual sensation of being in control in relation to her sisters. She realizes that, for once, she herself is not the object of concern.

It's Sunday. Another Sunday. Martha tidies up her flat, plumps up the cushions, clears away the cat-food remnants in the kitchen, vacuums up the very last feline hairs from the bed. There is some intricate paint-stripping on a chest of drawers with inter-esting filigree handles in the basement playing on her mind, so she dresses in her oldest clothes and goes down to tackle it. But she can't find the paint stripper. She looks everywhere. And at eleven A.M., the earliest she dares risk it, she calls April.

April says, "Sorry, who is it?"

"It's me."

"Who . . . ? Oh, Martha. Hello." Her voice sounds forced.

Martha asks her if she remembers where she put the paint stripper. April says it's in the cupboard under the stairs. Martha says she's looked. April says maybe it's behind the bucket, but that it's definitely there. Martha says she'll look again. Then she says, "Are you having a nice weekend?"

April says, "Er. Yes, thank you. You?"

"Fine. Have you done anything nice?"

"Um. This and that. Actually I've got to go. See you tomor-row, okay?"

Martha begins to say something else, to say what a funny thing it is that she doesn't know whether April has sisters, but she's already hung up.

The paint stripper *is* behind the bucket in the cupboard and she is hard at work, scouring away any lingering sense of un-ease about April, this colleague, this friend she's suddenly be-gun to realize she doesn't know, when she hears the doorbell upstairs. She's annoyed because she has to take off her gloves and lay them on newspaper; the paint stripper is lethal, and she'll have to slither them over her hands without getting it on her skin when she puts them back on. But it might be Geraldine in need of comfort. Or Eliza in need of another couch. Or—who knows?—some visitor from her past come to whisk her away.

So she goes upstairs and sees Fred standing on the pavement. He's wearing jeans, a T-shirt bearing the number 23 on the front (the sporting motif only highlighting the thinness of his chest), and espadrilles.

"I've begun," he says when she opens the door. His hair is sticking up at odd angles.

"What?" she says. "Begun what?"

"The basement." He points to two cardboard boxes at his feet. "You know . . . you said, er, the clutter."

There are chrome bath taps sticking out from one of the boxes, a moth-eared Afghan rug from the other. "Don't tell me I'm going to be the recipient of all your rejects," she says, more sharply than she intended.

His face falls. "No. No. Not at all. It's partly a joke. Partly, well, there might be something there of interest, something that might be sellable. Every penny counts." He finishes on a hopeful up note.

Martha stares at him. It's like looking at flotsam on the beach. He smiles doubtfully. She feels herself smile back. "Come on, then." Martha beckons him in. He bends down to lift the boxes into the shop, then goes back out to get something else from the street. "Coffee!" he says, passing her a cup of Starbucks cappuccino. "We like our coffee, don't we?"

"We do. Thank you." She's touched, as much by his phrasing—the assumption of a shared habit—as by the drink itself. "What would you have done," she asks, "if I hadn't been in?"

He sits down on the chaise longue and takes a sip through the hole in the lid. "I'd have drunk them both myself. Of course."

She feels let off the hook by that and relaxes. She sits down next to him and they drink their coffee and chat like two friends in a drawing room rather than two relative strangers in a shop setting. It crosses her mind to invite him up, but sitting here seems perfectly comfortable. In this room full of oddments, he seems to blend in.

"How's Kitten?" Martha asks.

"Settling in," he answers, rubbing the top of his head. "Quite demanding. Prefers room service to eating in the main restaurant. Still a little unsure about the other guests. And feels the plumbing isn't quite up to scratch."

"You have buttered his paws? You know, so he'll wash himself and then feel at home."

He grimaces. "Didn't have any butter. Used Flora."

He tells her he's had to get out of the house because his mother-in-law has come round to look after the children and, though he didn't have anything to do, he likes to appear busy around her, that it's her pity that depresses him most. Martha asks tentatively if his wife is going to be back soon and he replies that he doesn't know, that she's in New Zealand at the moment, working on a farm, so it doesn't look likely. "Hm," he says, and then there's a long silence.

A couple of women have stopped outside the shop and are peering in. Martha says, "Right. Downstairs with the boxes. If we hang around and notice them, they'll expect me to open up."

She takes one box, he takes the other, and they climb down

to the basement. Fred has to sit on the stairs because he is too tall for the ceiling. Martha, against her better instincts, has decided to be charitable, to humor him—it's very irritating usually when friends or acquaintances think they can offload any old junk on her. But Fred seems to need all the help he can get. "Which box first?" she says.

He starts going through the one with the taps. Inside are four wooden shoe trees, three throat pastille tins dating from the 1930s, a moth-eared album containing brown-and-white photographs of women in long dresses and men in hats ("some distant relative"), a shred of unfinished needlework, and a worn doctor's bag. Martha doesn't say anything as she inspects each item. In the other box are two dark, worn rugs—which jump with dust when she shakes them out—and a case containing about 100 old-fashioned toy cars.

"Well?" Fred asks finally.

Martha says, "I'm thinking."

"No obligation, obviously."

"Of course," she says sharply. She studies the cars a bit longer. Finally she says, "As it's you, for a favor, I can do something with the shoe trees, the tins, and the doctor's bag. No one will buy the needlework or someone else's family photos, I'm afraid. And the rugs are just wrong for my shop. People don't want old dark rugs anymore. They want stripes and pale colors. Try elsewhere or toss them. I'll put the other stuff on display and you never know. Sale or return, okay?"

"Great." Fred doesn't sound overwhelmed. "And the cars? They're Lesney, even older than Dinky."

"Yes. Interesting. I think the cars are, oddly, rather valuable. They are just not my thing. But if you leave them with me, I'll ask around."

"Thank you."

Martha has put on her gloves without thinking and gone back to work on the chest of drawers. Fred sits on the bottom of the stairs and observes her for a while. "That looks a bit toxic," he says.

"Yes, it is."

"Shouldn't you wear a mask?"

"I'm used to it," she says.

"That's good," he says. "I, er, gather you don't really want anyone to, er, take care of you, do you?"

She laughs then. She can hear the phone ringing upstairs. The machine will have to get it. She looks him in the eyes. "Haven't you got a life to lead, places to go, people to see?" she jokes.

He inspects his watch, that tacky electronic Casio. His wrists would look so much better with something chunkier. She should look out for something old and Swiss. "I've got a group of five-year-olds expecting me at three." His tone is dry, but also slightly maudlin. Martha looks up at his bony, worried face, still with the rag in her hand. She wants to rub the anxiety off. He needs filling out, too. She studies him like a piece of bric-a-brac that only needs the best to be brought out. The phone in the shop has stopped and started again. She hardly hears it. Has she been sympathetic enough about his wife?

"Might you, then," she asks, "have time to grab a sandwich in the cafe next door?"

CHAPTER NINE

the attic

"One person's junk is another's treasure. It involves
accepting cracks, chips and blemishes as part of an
item's attraction and as evidence that it is unique."

JUNK STYLE, *by Melanie Molesworth*

ON MONDAY Martha spends the morning in the market,
the afternoon in the shop, and the evening in Fred's attic. When
she goes to bed later, and looks back over the day, it looks like
a seamless whole, twelve hours of rubbing and poking and
refining.

At the market, she rummages in the back of the dealers'
vans for treasure, searching through junk for the gleam of a
candelabra. She finds an old watch in gunmetal, with a canvas
strap, as a present for Fred, and a set of eight ladder-back chairs.
In the shop, she finishes stripping the chest of drawers and begins the distressing process: a layer of paint, a dabbing of candle
wax, a roughing up with wire wool to make it look old. She

polishes Fred's objects—his tins and shoe trees—and places them at strategic points around the shop. The doctor's bag she fills with dried flowers and positions on a console table. Technically, she's closed, but she lets in the odd customer. She spends some time persuading a young couple of the aesthetic appeal of the lopsided shelves in the Welsh dresser. She wades through a pile of bills, has another moan with Nell from Sustainable Forests about the rent rise. "We'll be okay," says Martha, putting a polish on her words.

In Fred's attic later, where she has vowed to help clear some of the detritus of his life, she finds a vase that might be Lalique (but probably isn't), a wrought-iron cot (painted in peach gloss), and a sweet bedroom chair in need of reupholstering. The rest of the rubbish she says must go. Technically, she's closed to anything emotional—she's there on business—but when it gets late he comes up with a bottle of gin to keep them going and she spends some time persuading him of the aesthetic appeal of single parenthood. "I'm sure a lot of women find it attractive." He rolls his eyes. "You'll be okay," she says.

The day before, over ham and mustard sandwiches in the cafe next to the shop, he told her how young Lucy had been when she got pregnant, how she always resented not going to university, how he loved her but had always felt the tug of her desire to be elsewhere. Martha listened and saw some of the tension smooth out of his face. She told him about her sisters. "I've never been able to join in," she said. "Even now, as they battle over my mother's possessions, part of me wishes I could feel as emotionally *tangled* as they do." She told him about the bag of letters, how attracted she is to David but how fascinated by the thought of Nick she is, like something she's lost and needs to mend. Fred listened. When she finished, he asked her more about her father and Martha told him about the arguments through the wall and the girl in the car. He said, "Is it hard to let go?" She said, "I try to think of him as having gone into the next room."

He asked her if she had good friends in the present she could talk to. "This April?" he suggested. Martha laughed. He said, "You know, sometimes it's good to volunteer information, to get the, er, ball rolling. It's like when I do magic. People are open to persuasion, you just have to intrigue them first. If you confide in her, maybe she'll confide in you."

Now, perched on a box in the attic, she asks, "Do you think Lucy has found someone else?"

He doesn't answer. He looks at the floor and then away. When he turns back, she sees the shock in his face. All that soothing and now she's distressed him. She might as well stick to chests of drawers.

She stares at him, lost, until he says cheerfully, to show he's all right, to show he's been listening, "So if you're right about single parenthood, how about fixing me up?"

She points at the watch from the market, now on his wrist. "I'm doing that already," she says.

◆

ON TUESDAY, Martha spends the day at the shop and the evening with David. When she goes to bed later, and looks back over the day, there's not only a seam, she's like two different people on either side of it.

David has called twice since their drink on Saturday. When she played back the messages that were left while she was with

Fred in the basement, it was his low, reasonable voice on the machine. He felt bad, he said, about "running off" the night before. It had been so good to see her. He felt they'd only just begun to catch up.

Martha felt a twinge of guilt at not having answered. He always seemed to know everything about her, to be about to catch her out. He'll have known she was in when he called. She called him back straightaway. "How about Tuesday in my flat?" he said, but she held her ground. By the end of their relationship, they did everything "over at his place"—it was one reason she began to feel squeezed out. By stipulating her neighborhood, she was making a point. He has a girlfriend. She has a life.

She spends the day serving customers, cajoling April (in a sullen mood), finishing the chest of drawers, and painting Fred's cot. It is a good day. She feels busy, interesting, interested, on the go. She feels detached from David. It's only curiosity, and duty, that has led her to say yes.

So she is not prepared for the emotions, the sexual attraction, the tug of nostalgia, that arise in her when she sees him standing in the middle of her flat.

He had rung the bell and she had let him in, but the phone was ringing in the shop so she urged him up the stairs ahead of her while she answered. It was the electrician, to tell her the lights he'd mended were ready, so she isn't long. David is standing in the kitchen. He is wearing dark blue jeans and a dark gray cashmere sweater. He is leaning against the counter, with his back to the window, where he has so often leaned, half-naked, before. He looks so *dressed*. She wonders if he's thinking the same thing.

"I like the color scheme," he says.

It has all changed since he was last here. Martha's taste shifts, in relation to fashion, every two years or so, but she knows it's probably no coincidence that the last overhaul (from cluttered "Victorian House" to minimalist "Relaxed Home") took place shortly after she and David broke up.

"What's this?" he says, kicking at the garbage bag of letters still on the floor under the table. "Bit messy, isn't it?"

"That," she says melodramatically, "is the past."

But he doesn't pick up on it. He asks for a tour. She takes him into the sitting room, where he admires the linen cushions and the lamp shades. He walks around as if evaluating it all. In the bedroom, he's struck by an unsigned oil—lilacs in a blue vase. Martha picked it up for a song at Borough market. "Clever girl," he says appraisingly. He walks ahead of her into the bathroom. She watches the movement in his hips. He puts his hand in his back pocket; she sees the fabric tighten. She doesn't know if what she feels is familiarity or longing. This tour of her decorative details feels like an undressing.

"Oh, Martha!" Something has caught his eye. "What's this?" She follows him in. "I love the painted washstand," he says, "but this lets the whole effect down, don't you think?" He's staring at the mirror over the sink. It's functional, cheap, modern.

Martha is shocked, not by the observation, but by the fact she has let the eyesore through herself. "I suppose you get used to things; if they hang around for too long, you stop noticing them." She meant it as a clue to how she was suddenly feeling. He nodded thoughtfully. "Hmm," he said. But she suspected his mind was on something else.

She takes him to the bar around the corner for their drink. They eat tapas and try to hear each other above the music and the noise of the other, younger, people. Their first date was in

Leicester Square, in a noisy club—in those days, like now, it was the company, not the venue, that mattered. She has the same feeling today that she had then, the same thrill at the secrecy. It was two months until they confessed to Geraldine and Greg that they were seeing each other. No one here knows them; no one knows that they're here. Not that they're seeing each other now . . .

Conversation comes easily between them. The thing is, David and Martha have so much in common. Geraldine once said that if she didn't know better, she'd think David was gay. (Greg disputed this hotly; he'd played rugby at school with him, after all.) But he is one of those men who is interested in areas of life commonly considered "feminine." They talk, as they pick at bread and olives, about furniture and fittings, linen and linoleum, corbels, bangles, and semiprecious beads. Martha bumped into a former colleague of David's awhile ago at an auction in north London. He told her he was setting up on his own importing French furniture. "All very well in summer," says David. "Don't fancy those crossings in December."

Martha agrees. "And what happens when French furniture is no longer fashionable?"

"French furniture," says David, narrowing his eyes, "will always be fashionable."

They both laugh as if it's a private joke (which it isn't but the pretense is comfortable nonetheless).

He has started talking about Geneva, about the woman who owned an antique shop around the corner from his apartment. Martha starts feeling proprietorial toward him. He's like something that belongs to her, except that there is the extra frisson in knowing that he doesn't. Everything about him is familiar, and yet there is strangeness, too. These people she's never heard of.

"So then—" He's finishing off an anecdote, "Martina leaves a note on the door, which reads, 'Fondue at eight P.M.!'"

Martha smiles and then, so as not to hear any more anecdotes about Geneva, says, "I've got a bit of a problem with the shop."

He frowns with concern. "What?"

"The landlord," she says. She tells him about the rent rise. It works. He looks serious, taps her hand to comfort her. He tells her to appeal, to get a petition going. "If worst comes to worst," he says, "you can get rid of your girl or sublet your flat. We won't let you starve," he adds.

We? she thinks, or I?

"And anyway," he's saying, "we could always investigate other outlets for your talent. Sometimes it's important to move on."

She wonders if that's a clue to how *he's* feeling.

David drives an old 1960s Jaguar. It's parked down the road from the shop. When they leave the bar, the first thing he does is inspect it for scratches before getting in. "You never know," he says. "Round here." But the neighborhood vandals have controlled themselves and he gets in happy. "We should do this again," he says. "It's so good to be friends. Maybe lunch?"

But lunch doesn't really work for Martha, not with a business to run.

"Okay. Dinner," he says. "Saturday?"

◆

MARTHA HAS TAKEN Fred's remarks to heart and all week she has tried to express an interest in April's life and to open up about her own. But the more she has tried, the more she seems to squash out any air there already is in the relationship. April's answers are friendly but short. Martha, stringing some dried hops over the door, says, "So, where did you grow up, April?"

"Manchester."

"And was that nice?"

"It was all right." April smiles but doesn't elaborate.

One afternoon, Martha says, "My life's a mess."

April is polishing. "Aw, bless," she says. But the tone is off. Martha knows she isn't listening.

It's possible April senses she's of interest to her employer, and is keen not to make a connection because her behavior is definitely odd. April's usual pattern is a lurch from lethargy to animation. She can spend hours doing nothing but text on her cell phone or fiddle with her hair and then, suddenly, she will lunge into action, attacking and finishing some arduous sanding task in a matter of minutes. This week, though, she has slouched in, hungover, every morning and just seems to have sagged around. She groans when asked to do any painting. She says the Barley White Eggshell makes her feel sick.

Maybe Fred is wrong and David is right: April isn't a friend. And with things as they are, Martha can't afford to carry dead weight.

But she aches for a confidante. She doesn't want to speak to either of her sisters. She knows, from a brief house-related conversation with Ian, that battle still rages and she wants to keep out. She also doesn't want Geraldine to know she's seen David. She'll jump on it, that's the problem. It would be like the answer to her dreams.

She finds an old number for Nick Martin's brother and tries it. But he's moved.

On Friday, she calls her father. He's on the cell phone at the bottom of the garden. She can hear birds, the occasional plane, children's laughter.

"Darling, marvelous to hear from you," he says. "I'm coming over soon to buy some things for the boat. Did Eliza tell you? Hoping we can all get together. How's that lovely shop of yours?"

Martha tells him about the rent rise. The children's laughter has gotten louder. "Good. Good." he says. "Poor old Eliza. She's having a dreadful old time of it with Denis."

"Is she?"

"Well, you know what it's like, the strains of a toddler and not getting enough sleep, and keeping down that busy job. I'm sure they'll be fine, just a little bicker, I think. She was just a bit tearful when she rang yesterday. Tied up somehow with this ridiculous business about the picture with Geraldine. I don't think Denis approves. But honestly, darling, is there nothing you can do to smooth the waters? I know Eliza is demanding, but it's always so much easier to give in. Anything for an easy life, I say."

Martha listens. She longs to confide in him like Eliza obviously does—to tell him about David, about Nick, about Fred—but her voice comes out clipped and defensive. "I'm not getting involved," she says.

◆

SHE DOESN'T KNOW what she should think about seeing David—again. Should she ring up and cancel? But on what grounds? He has a girlfriend, after all.

On Saturday morning she drops in on Fred, with a check for the shoe trees (sold to a single woman with a new mantelpiece to decorate). They sit in the garden, in a patch of weak sun, watching Hazel and Stan kick a ball around. Fred is wearing shorts and she has to keep her eyes up, away from his bony knees and the dark hairs on his skinny calves. She tells him about seeing David. "We're just friends," she tells Fred.

"Hm," he says. "Be careful."

On Saturday afternoon, April runs the shop and Martha paints furiously in the basement. She has a couple of sleigh beds to do up and she slaps on the paint and scours their sides with sandpaper, as if physical activity will somehow produce an answer.

She doesn't leave much time to get ready. They are meeting in a restaurant near his flat in Kensington. David suggested they rendezvous at his place first, but she wanted neutral ground. She gets the train and then the bus. The number 11: her time chariot, her DeLorean, her Tardis. She has the newspaper with her, but she holds it in her lap and stares out the window in a trance.

The restaurant is perfect. He's made a perfect choice. If you were writing a guidebook to restaurants in which to meet your ex, you would give this one four stars.

It has (1) ambient lighting, (2) discreet service, (3) delicious food—or so it sounds on the menu. (She'll have the antipasto followed by the radicchio risotto.) And (4) one full wall of plate-glass windows so there is plenty to look at if conversation flails—cars, buses, passersby.

And here he is himself walking briskly along the plate-glass window to the door. He is frowning in that I'm-late-but-don't-be-annoyed-because-I'm-aware-of-it way that is very familiar to her. He has always had a thing about punctuality. Martha's mindless disregard for clocks used to drive him mad. He was a stickler for smartness, too, but the suit seems excessive. Even with no tie and the buttons of the plain white shirt underneath undone. David has a lot of plain white shirts. They are lined up in his closet, synchronized, like chorus dancers, swaying their arms in perfect time. At times, alone in his flat while he played squash or worked out (activities he would pursue with a sort of sheepish determination, as if he felt they were things that were expected of him), she would trail her fingernails along the shirts as you might scrape a stick along a fence. But she has the odd sensation now, seeing him wend his way across the room, still separate from her, but getting closer all the time, of wanting to bury her face in their clean starched whiteness.

"Sorry. God." He has arrived at the table, shaking his head in irritation. "The traffic coming down from the Cotswolds was murder." He kisses her on both cheeks and then looks at her directly. No glasses today. He rounds his mouth. "Hello." It comes out like a coo, like baby language, like the old days.

Martha notices that his shirt isn't plain white, but has textured stripes like expensive bed linen. She wonders what he was doing in the Cotswolds, in his suit, and whether she can ask. "Hello," she replies.

"God, but I'm hungry," he says. Sitting down, he plunges straight into the menu, running his eyes over it with his head nodding from side to side as if he just needed familiarizing with the details, and then casts it aside. "Ravenous. Brazed oxtail, I think. With Thai-style fish soup to start. So how are you? What happened to that set of ladder-back chairs you were telling me about? Did you get a buyer for all eight?"

Martha smiles. Not yet, she tells him. "But I'm not going to break them up. A family needs to stick together."

"Your kind heart," he says. "Now . . . guess what I found this week, tucked away in the attic of a town house in Bath."

"I don't know. Clue?"

"Something to reflect your glory."

"A mirror!"

"Yes. And what type?"

"Gilt?"

"No."

"Glass?"

"Ye-es." He's staring into her eyes, laughing.

"Venetian!"

"That's right."

"Old or repro?" asks Martha.

"Old."

Martha inhales sharply. "Square or oval?"

"Oval. Or rather, octagonal, if you can imagine it."

"I can." Martha closes her eyes. "With a fleur-de-lis crown and base?"

"Exactly." He has his head on one side.

Martha opens her eyes. "How much?"

He dips his spoon into his soup and says, "Tell you later."

She tuts. She says, "Oh, go on," and he says, "No," and she tuts again, shuddering in frustration like it's a game. When he gets up to go to the restroom, throwing his big white napkin on the table not in surrender but in challenge, he casts her a purposefully flirtatious look over his shoulder and narrows his eyes.

On the surface, Martha is lightness and little jokes. But she knows it's a sham—more of a sham than plain awkwardness—because underneath she is seething with questions. Why is she here? Why is *he*? Is she a possession that has slipped his grasp?

And Maddy Long Legs, what of her? As far as she knows, she is still floating around in his life, doing whatever Long Legs do, bumping into light bulbs, catching in people's hair. Have Maddy and David split up? But then the suit and "the Cotswolds"? Could Maddy be involved with those? If Martha has any grasp on her own feelings toward David, she loses it now. In her stomach, there is a sharpening of sexual interest, a keening, when she thinks about David in bed with someone else.

"So, the Cotswolds?" she says airily, when he returns from the restroom. "What happens there?"

"A lot of picturesque stone cottages." He sits down, fluttering his napkin again like a matador before a bull. "Some gently rolling countryside."

"Ha. Ha. An appraisal?"

"No. Um . . ." Their main courses arrive. David gives the waiter an acknowledging nod and then pulls at an eyelash in the corner of one eye. When the waiter has gone, he says, "A party. Lunchtime drinks."

"Lunchtime drinks?" Martha says it as if she means, "Oh, how posh," but she's thinking, Oh, who with?

"Yes. Lunchtime drinks." David picks up his knife and fork. "Quite nice. Some friends of mine have upped sticks and bought a place outside Chipping Campden. Lovely countryside and beautiful house. Bit of a schlepp, though."

Martha, thinking, What friends? New friends? Old friends? Friends of his? Friends of Maddy's? Do I mind? Should I care? Says, "Oh."

"Mm. Anyway."

"Was it fun?"

"Yes. It was. It was nice."

"Just drinks?"

"Oh, food as well. A sort of barbecue, I suppose. Children around. You know the sort of thing."

Martha feels a pang of something unfamiliar. "Have they got kids, these friends?"

"Er, yes, they've got two. Though there were others there as well." David frowns as if slightly baffled. "I'm not sure who the rest of them belonged to exactly. You couldn't tell who belonged to whom. Every time you opened a door there was another one. Watching a video or scribbling on the walls, or scratching toys across the original flagstone floor. Some of their friends were quite . . . Bohemian, I suppose. Not artistic Bohemian, just sort of a bit tatty? I was talking to one woman and she said she froze her breastmilk. Beautiful house, though, God."

Martha has put down her knife and fork and is looking at him. There is a pause. There are several things Martha thinks of saying. She wants to ask if he thinks it is possible to have children and keep them tidy; whether actually lots of people don't freeze their breastmilk somewhere along the way; whether he ever really wanted to have children with her. "Farmhouse?" she says finally.

David is wiping the remaining gravy on his plate with a mop of bread, clearing a dark unguent puddle into paler gloopy swirls. "More of a cottage, but a large one. In the middle of the village. Quite low ceilings. But the rooms aren't a bad size. And it's Grade Two listed."

"Century?"

"Early nineteenth, possibly late eighteenth."

Martha puts the other things to the back of her mind. "And have they got good taste?" she says.

David crosses his plate with another piece of bread and pops it into his mouth, both gestures neat and fastidious. The plate is altogether clean now. Dishwasher clean. He has placed the hunks of bone delicately on his side plate. There are crumbs of bread there, too, and scrapings of leftover butter, but in front of him, there is nothing. A circle of white: a helping of sticky, complicated meat reduced to a polished disk of milky porcelain.

"Oh yes," he says. "Their taste is perfect."

◆

FOR THE FIRST few days after the cat moved out, Martha expected to push against him when she opened the flat door, and when she didn't the door would swing wide too fast and bang against the far wall. In bed she would move her feet gingerly for fear of kicking him off and then, finding emptiness, would scissor them back and forth, tossing the duvet as if shaking some life into it. Funnily enough, she forgot to tell David about her temporary lodger. In all the "catch-up" stories and anecdotes, the cat has somehow slipped the net. The Saga of Fred and the Kitten is not something she has shared with her ex.

David wanted her to come back for coffee. His flat was only a couple of streets away from the restaurant—his lovely, light-filled (up-lighted, down-lighted, over-picture-spotlighted) flat, a draw in itself. But Martha was adamant. For all the muddle in her heart, in her head, it seemed important to play it cool, or distant, or ambivalent, to send out a message—whatever it was: she couldn't have said for sure.

"Please," he said. "I've got something to show you. To give you. A surprise." She shook her head. "Okay," he said, always the gentleman. "At least let me call you a cab."

But she set off, with a wave over her shoulder, to the bus stop.

He waited until there was half a block between them and then he called after her. "Martha!"

"What?" She turned, expecting more persuasions. The little-boy voice he used to adopt to engineer his own way.

"You've got paint on your face!"

"What?"

"Paint. On your face."

"What." She rubbed her hands over it. "You could have told me."

"I thought it was a style thing," he shouted, laughing.

Now home, she goes straight to the bathroom and looks at herself in the (functional, modern) mirror above the sink. She is poised with a washcloth when the phone rings. David, she thinks, checking that she got home safely. But it is Fred.

"Hellooo," he says, drawing the end of his greeting into a hum, a habit of his she has noticed.

"Oh, hello," she says. "You're ringing late."

"I tried you earlier, but . . . No. Answer." He says the last two words with import. (Another habit—sometimes there seems to be a rhyme and reason to which words he chooses to empha-size, other times not.)

"I've been out. I told you. With David. I've just been think-ing about you—or Kitten, rather. How is he?"

"I thought you'd be back by now. Kitten's, um . . . well, listen for yourself." There is a rustle and then the muffled vibration of a cat's purr.

When Martha hears human breathing again, she says, "I think that's almost as bad as putting your toddler on."

"I haven't got a toddler."

"You know what I mean."

"Oh, er . . . Hang on. Go back to bed. What are you doing?"

There is a clunk and Fred says, "I'll be back in, er, a second. I've just got to . . . sort out Hazel. Come on. Up."

Martha sits down on the bed. She has the phone to her ear and is holding the cooled washcloth across her face, feeling it balloon in and out against her mouth as she breathes. This morning Martha looked at the children playing ball and wondered about their mother leaving them. They are odd, nervy kids. Stan usually has a globule of green snot running from his nose. Hazel is jumpy and unpredictable. She can be sweet and charming, but if you ask her a question, about school, or friends, she might answer properly but she might answer in gobbledygook like a baby, or with her mouth stretched so that the words come out drawled and self-conscious. One day she repeated everything Martha said back to her until Martha felt her nerves were stretched to the screaming point. She couldn't wait to get out of the house.

But if they were yours? That would be different, wouldn't it? There has been the odd moment when she felt that, without even trying, she has connected with them and that, to her own surprise, they seem to like her. (She is, after all, the woman who brought them the cat and therefore, like some sort of Egyptian goddess, to be worshipped.) Once Hazel wanted to brush Martha's hair. Her strokes were so slight they hardly reached her scalp. Martha felt that, if she had had time, she would have let Hazel carry on, that the gentle fiddling could have been soothing, but actually, the slightness itself jangled her nerves and she pulled away before she could stop herself. At those moments she has felt a glimmer of what it must be like to love a child and yet feel suffocated by her. Maybe it is not the child but the burden of your own love you need to escape from.

"What are you doing? What's that noise?" Fred is back.

"I'm holding a washcloth to my face."

"Is that a nice thing to do?"

She rolls the washcloth up. "God, I've just remembered. When I was little, and used to stay with my grandmother, I would chew her bath sponge in the bath. It was my favorite thing. I remember her taking one away from me because I'd chewed the last one to threads. She said, 'When you're grown up you can buy your own sponges to chew.' Of course I don't. But I remember the texture of it, the warm taste of plastic and soap, the water squeezing out between my teeth." She laughs. "I wonder what that was about."

"Perhaps it just . . . felt nice."

"Yes, you're right." Martha chucks the washcloth across the room and through the doorway of the bathroom. It lands wetly on the floor. She follows after it, picks it up, and hangs it over the sink, wanders back into the bedroom and puts on a CD with the volume low. "Yes. Yup. You're right. I always read into things but you're probably right."

"Sometimes immediate sensation is all," he says. "What's that?"

"What's what?"

"That music."

"It's an overture."

"An overture to . . . er, what?"

Martha pauses. She answers in the form of a question. *"South Pacific?"*

Fred says, "Great film," and for a little while after that she can hear him humming.

Martha tells him that she talked to Jason earlier today and that he *does* know a man, and that he will come by to see the Lesneys sooner than you can say "offshore account." (Fred thinks selling them means Never Working Again.)

Fred tells her that might be lucky because he has had a disastrous afternoon. He thought he was doing a four-year-old party, but he walked into a room of eight-year-olds.

"Is that the end of the world?" Martha asks.

"So end of the world is it," he replies, "that from then on the parents decide it's three friends and a trip to the ice rink. Anyway, it was awful." He brought the wrong tricks with him and they all shouted that he was rubbish.

"You need someone there to protect you," Martha says.

Fred says, "Well, you could come one day. Be my lovely assistant."

It is a question, not a suggestion, but she doesn't answer. It hangs there in the silence for a bit. She is not stupid: she knows Fred is drawn to her. It's not vanity so much as realism. A man in his position with two small children and no looks, and not even a very nice house, to compensate, isn't exactly going to be fussy; all he needs is someone to clear out his attic with him, to rumple up his sheets and then help him change them afterward. Not that she doesn't like him. In fact, to her surprise, she finds she loves her friendship with him; it's something new to her she even hopes will last. But definitely not in *that* way.

So, after a pause, she says, to make her point, "So why am I seeing David when actually I'm still hung up on Nick? Should I settle? Or should I hold out for perfection?"

Fred says, "I thought you said it was a 'catch-up' date?"

"It is. But . . . three catch-up dates in a week? We've got nothing left to catch up *on*."

Fred doesn't say much in return—he's still humming *South Pacific*—so she makes a joke about "ex marks the spot," and he laughs vigorously. "The Ex Files," she improvises. And he laughs some more. His laugh is low, and fumbling.

She is trying to think of another pun to make him laugh some more—he has such a nice laugh—when she hears the shop bell ringing. "Come with me," she says. "In case it's a mad ax murderer."

"I expect it'll be a cab for someone else," he says. "Or a misdirected pizza."

"That's okay, I'm hungry," she says. "I only really had salad." But she takes the phone down with her anyway, through the shop to the door, and for a moment, she thinks it is a cab for somebody else, because a man is standing there next to a black taxi with its engine running. "Can I help you?" she asks through the glass.

"Delivery," the man says. "Delivery for Martha Bone?"

And out of the passenger seat he lugs a big brown package wrapped in string.

"It's half past eleven at night," she says, opening the door.

But the cabdriver just shrugs and hands it over. "Watch out," he says. "It's heavy."

Martha has the phone under her chin. She says, when she's closed the door, "I've got a mysterious package. Do you think it's safe to open it?"

"It's the middle of the night," Fred says. "Who sends a parcel by taxi in the middle of the night?"

Martha isn't listening. She has unwrapped the note. It says "To Martha in Balham from an attic in Bath. Love, David"; she can feel herself flushing as she reads it. And now she is pulling at the knots, tearing at the brown paper and pulling it aside, and there in her hands is the most precious, gorgeous, generous, antique Venetian mirror. Octagonal with a fleurs-de-lis crown and base.

"What is it?" She has forgotten the phone. Fred's voice is on the floor.

She picks it up. "Nothing," she says. "Look, I'll ring you in the morning, okay?"

She carries the mirror up to the bathroom—her palms against the pointed edges, her fingers caressing the felt back— and holds it in front of the mirror above the basin. It is the perfect size for the space. The glass is silvery when you look at it straight on, but green from the side, like water. The decorative leaves cast shadows across the surface, little pits of darkness that send sparks of light into the room. It brings everything together. It is perfect. She leans forward to look into the glass and scratches the last streak of paint off her forehead with her nails.

CHAPTER TEN

the conservatory

"A conservatory gives life a new dimension."
INTERIOR DESIGN SOLUTIONS, *by Ruth Pretty*

"IN, TWO, THREE. Out. Punch. In, two, three. Out. Punch."
The man on the video is lying on his back, lifting his pelvis and squeezing his perineum. Geraldine looks down between the double pendulum of her breasts to her own stomach muscles. Improving? Hard to tell, but she thinks so. She looks back at the television. "Now for the lower rainbow," the man says through his teeth. Hm. This part's hard. She forces the small of her back into an arch. It is the breathing she's got to crack. It seems to be the opposite of the breathing you're supposed to do for her yoga classes. That's more in for four, out for eight. Feeling the air ease out all the way down to your toes rather than punching it out from your solar plexus. The one relaxes, the other empowers. Relaxing. Empowering.

Punch. She still hasn't worked out if it's all right to do both. The woman at her new health club said it was fine. Dip in and out, she said. But maybe she should dip in there, in a proper class, before dipping out into stage two of the video. It may be called "Bottoms Up!" but it is her back she is worried about straining.

"Ow!" She feels a dart of exquisite agony—not her back, but in the palm of her hand, which has landed on an upturned ridge of hard plastic. It is a yellow piece of Lego. She bends across to pull out the new official Lego box from the immaculately tidy toy shelf and unclips the lid. A stray piece. A small hard yellow brick, easily overlooked, but essential to the construction of the Sky Ranger Propeller Plane. Lego deserters used to be chucked into a bright pink straw basket (Geraldine's summer handbag until one of the handles frayed away; like many middle-aged residents of suburban London, Geraldine likes the illusion that her weekly shopping is really taking place in an open-air French market), but Katrina, on her arrival from Poland two weeks ago, has imposed order upon the playroom. Hard boxes with lids that snap shut.

Geraldine doesn't know why she denied herself help for so long. She was always being told, by the kind of mothers who turn up at the school gates in lipstick and sneakers, that it is "the answer," but resisted it on the grounds that anything that applied the same criteria to motherhood as math couldn't be right. Also she wasn't happy with the thought of having a stranger in the house. Now she sees how wrong that was. Do everything yourself, you do nothing *for* yourself. And it doesn't feel like failure, letting Katrina look after the children, as she thought it would. It is liberation. Martha can think what she likes. Eliza can do what she likes. If she wants the chesterfield, if she wants the watercolor of the swans, *if she wants Graham's old slippers,* so be it. Geraldine is keeping *The Boy* and that's final.

She looks up at the mantelpiece where the picture now hangs. It looks fine here. Some might say the playroom is an odd place for it, but it works for her: not too showy, but somewhere she can gaze at it often. Susie, whom she has seen several times since the funeral, is right. She has to put herself first occasionally. It is extraordinary how free she feels not worrying about other people. She has put her sisters out of her mind. Since a furious conversation earlier this week, in which Geraldine made her position clear, Eliza isn't speaking to her. Martha is off in her own hermetically sealed world. Geraldine doesn't mind about either. She is in a different place now. Working out instead of cleaning up has changed her outlook on life. It has made her realize how important it is to look after yourself, how important it is emotionally to be in shape physically. Like the impeccable Camilla Quince, who caught Greg's eye at the funeral. She looks back at the person she was becoming before she met Susie— squashy and dimpled, her flesh flowing, her responses loose and uncontrolled. How could she have let herself go?

Geraldine replaces the Lego in the compartment of the box with the air travel parts, clicks the lid back, and gives herself a mental pat of satisfaction. Look after the little things and the bigger ones look after themselves. One L-shaped brick of Lego, one gyro-copter ready for takeoff. She puts the box, square and solid, back in its place on the shelf and inhales. One tightened perineum, one sex life on the up.

◆

ON THE TABLE in front of Martha are four bell jars, two watering can roses without the watering cans, and a plastic bottle of tomato ketchup. Her feet are bare because her sneakers are drying on the radiator. Kitten dashes in, shaking with indignation, and rubs himself against her calves. It is raining: one of those sudden, vertical October rains in which the whole world seems to be dissolving. In the street outside, drains are overflowing, gutters already blocked with autumn leaves are torrents, and the traffic is at a standstill. But here at the back of the house the rain is flat and still and it doesn't seem to touch them. Even with the door open, Fred's orange kitchen feels warm and enclosed, like the inside of a car on a long journey.

"So," says Hazel, who is sitting next to her eating a supper of fish fingers and Cheesy Wotsits. "We had painting. And then reading. And then we were supposed to have outside play, but it was too wet so we had *The Lion King* in the gym."

"You mean you acted it out?" Martha is studying the bell jars carefully. Fred found them in the shed at the bottom of the garden and, encouraged by the check he got for the shoe trees, is convinced he'll be able to sell them. Martha doesn't want to disappoint him. She's sure she can do something with them. There will be some decorative trick, some conceptual joke. She just has to think. Could she balance them, inverted, in wrought-iron mesh? Fill them with bulbs or attractively bound editions of Sylvia Plath?

"No. Silly. We watched it. The video."

Stan is licking the last orange dust out of his packet. He's got ketchup all around his mouth. "I hate *The Lion King*."

"Yeah, because it makes you cry."

"It doesn't make me cry."

"Yes it does. You're a crybaby. Crybaby, crybaby."

Fred, leaning against the back door, stubs his cigarette out on the doorjamb and chucks the end, still glowing, into the garden. It hisses into a lilac bush at the side. "Hazel," he warns mildly.

Martha looks up from the jar. "What's it about, then, *The Lion King*?" she asks.

"Don't you know?"

"No. I don't know anything. We didn't have videos in my day. We had 'Watch With Mother' or nothing. Though I do remember going to see *Fantasia* with my dad. Just me and him. That made a change."

Fred says, "It's good to remember things like that."

"Well." Hazel takes a deep breath and begins to tell her. After a while Stan joins in and at one point scrambles over to Martha until he's standing right next to her. When Hazel explains about the old lion dying, he closes his eyes as if he is trying to block out the sound and has got his senses muddled. Martha nudges him and holds a watering can rose in each hand to make them dance. Fred is watching from the other side of the kitchen. He is looking particularly pale and scarecrowlike today. The sleeves of his jacket are even shorter than usual— the knobbles of his wrists show—and there are pink rims under his eyes. He has lit another cigarette and when he inhales, his fingers have a slight shake to them. Martha knows he has had a postcard from his wife. From Bangkok.

He says, "Er . . . you two. If you've finished, go and get ready for bed."

"Oh-wa." Hazel hangs on his leg, then wheedles. "Can't we watch a video?"

"Sounds like you've watched enough today." After Martha says this she opens her eyes wide and jerks her head from side to side, as if to say, "Who said that?"

"Do you think we're all born with those phrases in our head?" says Fred. "Or are they learned? Anyway, Martha's right. Come on." He steers them out of the room.

Stan says, "Can Martha read my stories?"

Fred says, "I don't think so."

"I don't mind," she says.

"It's okay." He takes the children upstairs. There's the sound of water being run and lots of stomping. When it has quieted, he comes back in. "Drink?" he says. "A little beer, or a gin and tonic?"

"Oh . . . I'd better go. I'm seeing David. At his flat, too—first time. Very portentous. Oh, all right, just a little one, a very weak one because I'm driving. Have you got any more gin or did we finish it last time?"

"Er . . ." Fred opens the cupboard and produces an empty bottle of gin.

"Looks like we finished it," he says slowly. Then, he wraps it in a dish towel and, scooping some gel pens and coloring books out of the way, stands it, upright, in the middle of the table. He leans on it, pushing down, until it seems to be disappearing, and then there's a clunk and Martha bends down and there it is on the floor—except when she bends to pick it up, it's full.

"You're amazing," she says, holding it to her cheek. "Can you do it with everything? Must save a fortune on supermarket bills." She hands him the half-empty ketchup bottle. "Can you do it with this?"

"Er . . ." Fred makes a face. "Well, I can't actually."

"Oh. That's a shame. Do it again."

"No." He puts the empty gin bottle back in the cupboard and pours them both a drink from the full one.

"So how did you do it?" Martha is just teasing. She doesn't think he's going to tell her. But he holds out his hand. In it is the top of a gin bottle—a false top.

"It's an, er, illusion. I replaced the empty gin bottle with this, pretended to push it through, and then dropped the full bottle onto the floor with my other hand."

"But when did you swap the empty bottle for the false top?"

"Didn't you see me do it?"

"No. Not at all. And I was watching you the whole time."

"Well, there you go. That's the magic. Not the end result but the process. Doing things under your eyes without you seeing. One thing you learn as a magician: nobody pays attention. Look—"

He points at the fridge and then crosses over and opens it. From inside the door he produces a bottle of tonic and from the icebox, a tray of ice cubes, and brings them back to the table. He pours the tonic on top of the gin in the glasses and then hands her the ice-cube tray. Poking out of an empty section is a watch. Her watch! She feels her wrist. It's gone.

"How the hell did you . . . ?"

"You didn't notice me doing it?"

"No! But how did it get in the icebox?"

"Well, you didn't feel me slip it off because you were concentrating on the gin bottle and you didn't see me put it in the ice-cube tray just then because you were concentrating on the tonic. It's all about displacing the attention elsewhere." He smiles at her. "Something can be happening right in front of your eyes and you just don't see." He looks away. "Sleight of hand and misdirection."

"Oh, Dad." Hazel stands in the doorway of the kitchen in a

pair of pink pajamas. "Don't tell people how it's done. That's not what a proper magician does. Smarty Arty doesn't even tell people what his real name is."

"Yes, well." Fred is putting the children's plates in the dishwasher and wiping his hands on a dish towel. "There's ordinary magicians and there's . . ." From the cloth he produces a feathery red carnation. "Mr. Magic!" He brandishes it like a rapier, then places the plastic stem between his teeth and, sinking to the floor, skids on one knee across the tiles, to Martha's bare feet. "M'd'm," he says through the flower.

Hazel is giggling and Martha laughs so much the tonic tickles her nose. "Mr. Magic seems to bring out a different side of you," she says when she recovers.

He stands up to tuck the plastic carnation behind Martha's ear. She can smell the gin on his breath. Very slightly, she pulls away.

"Misdirection," he says, watching her carefully. "And sleight of hand."

◆

IN TRAFFIC TRYING to get across Albert Bridge into Chelsea, Martha pulls the rearview mirror down in order to study her face. She looks flushed (she shouldn't have said yes to the gin and tonic) and her eyes are bright. The carnation, which Fred said she could borrow, gives her an eccentric thrift-shop flamenco look. It's the sort of thing April might wear. She's still annoyed with April. The other day, she asked her if she wanted to go for a movie one night, and April gave her a funny look. "Bit tired," she said. "Maybe another time." Now Martha puts her head on one side and pouts, shrugging up a shoulder. The car behind beeps; she swivels the mirror back into place and moves up a few places on the bridge.

Fred asked her to stay for supper. He said, "I've got a whole chicken here, ready, glazed, and stuffed." But Martha reminded him she had a date and said anyway she never eats anything ready, glazed, and stuffed. She meant it as a joke, but Fred looked hurt. "Is it vulgar to buy something ready-stuffed? As vulgar as the horse picture and my taste in wristwatches?" Martha said, "No, just revolting. JOKE," because he hadn't laughed.

She had to put her sneakers back on before she left—warm now, though still wet and soggy inside. "Ugh," she said, resting her hand on Fred's thin shoulder to balance herself. He seemed to flinch. Hazel was sitting at the top of the stairs. "She gets in and out of bed all the time," he said suddenly. "She won't go to sleep. I miss my wife."

The rain hits the roof like static. There is green fractured through the windshield, clear and then blurred as the windshield wipers ratchet across and back. She rolls forward a few places. It dissolves to red. Of course he misses his wife. And those kids need their mother. There's really nothing she can do about that. The light changes again and this time she passes through it, the bulbs on the bridge disappearing through the sodden rear window like a pleasure boat going out to sea.

The traffic frees, as if undammed, as soon as she crosses the river. It doesn't take long after that to get to David's flat. There is nowhere to park outside so she has to leave the car a couple of streets away, hold a newspaper over her head, and run back. She is soaked when she arrives. There is papier-mâché all over her shoulders and newsprint on her fingers. Her shoes squelch.

David buzzes her in. Despite its chichi Kensington location, the building isn't as grand as it could be. Some of the apartments are rent-controlled, so no one has bothered to spend money on communal parts. The walls were once white but are now unintentionally rag-rolled with grime and the carpet is a sticky beige. An efficient person has organized a post system just inside the door: square wicker baskets below the occupants' names on neat white labels. There is an additional sign above David's box reading "No Flyers," which has tickled one of the other residents sufficiently to stuff the box with advertisements for pizza deliveries.

David has opened the flat door and is waiting there on the first floor for her. He is wearing jeans and a white shirt with the top two buttons undone. He has hooked his glasses there. (He doesn't wear them very often. Martha is beginning to wonder, with affection, if they are not just for show.) His sleeves are rolled up and his forearms have the remote blistered look of an old tan. Boat shoes, whitened with salt from a recent sea trip, are on his feet. Resting in his palm is a tiny cup of coffee, two fingers of the other hand crooked through the handle. His knuckles seem huge, his nails white scrubbed crescents.

He smiles. "You're late. I was worried you weren't coming."

Something garlicky and delicious wafts out of the open door. Glenn Gould is playing Bach. Martha puts her hand up to smooth down her wet hair and only then realizes she must have dropped Fred's carnation in the street.

◆

GREG OPENS THE front door to find the children's bags and school clothes regimented in the hall for the following day and a table set in the empty kitchen. There is a sweet meaty smell emanating from the oven and a bottle of red wine uncorked on the side.

He hangs up his coat, lines his briefcase up next to the other bags, and goes upstairs. It is all quiet. There are no children hollering in the bath, no wet towels strewn over the floor of the landing, no strip of light under the bedroom doors, no murmuring inside. He leans in to see Patrick and Ivor, damply tousled and openmouthed in their bunks. Next door, Anna is asleep, too, her arm curled around a naked doll, its plastic limbs flayed at an angle. Greg re-joints the doll's legs into a more comfortable position, rearranges the duvet, and kisses her hot cheek.

"Geraldine!" He stands on the landing. She doesn't answer. He has news she will find extremely gratifying. David told him at lunch that Maddy Long Legs has got the chop, that he's been seeing rather a lot of Martha, that tonight he is hoping . . . But where is she? She isn't in the bedroom, though there are signs of recent habitation—the bed is disheveled and shoes and garments are scattered across the floor, a trail from the open wardrobe to the door. It is getting a bit crowded in here what with Hilly Bone's dressing table and chest of drawers, all the additional knickknacks. He shuts the wardrobe, puts his hand for a moment on Geraldine's cello, which stands gathering dust in the corner, leaves the clothes, and goes downstairs.

Someone is in the kitchen, bent on her haunches with the oven door open, but it isn't Geraldine, it's Katrina. Her hair is scraped back in a ponytail and her normally whey-faced skin is flushed with the heat. They were lucky to get her at such short notice, and she is marvelous, he knows that. It's not very PC but he can't help thinking, God, if you're going to have a twenty-two-year-old living in the house, couldn't she at least be a bit sexier? Bit of a thrill over the old breakfast cereal? A little frisson as you pass on the way to the bathroom? Whatever happened to the Swedish au pair? You never seem to hear about them anymore. It's all Czechs and Turks and Poles. What do all those fit, young Swedish girls do instead? Play tennis?

Katrina, who is Polish, stands up when she sees him in the doorway. She has a tiny waist but huge thighs. "Oh."

"Hello!" he says jovially, coming into the room.

"Hi, Mr. Hewitt."

"Gregory. You don't know where Geraldine's put herself, do you? The kids are asleep, I see."

"Sorry?" Katrina's English is still formative.

"Geraldine? Where is she?" Gregory widens his eyes and stretches out his arms with his hands upward to illustrate vacancy and bafflement.

"Sorry?"

"GERALDINE?"

"Oh. G-em."

"Sorry?"

"G-em." Katrina stamps on the spot, moving her arms back and forth as if marching.

"The gym?"

"Yes." She nods. "G-em."

"Still?"

"Er?"

Katrina points at the clock and the oven and puts her hands on one side again, sadly.

"Right. Oh well, let's eat. I'm starving. Had a bit of a day at the paper and there's nothing like a bit of a day at the paper for building an appetite. There's nothing like a pint of bitter in the pub afterward, but there you go."

"Sorry?"

"Only burbling. Let's eat. I'll be OC crockery, you do the honors with the grub."

He gathers together a couple of plates while Katrina retrieves the dish—containing some sort of stew with dumplings—from the oven. As she slides it onto a mat on the table she catches her wrist on the side and says, "Ach."

"Hot?" he says.

She nods. "Hot." She enunciates the word clearly, rolling the "h," drawing out the "t." For a second Greg remembers Geraldine dabbing the children's fingers against a radiator to warn them. She would say "hot" just like that. It used to irritate him, actually, the way it always irritates one to hear a person one loves speaking in any way unnaturally—to children, or dogs, or foreigners. But the patience that she had with them when they were small was something to behold. She did everything slowly, still does, never a sense of urgency, moving through the house as if underwater. He would come in from work and he'd have to clap his hands to get things moving, to get the children into bed and the supper on. And then there would be the barrage of things hollering for his attention: batteries to be replaced, footballs to be blown up, basketball hoops to be fixed, children to take *back* to bed later (and in and out of their bed all night, Geraldine slumbering on), a whole maelstrom of inconsequential nothings.

It is a matter of both gratification and frustration to him that his home life is so separate from his work. "Good day?" Geraldine will ask when he comes in the door, or—in one of her little reductive jokes, taking a single idea of hers (foreign pages equal distant wars) and turning it into a cartoon—"Back from the battlefield?" What do you say? Where do you start? Because of course that isn't what it's about at all. It's about diplomacy and endless missed deadlines and failed fucking summits and train crashes on the other side of the world, hundreds dead, which you have to fight to get mentioned on the bottom of page two. He's feeling old and jaded. People used to say Greg Hewitt knows his stuff, but knowing your stuff doesn't add up to much these days. The new guy, straight from features, "an ideas man," thrusting his ignorance about like a trophy ("Where is Matabeleland when it's at home?"), facetious one minute ("Test me on my capitals?" he asked a secretary the other day), bullishly confident the next that he alone knows what the reader really wants.

Greg has served up two helpings and picked up his knife and fork before noticing that Katrina has not sat down. "Not hungry?" he asks. There is a little performance after that from which he gathers that she ate with the children and then she smiles and nods and leaves him there in the kitchen on his own.

He makes an involuntary snort through his lips, which he realizes, after he has done it, is a release of tension. The house is quiet. He wonders again where Geraldine is. And to be honest, for all his complaining, it feels a bit flat with the kids in bed. Because those inconsequential nothings aren't just a frustration, they are a gratification, too, a comfort. There is escalating tension in the Middle East, there is the nerve-racking petty intrigue of the office, and there is *here,* unaffected by it all, impermeable. He sighs, gets up to fetch the evening paper from his briefcase, and settles down to news and stew.

He is still sitting there, his empty plate thrust to one side, when there is a familiar clash and the sound of keys being thrown on the hall radiator, and Geraldine bursts into the kitchen, clutching handfuls of shopping bags.

"What happened to you?" he says.

"Greg! That is awful! What do you mean, 'What happened to you?' Can't you think of anything nicer to say?"

He simply meant to ask her where has she been. Now he sees that something *has* happened to her. But she clearly isn't offended by his tone because she has kissed him on the head and is twirling around the room, stopping only at the oven to inspect herself in the silvery blur of the stainless steel back-splash. "Look," she says, turning to face him. "Hair. Makeup. New top. And look—" She spins to the doorway where she has left the bunch of bags and pulls out a pair of pale blue baggy trousers that she holds up against herself. "Maharishis. All for me. Look—embroidery on the calves. Isn't that gorgeous? And—" She stuffs the trousers back and yanks out a blue jacket that she also holds up. "Denim blazer. Earle! You've got to go for quality with an item like this. There was one at The Gap but it wasn't a patch on this and Susie persuaded me. And—" She bends to rummage in another bag.

"So. Fun at the G-em Summit, then," Greg says.

"What?"

"The GM summit? The g-em? The gym."

"Oh, the gym." Geraldine gives a fleeting smile to signal that she has registered the joke, but she is too absorbed elsewhere to dwell on it. "Yes, it was fab. I had salsaerobics and a swim. But since then I've been playing truant. It's all right." She puts out her hand before he says anything. "I rang Katrina and she was fine about it. She's so brilliant, much better than I am. Did she put my casserole in? Fabby. Was it delish? Don't really fancy it myself. Bit off meat. So anyway, Susie and I dropped into Kingston for late-night shopping and they were handing out leaflets for a new salon offering free color with every cut. And after that, I thought I needed some more makeup and there was a demonstration at the Bobbi Brown counter in Bentall's and—voilà!"

She has come up close and this time she is clearly expecting a comment. Now that she mentions it he sees that her makeup, as well as her hair, is different. How exactly he couldn't quite say and whether it's *better* . . . he doesn't have an opinion. He tries to drum one up. He thought she looked nice before. Is that the sort of thing she wants him to say?

"Gosh," he says, raising his eyebrows.

"What?" Geraldine sits down next to him and holds her face up like a child waiting to be wiped clean. "What do you think? Be honest."

And if Gregory was in touch with his emotions—which he prides himself on not being—he would acknowledge now that he feels a pang, a twist, as if a small part of him has snagged on something sharp. But his subconscious tells him he is being ridiculous, that it must be something to do with the quietness of the house when he got in, with not having had a chance to see the children, with having to eat on his own, or the strain of making conversation with Katrina. Yes, it's probably something to do with Katrina—a sort of empathy; here she is far away from home, not being able to speak the lingo—because Geraldine looks fine. Her hair *was* a mess before, it had gotten very long and she had to twist it back into a knot all the time and when they made love it would fall forward into his face, into his eyes, into his mouth . . .

"So?" This new Geraldine is staring at him, hard-eyed, her hair sleek and jagged, her cheek and shoulder bones pointed. In this light, she doesn't look soft anymore, but all angles.

He turns back to his paper. "Very nice, old girl," he says.

◆

DAVID, unusually in a man, understands the importance of an enveloping towel. Stepping out of the shower, Martha wraps herself in something so thick and white she wants to bite it. When she was growing up, you dried yourself on cloth like sandpaper; the moisture she blots on this hardly dents the pile.

She folds it over the bath, twists her hair into a turban, and throws on the equally virginal bathrobe that is hanging on the back of the door. At the mirror she inspects her face for damage. She bares her teeth. A bottle of Listerine sits on the shelf above the sink and she swills a capful around in her mouth. Next to that is a small vial of aftershave with a French label. Unscrewing the cap, she breathes in the new nutmeg smell of David. She puts it back and is about to leave the room when she notices the bottle of Clarins Body Lotion (Lait Corps Soyeux) next to it. The label promises to revitalize your skin with 3.5 percent "plant-marine cell extracts." She unscrews the cap and dabs some on her hand. It smells sharp and clean like Band-Aid plastic. David has always been careful about hygiene, but even he is not the "plant-marine cell extract" kind. She considers this for a moment and then opens the bathroom cabinet. Inside is toothpaste, floss, antidandruff shampoo, a packet of razor blades—and a lipstick. "Barely There," it is called. But *there*.

The brand is expensive, the casing matte-brown with black

writing, and when she twists it up, she sees that the lipstick it-self is half-used, molded into a particular angle, leaf-veined with the marks of someone else's lips. These must be Maddy's lip prints. The intimacy of it takes her breath away. She puts it on. When she licks it, it tastes of powder and perfume on old dresses. The color is of a red wine stain. It makes her look dif-ferent, her eyes brighter. David will have kissed a mouth wear-ing this lipstick. Does he still?

Earlier today, Martha met with Karen and talked at length about David. Karen wanted to know what on earth was going on. Martha said she didn't know. She didn't know if he was free, or even if she wanted him to be. All she did know was that, since David had started filling up her life again, she has stopped thinking about Nick. There isn't *room*. "But you'll come to the reunion?" Karen begged. "Please tell me you'll still do that."

Now, Martha tries to remember exactly why she split up from David. It wasn't just Geneva and the shop. Faintly, as if catching on the wind the smell of a distant bonfire, she recalls something uneasy and heavy that might have been boredom. With the tingle of another woman's lipstick on her mouth, it seems spoiled, decadent, to have been bored. Not a real reason for leaving someone at all.

She clicks the cabinet shut and, her lips still flaming, goes out into the bedroom. Every piece of furniture in David's flat is a work of art, on display against the white walls and pale car-pet. The only thing out of place is her wet clothes, and even these, while she was showering, David has laid neatly over the radiators to dry. The bed is mahogany. The bedside table is wal-nut. It has a single drawer. Martha hovers. She thinks about opening it to unearth further evidence. But then her eyes focus on the picture above it, a small brilliantly colored portrait of a woman. It is by a sixteenth-century Venetian artist and the discovery of it, unattributed, in a house sale in Sussex ten years before, was one of the big moments of David's career. He could have sold it for profit and acclaim, but he chose not to. It has been carefully renovated, layers of old-house grime removed, so that the colors spangle. The woman is standing, with her right arm held across her body. Her cheeks are red, her eyebrows arched. There is light in her eyes and her mouth is angled as if she has just said something, or is about to. She is wearing an ornate cobalt dress, with jet velvet sleeves, puffed from the elbow—the texture so rich you want to reach out and stroke the fabric. Her white bosom melts above it. But David didn't keep it for any of this. He kept it for the necklace around her neck—a thick gold chain with an extraordinarily elaborate jewel-encrusted pendant on the end. Martha looks at it now and smiles with secret knowledge. You have to search hard for David's passion. Here it is, hidden in a small exquisite detail in a small exquisite picture. Does Maddy know where to look? She doubts it. And in her mind at this moment, a deep understanding of someone equates with love. So she doesn't open the drawer of the bedside table after all.

David is sitting in a fine Windsor chair at a small table on the large glass-roofed balcony he likes to call his "conservatory." When David first inherited the flat from his godfather, five years ago, they went together to buy a jasmine from the local garden center. It had just been his birthday and while he was paying, Martha slipped secretly to another register and bought him a terra-cotta pot—cylindrical with ivy engraved up the side—as a present. She sees now that the pot has been replaced.

This one is slate and rectangular and more modern. And bigger, which of course was probably the point because the jasmine is huge now—there are tendrils reaching down from the ceiling. The air is rich with a sweet, invasive smell. The rain hammers on the glass roof. Martha wonders if, now that she's clean and in a white bathrobe, they are going to have sex.

David says, "Well, I'm certainly free so that would be nice."

Martha starts. Then she notices the phone against his ear.

"Hang on a moment. Let me put her on." David is holding the phone out.

Martha says, "Hello?"

"Matt-ski. You dark horse. You're actually there, are you? Having a shower, I hear."

"Geraldine."

"Greg's just told me your wonderful news. He waited all evening. *Men*. He had lunch with David. I tried you at home to ask you everything but no answer so I thought I'd ring David to grill him, and then he said you were there, too. In the shower!"

"What wonderful news?" Martha takes the glass of wine David is holding out for her.

"About you getting back together. Martha, I'm so pleased. I've been longing for this. I knew you should never have split up. It's brilliant. Are you absolutely thrilled? Clever girl."

"Clever girl . . ."

"So I just asked David if the two of you wanted to come to supper on Saturday. I thought I'd have a get-together. Susie's about to fly back to Vancouver, and I thought it would be nice to have a little do to wave her off. And Dad'll be over; you knew that, didn't you? Just a short visit. He's got some stuff to organize for the boat. He's staying with Eliza because it's 'in town,' as he puts it. He says I'll have to ask her, too, but she won't come. She's still on her high horse. But you will, won't you? David says he's free."

Martha looks down at David sitting in the chair next to her. "He's free, is he?"

David is nodding and wincing at the same time. "Well, I'll have to check my diary," says Martha. "And anyway, I don't know if you're right."

"What?"

"About . . . you know."

"Oh, Matt. What are you talking about? David told Greg . . . Oh, piddle, am I jumping the gun? Have I got it all wrong?"

David bends down, ducking his head to adjust the feet of the table, as if to give Martha some privacy. It is a small circular occasional table. Four tapered legs. The top is marquetry and boxwood. Circa 1900. It is not dissimilar to the one her mother used to sit at playing cards. Solitaire, or the game David would play with her when she was ill in which you lay the cards in three separate piles. She has an image of his dark head next to her mother's buff-gray one, whispering about diamonds and hearts.

"Martha. What's happening?"

"What do you mean?"

"I mean, are you back together or not? And either way, can you make the do?"

David straightens and looks up at her from the chair. He smiles quizzically. She closes her eyes for a moment, a slow blink. When she opens them, he has diverted his attention to her naked leg. She watches as he reaches out his hand to touch it, rotating his thumb and finger on the skin just above her knee, and she stands very still. Their reflections in the conservatory window, his white shirt and her soft, thick gown—one white blur against the streaking rain. Martha's mother used to call a party a "do." Martha remembers the "do" when she introduced David to the family, the expression of disbelief on her mother's face that her problem daughter could have found anyone so "suitable."

She dabs the tip of one finger along her lipsticked mouth. Barely There still there. Geraldine is saying something, but Martha interrupts. "I think probably we are," she says.

She says good-bye and hangs up. David's hand has moved farther up her thigh. His head is dipped. She bends to kiss the top of it. She can hear his breath quicken.

When they first made love, eight years before, he took her to Paris for the weekend. He fed her oysters in this little place he knew in the Marais. Under the Arc de Triomphe, he told her she was beautiful. By the time they reached the hotel room, she was giddy with champagne and excitement and gratitude. In bed, she lost herself in his skin. All she thought about was the two of them, in the bed, then. It's not like that now. Even as she slips down to kiss him, she feels detached, as if she's watching herself from afar. There is the past to account for, the future to worry about. She feels embarrassed, too, but that will pass. And detachment is good. Detachment is wise, detachment is grown-up. She closes her eyes and finds his lips. Whatever happens, it'll be different this time.

◆

MARTHA'S CUSTOMERS, like her ghosts, obey a clock of their own. There is no telling when they will descend. On some Saturdays her shop is silent except for the sound of her own breathing. On other Saturdays, she can't hear herself think. Today is one of those days. All of Balham appears to have woken up with nineteenth-century French furniture on the top of its list of priorities and has charged down to pick up and put down her sconces, to open and close her cupboards, to test the springs of her reupholstered Victorian armchairs, to *fiddle*. A couple of long-nosed women are hot on the heels of armoires. They have been sent by their friend Charlotte Fraser. Does Martha remember? She asked them to tell Martha how much she "is loving" hers and to pass on her good wishes. She hopes Martha is getting over her loss.

Martha smiles and nods, but her eyes dart to their gaggle of children, who are holding garishly striped lollies. Fluorescent drips have begun to run down their hands and onto the sea-grass flooring. "Jo-lly good," she says, intercepting them on their way to the dappled-green-velvet-covered chaise longue with its smattering of antique chintz cushions. "Let's stand over here now, shall we?"

She is prodding them, teeth gritted, in the direction of the mat when the door swings open and there is Jason. Martha hasn't seen him for a few weeks. She has been buying prudently in view of the imminent rent rise, and has been holding off extra expenditure. He has a person with him.

"Mornin', all," says Jason. He is wearing an Iron Maiden T-shirt and a blue blazer. His friend, who is big and stooped and has thin shoulder-length hair with a small, round bald patch on top like a shiny coin in a patch of long grass, looks at Martha through his front fronds. Jason says, "I've brought you my Lesney man. Mark. Martha."

"Oh, your Lesney man. Brilliant. At last. Hello." Martha smiles and gestures to the back of the shop. "Sit over there for a sec and I'll just . . ."

She explains the rarity of that particular type of armoire

bought by Charlotte Fraser—"an armoirette," she calls it—to the two women, but says she will be on the lookout. She writes their names down in her book. She mops up the Day-Glo puddles of melted lolly. She sells a pair of bell jars (filled, in the end, with moss, compost, and hyacinth bulbs, and suspended from picture hooks), and answers questions on the dimensions of a nineteenth-century fruitwood dining table. And then, once she realizes that the young couple who are debating the decorative advantages of *this* marble console table in her shop over *that* contemporary oak-veneer console table in Heal's are going to be debating for some time, she goes down to the basement for Fred's toy cars and joins the two men at the back of the shop.

Jason's friend, Mark, who is sitting on a child's cot bed, his knees at his chin, cannot conceal his excitement when he catches sight of the box, when he sees that each vehicle has its own little cardboard compartment, a separate garage, so to speak. His voice comes out high and strangulated. "Novelty boxed! Can I . . . ?"

"Of course."

There is a sharp intake of breath from the man. "Ford Zodiac," he gulps. "Lesney series number thirty-three." And then, "Lamborghini Marzal, 'Matchbox' series twenty, 1969. Oh fuck, Kennel Truck, 1968, 'Matchbox' series number fifty. Oh boy. Oh boy."

Jason and Martha exchange glances as he burrows. Jason, who is leaning against a chest of drawers, says, "You're looking different. I've never seen you in a suit before."

"Oh." Martha smooths her skirt with her hands as if removing invisible creases. "Yes. Smart, isn't it? It was a gift from David."

"And heels? You fancy geezer you."

Martha waggles one for his benefit. "Thank you."

"Very grown-up. Designer getup, is it?"

"All right. You don't have to go on."

"I'm just saying."

"Yes, all right."

"I thought you were broke?"

"They were gifts."

"Tights, too. Or are they stockings?"

"I'll give you five thousand pounds for the lot." The car man's offer comes out in a rush. Martha and Jason look up from her legs.

Jason says, "Mark's a collector. I preferred how you looked before."

Martha ignores the last thing. It seemed to have come out by accident. She says to the man, "Oh, I see. You're not a dealer?"

"No. Toys. I collect vintage toys. Twentieth century. Vehicles and action figures mainly. It's been an interesting day for me. I picked up a 1973 Boxed Escape from Colditz Action Man Set at a toy fair in Sutton earlier. Complete with German and British uniforms, all the paperwork, and Sentry Box. Three hundred pounds. There was a tiny tear in the fold of the box, but otherwise perfect."

"Right. I see. Okay. Let me just go and make a quick call to . . . to the proprietor."

Martha says "proprietor" rather than "owner" because she is panicking. She has done some research and £5,000 is considerably more than she was expecting. From her desk, she dials Fred's number. His mother-in-law answers. Fred is washing the car. Martha tells him, when he comes to the phone, that in the future he can pay a Boy Scout to do it. "Whatever happened to 'Bob a Job'?" he says. She says he should stop nattering and get down to the shop right now. She hangs up with a satisfied clunk. "Sorted," she says to Jason and his friend.

As soon as she puts the phone down, Martha is accosted by another customer, a woman pushing a buggy who wants cutlery—bone-handled knives, that sort of thing. Martha tells her she rarely stocks it and the woman is about to lug the buggy all the way down again when Martha remembers the cutlery she bought from the Polish couple, still wrapped in the back of the car, and dashes out to get it. She and the woman are going through the bundle and she is trying to work out how much to charge when Fred arrives.

"Ah!" he says portentiously.

"Yes," says Martha.

They grin at each other—this could be his big moment—and, apologizing to the woman looking at the cutlery, she introduces him to Jason and Mark. Jason says, "How do you do?" and Fred says, "Very well, thank you," and Mark just stands there.

"Sit down," Martha says. They look so uncomfortable. She gestures to the child's sleigh bed at the back of the shop and they huddle onto it, with the cars laid out between them. She returns to the woman with the cutlery.

"Interesting handles," she says, to show she's back on track.

"Nice. Nice," the woman answers. "Oh no." Her baby has started crying and she fishes it out and starts bobbing it around, looking at the spoons over its head.

Mark says, "Mint condition, I notice. Are you a collector?"

"More of a hoarder," answers Fred. Martha looks in his direction and smiles.

She says to the woman, "It looks like they're dealing drugs. But it's only old cars."

But the door has opened again, and blowing off the street comes April, trailing scarves. "I've left my cell phone. Have you seen it?" she yells at Martha, who says, "Sssh."

"It's here, I know it is." She is shaking the cushions on the daybed. "It wasn't in my bag when I got home last night." The woman's baby is still crying. "Oh bless," April says.

Jason says, "Good investment, vintage toys."

Mark says, "I don't sell on."

"Maybe I shouldn't be selling them at all," says Fred. "Maybe I should give them to my son."

The baby is crying even louder now. The door keeps rattling as more people come in and out. "Poor lamb," says April. "Is she teething?"

Martha says to the woman holding the cutlery, "I'll let you have them for a good price."

But the woman isn't listening. She's looking over at the door. Martha turns. Standing in the doorway, a leather garment bag over his shoulder, his silver hair trendily short, his face tanned, is Martha's father.

Martha drops a fork. "Neville!" she says.

He hurls the garment bag onto the chaise longue, knocking over a bell jar and spilling some compost onto the marble console. He crosses the room to kiss her, smiling warmly over his shoulder as he does so at the woman with the buggy.

"Hello, Matty," he says, but really to the woman's baby, whose fingers he has already caught in his brown hand. "I know I'm seeing you later but I was passing by so I thought I'd pop in, see how things are. How are you, darling?" he says. This time to her.

"I'm fine. Listen, hang on. I won't be a second. We're just finishing off, aren't we?"

"Yes," says the woman, blushing slightly. "You know what, I think I'll buy the complete set."

Martha is used to the effect her father has on women. In photographs of him as a young man, he is the spit of Eliza: seal-like, sleek and dark (even under his dog-eared Afghan coat). His blue eyes are milkier now and the hair above the high arch of his forehead is gray, but age has, if anything, improved his face: the weightier jowls and the crinkled white ditches of his forehead adding interest to the bland, smooth surfaces. Add to all this the benefits of a young French wife: the jeans, the sneakers, the general air of fitness and sexual alertness, and it is no surprise that April should sashay over to be introduced. Even the baby has started cooing. "How old is she?" Neville asks the baby's mother. "Great age. I've got two little ones myself."

"Oh, so you're Martha's DAD, are you?" April says, holding her scarf at arm's length at either side of her neck and pulling it back and forth like a towel. "You're Martha's FATHER! She's kept you hidden! I can't believe you're her FATHER!"

"Yes, okay, April." Martha, processing the woman's payment for the cutlery, feels as if she is the parent in the situation. April has dropped the scarf and is holding out her hand to be shaken. Her cheeks are flushed and clear and her hair shiny. Neville picks up April's plump hand and kisses it. And now, with a little whistle, he is explaining the origin of the calluses on the pads of his fingers ("That's what happens when you spend your life messing about on boats"), and this leads to his yacht at Antibes, and his house in Grasse, *his whole life* in France. April and the woman who has bought the cutlery, and the baby of the woman who has bought the cutlery, listen entranced. "Honestly," Martha says.

She turns to the back of the shop where Fred and Jason and the car man are staring at them. She begins to roll her eyes at Fred—at least he won't be taken in by this ridiculous display. But he is frowning at her. His chin is at an angle. And for a split second she wonders why he looks so odd before she remembers: she told him Neville was dead.

Neville, very much alive, says, "Don't they, darling?"

She turns back, flustered. "Sorry?"

"My little girls. Agnes and Odaline. They speak French like natives, don't they?"

"That's probably because they are natives," she says, motioning frantically for Fred to come over. "It would be odd if they didn't."

But Fred is ignoring her. He finishes up with the Dinky obsessive. A check is signed and handed over. And then the three men stand, shake hands, and come to the front of the shop. Jason puts his hand up at Martha in a businesslike manner as he passes, ducking his head and breathing in through his teeth to show he is in a hurry. He and his friend help the woman with the all-terrain buggy down the steps and then the three of them are gone.

Fred is still standing there. Martha puts her hand out to touch his sleeve. She says, "Neville. This is a friend of mine. Fred. Fred, this is Neville, my father." She has her back to her father when she says this and she winces theatrically to show she knows she has some explaining to do. Fred's face is without expression. He says, "I thought you were dead."

Neville gives a shout of laughter. "Dead," he says. "Not the last time I looked."

April says, "Far from it."

Martha opens her mouth to explain. She puts her hand on

the back of her head and cups the other over her eyebrows. She grins at the floor. "Long story," she begins.

Neville, noticing the check in Fred's hand, says, "Been doing a bit of business?"

Fred says, "I've just sold my old toy cars. But now I wish I hadn't. I should have kept them for my son." He stares at Martha.

"Toy cars? How interesting. I used to have a lot of toy cars," says Neville. "I don't know what happened to them." He turns to Martha with his eyebrows raised questioningly, then faces back to Fred. "You know, just having girls. Five girls," he tells April. "From forty to four. Can you believe it?"

"And you so . . . boyish," April answers.

"You got children?" Neville asks Fred.

Fred has moved to the door, followed by Martha. He is ignoring her now. His hand is on the handle. "Two."

"I love children," Neville continues. "Particularly when they're little. You off? Nice to have met you." He clicks together the index finger and thumb of one hand and then shoots the arm out at Fred in a bonding gesture. He looks disappointed for a moment, then continues in the same intimately jovial tone as before. "But there is nothing like a baby in the house." He looks at April appraisingly. "You won't regret it for a minute."

Martha has been holding Fred's sleeve, but now she glances around quickly. She knows April is a bit chubby, but not *that* chubby. Neville is looking at April. April tugs her scarf tightly around her neck. "Sorry?" she mutters.

"Your baby, darling. When's it due?"

This time April pulls her coat across her middle. The cold is blowing through the open shop door. She mumbles something that sounds like "January."

Fred pulls away from Martha and goes. She hardly notices. She is staring at April.

"I can always tell," says Neville. "I've had enough experience. Well, best of luck. Got a nice man in the background, have you?"

April in a low voice says, "In Manchester."

"Fabulous. Well, I'm sure Martha's looking after you."

April hasn't met Martha's eyes but now she looks at her and then quickly away.

Martha lets go of the door. It begins to slide closed on its own with a quiet sigh, but at the last minute the wind picks it up and slams it. She says, "I have tried."

◆

GERALDINE'S LIMPID BODY glides through the blue water. She reaches and kicks, breathes in, breathes out. There are no windows here—the pool is underground—and the ceiling is low. The water hums when her ear dips through it; another swimmer passes her with a chirrup. But she feels all the sounds of her Saturday morning—the whining of small children, the barking of dogs, the thumping of both on the stairs—hit the water and stream away.

In, out. Before she felt faint pity for the mothers she met with their au pairs and their personal trainers, ready in their Nikes at the school gate. How narrow their minds must be, she thought; how thin the satisfaction of a sinuous upper arm; how empty their lives. But now she sees that it is not endorphins but the emptiness itself that is the drug. When she is here, or in the gym, concentrating on her body, she feels all other responsibilities peel off and leave her. Later, she will worry about tonight's supper and tomorrow's homework. She will face up to Eliza, who has reluctantly agreed to come to supper tonight and, according to their father, agreed to be on her best behavior. Next week, perhaps, she will get the cello out and think about playing again. But for now it's just her and the water—so warm it's like her own blood. And after her fifty laps, she will shower and transfer to the beauty clinic, where a woman in a pink T-shirt and surgical pants will talk through the latest "procedure" on Geraldine's list: plastic surgery without the surgery. Or, for that matter, without the plastic. "Micro-currents like the smallest currents you can get—an exercise routine for the face," she will say. "Ok-*ay*?" There will be an upward lilt in her voice because there are even different rules of intonation here.

Five weeks ago, Geraldine would have laughed at this. Not now. Now she will arch her (already "threaded") eyebrows with interest at each boast of "a natural ingredient." And then, face tingling, she will postpone going home a little longer. (Gregory is capable of setting the table; Katrina can handle the kids.) She will find herself on a quick detour to the shops. The new pants, perfect as they are, will be just a little more perfect with a new top. And the new skirt needs shoes. Each outfit, each "natural" procedure, keeps leading to the next.

She reaches the bars, turns and kicks away again. In, out. In, out. Once you start on the new you, it is almost impossible to stop.

◆

MARTHA INHALES THE smell of old leather and oil that permeates David's 1960s Jaguar. She rubs the cracks in the beige seat beneath her legs. David turns to smile at her, puts a hand on her knee, on her tights, just below her skirt, rolls it around gently like one might palm a mouse on a computer keyboard and then returns it to the steering wheel. On the car radio, people are discussing a new exhibition of tiaras at the Victoria and Albert Museum.

The lights on Tooting High Street are red on either side of them. Somewhere in the distance a water main has burst. Horns blare and the side streets are jammed with cars squeezed in at angles. The whole world seems to be heading in the same direction tonight, and no one is going anywhere.

Martha stares out her window. She thinks about April's belly growing and stretching without Martha noticing. Next to the car is a shop full of brightly colored saris. Sheets of blue and pink cloth, sheer and sparkling, stretch from the balletic fingertips of the plastic model to her pointed toes. Rolls of rich, gold-tipped fabric lean against the walls. David inches forward. From the open window of the next shop along, zucchini tumble out onto the pavement like jewels: long, tapered zucchini with orange plumes; heaps of ribbed green okra; mountains of bruised garnet grapes. There are two women chatting as they pick through the glistening red and yellow peppers; a middle-aged man in a cream shirt watches them from the doorway. On the radio, the presenter says, "So on to the Oriental Circlet designed by Prince Albert for Queen Victoria: a noble expression of the jewelry arts or an empty symbol of majesty?"

Martha thinks about April coming in late, her skin gray, spittle in the corners of her mouth. She remembers the sound of retching in the lavatory. She thinks about her on the phone, her muttered, intense conversations. The mood swings, the pink cheeks, the doughnuts! How can a person not notice something like that happening under her nose? What sort of person doesn't notice? Or what sort of person, working side by side with someone every day, isn't *told*? She told Fred she was a mother figure, for God's sake. Where did she go wrong? Is she so deluded? So unapproachable? So out of touch with the concept of motherhood, of *sisterhood,* that April couldn't tell her? When the anger goes, she feels desolate. Whose life can she say she is part of, if not April's?

When David arrived, she told him straightaway, relieved to have someone to open up to. "Shall I go and see her right now?" she said. "Tell her it's okay that she didn't tell me?" He shrugged. He said, "It's her life." Martha asked him why he thought April hadn't felt able to tell her. "Am I so cold?" she said, but David thought she was probably worried about her contract. "Is maternity leave built in?" he asked. Martha said their agreement was verbal, and he said, "There you go." After a bit, he added, "Silly girl."

"At least we're through the lights," he says now. "We might not be too late after all."

"Good." David's hand rests on the stick shift and she gives it a quick squeeze. "I hate being late for Geraldine."

They might have been later, and she might not have minded. Here is something else to worry about. She left David with a drink in the sitting room, and went to take a shower. With her head tipped forward, feeling the water stream through the soap in her hair, she willed him to push the door open. A connection with anyone at that point would have been reassuring. But when he didn't appear, she realized she was relieved. She had wanted to have bathroom sex not for itself but because it had seemed the sort of thing that *should* happen, like proof, like a vindication.

Sex, this time around, is embarrassing between them. She

wishes she could pretend otherwise, but she can't. Without his clothes on, there are stripes across David's arms and legs where his freckled summer tan ends. His white body feels cool, like a statue. There are bits of him, a triangle of delicate, almost translucent skin from his hips to his groin, that Martha feels she knows as well as her own. Naked he is beautiful, perfect, but she keeps her eyes tight when she kisses him. She isn't interested in discovering the intricacies of his body. No matter how much she tries, she can't recapture the erotic newness of that first time in Paris, jagged limbs and mouths. It is as if a sheen of politeness has come between them. Martha finds herself fantasizing about men she cares less about. She has put aside most of her ghosts (one of these days she is even going to throw out that bag of letters), but Nick Martin still lingers. At night when she can't sleep, she finds herself looking through the phone book. Karen says the two of them need to relax, to feel at home with each other again. Martha is working on this. He is, after all, perfect. They just need time.

"I can't tell you how glad I am that you're coming with me," she says. "It's terribly brave of you."

He says, still looking ahead, "I like your family."

"It's true, isn't it? You do." Martha smiles up at him. "How amazing."

They reach the highway and David at last puts his foot down. The houses behind the fences strobe past, one after another, front doors, leaded windows, Leylandii, gates, railings; everything upright and straight, lining their road to her sister's house as if in salute.

CHAPTER ELEVEN

the dining room

"Sitting at an informally laid table with a group of
friends has to be one of the most relaxing of activities.
And how better to enhance this treat, than by sitting in
a restrainedly decorated room surrounded by charm-
ingly grouped treasures and stored china and linen."

THE SIMPLE HOME, *by Julia Bird*

GERALDINE—or someone purporting to be Geraldine—
opens the door to Martha and David in what can only be de-
scribed as a new outfit, though this hardly does it justice.

David says, "Crikey, look at you!"

Martha says, "God."

Geraldine is wearing baggy beige trousers with pockets at
the knees and a vivid seagreen embroidered dragon crawling
up one leg. They are slung low over her hips and a pouch of
white tummy peeps out below a tight turquoise cap-sleeved
T-shirt. "Princess" is emblazoned in silver across her chest.

"What?" she says. She might be flushing under her bronzed

cheekbones. Her eyes look like eagle's eyes, or the markings on military planes.

"Your trousers." Martha opts for the least controversial item on display. "Are they combats?"

"No. They are Maharishis, thank you very much."

David says, "Ah."

"But if the Maharishi wasn't opposed to violence," says Martha, "you could call them . . . all I mean is, they look like combats."

"Well, they're not." Geraldine slaps her thighs, as if giving her cellulite a quick press. Painted nails flash crimson against the beige. "Anyway, leave me alone. Look at you. Miss Skirt. And congratulations—late as you are, for once you're not the last. Eliza hasn't yet deigned to turn up. Come and say hello to Daddy."

David and Martha follow her along the corridor. They pass the playroom. Martha pokes her head in. The children are in their pajamas watching television and don't look up. The dogs, in their baskets, are chewing their own feet. *The Boy* stares guiltily from the wall.

The atmosphere in the kitchen is that of a party waiting to happen rather than one in full swing. Greg is drying glasses at the sink. He is wearing pink sailing trousers and clumpy new sneakers that make him look awkward. His cheeks are heavy and there are beads of sweat on his brow. Neville is at the kitchen table. In his dapper dark suit and red tie, with his tanned raked face, he looks out of place, like a managing director having a cup of coffee in a greasy spoon. When he sees Martha and David, he says, "Ah! David, dear boy. Darling M!" and half makes to get up. But he ends up just rearranging himself in his chair instead, giving the fabric of his trousers a little tug. In the space between the fine blue wool and the fashionable laced shoe, there is a glimmer of scarlet sock.

He has been deep in one of his anecdotes. Graham's daughter Susie is sitting next to him. Martha knows Susie and Geraldine have been seeing a lot of each other, but if she hadn't, she thinks she would have guessed by her clothes. Susie is wearing the same trousers as Geraldine, only hers are white and have a snake instead of a dragon. Martha kisses her father, and greets Susie. Neville swills the wine in his glass and gestures to the pale young woman opposite. "Meet Katrina. The wonder-woman of Kingston."

"Our au pair," says Geraldine from the fridge.

"She has struggled across Europe to bring aid and harmony to this house, haven't you, darling?" Neville pats her hand. "Leaving behind her family, her friends, her fiancé . . ."

Katrina says, "I am from Poland."

"Can you believe it? When she arrived the family she was planning to come to had given the job to someone else. She was homeless, practically destitute. Out on the street, on her ear. Weren't you, Katrina?"

"Sorry?"

"Homeless."

Geraldine says, "Dad. Leave the poor girl alone."

Katrina decides to leave *them* alone. She is meeting some other au pairs at a bar in town. "A woman with a social life," sighs Geraldine when she's gone.

Neville says, "Goodness, all these young girls I'm meeting today."

"And some of them pregnant," says Martha. "Clever of you to notice that."

"It was obvious, darling. She had a little bump. And that sort of swollen look to her face. I'm amazed you didn't notice yourself."

"I guess I lack experience."

"Never mind," he says, smiling around the room.

"You, on the other hand, have known your share of pregnant young women."

"Now, now," Neville says lightly. Martha looks away. David and Greg are standing over by a rosewood bookcase that, until a few weeks ago, displayed Hilly Bone's Everyman editions of Dickens. These days it houses Jocelyn Dimbleby and Delia Smith. Greg is talking about work—something about a new boss. Geraldine is flapping around between the oven and the fridge and the dining room.

Neville has turned to Susie. "Fascinating country, Canada," he says. "God, I'd love to go there." Susie is chopping chives curtly. "Well, you should," she says. "While you can."

Through the window, outside in the garden, Julia and Ian are swaying up and down in formation, like a Scottish reel in slow motion.

"What are they up to?" Martha asks Susie.

"Getting the babies to sleep. Apparently, walking up and down helps."

Martha laughs. "Haven't they heard of babysitters?"

Geraldine scoops Susie's chives into a dish. "You're an angel. They use her mother sometimes."

Susie puts her head on one side and flicks her curtain of hair. "I think, Martha, if you had gone through what they've gone through"—she nods a couple of times as if to confirm Martha's sympathy—"you would be protective, too? Do you know what I mean? I know it's hard but we've got to try not to judge people."

"Yes, of course." Martha smiles grimly, thinking not just an angel but a saint.

Geraldine, clattering around with dishes and plates, says, "Isn't it time ours were in bed?"

Greg doesn't hear her and carries on talking to David. But instead of repeating the question, Geraldine says, "Oh all right, oh God, I'll do it," and flies out of the room. No one else seems to have noticed, but Martha is taken aback. Although she has always assumed that deep down her sister is unhappy, the surface impression in the house is usually relaxed to the point of chaos—family life at its most aesthetically hideous: dog-eaten toys, crayoned walls. Today everything is awkward and jagged. Geraldine won't keep still and Greg looks exhausted. Her father, the magnificently self-regarding guest of honor, is oblivious, but around him there is flitting and jarring.

She gets up and says to Greg, "Any chance of a drink?"

Greg says, "Of course. Sorry. What am I thinking?" and slugs out a glass of red wine for her. "She's given up," he hisses.

"Who?"

"Ger. She's given up booze and you'll notice she doesn't eat her food at the same time."

"The same time as what?"

He whispers, one eye on the door, "She won't eat meat at the same time as potatoes. She has to digest her fruit before she eats her vegetables. It's a bloody nightmare."

David looks alarmed. "So what are we eating tonight?"

"Chicken."

"Ah. Good. She does a good chicken. The usual, I suppose?"

Greg says, "She'll cook but she won't eat with you. She just sits and stares, like a disapproving dog."

Susie is looking over at them from the table. She says loudly (not just an angel and a saint, but a lip-reader, too), "Actually, it's called trophology, and there is a lot of medical evidence to support it." She turns to Neville. "I mean, at your age, you really should consider it. Combining the wrong foods, eating proteins with starch, the typical Western diet, causes havoc on the digestive system. It's the major source of fat and cholesterol accumulation in the body. Do you eat hamburgers?"

Neville says, "Never touch them."

"Okay then, steak and chips?"

"Steak frites, oh yes, of course. With a green salad, usually." Neville looks relieved. He breathes in to show off his slim waist and looks around for approval.

"Well, there you go," says Susie. "Sticky deposits in your arteries. Your colon lined with mucus. You should do something about it before it's too late."

She smiles sweetly at Julia and Ian, who are coming in from the garden. Julia is wearing expensive jeans with a crease down the front, but her eyes are tired and she has lipstick on her teeth. There is a scabby rash on Ian's neck. They mouth greetings at Martha and David and, limbs rigid, toes soft, move like moonwalkers with their bundles toward the kitchen door. Ian is just easing through it with his elbows when there is a loud peal and the rattle of the front door and the voice of Eliza coming toward them.

"Sorry we're late, everyone," she cries. "Burst water pipe in Wandsworth. Bloody nightmare. Julia! Ian! You've got the babies with you! Again! Oh! Sorry!" Julia's bundle has started crying. Julia looks as if she might be about to, too. She and Ian disappear into the house. Eliza says, "Oh dear. Never mind. It's about time they used babysitters like the rest of the world. Oh look, Mummy's little rosewood bookcase. Bit wasted for cookery books, wouldn't you say, Geraldine? Hi, Neville. How was your day?"

Neville says, "We've just been hearing about trophology."

"What's trophology?" Eliza is kissing everybody. She looks effortlessly relaxed in her faded jeans and white T-shirt. "Hi, David. Long time no see. Martha, what on earth are you wearing? What's happened here? There's Geraldine over there in her princess T-shirt and pop-star street clothes. And here's our reliable tomboy in"—she turns Martha around so she can look at the label at the back of her dress—"Armani. Very nice."

"It's to do with not eating steak and frites at the same time," Neville says. "Fatty deposits, mucus-lined colons." His suntan seems to have paled a little.

Martha says, "It was a present from David."

"Oh, you mean the Hay Diet. Are you on the Hay Diet, Ger?"

Geraldine is handing Denis a pile of cutlery. "I don't know anything about being on a diet."

Eliza taps her playfully around the waist. There is a cruel look in her eye. "Very brave of you, Princess. Seeing as you're intent on hipsters."

Geraldine pales. "I am involved in trophology. It is the science of food. All I am doing, Eliza, is looking after myself. Inside and out."

Neville says, "Girls, girls. Remember, you promised . . ."

"It's not me," says Geraldine, but Eliza is pretending not to listen. She has gone over to the table to join Neville. "Budge up, handsome," she says, perching on the edge of his chair. "Well, I hope we've got something decent to eat. I'm starving-wharving." She winks at her father.

Geraldine says, "Chicken."

David, comfortable in the thought of himself as Geraldine's favorite, steps forward and puts his arm around her shoulders. "Sometimes I dream about your chicken," he says. "Your world-famous Coronation Chicken."

"Grilled," she says.

◆

THEY DON'T EAT in the kitchen. Geraldine has set the dining room table for ten and lit the candles, even though it is grilled chicken and salad. Even though it is family. Even though she is wearing combats. There have always been distinctions in this house between "kitchen suppers" and "the dining room." Greg finds it hard to keep track of the rules. They seem to be laid out more in relation to the importance Geraldine wishes to bestow on an occasion than on any intrinsic formality within it. In the past he has been caught on the hop, about to chuck cutlery on the kitchen table for a takeaway to celebrate a neighbor's birthday, only to discover it has been "set" elsewhere; or, worse, ushering the editor of his newspaper (coaxed into the suburbs for a meal with one of his longest employees), into a cold, empty room.

Now, for this get-together, in honor of his father-in-law and his father-in-law's late ex-wife's stepdaughter (what *is* this about? What lengths will his wife go to to manipulate "The Family"?), they stream into the smartest room of the house (the *only* smart room in the house), forcedly jolly at the corraling. Geraldine flits about at the door telling people where to sit. "You can't go there, Denis," she says, "that's next to your wife," and "Oops, up you get, Julia; girl, boy remember." Everyone obeys her, but they stand by their allotted chairs awkwardly for a moment, too formal to sit down.

All, that is, except Neville. Steered by his eldest daughter to the head of the table, he plonks himself into his seat, flourishes his napkin, and says, "In Grasse no one ever bothers with seating plans. You just chuck some bread, some cheese, some pâté on the table, and whoever happens to be there—children, adults, *les voisins, le notier*—just help themselves. A plate of food, a glass of wine, the sunset, the love of a beautiful woman . . ." He tips back in his chair, with one elbow on the table. But the chairs, mahogany and satin-cushioned, passed down from Greg's mother when she went into the nursing home, are, like their former owner, a little unsteady on their feet, and he buckles for a moment, an expression of surprise on his face, before Susie, who appears to have taken it upon herself to behave like a nurse discreetly attendant on a wealthy if willful patient, slots him back in.

She says, mildly now, "Pâté, cheese, and bread. You might as well just block your arteries with a shovel."

Julia, at the other end of the table, says, "That's quite enough about arteries, thank you very much. You'll put me right off my food."

"You should listen," says Susie. "If you want to tackle Ian's eczema. Dairy is a known allergen. Smile, but if Dad had paid attention to his diet, then maybe he would be with us today. At this meal."

Martha catches David's eye. He blinks slowly and mouths something she can't read. It might be "God forbid," although she's not sure. It was always his role before—the outsider who sympathized with the sisters but was above prejudice himself— to be nice about Graham. But this time around his attitude is a little off, like a piano slightly out of tune.

Julia gives a radiant smile. She sets down her glass very

carefully on the table; it hardly makes a sound but her shoulder is rigid. "Yes, well, had you been here visiting him on a daily basis, schlepping up from Surrey, checking that he was eating at all, not to mention keeping an eye on his medication, trying to tempt him to eat anything—in the end he only wanted baked beans—then maybe you would have a point." She smiles again.

Martha, who has done none of these things, looks down at the table.

Geraldine comes in again with a plate of chicken and misses this. She says, "Sit," as if trying out a new jollying tactic on a room of dogs.

Greg and Geraldine's dining room is lined with dark red, gold-crested wallpaper. Martha considers it hideous and old-fashioned. A chandelier dangles dustily in the center of the ceiling. A pair of silver salt and pepper shakers stand to lilliputian attention in front of her place setting. She picks one up and studies it. It's familiar: it belonged to her mother and her grandmother before that. She puts it back on the table with a clink. When Geraldine, who is at one end, facing her father, passes the plates, they scrape and clank. Martha watches her elder sister hold a crystal glass up and turn it against the light, to check it for smears. Her mouth is gathered and a tiny frown flits across her forehead as she wipes it on her linen napkin.

Martha turns to Ian, who is next to her, and asks him how he is, and whether he has any news about "the house." He tells her they have just received two offers, one from a developer and one from the next-door neighbors, the Quinces, who would like to knock the two houses together. "Though only the ground floor, not all the way up the house," Ian adds, "because they wouldn't get a return on that."

Geraldine says, "Well, obviously we'll accept the Quinces'

offer, won't we? We don't want some horrible developer. There's no argument, is there?"

Eliza says, "Hold your horses."

Ian says, "The developer is offering another fifty grand."

Eliza says, "See?"

Geraldine jabs two spoons into the platter of grilled chicken and thrusts it to David. "I cannot believe I'm hearing this," she says.

"Hearing what?" says Eliza.

Geraldine throws herself back in her chair, her eyes casting around the table. She takes a gulp from her glass, which is holding a cordial of elderflower and ginseng. "You knew about this already, did you, Eliza? Martha? Did you? You didn't? Well, you agree with me, don't you? You won't let them sell the house, Mummy's house, to the highest bidder?"

Martha rubs her eyes. "Um," she says.

But before she can say anything else, David says, "I suppose selling something to the highest bidder is what is customary in these matters. And when it comes down to it, there isn't really room for sentiment."

"But my mother's house . . ."

"It was my father's house, too. In recent years at least." Ian hasn't spoken for a while.

"Yes," says Julia, nodding forcefully at her husband.

Martha, her mind on the rent rise, says quietly, "Graham would hate it to be sold to a developer. It was his thing, after all. Developers moving in and taking over the area."

But Susie, who is picking through a bowl of salad, says, "This is barking. Dad would have wanted us to get as much dosh for it as we could. He wanted the best for his children."

Geraldine says, "Susie!"

"I'm sorry, Geraldine. But money's money. And frankly, I could do with as much as I can get."

Martha says, "We all could."

Geraldine is looking tearful, her mascaraed eyes like daisies. "Dad?" she implores.

Neville gives his tie a flick as if shaking water from it. "Nothing to do with me anymore, I'm afraid, sweetie. Sold my say long ago." He puffs out his cheeks and reapplies himself to unpicking the chives from his portion of potato salad.

"Under the circumstances"—Ian's forehead has flushed red—"I've informed the estate agent to go back to Mr. and Mrs. Quince and give them an opportunity to match the developer's offer. I also believe we need to be in full possession of other information, such as how the capital in each case is being raised. And I would suggest that we reconvene at some point, when the position is clearer, for a final decision. Also, there is the matter of the remortgage. . . . Um . . . Over the last year, certain legal pressures have been brought to bear and my father was constrained, at one point, to take out a further loan against the house."

Eliza says, "He remortgaged the house? Fuck."

Martha feels a wedge of anxiety expand in her chest. "And there I was not worrying too much about the rent rise," she says, partly to herself.

Geraldine says, "What? What's happened?"

Eliza says, "We're fucked, that's what."

Everyone begins talking at once. Greg and David bend back in their chairs and talk practicalities behind Julia. Denis, in his own quiet way, tries to preach patience and understanding. But Neville, more because he is rendered uncomfortable by any subject that touches on his previous marriage than through any altruistic desire to defuse the discussion, slaps his thigh loudly and rests one hand on the top of his head. "I say," he says. "Did anyone else catch that program last night in which those two rather attractive girls threw away that poor woman's entire wardrobe? Did you? Said none of it fit 'the rules.' That she had to buy a whole lot of new clothes. What's all that about? And that was followed by that other program with that little camp Yorkshireman buggering up people's perfectly nice gardens. This poor elderly couple went away for the weekend and the television company constructed this hideous Japanese water fountain. We flicked over from that and on the other side that Carol Vorderman was doing the same thing to someone's front room. Painting it lilac! An army man, too! What is going on? I come back to England and all the media seems to do is go on about change this, change that, do this to yourself, do that, eat this, don't eat that, steak frites off the menu, wear this, don't wear that."

Everyone stares at Neville. Eliza laughs. She says, "You're right, Daddy. Get someone in, get a new garden, a new living room, and a new lifestyle might come, too. Find a new look and a new personality to go with it. The makeover artist is the new god. The question is, is it a benevolent god? Or one that makes people feel as unhappy as they are?"

Geraldine fingers the outsized purple diamanté cross she is wearing around her neck. She says, "Eliza, it is not 'a religion' buying a few new things to make you feel better about yourself. I saw the program, too, Daddy, and the woman at the end felt much more confident. She took off the wedding ring she'd worn since her divorce."

Neville, buttering another hunk of French baguette, says,

"Yes, but did you see her two weeks later? She looked just as much a mess as she did when they started."

Greg says, "Spent a fortune in the meantime. Expensive business, new clothes. Expensive business, the old me, me, me. Meanwhile in East Timor . . ."

Eliza interrupts. "It's the same as your shop, Martha, isn't it? People come in not because they *need* a bed or sofa—they'd go to a department store for that. They come into your shop because they want a *new* bed or sofa, one that fits into the current 'look.' One that will make their house 'look' different, that will transform the 'style' in which they live."

Martha says simply, "People find things comforting. Isn't that all it is?"

"But you're educating their eye." David laughs. "In a sense, at least. It's a style thing, not a value thing." He turns to Eliza. "Basically, attractive as a lot of it is, Martha sells junk. Dressed-up junk. Nobody is coming away with anything of any value, of any long-term significance—simply with something that looks pretty, for the moment. It's a sort of con. They are buying a lifestyle. Just like the fashion business. In fact, Martha's business *is* the fashion business."

"Sorry?" Martha looks at him. "I thought I was in the antiques business."

Eliza puts her head on one side. She and David always used to have a little sparring thing going on. "But isn't the grown-up stuff you do subject to fashion, too? I mean, what determines the value of a Regency desk or a pearl necklace? It isn't just their intrinsic value, is it? Rarity counts. Supply and demand, and demand goes up when something is in fashion."

Martha waits for David to fight back. That's what he would have done in the old days. But he just looks at her and winces.

Julia's knife and fork are clicking against the china. Ian, next to her, is trying to slice more meat off a chicken wing. Her father has picked his up with his fingers and is gnawing at it.

"So who are these gods, then, Eliza?" Susie asks. "The people who make the television programs? Martha with her funny little shop? I don't understand. If it's a tyranny, who are the tyrants?"

Eliza laughs. "Interesting question. Who determines fashion? Obviously designers, but they are responding as much as anything to what has gone before. Fashion itself creates fashion. But that's not what I'm talking about. I'm interested in this trend for complete re-creation, this culture of transformation. Where does that come from? All these books, telling you how to decorate, all these programs. I don't know. A new century, a desire for a new beginning? Or a godless society in which people flounder for excuses to change? I don't know. Possessions as the new gods. Household gods!"

That's when Geraldine stands up. Her chair makes a grinding noise on the floor. "If this is all just a dig at me, Eliza, why don't you say it?"

Eliza says, "It's not a dig at you."

"Oh really."

"Geraldine, it's not a dig at you. It was Neville who brought the subject up. It interests me. But if you want to get personal, it is also intriguing how a good Catholic girl like you can have become so grasping."

Geraldine swallows. She twists her face into a heavily ironic expression of confusion. "Sorry? Grasping?"

Eliza laughs again, more lightly. "I only mean the tea-leafing of Mummy's things. I notice the house is stuffed full."

"If this is about *The Boy* . . . ?"

"Which you have." Eliza has stopped smiling.

"And you don't have anything, I suppose? What about the chesterfield and the oak chest?"

The two of them are glaring at each other. Martha can't think of anything to say, and looking around the table at the blank expressions on the other faces, she realizes she isn't alone. It is as if this argument has been trying to get out all evening. She thinks she might say, "What about me? I haven't got anything, but I'll settle for the Penwork tea caddy." But she doesn't. As usual she keeps out of it. She's lost touch with who's right and who's wrong. It will pass. She picks up her wine and takes a swig. The glass has left a ring on the table.

And then Martha sees Julia start. In the doorway, Ivor is standing in his pajamas. His face looks startled, his eyes out of focus, as if the light is dazzling him. You would say he had "bed head" if he didn't always have bed head. He mumbles, "Mum. I need you."

Geraldine starts clearing away the plates angrily. "Run up. I'll only be a minute." But Greg has already scraped back his chair, and so has Neville and so has Denis and he's the closest. There is an undignified scrabble at the door, but uncle wins out. Ivor looks up at Denis like a supplicant. When Denis scoops Ivor under his arm, Martha sees the wet streaks down her nephew's pajama legs. Out in the hall, Denis can be heard saying, "Chase you up there, champ." And the clatter of the two of them on the stairs sounds like an escape.

◆

AFTER THIS, lots of people leave and Martha gets drunk. Ian and Julia remember they have a bad night ahead of them. Eliza doesn't bother with an excuse. At the door, she says,

"Well, I've taken the saltcellar so she can put that in her pipe and smoke it."

Geraldine has a cry in the kitchen. Susie comforts her, and Martha and Gregory clear the table. Neville says, "What are all these tears for, then? Don't like my girls falling out." David says, trying to make a joke, "It's only a saltcellar." Geraldine says, "What saltcellar? You mean, she's taken the saltcellar?" and then cries all over again. Martha hustles him into the sitting room, where Neville, shepherded in by Susie and told to "rest up in here for a bit," has taken over the sofa. He has managed to corral a bottle of wine and he leans forward to top up their glasses. Martha wonders idly whether he's going to drive home to Eliza's or stay over. He sees her looking. "Bugger arteries," he says.

It is cozy in here. Geraldine lit a fire earlier and, though it has given the bulk of its performance to an empty room, the embers are still warm. Martha sits in an armchair closest to the grate and nurses her glass. She feels the evening loosen. Conversation, which around the formal dining table was pinioned, swells and spreads. She can hear Geraldine laughing in the kitchen. Neville and David are sitting opposite her on the sofa. They are both slouched back; they are both supporting one ankle on the other knee. They both seem to be wearing red socks. David laughs at something her father says and afterward he gives the collar of his shirt a settling tweak. She realizes she is drunk. Her eyes half close, the room spins, and the two men seem to merge for a moment.

She hears her father say, "Well, Martha seems well, I must say. You must be good for her." And David nods and looks across at her but then, twisting away, says something she doesn't catch. He turns back and sees her watching. He says,

"Getting your life back in order, aren't I?" She curls her legs up and laughs. Even though a part of her wonders what he means.

"Let's get you home, then," David says. He pulls her out of her chair. Geraldine, coming to the door to say good-bye, says, "I'm glad you're happy, Martha. I'm glad one of us has got life sorted."

In the car, with orange street light on his cheek, David wants to know if she's free this weekend. "How about coming down to the beach with me? We could leave late Friday and come back early Monday morning and get two full days in. A long walk along the shore. A little putter around the harbor in the boat. Dinner in the pub. An early night. One of Mum's world-famous cooked breakfasts. I know the folks are longing to see you again."

"What about my 'funny little shop'?"

"Can't you close it for one weekend?"

She is not quite drunk enough to forget her responsibilities. She can't keep closing up. She can't ask April to stand in, not now that she's pregnant. "Well . . ." she begins.

David looks at her and smiles expectantly.

"Not really," she finishes.

David's face stiffens and when he turns the car into her road, the turning signal *tick-tucks* like a sound of disapproval.

◆

SHORTLY AFTER falling asleep, Martha surfaces abruptly, like someone bursting from warm water into cold air, and lies there, next to David, in her Victorian cast-iron bed, wide awake and sober.

At first she thinks it must be the sheets that disturbed her. Drunk and woozy, she found their lovemaking improved. They had undressed each other carefully, and then reached mutual climax with concerted passion. But afterward, David nuzzled sleepily into her neck and Martha hadn't liked to ruin the moment by moving him. Now the sheets are rumpled and uncomfortable. But there is something—not April's revelation, which fills her still with confusion, with a kind of murky unhappiness—but something else. Not the row between Eliza and Geraldine. She has a sense of discomfort, of being in trouble, of having been found out, just an *unease,* but it takes a moment to recall why.

Of course. Fred. It's nothing now that she remembers it. It's just a silly old misunderstanding. In the morning, she will go and explain to Fred how she just happened to end up telling him her father was dead. He is sure to understand. But, for the rest of the night, Martha lies awake in her beautiful bed, next to her perfect boyfriend, smarting with irritation.

CHAPTER TWELVE

the playroom

"Children live more fully in the
present than the rest of us do."
KIDS' ROOMS, *by Jennifer Levy,
Dania Davey, and Elaine Louie*

"WORK?" David says. "On a Sunday? Can't it wait?" He pulls
Martha toward him. He is sitting at the kitchen table in the
forest-green bathrobe he unpacked from his mock-alligator
Mulberry overnight case. A striped badger shaving brush, an
ivory-handled razor, and a wooden pot of lemon-scented
soap are already lodged on the basin, below the Venetian mirror, in the bathroom. This morning, after her shower, Martha
ran the brush across her cheek. It felt soft and seductive, like a
cat's tail.

"Okay," she says, pinioned between his knees. "I'll do it this
afternoon. After our walk." David likes a walk on a Sunday. It is
one of the things he and Martha have in common. They like

"Sunday walks" and "pub lunches" and "candlelit dinners," pursuits to be enjoyed in quotes, as if ordered by mail from Blissful Lifestyle, Inc. Keith once asked her, years ago, if she and David ever "just slobbed around." She repeated this to David, who said, "Slob?" and in his mouth the word sounded indecent. *She* hasn't seen Karen and Keith for ages now. She has tried not to feel too bitter—their life is full without her—and has spoken to them on the phone. They claim to be delighted that she and David are "an item" again, that her life is back on track. Keith referred to David as "your jeweler," which Martha found slightly patronizing, and Karen is thrilled because now, she thinks, Martha will accompany her to the school reunion. "Nothing weird to hide in your life now," she told her. "You're just like the rest of us."

David releases her and tucks the two edges of his robe into the gap between his legs. "Now," he says, "how about a nice 'leisurely breakfast'?"

The flat can't offer much in the line of breakfast, let alone a leisurely one, so Martha throws on some clothes and ventures out for papers and food. Bread, vacuum-packed bacon, orange juice with no pulp. The woman in the shop smiles hello at her and Martha thinks, Not a single woman in control of my life, but a hunter-gatherer returning to my man. The concerns about Fred, the need to tidy *that* up, don't seem as pressing in daylight as they did in the sooty shadows of night. She will worry about April later. There are piles of crinkled orange leaves in the gutter, and she kicks through them cheerfully. Only after does she realize there are puddles lurking beneath, spraying her shoes with muddy water.

When she gets back to the flat David is dressed and waiting

at the kitchen table. April called while she was out, but David tells Martha to ring her back later. In one of his characteristic lurches of impatience, he is aching to get on. They are at Pen Ponds parking lot in Richmond Park by noon. David hauls a pair of glossy Hunter wellies out of the trunk and takes in a succession of deep breaths, each one followed by a noisy exhalation. "Fresh air," he says with satisfaction, as if blowing his own trumpet.

There are dogs and children today. A couple of horses in the distance. Someone is flying a kite in the shape of a cow. David throws his arm around Martha's shoulders. She has forgotten how tiny he could make her feel. When he puts his arm around her like this—which he has always done, out of habit, whenever they walked anywhere—he hunches himself over her so that she slots in beneath him, like a piece in a jigsaw puzzle or a pastry cutter within the one the next size up. He is full of good spirits. As they circumnavigate the pond, swollen with fresh rain—not to mention Hilly's ashes and Graham's aftershave—he tells her he saw Maddy during the week at a sale of Indian artifacts. She turned her back on him. "I feel such a cad," he says happily. (Martha finds these revelations and others like it to be anticlimactic after a month of imagining the girl in his bed.) He has been asked to write a chapter on Cartier for the *Encyclopedia of World Antiques*. There are rumors that a Middle Eastern prince is thinking of taking his collection to auction, including a 32-carat pink Agra diamond that might reach a record price. The sky is an insipid blue and the air is still. A tiny plane crosses on the horizon and it takes ages for the miniature roar to reach them. "Penny for your thoughts?" says David.

When they get back to her flat, she thinks David might have

commitments elsewhere, leaving her free to have a day to herself, but he doesn't seem to. He digs into the Mulberry bag for his book—a novel, recently shortlisted for a prestigious literary prize, about eighteenth-century settlers in Tanzania—and lies on her Howard sofa in his socks saying things like "This is the life" and "What more could one ask?" She makes coffee, cleans the kitchen floor, flicks through the papers. After a while, he gets up, opens a bottle of wine, and shuffles through her pile of CDs. He chooses Barry Manilow (jesting, "Ah! Chopin's Prelude in C Minor") and settles back down. Eliza leaves a message on the answering machine wanting to talk about Geraldine. David tweaks Martha's thigh with his toes. "Go on, give us a massage," he says. When she goes to the toilet, she hears him on the phone trying to get a dinner reservation for eight o'clock. A table for two. She asks him who he's taking. "You, of course," he says. "Who else?"

At four o'clock, the phone rings and she answers as a distraction. It's April. She says, "I'm sorry to keep ringing, but I really wanted to talk to you about the baby and I'm sorry I haven't. It's just been difficult and it was hard to find the right moment."

Martha takes the phone into the kitchen and sits down at the table. There is a strange dull October light in the room. The weak mauve sky outside the window is full of crisscross wisps of cloud and airplane trails as if it doesn't have the strength to fight them off. She says, "I'm surprised you didn't tell me, that's all."

April says, "It's sort of none of your business," but there's no battle in her voice.

"April. You know, we see each other every day. I thought we were friends."

"Well . . . you're my boss." April says this flatly.

"Just your boss?"

There is a pattern of dirt on the linoleum by the kitchen table, a half circle of smaller circles. Martha stares at it until she realizes it's the mark left on the damp floor by her expensive new sneakers. She tries to think of something to say. She doesn't know if she's angry or upset. She feels hollowed-out, hopeless.

In the end, she says, "So is this chap in Manchester going to stand by you?" and April says, "Steve's a bit confused," and the name is a surprise to Martha, a shock that she's never heard it. She asks if April loves him, if he's "the one," and April laughs: "Whatever that means," sounding years older than she is, years older than Martha. "I've always wanted to keep it," she says. "My mum says I'm too young but I don't care. It's what I want."

Martha asks where April and the baby are going to live. "You're going to have to leave the squat," she says. "Will you move home?" April laughs again for an answer. "And what will you do for money? Will *Steve* be able to support you both?"

This time April is silent. Martha says, "Of course you can carry on working until the baby comes. I didn't mean that. But after . . ."

April's tone becomes cold again. She says she has to go and hangs up. Martha is left feeling restless and frustrated with herself. David is still reading his novel—he has a half smile on his lips. He says, "Hmm?" when she comes back in, without looking up. She tells him she's going out. She doesn't explain. She simply says she has to see a customer about some toy cars. "Don't be long," David says, which she takes to mean he doesn't plan on going anywhere himself.

Fred's tinny pistachio car is parked right outside his house so she rattles the letterbox. She is going to say, "Fred, I am so sorry.

There's been a terrible misunderstanding," and after that they
will be friends again and she can ask him what she should do
about April, about where she herself has gone wrong. But it
isn't Fred who comes to the door; it's a birdlike woman in a velvet shirt and leggings, long gray-blond hair tied up in a
chignon, kingfisher blue eyeshadow in an arch. The woman,
who must be Eileen, Fred's mother-in-law, looks at her without
curiosity, then bends and says, "Don't you dare. In. In." The cat
is trying to make a bolt for the great outdoors.

Martha makes a barrier with her arms and legs and steers
him back inside. "You must be Eileen," she says. Hazel is hanging on the banister and to her, she says, "Hi," in a high voice.

Eileen smiles halfheartedly. The lipstick on her lips has
seeped into the threads of skin above. "Hello, Martha," says
Hazel. She slides down the stairs to join her grandmother. She
has frilly white socks above her sandals. A long strand of pearls
dangles from her neck.

Eileen says, "Can I help you?"

"I'm sorry. I'm Martha, from the antique shop? I just wanted
a quick word with Fred. Is he in?"

Eileen says, "I'm afraid"—in the tone of one who isn't—
"he's not here."

"Three-thirty to five P.M.," Hazel says. "Molly Kitchener's
party. Number 57. I could have gone. Stan did, only Nan said we
could go through Mum's jewelry, so I didn't want to. Do you
want to see it?" Martha notices there are sparkly rhinestone clip-
ons dangling from Hazel's ears. Her pink T-shirt is too small and
the white edging on the collar is gray with overwashing. She is
wearing lipstick and rouge, too. She looks grotesquely pretty,
like one of those American tweenie beauty queens.

Eileen says, "You could come in and wait if you like."

"Oh." Martha looks over her shoulder. The last thing she wants to do is to go in to look at Fred's wife's jewelry. "Well, maybe I'll just wander down and meet him there. Or, actually, maybe I'll come back later." She backs down the step. "Thanks."

"As you like," says Eileen.

Martha does intend to go home, and maybe not to come back later at all, but she is walking in the direction of number 57 anyway, and as the house gets nearer, her pace slows. When she reaches 57, which has two balloons bobbing disconsolately at the front gate (there were three but one is sagging, wrinkled and deflated, like a used condom), she stops, for curiosity's sake if nothing else. It is a smarter than average house: the paintwork outside is iridescent white, and the hedge sharply clipped. And inside—she can see, as she peers through the hedge— there must be enough space to give the front room over to the children. The walls are circus-tented in green and white stripes, the overhead light is an airplane in flight. Furniture, which has been pushed to the walls, is elf-sized. Elaborately framed pictures of Babar and Tintin line the walls.

There are no children in evidence. But to one side of the window, perched on a miniature chair, is Fred in a flowery shirt and a pinstripe suit. He looks strange because he isn't wearing his glasses. He is leaning forward with his elbows on his knees, in one hand a pot of orange jelly and in the other a cigarette.

Martha goes up the path and leans over the garbage cans to tap on the window. Somehow she hadn't been expecting a costume. Fred looks up. He raises the hand with the cigarette in it, without enthusiasm, like a driver registering automatic thanks to a waiting car. Martha smiles and beckons him over. But he doesn't smile back. In fact, he turns away. Stunned, she taps again.

"Where are the children?" she says loudly through the glass. "Have you eaten them?"

He gestures with his head to the back of the house. "Having tea," he mouths.

"Fred." A car goes past. There is a smell of rotting vegetables. "I want to talk to you."

"You want to talk to me."

"Are you going to let me in?"

"What, now?" He's mouthing; she's shouting.

"Yes."

He frowns and shakes his head. "Not really a good time, Martha."

"Fred. Please. I've got to talk to you. I want to say I'm sorry."

He puts his palms upward.

"What, are you just going to mime at me now?"

He laughs, but not for long. He stands up and comes closer to the window. He says, "I'm not angry. It doesn't matter. I don't understand you, but, er . . . well, that's it. Look, I'm at work here. This is my job." He takes a last drag on the cigarette and twists it out in the frilly pot of orange jelly.

Martha is right up to the window. She is pressing her fingertips on the cold glass, as if trying to conduct her words through. "Please, Fred. Let me explain. About my father, Neville. It just happened. I didn't mean to lie. It wasn't him. It was my step-father who died. It was a misunderstanding. A woman was in the shop buying a very expensive armoire and she found out there had been a death and she got the wrong end of the stick and then you came in and . . . it just gathered pace."

Fred says, "Why didn't you just tell me? Why did you let me go on thinking it? You had plenty of opportunity."

"I don't know. I just didn't. It didn't seem worth it."

He turns away. "Well, there you go, then."

"No. No. Please—" She taps her nails on the window. He is leaning toward her and suddenly he puts his fist against the glass, near her hand. The window rattles in the casement. Martha's hand jumps away.

"Fred. Let me in, Fred. Just for a sec."

He looks at her and then gets up abruptly, as if impatient. She doesn't know if he is coming or has gone altogether but a moment later the front door opens. She brushes past the garbage cans. Hullabaloo comes from the house. She says (it is a relief not to have to shout through glass), "Fred. Fred. I'm so sorry. It was just a misunderstanding."

"I look stupid," he says.

Martha smiles. "I know you do. It's the purple suspenders that do it."

Fred pulls back into the house. "Stop, stop, stop," she says. "I'm sorry." She has her hand on his flowery sleeve. It's a batwing sleeve so he is still several feet away. "I'm the one who looks stupid. I didn't think it would matter. Everything you said about my father was really helpful. The fact that he was alive not dead stopped mattering. And I didn't think—"

"What?"

"That we'd become friends, I suppose."

She is still holding on to the sleeve but there is less resistance and she gives it a tug. Fred comes out onto the step. He is standing there, tall and thin and gangly, like a clown on stilts— though he is just a clown in shoes. Big black floppy shoes with black-and-white-striped laces. He seems unfamiliar, like someone she's never met before. It is partly the lack of glasses. His eyes look magnified without them. Martha notices his eyes again, one a shadow of the other, like the sea when there's a rock underneath it.

But he is looking at her with grudging sympathy, as if he doesn't want to see her upset.

He says, "You don't know what you are doing." His lips, surrounded by chalky makeup, look indecently naked, like the lips of someone with a beard. There is a golden fleck of tobacco on one of them. She reaches up to flick it away and before she knows what she is doing she has stretched up farther and put her lips to his mouth. It was supposed to be just a kiss, just an apologetic kiss, a kiss to make him *like* her again, but after a second he starts kissing her back and his hands are in her hair, and there is rushing in Martha's ears and her stomach turns to liquid, and the kiss goes on much longer than it should—though not as long as Martha would have let it. Because behind Fred, from out of the kitchen, burbles a stream of small children, chortling and screeching and blowing small trumpets, and here they are tugging at him and jumping up and down, "Mr. Magic, Mr. Magic!," and a couple of women have flustered up behind them and are saying, "Oh, the door, the door." Fred and Martha separate and he says, "Come in and wait for me." And Martha is swept into the house and into a playroom and onto a child-sized chair in the playroom, listening to twenty small children squealing and shouting and screaming at every word Mr. Magic utters (or every word he mimes), while inside she is squealing and shouting and screaming herself.

There is only half an hour left. Martha is aware of some juggling and some feather-duster activity and of the hilarity caused when Fred forgets how to clap. She can still taste the nicotine in her mouth. Molly Kitchener's parents, who are watching from the doorway, are tense with emotions of their own. Fred's routine has holes in it; you can see the wooden rabbit poking out of the bottom of its house when it's supposed to have "gone for a walk." They are not sure if he has all the children's attention. Little Harry there, who is inching his way closer to those "magic" cooking pots. Sasha, who won't sit still. Stan is sitting separate from the others. But when the children throw themselves sideways onto the floor at any joke that tickles them, Fred looks at Martha across the room and it is as if everything about her has disappeared apart from the bit of her that looks back at him.

At last, parents arrive, heads cocked, brightly smiling, in dribs and drabs, and the show ends. Somehow Martha is off her chair and nodding politely and helping Fred pass out balloons and cards bearing his details. Then he packs his stuff into his little leather suitcase and his big black magic trolley, and gathers together Stanley and his check and all his clothes, and the three of them leave the house and start walking down the road.

Stan skips on ahead. He has his hands full of party bags and ballerina cake. Fred says, "Were you at least close to your stepfather?"

Martha says, "No."

He darts her a look and then shakes his head. To Martha's relief he is smiling very slightly now. "So?"

Fred is having to push his magic-trolley thing along with his knees. The bottom shelf keeps slipping off and catching on the pavement.

"Um . . . Can I help you with that?"

"I'm fine as I am," he says.

Stan is way ahead of them now and has disappeared through the front gate of the house. They can hear him at the letterbox shouting, "Nan. Twig. They had marshmallow hats!"

Fred says quickly, "Have you got time for a quick drink?"

Martha says, "Not really, but okay."

Fred says, "I'll just change. Er, clean up. Eileen's here so we can go to the pub. And, um . . ." He makes a noise that is like the sound of air being released suddenly through his nostrils.

In the hall, he grabs her hand quickly and squeezes. Then thunders up the stairs and there is his voice and Eileen's voice and, intermingled, high-pitched, complaining, those of Stanley and Hazel. After a minute, Fred comes to the top of the landing and calls down. He tells her to wait in the sitting room, that he won't be a moment.

Martha goes in and leans against the back of the marine blue sofa. It doesn't give way softly like feathers, but bows energetically beneath her like foam. She moves away and, clearing some plastic toys (a Barbie with matted hair; a miniature brush with gray bristles), sits down on the edge of the winged armchair.

She tries to breathe properly. She can still feel the pressure of his hand on hers. When she holds it up she expects to see the impression of his thumb on her flesh. A door catches in a draft and slams. She hears the sound of running water overhead. Fred will be in the bathroom, stripping off his magician's outfit, wiping his soft mouth with a washcloth. The pipes in the walls crank and gurgle. She imagines him standing in the bathroom, just up those stairs, naked. In the shower, his long, thin pale body streaming. His bones. The sharp, moving point in his neck. The water stops. She imagines him drying his skin, and dressing. But then, Hazel's T-shirt dashes into her head. With its graying, fraying edges. She remembers the piles of washing that punctuate the stairs. She conjures up (he is not the only magician around here) something drab and holey. Something drab and holey intermingled with children's ratty T-shirts.

The room feels airless and hot. When she breathes in she has to do so in stages, as if there's an obstruction the air has to get past. In an upstairs room, Hazel is whining. Martha can't hear what she's saying but she can tell from the tone. Nobody has come down. She keeps thinking one of the children is going to burst in, but they don't. She can see the dust on the television screen. On the back of the seat, the imitation-tapestry upholstery is darkened and greasy where someone's head has rubbed. The sides of the sofa are dragged where Kitten must have sharpened his claws. On one corner there is a dent, thick with hair, where he must sleep. There is a stain—ink, felt-tip?—on the carpet by her feet. She pulls the corner of the rug, which has flipped over backward, to cover it. The tassels feel matted and grimy.

"No!" Hazel suddenly shouts from upstairs. "I don't want pizza!"

There is the sound of muttered adult voices. More shrieking.

Martha looks around her at the flesh-pink walls and the huge television; the junk, the toys, the cheap sofa, the cat hairs. Abruptly, she stands up. She makes for the door and at this point she may only be going to call up, to check that Fred is almost ready, but her eyes fall on the picture on the far wall: the purple horses, the spiked paint, the white-tipped waves crashing onto the shore. Only, in the picture, there doesn't seem to be a shore. It is all choppy and jagged; the horses' feet disappear. There is no still point. And as she stares at it, each brush stroke seems to separate and move until she can't even see the shapes anymore, until she can't even see what the picture is. She rubs her eyes and it clears. She can see it now all right. She takes a step back. It is the worst picture she has ever seen in her life. How could anyone like this picture? How could anyone *live* with it?

She takes a deep breath. She sees herself from afar, a woman in dry-clean-only black trousers (given to her by a handsome, rich, abandoned boyfriend), hanging around in this vile room while a sweet oddbod, an accountant, a *clown,* with whining children, takes off his baggy trousers. She runs her hands through her hair and smooths it back behind her ears. In the hall, she can hear the sound of a television and small splashes from the bathroom, the staccato sound of a blade in water. Stepping past the bikes and the bags, freeing herself from the snare of hanging coats, Martha Bone opens the front door and closes it behind her.

She walks quickly, then runs past number 57, down the road and around the corner. Her throat hurts with the sudden exertion. She slows. Her stomach clenches with nerves, and dread. Her head is filled with everything she was about to do and everything she *has* done. She feels sickened. He was right, she thinks: she doesn't know what she is doing.

◆

MARTHA'S TURMOIL LASTS until mid-evening. It is only when sitting opposite David in a restaurant by the river in west London, dipping chunks of charred ciabatta into velvety green olive oil, that she begins to put her life into perspective.

David is telling her about a staff reshuffle at his office, while she runs things over in her head. It is not surprising that she and Karen should be distanced from each other. It's just a stage.

April *is* a silly girl not to have told her. And as for Fred, she considers the sequence of events carefully and concludes that she was the victim of inappropriate emotions: guilt, pity, and hysteria. She overreacted to the kiss—which was just a kiss, after all—and leaped to certain conclusions regarding Fred's motives, which were, undoubtedly, wildly inaccurate. She had imagined that the drink would lead to some sort of declaration, whereas in truth he probably wanted to discuss the father thing, apologize for overreacting about that himself, maybe even reopen negotiations with regard to the ongoing clear-out of his attic. In the morning, or maybe later in the week (after all, she convinces herself, there is no hurry—no hurry at all), she will call him to explain. She will say something about the lateness, her realization that his children needed him, about David waiting at home, etc., etc., remind him that he was in the bathroom and she hadn't wanted to, well, burst in on him, and that he can bring any more bric-a-brac over anytime.

Establishing this in her mind, she smiles warmly across the table at David. He puts his hand on hers. He says, "So what do you think? Are you up for it? Do you think it's a good idea?"

She shakes her head slightly. "Sorry?"

"Shall I put a word in for you at South Ken? I know they want fresh, uncynical eyes. Obviously, you're not trained in any sense of the word, and we may have to blur your lack of qualifications, but you are very experienced and you can learn on the job."

"The job?"

"The one I've just been talking about. In Garden Statuary."

"Oh." Now that he mentions it, various phrases from his conversation parachute into her brain, late, but intact: "business-getter," "recent opening," "an eye for," "angels and urns."

"Oh, I see," she says.

"Because honestly, I don't know." He shakes his head, still smiling. "It's a dodgy business, isn't it, the old shop? The landlord's clearly being a complete pig. And even if you restructure somehow—get rid of April once she gives birth—you're only going to cover your overheads. And all those odd characters who wander in and out. I don't really like to think of you there on your own, prey to whatever."

"Don't you?"

He stops smiling and gazes into her eyes. He puts out a finger and traces a line from her forehead, over her nose to her mouth. Martha tries to bite it. He still looks serious. "No. I don't," he says.

"You are very kind to me," she says.

He shakes his head. "No. I'm not."

He takes the wine out of the silver cooler and tops up her glass and his. Then he wipes his hand—a little wet, probably, from the bottle—on his stiff white napkin, and returns it with a clumsy flourish to her knee. And after he has done that, he tells Martha that he loves her, that he realizes how much happier he has been since they have been reunited and that he has been thinking recently how nice it would be if she gave up her flat in Balham and came to live with him in his flat in Kensington. He doesn't want to hurry her, but they could "reopen negotiations" with regard to marriage, maybe even think about starting a family. It would be good, wouldn't it? he says, to get things on an "even keel." After all, neither of them is getting any younger, and you know—he gives her a sweet smile—"Important Clocks" ticking.

Martha hides behind her bangs. She doesn't even look up when he makes this little joke. She can hear the nervousness in his voice. She tears the warm olive bread on her side plate into tiny crumbs. She builds the crumbs into castles. She demolishes the castles with her thumb. There is a piece of loose skin in the corner of her lower lip that she is ripping with her teeth. She wants him to stop talking, but she knows, if he does, she will have to answer. She wants to run out of the restaurant but she knows, if she does, she'll never see him again. Anyway, what kind of person runs out on two people in one day? What kind of person runs out on people *all the time*? She still has to yank her mind back from Fred. She realizes that David has always provided her with a structure. He grounds her within her own family. And now he's talking again about starting one of their own. Her heart tightens. Is this how she could start again? In the two years in which they were apart, she was adrift. She has an image of her basement, filled with three-legged tables, chairs with the stuffing spilling out: messy, chaotic, frightening, full of potential but unfinished. Unfinished business.

"So?" David must have sat back because his voice sounds farther away than it did. She is going to have to say something. She pushes her bangs aside and glances up and, in doing so, catches the expression on his face. His mouth is smiling, but the rest of his face is still, as if he has to keep it like that or it might crack altogether. And with the tenderness in her that this evokes, it all suddenly seems so simple she can't imagine what she has been worrying about. The piece of tangled thread that is her life tightens and straightens. The chafing anxieties about the shop, about Fred, about Nick, about April fall away. There is no call to change. David loves her as she is. With the side of her hand she sweeps the bread crumbs into a neat line: "Yes."

CHAPTER THIRTEEN

the garage

"At the risk of sounding sexist, garages are scary
places created mostly by men. They are often
bolt holes where they can spend time alone
and pursue their own interests."

THE LIFE LAUNDRY: HOW TO DE-JUNK YOUR LIFE,
by Dawna Walter and Mark Franks

OVER THE next few days David is away on business in Italy,
which gives Martha space to prepare herself—mentally and
practically—for the big move. The important thing, it seems, is
to inform other people, to study their responses.

The first person she tells—Nell from Sustainable Forests—is
all for it. "Good on you," she says. "You get out while you can."

Jason is less enthusiastic. He arrives to deliver a pair of wal-
nut bedside tables while Martha and Nell are on the pavement
outside the shop. "You're joking," he says when Martha tells
him her career plans.

"No, I'm not," she says. "Pastures new and all that. Putting
my talents to different use."

"But—" Jason looks aghast. "What about the clients you've built up? You're going to chuck it all in just like that?"

Martha laughs lightly. "I haven't got the job yet. It's just an idea."

"Rent's going up anyway," says Nell, turning to go down the road to her shop.

Jason is still standing, staring at Martha. "I'm moving to Kensington," she says. "To be with my boyfriend David."

He's scuffing his feet on the paving stones. She remembers April's theory that he "likes" her. "We can still be friends," she adds.

Jason doesn't say anything. He goes to his van and starts bringing out the bedside tables. "His and hers," he says bitterly.

April comes in, sighing and heavy, shortly after he's driven off. Martha tells her to sit down on the sofa. "I'll get you some coffee," she says. "My turn."

"I'm off coffee."

"Tea?"

"Okay."

Martha gets it from the cafe next door and buys doughnuts, too. April says, "Oh bless, thanks." She sits and eats slowly, like a cow chewing the cud. Her stomach, above her hipster jeans and below her T-shirt, is so rounded Martha can't believe she didn't notice it before.

"Look," she says, crouching at the floor by April's feet. "I've got to tell you something."

April looks at her. "What?"

"It's not definite, but I want to keep you abreast of my plans. The thing is, I'm thinking of selling the shop. I'm moving in with David in town and it's just not practical to schlepp out here every day. And, what with the rent increase . . ."

April's mouth is hanging open. There is sugar in the corners. "What about me?" she says.

Martha becomes more strident. "Well, let's be realistic. You couldn't carry on working here with a baby, could you? It's just not practical. Not around all these precious things." She gestures to the contents of the shop. Her eye falls on the rocking horse at the back (it is odd, she thinks fleetingly, that it hasn't yet sold).

"But what shall I do?" April seems to have sunk back into the sofa, to have shrunk a little. Martha feels a wave of pity, but then remembers what David said about April taking advantage. "Surely you can move back in with your mother?" she says. "Let her look after you for a bit. Until you find your feet, you know, get your life in order." April's not her responsibility, after all.

April looks into the distance now. "Yeah," she says. "Maybe. Thanks."

Martha stands up. "Another doughnut?" she says.

"Thanks."

"You never know, I might be starting a family of my own soon." As she hands April another doughnut, she has a mental flash of a group of children, in gingham, crabbing on a Cornish beach. "We could go on holiday together, or meet in the park."

April gives a small smile, and before biting says with what almost sounds like pity, "Yeah. Whatever."

Martha, turning to go up to the flat, doesn't feel this conversation has gone as well as it might. To cheer herself up, she sits down in the kitchen for a moment and calls Karen and Keith. "I haven't seen you for ages," she says when Karen answers.

"No," cries Karen in mock distress. "Where've you been?"

"Well . . ." Martha fills her in on the latest regarding David.

"That's fantastic!" Karen says. "I'm so pleased for you. That's brilliant. Kensington! How posh!"

Karen has to go because the baby is crying. Before she does so, she makes Martha promise, now that *her* "life is in order," to come to the school reunion with her the following week. Martha agrees. She wonders after she has hung up why she feels irritated. It's not the reunion: she's come to terms with that now. It's something deeper. Had Karen been sufficiently upset at not having seen so much of Martha recently? Seeing Martha, or not seeing Martha: it all seems much of a muchness. She has thought of herself as fundamental to Karen and Keith's life, as something they couldn't do without, like a sofa, or a fridge, but maybe she has never been more than an accessory, or an ornament. She stands up and pushes her chair in. She looks at her watch. David will be landing in Turin about now. She has her own life.

◆

TWO DAYS LATER, driving back from her interview with Garden Statuary, she passes the end of Eliza's road. Most of the houses are Victorian redbricks, so Eliza's house—a stark palace of glass and poured concrete—stands out like a beacon. Martha pulls her beaten-up old car off the road into the forecourt and rings the intercom.

"Matty!" Her father opens the side door. "*Quelle* treat!" He beckons her into the garage that forms the first layer of the house, where there are coils of rope and bunches of sail on the floor. "Just sorting through the stuff I've bought for the boat. Eliza won't let it in the house."

"Has she left for work?"

"Yes. And Denis has taken Gabriel to Monkey Music. He'll be back at lunchtime to take me to the airport."

"I'm glad I caught you." Martha sits down on the steps leading up into the house. "I've got News."

"News? Nothing I like more than News."

She picks up the end of a piece of rope and twirls it. "I'm moving in with David. I may sell the shop. I've just been for an interview at David's auction house. They seemed to like me. They said my knowledge of decorative stone lions was impressive. I can start anytime."

Neville stops what he is doing, which is something complicated with a sail. "Darling!" He bends to wrap his arms around her. "Three bits of news!" He plants a loud kiss on the top of her head. "Ah! I can't wait to tell Eloise." He rolls his eyes. "At least I can go home with one of my daughters sorted."

"What's wrong with the others?"

"Oh, this ridiculous row over the painting. I wish they would give it up. They're both stubborn, that's the problem. They take after your mother. Couldn't you step in, Matty?"

"I've told them I won't be piggy in the middle."

"You've never liked getting involved, have you?"

"No. I suppose I haven't."

"My middle child." Neville looks at her fondly.

Martha smiles at him. "Yes."

He sits down on the step next to her. "You've always found life hard, haven't you, darling?"

Martha, close to him, says shyly, "I don't know."

"I took Geraldine's Ivor out yesterday for lunch. McDonald's." Neville raises his eyes to the ceiling. "He's a funny one, too. Wetting the bed, you know? He's the middle child, too."

Martha pokes Neville in the side. "Yes, but *I* don't wet the bed."

Neville doesn't laugh. "Thank God. It's easier when you've

only got two. That's why this time round I've just got my two little girls."

"For now."

Neville looks at her. She widens her eyes. "I mean, Eloise is a very young woman. . . ."

He breathes in sharply. "Don't!" he says.

◆

IT ISN'T UNTIL Thursday night that Martha rings Fred. She has been putting it off all week. It is like a big, insurmountable thing she has to get over. David is coming back the next day. She has to do it once and for all. Unfinished business.

It's late. His voice sounds strained when he answers. "Hello."

She says it quickly in one go. "Fred. I'm sorry I left like that."

"Martha?"

"I'm sorry. I keep behaving very oddly around you and I wanted to apologize. It's just that you have this effect on me."

There's a silence. When Fred answers, his voice cracks. "You have that effect on me, too."

Martha feels something inside her tug. She is in bed. She bends forward so that she's doubled up. "I just wanted to say sorry."

"I go to pieces around you. It's never happened to me before. With anyone. I've never felt like this before."

Martha closes her eyes. "If things were different, I'd say I'd come round and stick you back together, but . . ."

Fred clears his throat. "But they're not."

There's another long silence. She says, "I've got to go."

"The kids miss you."

She is biting her lip so hard she can taste blood.

"*I* miss you."

Her face is wet. "I'll miss you, too."

◆

ON DAVID'S FIRST Saturday back, he has tickets for the opera. *Tosca* at Covent Garden. Martha meets him and the clients there. She's late and has to run from the station. Her coat flaps. Her face feels red. People stare. She steps in a puddle and splashes water up the back of her tights.

David is standing in the foyer, looking at his watch. "Hurry up," he snaps, already turning for the stairs.

"I'm sorry, I'm sorry, I'm sorry." She rushes up and puts her arms around him. "The Tube stopped in a tunnel. There weren't any announcements. I ran—"

"It's okay." He flashes her a smile. "The Gunters are in their seats." He pauses outside the door to the auditorium and appraises her. Tucking a piece of stray hair behind her ear, he says, "We need to get you some new clothes, don't we?"

"But this is the Armani you bought me for dinner at Geraldine's."

"Is it?" He looks doubtful. "It must be the shoes, then."

She leans forward and whispers, smiling, "Or the mud on the tights."

He kisses her on the head. "You funny thing."

The Gunters, who are in their fifties and wealthily dressed, speak very little English. Martha's German is nonexistent so they smile at each other and nod their heads. She suspects they enjoy the opera not much more than she does. Mr. Gunter's heavy eyelids have dropped by the third act. Mrs. Gunter, who is wearing a necklace so bright and ornate it looks fake, spends much of the time scanning the rest of the audience. Martha wills herself to enjoy it for David's sake. The education of her musical tastes has always been one of his ongoing projects. He is seated on the other side of the Gunters from her and from time to time she eyes him. His whole body seems to be absorbed in the music, occasionally his fingers twitch, his shoulders sway. She feels she lets him down.

At the Italian restaurant afterward, he is full of bonhomie. He claps Mr. Gunter on the shoulder and tells him something in German that makes him roar with laughter. (Martha marvels at his ability to speak the language; is there no end to his accomplishments?) Breaking into English for Martha's benefit, he tells them that she is his "fiancée."

"Am I?" she says, but Mrs Gunter just beams and pats her on the shoulder.

Martha has chosen linguine and keeps getting sauce on her chin.

In the taxi home, David puts his arm around her, so that her face is tucked into his neck. She can feel his fingers moving on her arm; he still has music in his head. She wonders what Fred is doing. She feels so tired. She can't wait to go to sleep.

"I've got tickets for *Don Giovanni* next Saturday," David says. "Will you come?"

"Oh, I'm sorry." She sits up. "I've got that school reunion. I promised Karen."

"Oh." He makes his little-boy face. "I'll see if I can change them. But Thursday we've got dinner with the Ascots."

"Oh yes."

"And Friday, my godfather has invited us over."

"Great." She smiles. She had forgotten how pressing David's

life could be, how easily squashed her own. Her market friends and auction connections, her feuding sisters, her Sunday routines with Keith and Karen, so scrappy in comparison to the many engagements with David's godparents, the regular meetings with his colleagues and the university crowd, the tickets, the advance bookings. And she knows that his enthusiasm to involve her is evidence only of his commitment. But it still demands effort to work out where her own stand should be. She doesn't want to be overpowered, but still less does she want to demonstrate the intransigence that, in Greg's words, "buggered them up last time." She just wishes she could clear her head to see what would be best *now* without feeling the pressure of *before*.

"And Sunday . . . I thought maybe we'd move you in."

Martha leans forward to open the taxi window. It feels so hot all of a sudden. She breathes in the damp October air. "Okay," she says.

◆

MARTHA PEELS BACK the foil and sniffs. The smell is pungent. On the phone, Greg said he didn't know the recipe for Coronation Chicken himself but he was sure there was curry powder and raisins. "You'll have to wing it," he said. "Ha, ha." Geraldine was on a retreat and wouldn't be back until the following day. "With her yogi," he added manfully (or maybe just loudly to be heard above the family battle cries in the background).

Martha puts the foil back and returns the dish to the satisfyingly bare fridge. She dries the spoon she used for stirring and lodges it in the top of the half-full crate on the floor. She ties up the bag she has used for the last bits of trash and leaves it by the door to take down later. The other bag, the one that has lived in her kitchen all autumn, is still under the table. She eyes it guiltily. It looks so huge and cumbersome, she doesn't know what to do with it.

She goes into the bedroom to change. There are two outfits laid out on the bed: a simple pale pink sheath dress for the evening (a moving-in present from David), and jeans and a T-shirt for the following day. Everything else is in the suitcases lined up on the floor.

The dress is halfway over her head when the phone rings. It is David, who has only been gone a couple of hours but sounds anxious.

"Everything's fine," she says.

"And you're sure you don't want to come over here later? Or for me to come to you?"

"David, I'm sure. Honestly. I'd like to spend one more night here on my own."

She has gone to look in the mirror. The dress has little pearl buttons down one side and she does them up while she is on the phone, watching herself push each fragile disk into place one by one, each exquisite brittle shell representative of David's love and concern, until the fabric is secure and tight around her.

"We'll have a little weekend away soon. How about that?" Lots of women, Martha suspects, would pinch themselves if their lover started thrusting City Break brochures at them over the cornflakes, would leap into comparative studies of Vienna versus Venice with delight and abandon. She says, "Could we talk about this later?"

"Tomorrow, then. I can't wait."

"I can't wait either," echoes Martha.

It is early in November now, the first Saturday after Guy Fawkes Night, and there is a damp, woody smell in the air, the scent of old canvas and charred leather. As she drives over to Karen's house, distant unseen rockets explode like machine-gun fire.

Karen looks jumpy when she comes to the door. Her face is blotchy and her red hair is pulled back in a messy ponytail. She greets Martha, then shouts back into the house, "Controlled crying, Keith. Don't forget. Don't give in."

Martha says, "That sounds a bit violent."

"Desperation," says Karen.

She puts the tray of cheese in her hand into the backseat and gets into the front. "Feeling better about this?" she asks.

"Yes." Martha tries to put some enthusiasm into her voice. "After all, I could be at the opera with David. Again."

Karen laughs. "I suppose you're not interested now even if Nick Martin is there."

"Be still my beating heart." Martha puts her hand on her chest. "He won't be, anyway."

"What happened to that nice bloke Fred you said kept coming round?"

Karen is rummaging in her handbag. Martha puts the key in the ignition and pulls out into the road. "Oh," she says. There is a sharp pain in her chest. "He stopped coming round, I suppose." Karen is putting on some lipstick in the overhead mirror and luckily doesn't notice the flush in Martha's face.

Martha rubs her eyes. "Your hair's got a bit long," she says. "I think I prefer it shorter." It's the sort of comment they often make to each other, but Karen, snapping the lipstick back in her purse, says rather sharply, "Yes. All right. I haven't had time to go to the hairdresser, that's all. You know? There's always the next feeding to think about and the next appointment at the clinic and how much Kit has slipped off her growth percentile—which she has—and I don't know whether I shouldn't try formula. And God knows when I'm going to get a good night's sleep or whether Keith and I are ever going to have sex again or how I'm going to get rid of this—" She grabs the fold of skin above the drawstring of her pants and then sighs and sinks back into the car seat. "A haircut is the last thing on my mind," she says.

"Sorry." Martha looks at her.

Karen looks back. "It's not easy having a small baby, you know. Keith's at work and, well, it can be pretty bloody lonely."

"I had no idea. I'm so sorry."

"Drop in sometime. We miss you."

They're at a light. Martha puts her hand on Karen's shoulder. "I've been very selfish. I didn't realize. I thought you'd dropped me, but—"

Karen shakes her head. "No. It's not like that."

"I do see. I'm the one who has to adapt here. I've been feeling . . ." She is going to say that she's been feeling annoyed with Karen and Keith, but it sounds so awful to admit it so she doesn't say it out loud. She lets the sentence trail off, then she starts again. "I've been expecting you to carry on as before and I should have done more to help and understand. I am really sorry."

"It's all right." Karen reapplies her attention to her makeup.

"I've been really passive, haven't I? It's the same with my sisters . . ."

Karen smiles. "It's fine. Bring David round for supper soon."

"Yes. Okay."

"You don't sound very enthusiastic."

Martha squirms in her seat. "No, that would be great. I think we're engaged."

"Fantastic!" says Karen, not looking at her.

Martha drives them to the house down the road from their old school where the reunion is taking place. Jane and Phil Dunstan, old alumni, who married shortly after graduation, haven't moved far from where they grew up. The house, a 1930s semi, pebble-dashed with mock-Tudor beams across the front, is identical to the house their parents might have lived in.

A girl about the same age as Hazel opens the door. She is wearing the same Barbie-styled teenybopper kind of clothes that Hazel loves. Martha says, "Great crop-top," and the girl gives her a gap-toothed grin. "It's my favorite," she says.

Karen has moved past the girl toward the kitchen, where there is chatter and the occasional shriek over the Cars. "Come on," she says.

Martha says, "See you" to the girl, who ducks back into the TV room, and follows. "My Best Friend's Girl?" she says to Karen.

"Sounds like . . ." Karen pushes her forward. She has her fingers at her back like a gun.

The kitchen is packed with people. Everyone seems oversized, not ghosts at all, but solid, fleshier than they should be. Martha stands at the door, with Karen just behind her. There is a large pine table, very like Fred's. And people she vaguely recognizes everywhere. Features that are familiar to her—a nose, a mouth, a chin—all look as if they've been kidnapped by strangers. That man over there too bald surely to be Mark Leonards; the woman too old to be Danielle Lawrence. . . .

"Hi! Look, everyone, Martha and Karen are here!" A person of their age in bright red lipstick, wearing a school tie and a short school skirt over stocky thighs, hurls herself toward them.

"Jane!" says Karen weakly. She eyes Jane's school uniform. "Well, you're certainly in the spirit of things."

"Oh well, God," she says. "It's only a bit of fun, isn't it?"

She grabs a familiar man, with brown hair cut straight across his brow like a skullcap and one of those faces that starts off bold with a big forehead and disappears into a small chin. "You remember Phil, my hubby, don't you? Not that he was my hubby then."

"Yes," says Martha.

"Yes," says Karen.

"Drink!" says Phil. He is standing beside a large range of spirit bottles. "School Cup all right for you? It's a homemade punch. Lethal, let me warn you."

"We'll all be puking," giggles Jane.

"Very authentic," says Karen dryly.

Another couple have come in and Karen and Martha move away to the door to the garden. Martha smiles at someone who is also standing there before she remembers who it is and re-grets it. Amy Blanket, from her French class, who has a flat col-orless face and a habit of speaking French with her mouth puckered up like a cat's bottom. "Hiya, Martha!" Amy says.

"Oh, hello," says Martha. "Do you remember Karen?" Too late, she realizes Karen has moved off to talk to a woman in a floral frock on the other side of the room. Martha turns back. "Oh. She's gone. How are you? What are you up to these days?"

Amy launches into a long description of her busy, busy life— three kids, a frantic, highly successful business cooking freezer meals for other working women, the lovely house in Oxford-shire, her husband's long, long hours in the City. Martha nods and smiles politely. Inside, she is saying to herself, "What am I doing here?"

"And you?" says Amy finally.

"I run a shop," Martha says without thinking. And then remembers herself. "Or rather that's what I have been doing. But I've just got a job working for a well-known auction house."

"How fascinating. And are you married?"

"No." She sees a fleeting expression of pity float across Amy's eyes. "But I'm going to be. I'm moving into my fiancé's apartment in Kensington, and, well, let's just say, we're making plans." Why is she talking like this? Who is she trying to impress?

"Golly. Posh." There's no denying it, Amy does look impressed. "And I expect you'll be starting a family soon, won't you?"

"Absolutely," smiles Martha. "Important Clocks ticking and all that."

"Sorry?" Amy looks confused.

"It doesn't matter," says Martha. "But yes, children are high up on our agenda." What has she just said? Who is she pretending to be? "Oh. Karen's beckoning me. Hang on."

Karen hasn't turned around or made any gesture at her at all. But Martha crosses the room quickly toward her. She needs to leave. She needs to leave now before she turns into any of these women. "Save me!" she says when she gets to her. Karen, who is talking to Phil and the woman in the floral frock, downs her drink and says, "Martha, do you remember Tracey?" The woman in the floral frock narrows her eyes. "Gosh, mousy little Martha," she says. "You look different."

Karen and Martha both laugh. The woman slaps her hand over her mouth. "Sorry, that sounds awful. I just mean you were always a bit on the sidelines, an observer rather than a participator, shall we say."

Martha remembers Tracey now. She was very sporty, a dreadful flirt, and terrible at math. "You're right," she says. *"Plus ça change."*

She is about to pull Karen to one side and ask if they can leave when she notices a man staring at her. He is wearing jeans and a green T-shirt. "I know you," he says. He is good-looking, with nice eyes, but that bullet-marked skin that comes after bad acne.

"Do you? I don't . . ."

"Yeah. You went out with my next-door neighbor."

"Did I? Were you at the boys' school?"

"Yeah. I had bad acne, you wouldn't have noticed me. But you noticed my next-door neighbor. Nick? Nick Martin?"

The room seems to go still around Martha.

Karen waves her empty cup. "Ah. The elusive Nick Martin."

Martha says, "So do you, um, ever see him?"

The man feels in his back pocket for some matches and lights a cigarette. He nods as he inhales. Then he lets the smoke out slowly and says, "When he's in the country."

Martha's throat feels dry. "When he's in the country?"

"Yeah. You know he's an economic advisor? After his Ph.D. at the London School of Economics, he went into local government. Now he advises governments all over the place. For a long time he was in America. I'm not sure where he is now."

Karen says, "So, is he married with a string of kids?"

"Not last time I heard. Still single. Still chasing Ms. Right." He gives Martha a piercing look. "Maybe you broke his heart."

"Do you have his number?" Martha can't believe she's asked but she has.

"Ooooh," the man says suggestively.

"It's all right," says Karen. "She's engaged."

"It would just be nice to see him, that's all," says Martha. She is sure her face is red.

The man feels again in his pocket and brings out his cell phone. He goes over to the window and presses some buttons. Martha leaves the others and follows him. She watches as he writes a number down on the packet of matches. He hands it to her. "Good luck," he says.

She is staring at it when she hears Karen call her back over again. She is just with Phil now. "Martha!"

"What?"

"Phil has got something special to show us in his garage."

"Oh really?"

"Yep," says Phil.

"We were talking about you and Nick and I asked him if he had any secret passions in the past and he said this."

"Passion," says Phil, "is an understatement."

He gestures them to a door on the other side of the kitchen. His wife, Jane, still picking at the food, says, "Oh no, Phil. You're not!"

"I am," he says.

"Oh, Phil." Jane tuts loudly and dramatically, a woman with no time for her husband's foolishness. She rolls her eyes at the people she is with, as if to announce that others may be taken in by him, but not her. Karen is busy refilling her drink, but Martha finds this moment touching: a gesture that looks like contempt but is actually love.

Phil has unlocked the door, pushed it open, and stretched his arm in to turn on a switch. He stands aside for Karen and Martha to go in first. "Ta-da," he says.

The door has opened into a garage, one as clinically clean and organized as a pathology lab. There are rows of shelves for boxed implements and ointments and lines of jars filled with nuts and bolts. The walls are painted white and the floor is pristine concrete. But in the middle of it, where you might expect a body to be, is a big pink car.

Karen says, "It's a car! You've got a car in here. A garage with a car in it; how amazing. You devil, you."

"This," says Phil, running his hands over the shiny chrome strip along the side, "is no ordinary car. This is a 1956 Ford Crown Victoria. 312V8. In sunset coral and colonial white. Fully automatic. Power steering, power brakes."

Karen laughs. "It's just a car," she says. "A big old American car."

"You may say that." Phil spits on his finger and rubs a tiny mark on the wing. "But you would be wrong. This is an extremely rare, valuable classic motor. In prime working order. There are people who would kill to get their hands on this car. You could take this car out of the garage right now and drive it anywhere you wanted and it would get you there in style, comfort, and without a hitch. It could drive from Albuquerque to Oklahoma City, from Baltimore to Philadelphia . . ."

"I thought you told me," says Karen, "that you never took it anywhere."

Phil runs a hand over the wing where the mark was. "That's true. It is my little piece of perfection. My little slice of history. I want to keep it safe. Five minutes out there in the real world and it'd be scrap iron. You'd have some wanker run a key down the side or bash into the back in a parking space. No." He shakes his head and makes a satisfied clicking noise with his tongue. "My little baby's staying here."

Karen, solemnly, says, "She's very lovely. You should be very proud."

Phil is gazing at the car as if he could do so all night. "I mean, look at those fins."

Martha shakes her head. "Fins ain't what they used to be."

Karen, giggling, says, "It's the fin end of the wedge."

Martha says, "These foolish fins . . ."

Karen throws her arms out. "Remind me of you."

Phil doesn't seem to hear them. "One day," he says, "if we move to a house with a bigger garage, I'm going to get a 1949 Buick Roadmaster."

He turns to go back to the kitchen with Karen, still grinning, behind him. But Martha doesn't follow immediately. She stares at the car for a moment longer. It looks ridiculous in this small, neat garage, like a beached blancmange or a huge pink balloon that has floated away from a carnival float and become entangled in the chimney of a factory. She is reminded for a moment of the man Jason brought along to the shop and his passion for Lesneys. She thinks about the sort of person who hoards things from the past. That man, Phil, herself. Why would you do that? Why would you keep an object locked up like this, perfect, apart from the real world? Does it provide him with some sort of comfort? Does it make him feel better about himself? In control, perhaps?

Karen, swaying, says, "Are you coming?"

"Yes," Martha says, and turns her back on this piece of 1950s

America behind a garage door; this sunset coral and colonial white vehicle of stationary dreams; this glorious piece of nostalgia kept in a box.

◆

AS IT TURNS OUT, Martha doesn't spend "one last night" in her flat. When she draws up outside Karen's house, her friend flounders around in her pockets, says she has forgotten her keys, and decides it's all right to rouse Keith.

He comes to the door looking tousled and bemused in bare feet and a bathrobe. He doesn't seem annoyed. He smiles affectionately when he sees Karen leaning against the door frame and says to Martha, "Don't go. Come in and tell me everything."

They sit in the kitchen for an hour or so, with Karen saying things like, "I love all those people. I think we should see them all the time. Martha, why don't we see them all the time? Jane and I think we should have a reunion every month. The next one's here. What do you say? And then after that, yours! And then after that, here again! Lots of lovely, lovely reunions."

"There was punch called 'School Cup,'" Martha tells Keith. "It was very authentic." To Karen, gently, she says, "There's usually a reason why you stop seeing people. Remember?"

Karen lolls back in her chair. "You're one to talk. Ms. Meet My New Ex."

Martha laughs. "I hated it," she tells Keith. "For a while there I saw my life as it might have been, following the same pattern—nice job, nice kids, nice husband—as everybody else's."

Keith raises his eyes at her but doesn't say anything.

It is warm and cozy in Karen and Keith's kitchen and even

the sound of the baby wailing in the distance doesn't ruin it. Martha is initiated into "controlled crying"—making one or two of the ten-minute checks herself. She kisses Kit's warm damp head to try to soothe her on one visit and feels, for the first time in ages, how lucky she is to have these friends, with their sweet little baby. She remembers the woman at the party saying Martha was "an observer"; it's time she is more than that. She has to make the effort to involve herself in other people's lives. You can't just always wait for them to come to you.

"You must let me babysit for you one night," she says when she gets back into the kitchen. "It's so obvious. I can't believe I haven't suggested it before. You and Keith can catch a movie or something."

"That would be nice," Karen replies. Then, when it's Keith's turn to go upstairs, "So do you think you and David might start a family?" and Martha, who has picked a baby blanket off the back of the chair and folded it neatly into squares, breathing in the smell of talcum powder and milk, says yes, she thinks they will.

"What about Nick Martin?" says Karen, and Martha laughs. She says she has put him out of her mind. A little later, Karen, who is beginning to fade, asks if she wants to spend the night. There is no real reason to—it is a short drive home and Martha has only had a couple of drinks—but the offer is held out like an olive branch and suddenly her flat, the floor a shifting sea of suitcases and boxes, seems an unattractive prospect, and she grabs it.

In the night, as she lies on the sofa in her friends' house— "this work in progress"—she realizes she's lied to Karen. Nick Martin is all over her head. He is, finally, only a phone call away.

She has never felt so confused. She keeps thinking about Phil's ridiculous boxed-up car in his pristine garage. She keeps thinking about Fred. Fred and Nick. Nick and Fred. They are becoming interchangeable. But she is moving in with David the following day. There is a future unfolding before her involving baby blankets of her own and Cornish beaches. The light springing off wooden floors. White linen on a mahogany bed. Until a month or so ago she hadn't thought about Nick for years. She tries to block him, and Fred, out with David. She remembers David quizzical, at Geraldine's wedding, intrigued by her "aloofness" (but aloof, too: talking down to her as if she were a child?), and on holiday together, the weekend he "showed" her Rome. It was spring and the plane trees that lined the streets were spraying out seeds; it was like confetti, but Martha's eyes streamed. Christmas with his parents. There was a fire and sherry and cards hanging on ribbons on the back of every door. Martha, edgy with the need to be helpful, cut the carrots not into batons but coins. David's mother breathed in sharply. "I'm sure they'll taste just the same," she said.

Will they go there this Christmas? No, they will spend it "at home." They will pull a tree, tall enough to reach the ceiling, back through snowy streets. They will strew his flat with garlands of ivy and pinecone, cinnamon stick and gilt. They will stab oranges with cloves. The decorative possibilities are endless. Martha, with the matchbox clutched in her hand, falls asleep with thick, buttery church candles flickering in her head.

CHAPTER FOURTEEN

the doorstep

"The door is both the first thing a visitor sees on
entering your home and the last thing on leaving.
Yet most of us seem to take no notice of them."

CONTEMPORARY DETAILS, *by Nonie Niesewand*

THE SHOP feels cold when Martha, wearing a crumpled
pink sheath dress and carrying a plate of devastated Coronation Chicken, opens the door early the following morning. It is
drizzling, but lightly, so that the rain doesn't so much fall as
buzz irritatingly around your head like midges. Behind her, the
street is empty but has a sordid lived-in air. There are pieces of
market debris—squashed fruit, rotten vegetables—in the gutter. Someone has left an empty carton on the pavement by the
step and it has dissolved into soggy, gray crumbs. Martha wants
to shut it outside, but when she closes the door, the smell of
mildew drifts in with her, seeps into the joints of the furniture.

The shop seems to know that something is up. Martha has done her best to make the existing stock look inviting, but the bulb in a table light at the back is flickering, and the dried hops that were garlanded across the ceiling have begun unexpectedly to molt: dusty, empty, dried-up seeds scatter the floor as fast as she can clear them. Spaces have begun to materialize: the pile of Welsh blankets is getting low; hooks look jagged with nothing on them. When she closes the door behind her, even the bell sounds rusty, as if it is tinkling in reproach.

Her flat, in its state of suspension, doesn't welcome her either. She leaves the plate and the box of matches bearing Nick Martin's phone number on the kitchen table. She takes off her pink dress, puts on her jeans, and chooses some music to cheer herself up. Reluctantly, she passes over Andrew Lloyd Webber's *Aspects of Love* in favor of *The Puccini Experience,* a CD she has bought to humor David. She moves about the flat. To put off thought—she's not ready for that—she strips the bed, cleans out the drawers, scrubs the bathroom floor.

She doesn't hear the bell at first. Or if she does, her ear tells her brain it is part of *Madame Butterfly.* But after a while, the ringing peels away from the music and she realizes it must have been going on for a while. She taps down the stairs, assuming it is David. But outside the front door is a sight both normal and incongruous, like a pair of shoes on the pavement, or a child's soft toy abandoned in the park. It's her nephew Ivor. He's wearing shorts and a T-shirt and no coat.

"Hello!" she says. "What are you doing here? Where's everyone else?"

He mutters something.

She looks up the road. Have they parked around the corner? No. It's empty. "What did you say?"

"At home," he says.

Martha's confusion rubs against something rough, creating a little spark of panic. Nothing is in the right place this morning. "What do you mean, 'at home'? Who are you with?"

Ivor kicks at the dissolved carton on the pavement. He says truculently, "Nobody."

Martha grabs his shoulder. "God, you're soaked," she says. "What's the matter? What's happened? Who knows you're here?"

He mutters something else.

She pulls him into her shop and bends down. She puts her other hand on his other shoulder to make him face her. "What?"

"No."

"What do you mean?"

"I've run away."

"Fucking hell." Martha stands up and heads for the shop phone.

Ivor looks up at this. "NO, DON'T."

She pauses, her hand on the receiver. "Don't be ridiculous." She feels a bolt of irritation toward him. "They'll be going out of their minds with worry."

Ivor kicks his shoe backward against the door. "They won't even have noticed," he says. "They think I'm at Sunday soccer."

"Well, I'm going to ring them anyway." She starts dialing. There is the sound of the door. Ivor is halfway out. "Come back right now."

Ivor pauses, his hand on the handle. His teeth are gritted. "If you ring them I'm going."

Martha has a moment of indecision. She could still phone them and physically make him stay. He is only a child. Not even seven. But she sees him rub his eyes, leaving a smear of dirt across one cheek. What did Neville say about him? Something about a fucked-up middle child. On his feet are soccer cleats. She thinks of him hobbling all the way here. "Okay. Look. Come upstairs. Let's get you warm. Are you hungry?"

She continues to fire questions at him as they climb the stairs. Greg left him at a drop-in soccer club at the local park, but he slipped off before the coach noticed him. He caught a train at Kingston—"no one looks at your ticket on Sundays"—and meant to go to Victoria but the ticket inspector was coming so he jumped out at Clapham Junction. He got through the barriers by sticking close to a couple with suitcases. And then he walked. He remembered the way from the time they visited that playground on the common. The babyish one that doesn't have swings.

Martha says, "You walked all the way here from Clapham Junction?"

"Yes." He looks defiant, but also as if he might be about to cry.

"You must be exhausted."

Martha strips Ivor of his sopping clothes, puts them in the dryer, and runs him a bath. It must be hotter than he is used to because when he first gets in—lowering his thin, pale limbs—for a few minutes he sits very still, with an expression of concentration on his face. She leaves him and goes downstairs to use the phone in the shop.

"Hello, yes?"

"Katrina. It's Martha, Geraldine's sister. I've got Ivor here. Is Geraldine or Gregory there?"

"Ivor is at soccer?"

"No. No. Katrina. Can you get me Geraldine? Or Gregory?"

"No one is here now. Geraldine is on retreat."

"Oh shit, yes. Okay. Katrina. Listen carefully. This is important. Can you understand me? Tell me if you don't."

"Okay."

"Ivor. Is. Here. With. Me. He is at Martha's. Not soccer."

"Ivor is not at soccer?"

"No. So don't go and get him. And tell Gregory the moment
you see him? Ivor's fine. He's at Martha's. Tell him that, too.
But I'll keep trying."

Martha thinks Katrina understands. With any luck Martha
will be able to persuade Ivor into the car and drive him home
before Greg gets in. She is about to go back upstairs when she
thinks of something else she can do. She dials.

"Hello?"

"Eliza. It's Martha. There's a bit of an emergency here. I
think I need your help."

Eliza, sounding defensive, asks what. Martha explains the sit-
uation. She slightly exaggerates Ivor's state of distress. She says,
"So I can't get ahold of Geraldine—she's at this retreat thing.
And, well, Ivor's asking for you."

"Is he?"

"Yes. He is. I know how close you two have got. And I'm
sure Geraldine would appreciate it. Also, I could do with some
moral support. Could you come round?"

"Yes, of course." Eliza sounds surprised but pleased. She
says she'll come straightaway. Martha finds she's smiling when
she hangs up.

In the flat she hears abrupt splashings and slurpings and
when she goes back into the bathroom Ivor has tipped onto his
stomach and, head down, is shooting himself from one end of
the bath to the other, like a snorkler or a human submarine.

She watches him for a bit, thinking about Hazel and Stan and the mess they leave in the bathroom, and then says, "Right. Out," and lifts him into one of the clean towels beautifully folded in a suitcase, and puts him on the sofa in front of the television. It is 10:10 A.M.

"Are you hungry?"

"Starving."

"What would you like?"

Ivor doesn't look up from the *Powerpuff Girls*. She has to repeat the question several times. Finally, she gets him to answer. He says, "What have you got?"

"I haven't got anything. But I can get something. What would you like if you could have anything?"

"A sausage and egg McMuffin."

"From McDonald's?"

"Yeah. But hold the egg. And can I have Coke with it?"

"Coke for breakfast?"

"They let you. It's in the price."

"Okay. I'll be five minutes."

She locks the door, in case he takes it into his head to run away again, and sets off for McDonald's. There's a woman with a tray of poppies outside. It is Remembrance Sunday, a day to remember the dead of both world wars. Martha had forgotten. When she gets home, with a poppy in her buttonhole and the McBreakfast in a small paper bag (it feels so light and insubstantial she can't imagine it is enough to sustain him), Ivor is still huddled in his towel staring at the television. She tells him he has to eat in the kitchen but the look he gives her is so abject, she says, "Oh, okay, just this once."

She sits next to him as he opens the bag. When he brings his hands out, the towel falls away from his shoulders and she tucks it around his body. It wraps around several times. His upper arms are so skinny they look like they might snap. The tips of his ears are pink. She feels her heart twist. He devours his hash brown slither in its paper bag quickly, with small quick bites. It smells of the air you get in McDonald's—fried grease and paper and air-conditioning. When Ivor comes to his muffin, he says, "Oh-wa. I said no egg."

Martha peers over, concerned. "Oh sorry. I forgot. Can you take it out, or has it dripped over everything?" But it hasn't. It is a symmetrical white floppy disk—no sign of yolk, dripping or otherwise, and it slips out without leaving a trace. She sits back, watching him. She worries about the ketchup on the raw skin below his mouth. Once she dabs it with a napkin and he darts his head away as if stung. "Sorry," she says.

She waits until the cartoon has ended (it keeps stopping and starting; she thinks it will go on forever) and then switches off the television.

"Okay," she says, when he has given up complaining. "What's going on? Why have you run away?"

Ivor takes a long time sucking up some Coke and then he says, "I dunno."

"Ivor, you must know. No one runs away without a reason. Is it something at home?"

"No."

"At school? Is anyone being horrible to you?"

"No."

Martha tries to remember what troubled her when she was six. "Are Mum and Dad arguing?" She thinks back to the tension between Geraldine and Greg at the dinner party. "Is that what's upsetting you?"

"No. Not really."

Martha asks him if there are problems with Patrick, if he is ever bullied, if there are any teachers he feels uncomfortable with. She says if there is anything that's worrying him that he feels he can't for whatever reason tell people, to tell her now.

Ivor looks increasingly sulky. He says, "Can't I watch *Hollyoaks*?" But she says she wants to know what's bothering him first, and finally his answer comes out in a rush. He pushes his cup of Coke away from him. "I hate soccer and Dad knows I hate soccer and he still made me go."

Martha looks at him in surprise. She wants to laugh with relief. "But that's what dads are like," she says. "You just have to tell him. He probably thinks you want to go. We'll tell him today."

"But I have told him. It doesn't make any difference. . . . Mum doesn't make me go. She lets me stay at home, or go with her to watch Patrick at tae kwon do."

Martha has picked up the television remote control ready to hand it to him. "At least you've got one parent on your side. That's all that matters."

"But she's not there. It's always Katrina. The other day she made me take a bath in her bathwater and it was oily and had bits floating in it."

"She's just at this yoga thing. She'll be back later today."

Ivor stares at the dark television screen. "She's not like my mum anymore. She looks different, her hair is all funny, and she smells different."

Martha puts the remote control down. "Of course she's your mum." She strokes his hair, because it seems like the sort of thing she should do, and as she does so she feels a pull of love, not really for Ivor, although he is implicated, but more, surprisingly, for Geraldine. "She's always going to be your mum."

Ivor doesn't say anything. He seems suddenly very inter-ested in the McDonald's bag on the table.

"The thing is, you can't always expect people to stay the same. That would be boring, wouldn't it? I think her new hair's great, though I haven't told her." Martha puts her finger to her mouth and adds conspiratorially, "I mean that's the thing about sisters, sometimes you keep that sort of thing to yourself." Ivor looks at her then. Encouraged, Martha carries on: "I know she seems busy at the moment with this yoga thing and you might think you have less of her than before, but you don't, you know. You really don't. Because I know your mum very, very well and I know how much she loves you. And that, even when she isn't doing all the things she does all the time, like cooking your meals and getting your clothes ready for school and making your bed and tidying your toys, she is thinking about you. Even when you're not there, she's thinking about you." Ivor is still staring at her. His face is blank and pinched, but his mouth is moving very slightly.

He says, "Not me. Anna and Patrick. Not me."

Martha thinks how fortunate it is that she is here to answer him. "She does think about you, too, Ivor. She loves you just as much as them. And your dad does. Maybe differently. But just as much. You just feel as if they don't because you're in the mid-dle." She puts her finger under his chin so she can look at him. "But it's great being the middle child. You don't have to be any-thing you don't want to be. You don't have to be 'the grown-up one' or 'the baby one.' You can be anything you want. You're the free one. The freest of all." There is an obstruction in Martha's throat. She swallows to clear it. "And the thing about families is that they are often all mixed up and fathers and mothers and brothers and sisters can sometimes be awful, and bossy, and horrible to each other, and not even like each other very much some of the time. No one's family is perfect." She takes Ivor's hand and squeezes it. "And, goodness, you're lucky to have your family with a mum and dad and a brother and a sister. I've got half-sisters and stepbrothers and stepmothers young enough to be my daughters. But families can be like that. And you know something, poppet?"—this poppet just slipped out— "They never go away. They'll always be there. I mean—" Martha breaks off as she realizes something momentous and touching. "You came to me, didn't you? I'm your family, too."

Ivor doesn't answer.

She says, "Was it the Harry Potter wand?"

Ivor has been eyeing the television remote, but he flicks her a look. "I'd've gone to Denis and Eliza's," he says, "if that ticket inspector hadn't come."

❖

MARTHA AND IVOR are watching the Remembrance Day service at the Cenotaph on the BBC when a car pulls up outside and she hears the jangle of familiar voices in the street. Throwing open the window, she sees Greg and Geraldine already on the pavement, white-lipped, loose-cheeked with anxiety, and Patrick and Anna clambering out of the backseat. Anna is carrying a pink balloon and it bobs on the end of the string. There are shouts of "No. Bradley. Back. Monty. Stay," but it is too late: the dogs, frantic as everyone else, have bounded out, too.

Martha calls down, her voice as calming as she can make it, "It's okay. He's fine. He's fine."

Geraldine looks up, her eyes squinted against the drizzle.

She is wearing loose drawstring pants and a pink sweatshirt—no makeup. She says, "Thank God."

A few minutes later the flat is full of damp people and wet animals. Monty, Bradley, and the two new children are in and out of doorways, getting tangled in legs. Anna's balloon, which she says was her special one but she's brought it for Ivor, bumps against the ceiling. And Geraldine and Gregory sit on either side of Ivor on the sofa, talking in low, steady voices, telling him how much they love him and how he must never, ever, ever do anything like that ever, ever again. Martha stands listening to them in the doorway.

"I was out of my mind with worry," Geraldine says.

Greg says, "You didn't even know he was missing until he was found."

Geraldine glares at him. "That's enough from you. You big bully. If it hadn't been for you—"

She stops. "Anyway, darling, if you don't want to go to Sunday soccer you don't have to."

Greg tucks Ivor's head under his arm, as you might do with the ball in a game of rugby, and gives it an affectionate squeeze. "Maybe when you're a bit older, old man," he says.

Ivor's face has already lost its pinched look but at this a patch of color appears in his cheeks. He bashes his squashed head against his father's chest and says, "Help!" but he's grinning. Greg frees him and runs both hands through his own hair. He says, across the room to Martha, "Walked from Clapham Junction, did he?" Then, with a small note of admiration in his voice, "Little tyke."

But Ivor hasn't heard this. Extracting himself from his mother's arms and trailing his towel like a train, he has careered off to join his siblings, who are up to something in the bathroom. There is yelping and splashing in there as if it is the dogs who are having a bath now. (Maybe because it is the dogs who are having a bath now.)

Geraldine gives a great, trembling sigh. "I keep imagining what might have happened."

Greg says, "Well, it didn't, did it?"

"Yes. But . . . okay." Geraldine begins forcefully, but she grabs Greg's hand and kisses it impulsively instead. He puts his other arm around her. "Our kidlets," she says.

"I know." Greg shakes his head, as if to stop her from saying anything else.

He has taken his arm from Geraldine's shoulder and the two of them are holding each other's hands now—not romantically, but tightly in a fist, half-raised like team members. Geraldine is resting her forehead in her other palm, away from him, and Greg bends so that he can see her eyes. He says, "Come on, old girl. It's okay. Nothing's happened." And Geraldine nods very slightly.

Geraldine spots Martha watching them. She sighs again while raising her eyes to the ceiling, simultaneously an expression of her own anxiousness and exasperation at her own anxiousness. Martha smiles. She thinks, They are happy after all. All along she had thought they weren't, but they are.

"So what's going on here, then?"

They all turn. Eliza is standing in the doorway—black leather jacket, black boots, black jeans: an avenging angel. "I walked straight in," she says to Martha. "The door of the shop is wide open. Anyone could have come in and nicked what they liked."

Martha, startled, makes for the stairs.

"It's all right," Eliza says crossly. "I've closed it now."

Geraldine has stood up. "What are you doing here?"

Martha says quickly, "I called her. When I couldn't get ahold of either of you, I called Eliza. Ivor mentioned her and—"

"Oh. I see." Geraldine looks slightly mollified. "Oh well. Thanks. It was kind of you to come."

"Very kind," repeats Greg, nodding.

"Where is our little Papillon?" Eliza casts around the room. It's the cue for more noises from the bathroom. "Ah. He's okay, then." There's a pause. She turns for the door. "Well, I'm glad he's safe."

"Eliza!" Geraldine has taken a step toward her.

Eliza stops. "What?"

"Um. Well. Now that you're here, how about coffee? If Martha can stretch to it?"

"I thought you'd given up?"

"Well, I sneak the odd one in here and there. Got to have some pleasures in life."

Eliza makes a show of consulting her watch. "Yes," she decides. "Yes, I've just got time for that."

Martha goes into the kitchen. Has she done her bit? Does she have to do anything more? She puts on the kettle and rummages around loudly in a box for her coffee plunger and the bone china mugs. She has to get the Le Creuset saucepans out, and the Magimix: it lies scattered across the floor like the pieces of some medieval instrument of torture.

Geraldine and Eliza have followed her in. They don't seem to be able to make conversation on their own. "Got any milch?" Geraldine asks.

Martha hasn't (no milch, no milk, no Coffee-mate). Eliza asks Geraldine whether it is permissible to combine caffeine with dairy. Geraldine narrows her eyes and goes into the sitting room to send Greg. "Off you go, Gregorian," Martha hears her say. "And take the dogs. And your coat. It's a bit cold out. A bit chill on the will."

Eliza surveys the boxes. "So today's the day, then?" she says.

"Yep. Looks like."

Geraldine comes back into the room and steps over the cutting attachments. "Ivor was the last thing you needed, then. Thanks for being so brilliant."

Eliza is warming her hands on the heating kettle. "She didn't do anything. She was just here."

"She's right," admits Martha. "All I did was be in."

"You did more than that. You calmed him down, which is quite an achievement. Particularly Ivor. He's such a touchy little chap. Anyway, being in—it's a greatly underrated virtue."

Geraldine breaks off because Ivor himself has come into the room. "I need a drink," he says. *"Please,"* adds Eliza. Martha lets him choose his cup. She lifts him onto the counter so he can turn on the tap himself. "Don't get drunk," she says as he glugs it down.

After he's gone, Geraldine, who has been watching, says, "Actually, you have quite a way with him, Martha. I've only just noticed that."

"Yes," says Eliza, studying Martha. "You do. You're quite good with kids."

Martha laughs. She is aware of a shift somewhere in her sense of herself. She *managed* something with Ivor today. He didn't run off. More to the point, neither did she. Maybe she isn't as hopeless as she has always believed. Her friends and family seem to open up to her—to be full of possibilities. There

are all those children to get to know. Not just Ivor but Patrick
and Anna. And Gabriel. She should invite them for sleepovers.
Give her sisters a break. And the twins! And Kit! She spoons coffee into the Cafetiere, dark, heaped grains. "Next time you're
on your yoga retreat," she says, "they can come and stay here."

"Oh God." Geraldine sits down on a chair. Her new haircut
is beginning to grow out. It is curling over her eyes, frizzing at
the back. "I feel awful. Thank God I walked out when I did. It
was freezing cold and I was bored and I suddenly thought,
What am I doing here? I should be at Mass, or with the kids.
I've let everything slip. I'm a terrible Catholic and a terrible
mother. All I've been doing is thinking about myself—my yoga,
my gym, my diet, my new clothes. I haven't been thinking
about the children at all. It's as if once I started—getting Katrina
to pick them up from school; not being there at dinner; leaving
them for Greg to sort out on weekends, I couldn't stop. It seems
to be all or nothing. It was such a relief not to have to worry
about them at all, to know that someone else was in charge of
all that. It seemed so easy once I'd started. I mean this thing
with Ivor, I've just let them slip away from me."

Eliza is leaning against the counter, her back to the window.
She says, "Some might say you're lucky to have all that time to
indulge in your own interests. Some of us don't see our kids because we have to work."

"Yes. I know. I . . . look, I don't want to get into an argument.
I've had a hard enough day already." The kettle has boiled.
Martha pours steaming water over the coffee grains, watching
them dance and sift. "Geraldine, I'm sure you're exaggerating."

"No. I'm not. I lost touch with Ivor, with all of them."

Martha carries the Cafetiere and the cups over to the table

and sits down. The plunger is still too stiff to push. She says, "It could be worse. This magician I know, his wife has just buggered off. The children haven't seen her for months. I don't know how someone could do that."

"You start leaving them by degrees."

Martha looks up. Geraldine's lips are tight and her eyes are bright.

Eliza sits down at the table, too. She says, very softly for her, "You're being too hard on yourself. Kids are adaptable. We're all allowed some things, some time, that's just for ourselves. Look at me! I'm not there in the week, and I'm not there now. You don't say I'm a bad mother. Do you?"

"No." Geraldine answers just a little too quickly. "Of course not."

"It's just a different way of doing things, that's all," continues Eliza. "Anyway, Ger. It could have been worse. It was only a weekend yoga retreat in Collier's Wood."

Geraldine doesn't smile. Even the "Ger" hasn't cheered her. (Some sort of truce is taking place. It's been a long time since Eliza has called her "Ger.") One of the laces of her sneakers is undone and with the other foot she is rubbing it back and forth along the floor so that a section of it is flattened, not white anymore but gray. "Then why did he run away?"

Martha says, "Isn't that just the sort of thing kids do?"

"Not really."

Martha slowly, carefully, pushes the plunger into the coffee. This time it moves down smoothly. She says, "Could it be something as simple as the hair? He seemed a bit obsessed that you were 'different.'"

"Did he?" Geraldine puts her hand up to it. "Kids hate

change. There's nothing worse for them. They like routine and . . . things to carry on exactly as they were yesterday and the day before."

"I know how he feels," says Martha. There is a silence. It is suspiciously quiet in the bathroom. Eliza rolls her eyes from side to side in an exaggerated demonstration of listening. Geraldine sighs and says, "A camp. They'll be making a camp. They're obsessed with camps."

Eliza says, "Well, you have to show them that nothing ever stays the same. Show them that change is a good thing. How boring life would be if we always knew where we were. If we were always looking *back* . . . New is good."

"Here you go, girls. Milko." Greg bundles into the kitchen with a bottle of milk and an armful of papers. The dogs, un-leashed, snuffle excitedly toward the bathroom. Greg has bought them all poppies. He pins one onto his wife's sweat-shirt, leaves Martha's on the table, when he realizes she already has one, and then gestures to the sitting room with his copy of *The Observer.* "We'd better be shoving off soon, but I'll leave you girls for a minute, then, shall I?"

Martha, pouring the coffee into four cups, says, "We're put-ting the world to rights."

"Get her to start playing the cello again, won't you?" Greg says as he wanders out.

Geraldine gets out a tissue and blows her nose. "He's right. That's what I should be doing with my extra time. Not preening."

"She's letting her talent go to waste," shouts Greg from the sofa. "Nothing sexier than a woman with a large instrument be-tween her legs."

"Greg." Geraldine frowns but looks pleased. Martha laughs.

For a while after this, the three of them discuss where Geraldine might take her cello-playing now that the children are at school: local orchestras, teaching, guest appearances. But then in a pause, Eliza says again, "So today's the day, then?"

For a moment Martha doesn't know what she's referring to, but then with a shock, remembers. "Yes."

"Are you pregnant or something?" Eliza looks at her quizzically.

"No."

"So why the rush?"

Martha wishes they hadn't got on to her. She says, "Well, I am getting on. I am thirty-eight. And I suppose we are thinking about starting a family."

Geraldine says, "Lovely!" Her tone is bright and breezy, but it strikes Martha that she expected more from her sister, that Martha brought the subject up to make her happy, that Geraldine, emotional as she is, should be *moved* at the thought of Martha and David conceiving. She says, to nudge her along, "You would lend me all your old baby stuff, wouldn't you?"

Geraldine gives a small smile. "It's a bit ratty," she says. "I don't think you'd want it really."

Martha says, "Don't you think we'll make good parents?"

Geraldine says, "Of course I do, Matt. You'll make lovely parents."

"Absolutely," says Eliza.

But then there is a silence. Geraldine pushes her chair back and looks out the window. She says, "It seems to be lightening up." Martha stares at the matchbox with Nick Martin's telephone number on it. And then Geraldine turns back and says, "Are you sure you're doing the right thing?"

"What?" For a moment, Martha is confused.

"You moving in with David."

"What?"

"Is it what you really, really want?"

"What do you mean?" Martha takes a sip of her coffee. There is a bitter taste on the tip of her tongue. "It'll be nice."

"Exactly. Nice? I may be speaking out of turn, but it's as if you're both pretending, playing a part with each other. I feel terribly guilty because I pushed you together, but when you came to supper you seemed so stiff."

"Yes. They did," agrees Eliza.

"And seeing you now, well, I just would expect you to seem more excited. It's as if you're trying to please everyone else and not yourself. And all this about giving up your wonderful shop."

"My wonderful shop . . . I thought you liked David?"

"I do. I really do. He's the sort of man I go for. You know, in many ways he's just like Greg. They are both organized and tidy and . . . everything I'm not. It's why I like David. It's why Greg and I rub along so well. I know I exasperate him and he drives me mad . . ."

"Cards on the table," says Eliza. "I'm not mad about him."

Martha is still looking at Geraldine. "And that's a good thing?"

"If you let each other be different, you can see each other's virtues and vices without them being muddled up with your own. You don't get fire without friction, you don't get passion. What do I mean? What do I know? If you're happy, Matts, then I am, too. But, maybe, I was just worried that what we were just saying applies to you, too. About always looking to the past, sticking with the familiar and—"

"I thought you wanted me to get back with David?"

"I do, but . . ."

"What are you saying?"

"Don't do anything you don't want to do."

Martha puts her cup down on the table. Some coffee jerks over the rim. She stares at the drops, but she can't tell if it's a drip or a flood, if it's going to spread and stain and engulf the tablecloth, or whether it's nothing. She knows she is sitting on a chair, but she feels disembodied for an instant; she can't feel her feet; the air is full of particles of noise. There are Magimix blades all over the floor. Her voice comes out high and twisted. "I don't know what I want."

Geraldine gets a cloth and mops at the spillage. She doesn't look at Martha. "I just mean if it doesn't feel right, don't do it. It doesn't matter how it looks. You don't have to hold it up to the light and inspect it. It doesn't have to *look* right. It's not a china bowl you're thinking of buying. It's your life we're talking about. You don't know what it's going to look like in five years' time. Sometimes things feel right when they look all wrong. You have to go with what *feels* right now."

A minute ago, Martha felt warm and affectionately protective toward her sister. Now, she wants to say something to hurt her. She says, "I'm going to vote for the developers. If it comes down to it and there's a vote, I think 'Mummy's house,' 'the family house,' should go to the highest bidder. Bugger sentiment."

Eliza says, "I've been saying that all along."

Geraldine puts the cloth back in the sink. She leans against the counter for a moment. When she turns back, her face is calm. "And I agree," she says.

"What?"

"I agree. There's a place for sentiment—which is in relationships. And there are other aspects of life where it has no place at all: houses, property, objects."

"So what about *The Boy*?" Martha throws this out like a challenge.

"I'm giving it to Eliza."

"Are you?" says Eliza.

"When did you decide this?" Martha stares at her.

"Just now." Geraldine sits down at the table. She puts her hand on Eliza's. "Today. It has made me see how silly I've been, falling out with you over an object. I know our mother's dead. She's not in the house. Or in *The Boy* . . ."

"You can have the chesterfield." Eliza is smiling, like a five-year-old with the biggest ice cream.

"It's just bricks and mortar. Mummy's not in the things she loved. They are just things. And things, like clothes and makeup, aren't what matter. They're distractions."

"Yes, but things are important," says Martha. "I love my things. I don't know where I'd be without—"

The noise in the flat, the timpani of children and dogs, against the percussion of running water and the rattling drone of the pipes, has been getting louder. The sisters have had to raise their voices to hear one another. But as Martha pauses, she hears Ivor's voice—the loudest of all, a Tarzan cry above his siblings'. It's a voice on the move, and in the drama in the bathroom the others hush as Ivor attempts whatever he's about to attempt. He yodels with all the daring, unbridled enthusiasm of a naked six-year-old. And then there is a resounding rip. A thump, a clatter, and then the sound of a mirror falling to the floor and breaking: a splinteringly loud, gloriously thrilling, monumental crash. A split second of shocked silence follows. Greg says, "Fuck." Then, one of the dogs starts barking, and Patrick says, "Sssh. Sssh." Ivor yells, "Hide. Someone's coming," but in the kitchen, the three sisters haven't moved. They're too busy laughing.

◆

IN THE ENSUING commotion Martha misses the arrival of David. Someone has switched off the television, chucked *The Puccini Experience* to one side, and put on *The A–Z of British TV Themes*. The dogs are tied to chair legs, but keep tangling themselves up and yapping, and the kids are in the bedroom, playing "a nice quiet shopping game" ("Fat chance," says Greg), involving Martha's bed, a box of her price tags, and the contents of her suitcases. Martha and Geraldine "deal with the worst" in the bathroom. The camp—an elaborate construction centering on the bath mat, the shower curtain, and several towels, has imploded in the tub. The toilet seat is askew and the bottle of scented bath oil is on its side in the sink, leaking a blue trail across the porcelain. And all over the floor are silvery green fragments of Venetian glass. The felted back is intact and there are gashes of etched mirror still affixed to it, like old teeth, but the rest has shattered into glinting splinters. Martha wonders for a fleeting moment whether to preserve the separate pieces, to collect them together carefully, but it's a headachey, scratchy thought, and in the end, when she sweeps the whole lot up—so carelessly she cuts her finger on a tiny shard (the drop of blood tastes warm and salty like sweat)—she feels nothing but relief.

She is on her way to the kitchen, with a loaded dustpan, when she comes across David looking shell-shocked in the sitting room.

"I've just been hearing about Ivor's escapade," he says loudly over the theme tune to *The Avengers*. He is wearing pale gray chinos and a white shirt with parallel ironing lines on each side of his chest. "I could have been here earlier if you'd rung." His hand is over one of the dogs' muzzles—trying to stop him from burrowing in his crotch.

"Bradley!" Greg says, yanking on a lead. "Stop rogering David!"

"Oh, how sweet of you," Martha says. It occurs to her that it hadn't even crossed her mind to do so. "Isn't it awful. But at least he's all right. And hasn't he been brave?"

When Martha bends down to kiss him, David whispers in her ear, "I've got a little welcome lunch, a rack of lamb, waiting for us at home."

She says, "I don't think we can get away just yet."

But Greg has heard this and, once Ivor's clothes have been retrieved, starts rounding up his troops. A plan is made: Eliza goes home to collect Denis and Gabriel and will bring them around to Geraldine's for lunch. "You can take *The Boy* then," Geraldine tells her, and Eliza, all smiles and kisses, says she will.

"Well done, Martha," Eliza says as she leaves, and Martha feels satisfied at something else she's achieved today.

But then the others all leave. Patrick and Ivor jostle on the stairs and Anna is whining because, since Ivor has had a McDonald's breakfast, she wants a Happy Meal, and Greg shouts, "Order, you lot," so the events of the morning appear already to have been swept up. Geraldine comes down behind them, with a handful of crumpled newspaper and glass. She says, "Sorry about the mess."

Martha takes the rubbish from her and says it doesn't matter and at the door of the shop, Geraldine hugs her and says, "Thanks, M., for 'being in,'" and Martha says it was nothing, and Geraldine says, "I just want you to be happy; do whatever you think is right," and something pricks behind Martha's eyes. She squeezes Ivor's shoulder before he gets in the car and then stands back to wave them off. It seems her role in life is to wave off families from her step. Geraldine has let Patrick sit in the front and has gotten into the back herself, and wraps her arms around Anna and Ivor on each side of her. But she bends her head so she can see her sister. The two of them look at each other as Greg turns the car around, and Martha makes a face that isn't quite a smile, though it is closer to that than anything.

Martha puts the paper-wrapped glass in the trash and, alone in the shop, takes a moment to sweep up some of the molted hops. She straightens a pair of toile de Jouy cushions on a mid-nineteenth-century neo-rococo chaise longue. There is a foot-stool beside it, which she left with its original needlepoint seat. It strikes her that it would be more attractive with some bright, modern Ian Mankin checks. It hadn't occurred to her until now. And along the tapered treads of the fruit-picking ladder over there, which she always considered so delicately decorative, she could hang linen tea towels, give it a *use*.

As for that old rocking horse: she crosses the room and sits on it. It creaks halfheartedly beneath her. She must get it working properly. What's the point of a rocking horse that won't rock? No wonder no one will buy it. She will get Jason on the case, maybe even respray it (bugger authenticity). And then—a wonderful idea comes to her—she will give it to April, for the baby. Is this furniture really so vulnerable? Isn't it the fear of something breaking rather than the breakage itself that ties you? For that matter, why on earth couldn't April continue working once she's given birth? Would a child be so much in the way? Looking around her now, at this room full of *stuff*, it all seems so adaptable, so robust.

When she gets upstairs, David is still sitting on the sofa, with one leg crossed up high on his thigh. She stands in the doorway looking at him. He makes a noise like a horse blowing through its lips when he finally sees her. "Chaos!" he says. "Have you seen what they've done in your bedroom? And the bathroom! I don't believe it. Shattered. Bloody chaos."

Martha still doesn't move. "You match my sofa," she says.

"You're going to have to pack all over again, you poor love."

"Different fabric, obviously. Though haven't you got some summery linen ones that match exactly? A suit?"

"Er?" David laughs. There are bristles on his cheek—his only-on-a-Sunday beard.

Martha turns her back and goes into the bedroom, which is a mess. The dogs have chewed the pashmina throw; the children have been in the suitcases; the floor is a sea of clothes and sheets and bits of paper. She picks something up. It's one of the labels they used for their game. "A delightful brass bed with unusual barley twist posts" it reads. David calls, "Are you talking about my Paul Smith?"

"Maybe," she says.

Under the pashmina, she finds a pair of wet orange-red underpants with a picture of a racing car on the front.

"Look," she says, taking them into the sitting room. "Ivor forgot his knickers." She puts them on her head and does a stupid dance. She hums "The Ride of the Valkyries." She smiles at David, camouflaged against her Howard sofa. David watches her guardedly.

"Come on," he says. "Let's get you sorted, shall we?" He

makes as if to stand up, but frowns and leans down. Under his foot is a white rubber object, which he picks up by one corner and holds out. "Oh God," he says mournfully, sitting back down. "Now, what's this?"

Martha takes the underpants off her head and lays them across one of her scallop-edged cushions. She considers them, with her head on one side (the color goes well, actually). Then she sits down next to David, takes the object from him, and says, "It's the egg from a McMuffin."

"Bloody hell."

They sit side by side in silence for a moment. The flat seems very quiet now that everyone has gone. She says, "What a morning."

"God. I know. And I wasn't even here."

"I'm so sorry about your mirror."

"It's not my mirror. It's yours. I'll find you another one."

"You are very sweet. But please don't." His eyes meet hers. There is a blackhead in an odd place just below the smile lines under his eyes. "Sometimes I think you buy me things, you load me up with possessions, to possess me, to make me something I'm not."

"Don't be ridiculous." David cups her face and kisses her—a warm, dry kiss on the mouth. He darts the egg, still in her hand, an anxious look. He says, "I buy things for both of us. We're a couple. We're an item."

Martha says, "An item. 'A delightful twenty-first-century couple, English.'"

David laughs. He holds his hands flat between his knees and twitches his legs. "Shall we get going?"

He starts to lever himself up. Martha doesn't move. She says,

"You make me feel vindicated. Like a proper grown-up person. David, I do love you. When I'm with you, I feel like a delightful couple. We match. We blend, like your trousers on my sofa. And I know that our life together will be just fine."

David says, "Good."

"But . . ."

"What?"

"I'm not going to take that job at the auction house. I'm not going to give up the shop. I love it. I'm good at it. It's something I've built up myself. I know you think it's shabby and tacky and..."

"Martha, that's okay. I can drop you here in the mornings, you can get a Tube pass, like normal people. You can drive. We could find you a site nearer home. Just as long as you're living with me we'll be fine."

"And April—I want her to carry on working here, too. I might not be her friend, but I'm going to be a great boss."

"Whatever," David says, impatient now, getting up. He marches, a man of action, into the bedroom, where he starts repacking suitcases. Martha still has the egg in her hand. She gets up, walks into the kitchen and, levering the trash can open with her foot, drops it in. She realizes after she has done it that there's no bag there; that the egg has fallen to the bottom and bounced on the metal. She makes to pick it up but then stands there not moving.

David follows her in. "What's going on?" he says.

She doesn't turn around. "I don't know."

"Shall we get this place re-sorted and go?"

She doesn't answer. She stares at the wall behind the trash can, where she notices for the first time that some misaimed tea bags have left brown smears.

"Are you coming with me or not?"

"Oh, David," she says, still not turning around.

"Martha, history is not going to repeat itself. You are not going to do this to me again."

"David, I'm sorry," she says.

There is a silence. She hears the street cleaner going past downstairs. Finally she says, "We are too similar, David. I thought that was a good thing; actually, I thought it was essential. But it isn't. You bring out the side of me that is too tidy. You want to put my life 'in order,' as you told Neville. But I've begun to think a bit of mess, a bit of disorder, the occasional Mc-Muffin wrapper, you know, the odd splash of orange in an interior, is a good thing. You are a terribly nice person, oh, perfect in lots of ways, and I'm a coward. I just think you can't always stick with what you know, that sometimes you—I—have to take a chance on the unknown." He is so quiet she thinks he must be staring at her in horror. She can hear a slight squeaking noise, like a finger on paintwork, and for a moment she imagines him rubbing at a mark on the wall. But when she turns around, it is Anna's balloon that is making the sound, still bumping quietly against the ceiling, and she sees that the door is open and David has gone.

◆

THE MATCHBOX WITH Nick Martin's phone number on it is still sitting on the kitchen table. Martha has tidying up and unpacking to do, the shop to get to work on, April to call and cajole, but her eyes keep finding their way back to it. She picks it up and stares at it. The numbers dance like hieroglyphics.

She isn't going to phone him. She has known that all along. She finds that when she thinks about him, when she tries to summon him up, nothing comes. All the memories that seemed so interesting and unfinished elude her. The ghosts have gone. It strikes her that memory is actually the biggest spin of all. When she took that taxi ride through Hyde Park and she felt as if the past had been "unlocked," when she wondered at the selection of memories that bombarded her and concluded it was something to do with the past moment itself— some special quality in it that put her outside herself—she couldn't have been more wrong. It had nothing to do with the nature of the remembered experience and everything to do with the state of mind she was in when she remembered it. She picks up the spare poppy on the table and twirls it between her fingers. And what a waste of memory, she thinks, to spend it on yourself.

The big black garbage bag still sits, heavy and unwieldy, in the middle of the floor. She pokes a piece of newspaper into the top of it. And then she decides. There is nothing in here she needs. Only false corners and dead ends. You carry people around with you in your character; all the people you have been close to have made you a little bit of what you are. That is how the past is kept alive, not through reunions or self-indulgent reveries or the chasing of old boyfriends. She bends, screwing the plastic into a handle, ready to heave it over her shoulder, to lug it down, banging against her knees, to the car and to the dump. But when she picks it up, it comes off the ground easily and she finds that it is much lighter than she was expecting, that actually it has no weight at all.

◆

THE STREETS SHINE as Martha walks along them later that afternoon. The thick dark clouds have cleared, sucked up into billowing factory-white cumulus, and there are chinks of cold blue sky reflected in the windows of some of the houses. Droplets of water gleam on car roofs and every other paving stone—the hard pink squares among the porous gray slabs—glistens. Martha found one of April's stripey scarves on the back of a Victorian chair and she grabbed it as she left, wrapping it around her neck like someone spinning sugar, and now she keeps catching fragments of herself in car windows and side mirrors, not braced, but open, her pale, white face peering out of a knitted rainbow.

She turns onto Fred's road. Every house looks different to her today. The elaborate cheeseplant standing watch at the window of number 17; the lemony plaster lions poking their heads above the parapet at number 19; the wind chimes at number 21; the Chinese lantern at 23; the doors, moss-green and canary-yellow and peach; doorknockers shaped like hands or urns; the curtains, velvet and floral and polka-dotted, ruched or folded or slatted; and the snatch of alcove she can just see beyond, filled with photographs or books or mirrors or paintings. And rather than sad, it seems vital to her suddenly that not all the houses should have railings; how varied the unruly run of hedge and picket fence and red-brick wall. How dull if they all looked the same.

And here she is at number 35. She hasn't felt nervous until now. But now, when she stops walking, the excitement tightens. The lids are off the garbage cans again and the weeds in the front are still strangling the railings. Someone—Hazel, of course—has left her Barbie bike out front, thrown undignified on its side, and it is smattered with magnifying drops of water. In the upstairs windows, Martha can see small squares and circles randomly dotted at a child's eye level, which she guesses are Stanley's stickers. She starts walking toward the mauve front door. But at the last minute she hesitates, and turns, and bends to pick up the bike. And as she straightens up, she looks in at the front window. Perhaps she always intended to do this. Perhaps she hopes to catch Fred for an instant, his face unguarded, before he sees her.

And she does catch him. She is fortunate because he might have been in the kitchen, or the garden, or upstairs in the bathroom. She sees him, on this end of the sofa, his long legs drawn up sideways as if there was nowhere else to put them, his big black glasses perched on the end of his nose, with Kitten curled up like a fossil on his knee. And on the other side of him is Hazel—in some sort of silk garment, a sari?—and beyond her, Stan. She can only just see Stan's head because taking up the floor in front of all three of them, gesturing, bangles glinting on her arms, is a woman. And it takes a second for Martha to register this, but it's the woman from the photograph on the fridge, with the gums and the open smile and the shoulder-length blond hair (though it's longer now, halfway down her arms, in fact, and darker on the top). Hazel and Stan's mother, Fred's wife. Martha looks at Fred again. She has an impression, like a photographic negative, of his face a second ago, guarded and defensive, not open and longing as when he gazes at her, and she looks back at him to be sure, but he has bent to stroke the cat now and she can't see his face.

Martha crosses back to the doorstep and stays there a moment, her heart thudding. Her instinct is to turn and run, to leave again—that's what she has always done, isn't it, when things got hard? But she doesn't leave. Life isn't as easy as she used to think it was, or as straightforward. She thinks about the time Fred kissed her, the time Hazel brushed her hair. She thinks about Stan sitting on her knee. Will their mother stay this time? Or is she just passing? Through the paler sections of stained glass, she can see the jumble of coats and bags in the hall, Stan's Fireman Sam bike, the piles of washing. She can make out the shape of Fred's magic box at the bottom of the stairs: all the chaos and complications of the life within. She hesitates. What should she do? Then the sun comes out behind her and the panel brightens. In the green pane now, all she can see is the shiny, hard reflection of the house opposite and she has to put her face right up close to the glass to see behind it into the messy hall.